"HOW

Lazily, he lifted a hand, pointed the forefinger, and tipped his hat back a mite, just enough to uncover his eyes but leaving it far enough down on his forehead to show her who was in control.

So this was the man she'd hired over the wire—this cowboy with a bearded stubble and mud splattered all over his chaps. This *chauvinist* who hadn't even risen from *her* chair when she'd walked into the room, let alone removed his hat or taken his spurred boot heels off her desk.

Kate let her gaze roam leisurely over his long legs, up his buckskin vest, and across his wide shoulders, finally settling on a pair of the biggest, darkest brown eyes she'd ever seen. She'd been taken in by a pair of dark brown eyes before. . . .

Witnessing his reaction when he found out *she* was the mayor was going to be a pleasure. And then she'd see to it that Mitch Dawson learned some manners.

ELIZABETH LEIGH

PRAIRIE PARADISE

ZEBRA BOOKS
KENSINGTON PUBLISHING CORP.

ZEBRA BOOKS are published by

Kensington Publishing Corp.
850 Third Avenue
New York, NY 10022

First Printing: July, 1994

Printed in the United States of America

For my agent extraordinaire,
Evan M. Fogelman

Acknowledgments

Many thanks to Julia Williams, who provided the initial research material that became the historical backbone of this story; to my editors at Zebra: Ann LaFarge, Tracy Bernstein, and Amy Van Allen; to David Tweedie, Construction Project Manager, who explained the use of acetylene gas for lighting and the method used in paving streets before the turn of the century; to the University of Kansas Library; and to Alfie and Dan Thompson, who so patiently answered all my questions about east Kansas.

And my undying gratitude to my critique group: Donna Caubarreaux, Vicky Evans, Norma Franklin, and Natalie Salley, whose suggestions and input strengthened this story and whose encouragement and support kept me writing when it seemed the real world was falling apart on me.

Prologue

November 1887

In the depths of his soul, Mitch Dawson knew he would forever live to regret arresting those two temperance women. He knew equally well that all the beer in Nebraska wouldn't make this particular turn of events any easier to swallow, but he was damned sure willing to give it a try, which was exactly what he'd been doing for the past three days.

So far, all he'd gained was a sour stomach, evidenced by the periodic expulsion of foul-smelling air from one end of him or the other, and a rather sore posterior, spawned by sitting overlong in one of Shorty's hard wooden chairs. Had there been ladies present, Mitch would have taken his gaseous condition to the privacy of his room upstairs, but Shorty didn't allow members of the weaker sex, even soiled doves, on the premises.

That one hard-and-fast rule was what had started the whole mess.

"There are three kinds of women," Mitch told his former deputy, Earl Woody, between sips of dark, foaming beer. The two sat facing each other at a small, round table in Shorty Moss's Webfoot Saloon.

Following the fiasco and Mitch's subsequent dismissal, Woody had stepped in to replace Mitch as marshal for the town of Dry Creek—not because he wanted the job but because he was the only deputy. Now, he was the only lawman in Dry Creek.

Mitch wasn't about to let his recent downfall interfere with a long-term friendship, even if that friendship was with the man who now had his job. Woody might be a bit dense, but he had a good heart. Despite Woody's reservations, Mitch knew he'd do a good job.

Woody tried not to wince. He had heard this particular speech so many times in the past three days that he knew it by heart, a worthy accomplishment for a man who had experienced true difficulty memorizing "Now I Lay Me Down to Sleep" and who had given up on getting past the first verse of "Mary Had a Little Lamb." Perhaps, he mused, if Mitch would recite the rhyme for him as often and as fervently as he did his "three kinds of women" speech, he could at long last amuse his grandchildren with the poem. And then he could learn "Jack Sprat" and "Little Bo Peep" and . . .

"You ain't paying attention!" Mitch accused, his voice so sharp the calico cat he'd been stroking shot off his lap and darted outside through the open doorway.

The older man smiled behind the thick rim of his beer mug, took a long swallow, and erased the lower portion of a foam mustache with a leisurely journey of his tongue across his upper lip before he answered. "Yes, I am."

Mitch's eyes squinted into narrow slits. "Then what did I say?"

" 'On the one hand,' " Woody quoted confidently, inordinately pleased with himself for recalling the words so clearly, " 'there's the kind of women who know their place—' "

"Who always behave in a ladylike manner," Mitch picked up, ignoring Woody's displeasure at being interrupted before he could finish. "Ladies mind their own business. They stay out of politics and other men things. Then, there's the kind who know how to pleasure a man and take great delight in charging an arm and a leg for the benefit of their knowledge, but they're basically harmless. Besides, any idiot," he said with self-derision, "can tell a whore from a lady. But it's the third kind that's dangerous. The third kind—the kind I've managed to avoid now for thirteen years—spells disaster with a capital *D*."

The reason, as he'd said often enough in the previous seventy-two hours, he'd managed to avoid this third variety, was that his intuition hadn't failed him since Jennie Clark had educated him on that particular score. Why it had deserted him that fateful afternoon he was certain he'd never understand. For thirteen years, he'd been able to spot one of the number-three variety as easily as spotting a Jersey cow among a herd of Texas longhorns.

Usually, this wasn't too difficult, since many of this variety dressed in trousers, toted six-shooters, and towered over most men. The ones who didn't fit that particular description swaggered or chewed tobacco or possessed some other habit that should, by all that was right and holy, belong only to the male of the species. But the two he'd arrested were like Jennie Clark; they didn't fit the mold. How was a man supposed to know anymore what he was up against if women refused to fit their appropriate molds?

"You just didn't see it coming, Mitch," Woody consoled. "No one sees everything coming. Sometimes you only see it going, and then it's too late." Earl took another swallow of beer, and though he backhanded his entire mouth this time, traces of foam still clung to the reddened skin just under his wide nostrils.

"I shoulda seen this coming," Mitch said, his words somewhat slurred from an excess of beer. The beer, however, had failed to erase the thirteen-year-old pain of rejection from a member of the third variety. In all the years they'd been together, Mitch had never told Woody the details of his bittersweet love affair with Jennie Clark. He considered telling him now, then changed his mind. Woody knew Jennie had soured Mitch on women with causes—hell, on women, period—way back yonder, and that was all he needed to know.

"I shoulda known those two women couldn't possibly be whores. Hell, whores don't cover their ankles or wear sensible little hats."

"You knew they warn't ladies. You got that part right. They was new to town. How was you supposed to know they was temp'rance leaguers? Or that one of them would turn out to be the governor's wife?"

Mitch ran long fingers through unkempt dirty-blond hair that could stand the attention of a barber's shears. "I shoulda known, that's all."

Shorty Moss, who carried a clear glass pitcher half full of foaming beer, stopped on his way past their table to put his two-cents' worth in. "Don't blame yourself. I was the one started all the ruckus. I was the idiot who first accused them of being whores. It's all my fault."

Woody flashed Shorty a look of pure gratefulness while his former boss held up his mug for a refill from the pitcher.

Shorty ignored the raised mug. "Don't you think you've had enough?" he asked, his voice quiet.

"No, I haven't, and no, it ain't your fault," Mitch

insisted, his wide mouth set in an obstinate line that defied argument on either issue. "If it's anyone's fault except mine, it's the fault of those temperance women, damn their ax-grinding hides. Women are supposed to stay home and take care of younguns, cook and clean and such like. I don't have no use for no women preachers."

"They ain't preachers, Mitch," Earl Woody argued.

Mitch Dawson's stubbled chin popped up and he fixed his bloodshot gaze on the marshal's face. "You defending 'em now, Earl? What else you gonna call folks who go 'round moralizing, trying to mold everyone else's thinking into a replica of their own? Sounds like preaching to me. It's bad enough when a man's doing it, but women preachers—well, they really get my dander up."

While Woody wriggled uncomfortably in his chair and tried to think of a rebuttal, Mitch raised his mug higher in the air, tossed his head back, and let the bit of brew left in the mug trickle out and fall into his open mouth. A loud belch that smelled worse than rotten fish followed.

"You got better manners than that, Mitch," Woody admonished.

Woody's quiet, gentle voice grated on Mitch's bruised nerves, and he slammed the mug down hard. "What's got into you?" Mitch demanded. "Suddenly, you're taking exception to everything I say and do. You and Shorty." He turned his attention to the contents of the pitcher Shorty held and nodded toward his empty beer mug. "Fill it up, Shorty."

Though the saloon owner complied this time, he poured the beer with a caustic remark. "It's your funeral."

"My career as a lawman is already dead and buried," Mitch countered. "And those two no-account varmints in skirts who killed it didn't even have to stand trial. Thanks to them, I'm the laughingstock of this town. I ain't never gonna live that down." Mitch wagged a pointed finger at Woody's chest. "And I ain't never gonna wear that badge again."

"Don't you know I'd give it back this minute iffen I could? This binness will all blow over in no time, and you'll get your job back."

"No, I won't," Mitch argued.

"Then you'll get a job sommers else. Since your mama died last year, there ain't been nothing holding you in Dry Creek 'ceptin' your job."

Mitch shook his head. "I ain't never gonna be a marshal again. I got me a reputation that'll follow me around all my days. No one will even hire me as a deputy. I'm doomed. Just wait. You'll see."

"I'm tellin' you, Mitch. It'll all blow over."

"Like it did for Wyatt Earp? He ain't never gonna be a marshal again and I ain't neither. I might as well face it, 'cause no one's ever gonna forget that Mitch Dawson arrested the governor's wife on grounds of prostitution."

Chapter One

Paradise, Kansas
1888

It started like most other election campaigns that the thousand or so folks in Paradise, Kansas, had ever known. The same men were running for the same offices and making the same promises they made year after year but never intended to keep.

Mort Moffet, who finished out old Jehosaphat "Jump" Barnett's term when a heart attack caught him unawares, and then had continued to serve as mayor for nigh on to a dozen years now, was seeking reelection, as were the five town councilmen who had served under Mort for several years' running. Everyone expected the six would be in office for some years to come. Folks had no call to expect otherwise; after all, no one else was running despite the fact that most townspeople blamed the present administration—and rightly so—for the deplorable state into which the town had fallen.

And what a deplorable state it was. The farming community of Paradise, Kansas, was going to seed.

The two-story, red-brick Madison County courthouse, situated almost dead center in the middle of town, was the only brick building in Paradise and, therefore, the only one that didn't need sprucing up, but the deep yard that surrounded it had never seen a sprig of grass, let alone a shrub or a flower. Most of the businesses and professional offices faced the courthouse square, so that anyone going or coming couldn't help seeing the bare yard, but the municipal government never made a move to improve it, and no one else had the time or the money—or the authority.

Anyone coming or going from the courthouse couldn't help seeing the long streamers of peeling paint hanging from the walls of the business houses. What shingles and signs there were should have been chopped up and used for kindling a long time ago. For the most part, their lettering reflected the hands of the uneducated and inartistic, what lettering hadn't practically faded into oblivion, anyway.

Anyone daring to cross the narrow streets on foot had better be wearing boots, so deep was the mud from lack of proper drainage. The absence of street lamps or other outside lights to illuminate the way made the going even more treacherous after dark. Unfortunately, a body couldn't always move from one store to another without avoiding the mud, for the construction of boardwalks had been left up to the discretion of business owners, many of whom had never bothered. Of the existing boardwalks, a number were in such a sad state of rot and disrepair that a pedestrian never knew when he or she might fall right through.

It was just such an occurrence that started Dr. Wilbur Myers to thinking about the deplorable state of affairs in Paradise and what could be done to change the town.

Shortly after noon on the last Friday in March of 1888, three days before election day, two of the townsmen hauled Billy Fink, a shrimp of a man if ever there was one, into Doc's office, which was next to the unimposing town hall. Billy had placed his slight weight on a rotten board on the walk outside Youngblood's Mercantile. The board broke and so did his leg.

The doctor mashed a particularly sore spot.

"What this town needs is a new sawbones!" Billy screamed.

"Save your breath," Dr. Myers said. "You're going to need it when I set this leg." He continued to probe and mash along Billy's calf. Billy ignored Doc's admonition.

Amid his patient's ranting and raving, Doc offered his own observation. "What this town needs is a new mayor who'll make folks like Al Youngblood fix his boardwalk so this won't happen anymore. Of course, I wouldn't get nearly so much business, but it would be worth it. Yes, indeed, it would. If someone doesn't do something, we'll be forced to change the name of this town. It's certainly no paradise—not anymore. Billy, quit wiggling. Hold his arms, Jethro."

"Don't I get a stick or something to bite down on?" Billy cried.

Since Jethro Smith's hands were otherwise occupied, Doc handed a chewed-up piece of dowel to Tully Patterson, the other man who had carried Billy to the doctor's office.

"I ain't puttin' that nasty thing in my mouth!" Billy declared.

"Then scream bloody murder for all I care," Doc Myers said disgustedly. "I hope they hear you next door and come running. I wouldn't mind giving Mort Moffet a piece of my mind. Here goes . . ."

Billy did scream bloody murder, along with some rather vile oaths, but if Mort heard, he didn't pay any mind. Around mid-afternoon, Doc strolled next door to talk to the mayor but found his office empty.

"He's over to Mission's Drug, stocking up for the big day," Hardy Osborne, the town clerk, explained.

Doc assumed the "big day" was Monday, Election Day, but with Mort it was anyone's guess. To the esteemed mayor of Paradise, every day was a big day when it came to the consumption of demon liquor. Doc put out his "Closed" sign and walked a short piece down the street to Mission's Drug, one of three drugstores in Paradise. All three owners sold illegal whiskey out of their storerooms at the back.

Although seven years had passed since the Kansas state legislature had enacted Prohibition, whiskey remained readily available all over the state. Indeed, many Kansas towns boasted regular saloons, but most violators saw fit to shroud their illegal trade behind the facade of a legitimate business.

Since Mort was purchasing whiskey, Doc didn't bother going through the front door. Instead, he walked down the alley to the back, where he found the mayor climbing aboard his buggy. A wooden crate occupied half the seat, and when Mort plopped his wide rump down on the remaining portion, he set the bottles in the box to jiggling so it sounded like they would all surely break.

"Hold on there, Mort!" Doc Myers called.

The Honorable Mortimer Moffet peered down the beak that was his nose and frowned at Doc, whose expressive face bore evidence of his consternation. "I'm kinda in a hurry. Can't it wait till Tuesday?"

Mort reached for the reins, but Doc was quicker. He snatched up the reins and held them firmly in hand. "No, it can't. By Tuesday the election will be over for another year, and I want to know now what you and your council are planning to do about the sad condition of this town. And don't give me any of your empty promises."

"Look, Doc," Mort said, his tone condescending, "you take care of influenza and broken toes and let us take care of the government. They ain't nothing wrong with Paradise that a few drainage ditches won't fix, but the town don't have the money to pay for 'em. 'Sides all that, you know the economy's a mite depressed right now. Now, hand me them reins."

Doc clutched the strips of leather tighter. "What exactly can the town afford to pay for, Mort?"

Mort pursed his lips and looked off down the alley. "Not much, Doc Myers, not much."

"And why not? We all pay property taxes. What does that money go for?"

"Salaries and upkeep on the town hall. After that, there ain't much left."

"How much?" Doc pushed.

"Not much. Now, let me go. I'm having a little social gathering at my house tonight, but my wife doesn't know it yet. I've got to get home before the men start arriving."

"How much?" Doc repeated. "How much money do we have in the treasury, Mort?"

The mayor hung his head and mumbled, "Thirty-six cents."

"Thirty-six cents!" Doc bellowed.

"Sh-h-h!" Mort admonished, his face suddenly a deep shade of raspberry. "We don't never have no excess, Doc. You know that."

Dr. Myers bit back a retort, handed over the reins, and turned to walk away.

"Hey, Doc!" Mort called. When Wilbur Myers turned his head Mort said quietly, "I'm sure I can count on you to keep this conversation under your hat."

Doc gave the mayor a long, assessing stare before replying. "I don't wear a hat, Mort. You know that."

As was true of any frontier settlement that had one, the post office served as the hub of gossip for the town of Paradise. When Doc Myers left Mort Moffet sitting in his buggy with his mouth wide open, he went straight to the post office. Once the usual amenities had been dispensed with, Doc got straight to the point.

"We have to do something about this town," Doc announced to the small crowd gathered out front. He paused and assured himself he had everyone's attention before proceeding. "I can't be the only person who's suffered severe disillusionment with our present administration."

"What's that mean?" Gabby Dahlmer, who was both hard of hearing and poorly educated, whispered loudly to his son Ebenezer.

"Means he's fed up with the mayor and the council, Pa," Ebenezer shouted in Gabby's ear. At his booming explanation, a few more citizens within earshot joined the small group.

"Me, too!" Gabby declared. His broad grin melted into a troubled frown. "What you reckon we ought to do about it, Doc?"

"I reckon we can field another ticket," Doc offered.

Thomas McWilliams, who owned a farm just outside town, shoved his straw hat back a mite and scratched the front of his nearly bald head. "We tried that a couple years ago, but it didn't work. They was all defeated."

"Maybe we ran the wrong candidates," Doc suggested.

Thomas resettled his hat. "Pert near everyone around here's too busy with their farms or their binnesses to have time to run this town. 'Sides, mayorin' don't pay worth a tinker's damn and the councilmen make even less. Ain't no incentive in it."

"No incentive at all," Dr. Myers agreed, "except for those who want to see things change."

"We're all with you there, Doc," the owner of the livery, Josiah Keane, put in. "Fact is, like Thomas said, ain't no one else wants to run, lessen you do. I'll vote for you, Doc. But don't think you're gonna talk me into running for no public office. I ain't got the time or the know-how."

Doc smiled. "I expect you could do better than those we have in office now, Josiah, assuming you had the time. But I wasn't thinking about any of us."

That remark got everyone to scratching their heads.

"Then who were you thinking about?" Tully Patterson ventured. Better educated than most of the townsmen, Tully ran a bookkeeping business and sometimes offered legal counsel to folks who couldn't stomach James Larue, Paradise's only real attorney.

Though Doc was no farmer, he knew you couldn't expect to produce a full-blooming plant without some sowing and nurturing. In order to harvest his idea, he needed to employ a full share of both, but first he had a bit more harrowing to do. The smart thing, he decided, was to make these men think the idea was theirs.

"Who's eligible to vote in this election?" he asked.

This would be Ebenezer Dahlmer's first time to vote. The young man puffed out his chest and tilted his square jaw in an attempt to look his full twenty-one years. "Why, all the men my age or older who live hereabouts," he said.

"That's right, Eb. *All* the men, including the colored folk," Doc reminded them. "Who else?"

"Who else?" Max Smart, the barber, echoed.

"Yes, who else?" Doc repeated, then held his breath for the response.

Gabby's watery blue eyes brightened. "I know!" he shouted with the unbridled enthusiasm of a primary student who's just learned his alphabet. "The women! The state done priv'leged 'em with that last year."

"But they'll vote the way their husbands do," Skip Hudson, a harnessmaker who had only recently married, proudly pointed out.

"Not my Sally," Doc argued. "Everyone knows she's an uncompromising Democrat and I'm a Republican. Sally will vote the way she pleases."

"But that's rare, Doc," Thomas said. "What I want to know is who you're planning to talk into running."

"I'm getting to that," Doc assured him. "Gabby, you mentioned that the state gave women the right to vote last year. Do you recollect the details?"

"Sure as shootin', I do! They can't vote anywheres 'ceptin' mu—munis—, dang it, *town* 'lections."

"It's 'municipal,' Pa."

"And what else?" Doc prodded, his sweeping gaze daring anyone else to answer for the old man.

Gabby screwed up his weathered face for a moment. "They can run, too?"

"That's right! They can!" Max said.

"Didn't they elect a woman mayor over to Argonia last year?" Josiah asked.

"Yeah, but they did it as a joke," Thomas said. "The council's still all men, so they make all the decisions. She ain't nothin' more'n a figurehead."

"But what if we fielded an all-female ticket?" Doc suggested.

His all-male audience erupted in laughter. When they quieted Tully offered the first rebuttal. "Even if you can find six women who can do the job, you'll never find six *men* in this town who will allow their wives to run."

"I will," Doc countered.

"I will, too," Skip said. "Julia's getting awfully bored with nothing but housework to occupy her time. Course, once we start up a family, things'll be different."

"But will your wives want to run?" Thomas asked. "And even if you can get six women—and their husbands—to agree, how are you planning on getting them elected?"

"Campaign for them," Doc said.

"When you've only got a couple days?" Josiah's voice rang with skepticism.

"If we all work together on this—" Doc began.

Ebenezer interrupted. "I want to know who you have in mind for mayor."

"She'll have to be smart."

"And politically minded."

"And not have a houseful of younguns to look after."

Doc flashed the group an enigmatic grin. "Leave that to me," he said. "I have the perfect person in mind."

Although it hadn't occurred to her, Kate McBride bore the distinction of being the youngest widow in Paradise. Nor had it occurred to her that her tall, slender frame, glistening strawberry-blond hair, and classic oval face made her one of the most attractive women in the county. And though she was unfashionably intelligent, this she'd never quite realized either.

She was aware that she didn't exactly fit in with the Paradise crowd, though she didn't understand why.

She had friends, but none she could call a bosom buddy. She was invited to most social events and was an active member in the Episcopal church, yet, after nine years of residency in Paradise, she still felt like an outsider.

But there was one distinction that truly pleased Kate: that of having her name emblazoned on an office door at the Madison County courthouse.

She stood before that door late that Friday afternoon, her right hand still holding the key she'd turned in the lock, her gaze fixed upon a placard that read KATHERINE G. MCBRIDE, REGISTRAR OF DEEDS.

Though well deserved, it was a position she knew she wouldn't hold had her husband not held it before her—and had she not served on his staff as deputy registrar of deeds. Sometimes she thought that this was the only good thing to have come of their marriage.

But, she reasoned, the county commissioners could have offered the position to someone else when Arnold McBride caught the measles and died last year. The unadorned truth of it was, however, that no one else in the entire county was as well qualified as Kate.

Despite her qualifications, the job wouldn't be hers after the election on Monday, for women were not allowed to run for county office. And even if they were, Kate figured she would more than likely be defeated. Women might be making progress, but they hadn't made that much yet. Nevertheless, she wouldn't mind being afforded the privilege of losing.

Reluctant to leave, to bid good-bye to her position, she lifted her left hand and placed her forefinger in the groove of the K on the placard. Slowly, she moved the finger, pushing its pad along the grooves of each letter in her name. Her breath caught in her throat and a rush of tears gathered in her eyes. Kate swallowed hard and fought back the moisture.

"What will you do after the election?"

Startled, Kate dropped her left hand, but she wasn't fully composed enough to face the voice, which she recognized as belonging to Dr. Myers.

"I'm not sure," she said simply, biting her lower lip. "I've thought about becoming active in the suffrage movement again."

This task, as she well knew, came without pay and required the dedication of much time and energy. Still, the recollection of her days as a suffragist begat the pleasant tingle of challenge and purpose. She'd quit only because Arnold had refused to allow her to continue. Now, thanks to her own foresight, she had the money to support herself, and without either husband or career to stop her, she had the time. Kate had never lacked energy, yet something held her back . . . something she couldn't quite put a mental finger on. Not a lack of conviction in the cause, which, despite recent success in several areas, had yet to reach its full intent. Something else . . .

"Really?" Doc asked, almost sounding disappointed.

She nodded, and the positive gesture lent her enough confidence to turn around. "It's high time I make a change. High time I channel my energies into something that will make a difference in my life and the world I live in. Don't you agree?"

Doc Myers grinned. "I certainly do!"

Kate admired Wilbur Myers. Having his blessing felt good. "I'm glad you think I should rejoin the movement."

"Oh, but I don't."

She frowned, confused. "But you just said—"

"I think you should run for office."

She couldn't have heard him correctly. Surely Doc knew she couldn't run. Surely he knew her name would be on the ballot if she could legally put it there.

"Not this office," he explained, gently removing her hand from the key and then turning it himself. The opening click resounded loudly in the empty hallway. "I have something else in mind."

Nothing else could have restored her composure so completely yet confounded her so thoroughly.

Doc turned the knob and pushed the door open. "Do you want to hear more?"

Kate nodded and followed him into the office she'd vacated moments before. When they were both seated she folded her hands together in her lap and squeezed them until her knuckles turned white. "What, exactly, do you have in mind?"

She heard the squeak in her voice and swallowed hard again.

Doc suffered no such affliction. His voice was firm, his tone enthusiastic. "The mayorship."

Kate laughed, a silly, high-pitched giggle that rang in her ears. Quickly, she squelched the eruption.

"I'm serious," Doc continued.

"I'm sure you are," she commented dryly, "but for the life of me I can't understand why."

"Because you're the best candidate, Kate, bar none. You're intelligent. You've worked with the women's suffrage movement. You don't have a family to tie you down—or a husband you must clear this with. And you have public office experience. I don't know anyone who doesn't hold you in esteem. I've already discussed this with a number of men, and we're all in agreement."

Something akin to hope and purpose pierced her heart, but Kate refused it full admittance. She shook her head. "I'm not a strong leader, Doc."

"So? Is Mort Moffet?"

"If I can't do any better than Mort, there's no sense in my running," she countered.

"But you can do better, Kate. You could be a good leader if you worked at it. We need someone new, someone with a vision, someone who can change things around here. I think you could do it."

She shook her head again. "It would end up like Argonia, Doc. Susanna Salter may have become the first woman mayor in this country, but she hasn't made a difference."

"Mrs. Salter isn't politically minded, Kate. You are."

"So? With an all-male council—"

"Exactly."

Kate frowned. "I'm not following you."

Doc Myers leaned forward in his chair, rested his forearms on his thighs, and set his unwavering gaze directly upon Kate McBride's bewildered face. "What if you had an all-*female* town council to work with?"

Doc watched sparks of hope gather in Kate's green eyes and the hint of a smile lift the corners of her lips. "Do you think it's possible?" she breathed.

"Indeed, I do." He slapped his thighs for emphasis.

"But . . . who?" It was all she could manage, but Doc understood.

"My Sally, for one. Perhaps Julia Hudson. Skip thinks she might be interested. He's already given his consent. There must be three other women who are willing to clean up this town."

"Have you asked Sally?"

"No."

Perhaps, Kate thought, running for mayor was the *something else* that had stalled her decision. Winning this election was an unrealistic expectation. Mort Moffet was too powerful, and people were too resistant to change. But merely running for public office would further the cause of equal suffrage. She owed the movement that much. And when it was all over she'd pack up and go to Kansas City, join forces with the leaders of the movement there.

Kate stood up. "Then let's go talk to her. Time's awasting."

The way it turned out, Monday wouldn't be just another election day.

Since editor and publisher Herman Stockley had already put his weekly *Paradise Chronicle* to bed before Kate and Doc confirmed the women's ticket, the paper hit the streets Saturday morning without carrying the unprecedented news. Folks seldom read anything in the *Chronicle* they didn't know already, however. More news was exchanged on the boardwalk in front of the post office than ever found its way into the pages of the *Chronicle*.

All day Saturday people talked about the women's uprising, and by Sunday night hardly a soul wasn't aware that Kate McBride and five other women were running against Mort Moffet and his bunch of deadheads.

Of course, that meant that Kate's mother-in-law heard about it. Knowing the elder Mrs. McBride as well as she did, Kate fully expected a visit from the old busybody and prepared herself accordingly. All remained quiet at her lonely end of Elm Street until around three o'clock Sunday afternoon, when she answered a rapid-fire knock to see Adelaide McBride standing on her porch, the quick rises and falls of her large bosom and the tightness of her lips indicating her displeasure. As befitted his subservient attitude,

Arnold's father, Horace, stood beside his wife, but a step behind her.

Actually, Kate was relieved to be getting the inevitable scene behind her. The relief brought a brief, though deceptively gracious smile to her face. Then reality gave her heart a swift kick, and she experienced some difficulty summoning her voice. She covered her discomfort by taking a step backward and opening the door wider.

"What a surprise to see you," she finally managed, refusing to feel guilty about the falsehood. She wasn't about to admit she'd been expecting them sometime that day, nor was she about to say she was glad to see them. Kate could go the remainder of her life without seeing the McBrides and never miss them at all. Still, they were her kinfolk and her elders. Her mother had taught her to respect both. "Do, please, come in."

Still huffing, Adelaide pushed her way past Kate. Horace lagged behind, his gaze on his shuffling feet as he followed his wife into the parlor. Kate wanted to tell him that if he'd stand up straight, he might be as tall as Adelaide. This she wasn't too sure of; she'd never seen him with his back completely plumb.

She busied herself opening the heavy parlor drapes while she willed her heart to behave. Behind her, the settee groaned in protest, a sure indication that Adelaide had chosen it to light upon. Kate prayed the delicate piece held up under the unaccustomed weight.

"It's a little early for tea," Kate said, her back to the McBrides, "but I'll be happy to make us a pot."

"This isn't a social visit!" Adelaide snapped.

Damn, but she was a pompous ass! Kate wished she had the nerve to tell her so. She almost laughed out loud at the very idea, but settled for the smile of pure pleasure the thought had given her. The smile, however, represented an inappropriate reaction.

Slowly, deliberately, she pulled the heavy gold cord around the folds of claret-colored velvet and draped the tasseled end over the wall hook, all the while adjusting her features into what she hoped was a look of pure shock. Then, just as slowly, just as deliberately, she turned to face her in-laws.

"Oh?" she said with what she hoped was a suitable measure of innocence, her eyebrows stretched upward and her jaw slackened downward. "It isn't?"

Despite her bravado, Kate winced inwardly at Adelaide's piercing black gaze.

"You must know why we're here, Kate. Sit down," Adelaide added. "You're making me nervous."

Good! Kate thought and remained standing in front of the window. It was the first time she'd ever defied Adelaide, and it felt wonderfully exhilarating. "Why don't you tell me."

Adelaide sighed dramatically. "We didn't say anything when you decided to complete dear Arnold's term of office because it seemed a fitting thing to do for our son. But to run for mayor!" Adelaide clucked her tongue. "That's something else entirely—and quite unseemly for a woman of your social and financial stature."

"I don't see how my stature has anything to do with it," Kate said.

"It has everything to do with it!" Adelaide averred. "You *had* no social or financial stature until you married my son!"

Kate wished she could dispute that fact, but the truth was her father had been nothing more than a Topeka saloonkeeper who imbibed a bit too heavily from his own stock, and her mother had been a lowly washerwoman. Nevertheless, the two had recognized the need for education and had spent every dime they'd managed to save to see her through two years at the University of Kansas in Lawrence.

That was where she'd met Arnold, whose parents had never met Kate, much less known anything about her family, until the wedding. Shock was too mild a word to describe Adelaide's reaction when she'd met the Gillises. Despite the fact that their having met provided Adelaide with additional ammunition against her, Kate was glad her parents had lived long enough to see her married—and then mercifully died without knowing how miserable she was.

"Arnold saved you from a life of drudgery!" Adelaide declared. Kate didn't think she'd ever known anyone who used as many verbal exclamation marks as her mother-in-law. "Then, he left you a comfortably wealthy woman. And this—*this* is the way you repay him! By disgracing his good name!"

The blood drained from Kate's face and she clutched the drapery for support. "That was never my intention," she began, sounding far meeker than she'd intended.

"I knew you'd come to your senses, Kate," Horace said, rising from his chair. "Recording deeds is one thing; running a town is another. I'm glad you see the difference. Come on, Adelaide."

"But—" his wife sputtered. "I'm not through—"

If Horace heard her, he gave no indication. Instead, he headed for the door.

"Well!" Adelaide huffed, standing herself and following him.

That must be a first, Kate thought, proud of Horace for asserting himself but outdone at her own lack of posture. Perhaps they were right, she thought. Perhaps she had no business running for mayor. Maybe she should pull out of the race. . . .

The front door slammed hard into the frame. In the

wake of its booming echo came the tinkle of shattering glass. Kate ran to the door, then stopped short and watched in horror as shards of glass from one of the narrow sidelights rained onto the floor. Fighting back the sting of tears, she knelt and picked up one of the fragments. She laid the piece in her palm and stared at the delicately etched tail of a hummingbird.

The glass had come all the way from Baltimore, special-ordered and hand-etched to Kate's specifications. A matching panel hung in the other sidelight, while coordinating pieces had been made for the door and the fanlight over it. She'd waited over a year for the busy craftsman to get to her order, and she'd most likely have to wait another year to get a replacement. And even then, the odds of matching the existing pieces of glass were slim.

"Damn!" she whispered fiercely, shocking herself at actually giving voice to the curse. But doing it felt so good, she swore again. "Damn!"

Did the McBrides know how close they'd come to dissuading her? Did Adelaide realize her temper had cost her a victory?

Kate doubted it. She jerked the door open and, not really caring whether Adelaide heard her or not, she hollered at the retreating buggy. "I'm staying in the race. Do you hear? I'm running for mayor of this town!"

Chapter Two

Shortly after four Monday morning, Kate gave up trying to sleep. She threw the covers back and swung her long legs out of bed, but a loud screech from the vicinity of the footboard delayed her rising. She scooted down and reached across the bed with a tentative hand, feeling along the quilt until the tips of her fingers encountered fur.

"Sorry, Hobo, old boy," she whispered, sliding her hand upward in the thick fur and giving the cat a pat on the head. "I'm surprised you managed to sleep through my tossing and turning."

Beneath her stroking hand, the fat tabby, whose ancestry was as mottled as his brindled gray coat, stretched with exaggerated drama. Kate patted him one more time for good measure, slipped off the high bed, and lit the coal oil lamp on the bedside table. Hobo made a great show of squinting against the light, then hiding his eyes with a well-placed paw. Kate laughed lightly at the cat's antics before taking the lamp and padding off to the kitchen to make coffee.

Never, she thought as she stuffed kindling into the stove's firebox, had any day in her life held more promise or its potential outcome made her any more nervous than this one—not even her wedding day.

That admission caught her unawares, and without her guidance, Kate's musings traveled back to the day she had married Arnold McBride nine years ago.

It had been a warm, clear day in June, a day so perfect only God could have ordained it. Just as He had ordained her marriage to Arnold . . . or so the preacher said: "What God hath ordained, let no man put asunder."

Perhaps no man had put it asunder, but the marriage was doomed from the beginning. She was entirely the wrong kind of woman for Arnold. He'd needed someone to fawn over him, to depend on him, someone he could coddle and mold. And intimidate.

Maybe she was being unfair. Her granny had been fond of saying it didn't bode well to speak ill of the dead, but it hadn't taken Kate long to discover she'd made a grievous error in judgment when she'd said, "I do" to Arnold. And she couldn't help feeling his unexpected death had set her free.

Though Kate didn't honestly believe Arnold could reach her from the grave, she nevertheless put her reminiscences aside. Today was entirely too special to allow the cloud of dark memories to overshadow it.

If she was to become a leader, the first step was organization. While the water heated, Kate collected paper, pen, and inkwell from her desk, sat down at the kitchen table, and began making notes on the outside chance her all-female ticket was elected at the polls that day.

First, she listed two broad goals: "Enforce present laws that have been conveniently overlooked" and "Make Paradise a safe, clean, attractive place to live."

Next, she listed her five running mates: Sally Myers, Julia Hudson, Stella Carey, Liza Ziegler, and Martine Pence. She wrote their names in one column and left ample space between them. Beside each name, she listed ages, talents, and interests. The six ranged in age from twenty-three, with Julia the youngest, to forty-nine, Stella Carey being the oldest. Sally was a born organizer; Julia's youth would provide enthusiasm; no one managed to pinch pennies as well as Stella; Liza possessed the best public-speaking skills of them all.

A smile played upon Kate's lips as she wrote in the space next to Martine's name. She'd never met a woman who wanted to be a man quite as much as Martine Pence did. Kate wondered if Martine, who preferred to be called Marty and often defied the law by wearing trousers in public, had ever sewn a dress or arranged flowers in a vase. Though she tried, she couldn't conjure an image of the woman sitting still long enough to ply a needle or caring enough about aesthetics to decorate her house. But give Marty Pence a sewing machine to repair or a garden shed to build, and she was in her element. Marty would head up all engineering projects, from drainage improvement to street repair. Kate couldn't think of anything that would make Marty Pence happier.

If this thing were only possible, Kate thought, chewing the end of her pen. But it wasn't. Oh, there were plenty of folks who *said* they supported the women's ticket, but when it came right down to marking the ballot, Kate wasn't the least bit certain they'd actually vote for them. After all, nothing like this had ever been done before. Never had any town, at least not in the United States, elected an all-female administration. Kate had never heard of such a thing happening anywhere in the world.

Mort and his councilmen had derisively dubbed them the "petticoat" ticket, and the term had caught on. All over town, men were laughing and saying they weren't about to allow no "petticoats" to rule them.

No matter how much Kate and Doc and these five women wanted it to happen, it wasn't going to.

Kate was a realist, and she knew in the depths of her soul that this was to be the way of it. It was too outrageous to consider even remotely possible. It wouldn't happen.

At least she'd been given the opportunity to lose an election—she and five other women. They were taking a stand for feminism, for women's suffrage, for equal rights for everyone. And the world would hear about it, even though they wouldn't win.

That was far more than she had bargained for.

"Hey, Mitch!" Jabez Smiley, Dry Creek's blacksmith, called. "You mistaken any of them temp'rance women for whores lately?"

Mitch Dawson laid his pencil down and glanced up from the ledger, a pulsating tick at one temple in direct contradiction to the limp smile that hiked up the corners of his mouth. *Good Lord!* he thought. *It's been more than four months now. Do the people in this town ever let sleeping dogs lie?*

A lifelong resident himself, Mitch knew they didn't. Some of them still teased poor old Annie Mae Wilbanks, who'd recently turned forty-six, about wetting herself in the lower third grade. No, Dry Creek folks seemed to take a perverse enjoyment in cutting their teeth on the living flesh of human error and then tearing at the carcass until it was nothing more than an unrecognizable mass of tissue and bone. And even then . . .

At least he didn't blow up anymore. At least he could paste that silly grin on his face now and pretend he didn't care. Shorty had assured him that a lackadaisical shrug and a self-mocking smile would put an end to the harassment, but so far it hadn't worked. Not completely. The heckling had tapered off some, Mitch grudgingly admitted, though—to his way of thinking—not nearly enough. It was high time the people in Dry Creek chewed their fill of dog meat . . . *his* dog meat, anyway.

Forgetting to shrug, he stood up and ambled toward the counter, his sluggish pace deliberate. "You need something, Jabez?"

"Shore as shootin', else why would I be here?"

Mitch could think of a whole slew of caustic responses to that question. Despite his resolve to act indifferent and maintain a facade of cordiality, he would have voiced one of them if he hadn't taken so much time deciding which one to use.

"Need to send me a telligram," Jabez said, his round red face beaming and his barrel chest puffed out with pride.

This was the first time in the four months Mitch had been working at the Western Union office that the blacksmith had had reason to send a telegram. Still and all, Mitch couldn't understand why such a simple, everyday thing as sending one should elicit a vainglorious attitude. There was just no figuring some folks.

"Got it all writ down, nice and proper like. Checked ever' word agin Noah Webster, too, so don't go changin' nothin', you hear?"

Weary of faking tact, Mitch replied in a voice dripping with sarcasm, "I wouldn't dream of it." He took the block-lettered message from Jabez, then looked up at the jingle of the bell on the door. "Morning, Mrs. Shaw," he said, nodding absentmindedly at the storekeeper's wife, who was the town's busiest gossip. "I'll be with you in a minute." Mitch returned his attention to the paper in his hand and started to read it out loud. "Myra Sedgewick, Spring Street, St. Louis—"

"Now wait just a goldern minute! What you think you're doin'?" Jabez bellowed, his complexion suddenly far redder than usual.

Mitch blinked in confusion. "Reading this to you," he explained in an adult-to-child—or, more appropriately, genius-to-idiot—manner.

"Why?"

"Because I want to be sure I send the right message."

"I done tole you I writ it right. Just send it," Jabez demanded.

"Regulations say I've got to read it back to you first." Mitch glared at Jabez, daring him to argue. If Western Union had any such regulation, Mitch didn't know about it, but he'd made the practice a habit since the fiasco with Reverend Hunsaker's message, just before Christmas.

Until that incident, Mitch figured no one in Dry Creek had more education than the Methodist minister, who delighted in sprinkling his sermons with long, virtually unpronounceable words that no one knew the meanings of. Words like *prototypical* and *obfuscation* and *interpellate*. Occasionally, he threw in some shorter, though equally obscure words like *cymatium* and *eschew*. The man's extensive vocabulary, coupled with a pompous air, had convinced the townsfolk of his superior intelligence, even if they didn't have the slightest notion what he was talking about.

So, when Mitch sent Hunsaker's message, he didn't question the minister's spelling or word choice. The long missive, addressed to Bishop Kerr, read in part, "You will be pleased to know that I have successfully fecundated those members who have heretofore exhibited fickleness."

On Christmas Day the bishop himself arrived on the train from Kansas City and marched right into the church in the midst of opening prayer. The congregation, Mitch among them, sat stunned as Bishop Kerr interrupted the minister's long-winded invocation with a loud "Amen," and then faced the crowd and announced his intention to remove Reverend Hunsaker from his post before he impregnated another female member of his congregation. That action, the bishop assured them, had not been sanctioned by the church, nor would it be tolerated.

Elias Hunsaker gasped and clutched his high-collared throat. "I've done no such thing! Wherever did you get that idea?" Though it took some doing, Hunsaker eventually convinced Bishop Kerr that the word *fecundated* in his telegram was supposed to have been *secundated*.

"I'm sure that's what I wrote!" he averred.

"There's no such word!" the bishop argued.

The two battled loudly from the pulpit while the members of the congregation attempted to stanch their mirth. Before the quarrel was over, they came to understand that the minister's wire was supposed to tell the bishop that those who were lacking a steadfast faith had been brought to their senses and were now following the straight-and-narrow path.

Although the incident gave the townsfolk someone else to rib, there were those who blamed the mistake on Mitch. He counted himself lucky not to have lost *this* job on the basis of human error. Trouble had become his constant shadow. Now that he knew it, he wasn't about to take any more chances. For one thing, he needed the wage. But there was another, far more important reason Mitch Dawson wanted to hold on to his job with Western Union.

Decoding telegraph messages allowed him to know about some things before anyone else did. Sometimes, it was a job opening. Sometimes, the job was that of town marshal. Eventually, he would answer such a message, and no one on the other end of the wire would know anything about Mitch Dawson's downfall. And then he would go back to doing what he wanted to do—marshaling—because he'd been Johnny-on-the-spot and answered the advertisement before it ever even got printed in the newspaper or tacked on the wall in the post office.

Deep down, Mitch didn't honestly believe he'd ever work as a lawman again. After all, Wyatt Earp hadn't come close to offending a governor, and look what had happened to him. He'd just been doing his job, to Mitch's reckoning, when he shot the Clantons at the O.K. Corral. That had been over six years ago, and Earp hadn't worked as a lawman since. Probably never would again.

Mitch supposed he'd spend the remainder of his days working at the Western Union office in Dry Creek . . . assuming he could manage to hold on to this job. He didn't expect to ever be happy again, but maybe he wouldn't always be so miserable.

When Mitch finished reading Jabez Smiley's message aloud, he was grinning and Jabez was squirming. So, the blacksmith had a lady friend in St. Louis, but he didn't want anyone to know about it. Mrs. Shaw "ahemmed" rather obtrusively, and Jabez turned redder.

"I'm gonna git you for this, Dawson," Jabez spat out. "There ain't no such regulation. Telligrams're s'post to be private. Now, thanks to the two of you"— he twisted his neck and pierced Mrs. Shaw with a knowing look—" the whole town's gonna know 'bout mine!"

Mitch cringed inside and wondered if he'd made yet another serious error. "Just tell me if this is right," he said, his jaw clenched.

"I done tole you it is! Ere you gonna send it or not?"

Mitch nodded, one part of his mind counting letters with his pencil point while another part counted his remaining hours in the employment of Western Union.

From the moment the polls opened people stood in line to vote. Kate couldn't remember a single election in the history of Paradise that had fostered such a heavy turnout. A few hours after the polls opened some of the anti-Prohibition men, worried about the number of women casting ballots, attempted to split the female vote by fielding another all-female ticket. The women they approached, however, refused to run, and the ploy failed.

This attempt tickled Kate and her running mates, but none of them seriously thought the men had anything to worry about. Too many of the women voters apologized for not voting for the females. They had to live with their husbands—or their fathers or their elder brothers, they explained. And surely the men—at least those outside the immediate families of the women whose names appeared on the ballot—were voting for Mort Moffet and his bunch. By her calculations, her ticket might glean as many as thirty or forty votes, tops. There was simply no way on God's green earth the women could win. But she was determined to try with everything she had to offer.

"When I moved here nine years ago," Kate told the small crowd gathered around her, "Paradise was a pretty little town and a decent place to raise a family. I loved this town then and I love it now. But somewhere along the way we lost our pride. For too long we've allowed the wrong people to run this town. Paradise is no longer an appropriate name for our community. Sally, Julia, Stella, Liza, Martine, and I pledge to restore pride in our town, to clean it up, widen the streets, provide proper drainage, install street lamps, and see that the law is enforced and violaters are prosecuted."

It was a speech she'd repeated often, but she believed as strongly in her words then as she had the first time she'd uttered them that morning. Her voice rang with fervency and purpose, and her heart thrilled each time someone nodded in agreement and wished her luck.

"You realize," Doc Myers had said that morning to all six women who were seeking election, "that if you're elected, you're in for a passel of trouble. Cleaning up this town the way it needs to be cleaned up isn't going to be easy, and you'll face more than the usual share of opposition simply because you're women."

Doc's words stayed with Kate throughout the day, and each recollection of them strengthened her purpose. She supposed her attitude might be considered a bit insane by most, but she saw it as the greatest challenge of her life and embraced it wholeheartedly.

No matter how much she and her female cohorts believed in their cause, however, Kate continued to harbor little hope that they would be given the opportunity to meet the challenge. There were simply too many men supporting the present government, and they had all turned out to vote.

The boardwalk and street in front of the town hall were both so congested, some folks experienced true difficulty making their way through to the door and then out again once they had cast their ballots.

Mort Moffet's food and liquor wagon, parked on the right side of the door, right up next to the boardwalk, contributed to the bottleneck, as did the throng of men gathered around the vehicle. As the day wore on, that assemblage steadily grew, until by midafternoon the men stood so thick, Kate wondered how they managed to breathe.

The loud buzz that rose from their ranks, punctuated quite often with raucous laughter and the loud slap of open palms connecting with backs and thighs, testified to their vitality—at least for those who were still on their feet. Occasionally, someone managed to wedge a wide enough opening in the crowd to reveal several of Mort's cohorts sprawled on their backs beneath the wagon, their open mouths sawing logs. During one such gap, Kate watched Billy Fink dribble whiskey into an open mouth until the poor fellow gagged. Billy giggled, then turned the bottle up and guzzled. The amber liquid ran out of the corners of his mouth and onto his shirt collar.

In disgust, Kate went looking for Obediah Stringfellow, the town marshal. She found him near the wagon's tailgate, a battered metal flask in one hand, a half-eaten chicken leg in the other, and a dark blue chicken vein hanging off his lower lip.

"Welp, the enemy's done infiltrated our camp," he drawled, tearing a strip off the leg with half-rotted teeth and chewing noisily. He wore a three- or four-day-old beard on his grizzled face, a battered felt hat with a wide sweat stain where the crown met the brim, and dirt-smeared khakis that didn't look like they'd ever seen an ounce of starch or a pair of stretchers.

Though it took all the stamina she could muster, Kate looked him square in the face. "I want to know what you're going to do about this chaos."

Some of the men pressed closer, their faces suddenly stony, their eyes daring the marshal to side with her. Kate's heart skittered to a stop as a wave of panic washed through her, but she took a deep breath and stood her ground.

Stringfellow chewed, washed the chicken down with a slug from his flask, then let his gaze roam the contingent of men standing closest to them. "Chaos? I don't see no chaos, ma'am."

Kate extended an arm and swept the narrow vista. "What do you call this?"

"Good food, good whiskey, good company. Hell, it's election day, Miz McBride. Why don't you just go back over there where you came from and mind your own binness?"

She planted her feet as firmly as she could in the squishy mud and flashed him what she hoped was a look of pure defiance. "Not until you break up this crowd, marshal."

"If I break up this crowd, ma'am, I'm gonna have to come over there and bust up that pitiful little group on your side, too."

"Why? We aren't blocking the doorway."

"That's only because there ain't enough of you. We're just exercisin' our cons'tutional right to assemble, and we aim to keep right on exercisin' it."

"Who gave you the right to ignore the state Prohibition law?"

Everyone within hearing distance guffawed, including the marshal. "You cain't be serious."

Kate's voice rose with her anger. "Oh, but I am serious, Marshal Stringfellow. You and these other men are in direct violation of state law. I demand that you assume the responsibility that goes with your office and enforce that law."

Her outrage earned her the attention of more of the men, including that of the mayor. Without bothering to apologize for the toes he stepped on or the ribs he elbowed, Mort Moffet shouldered his way through the crowd until he secured a spot mere inches from Kate

McBride. "You cain't honestly believe anyone's gonna take you serious."

"Folks already are, Mr. Moffet," she said, taking courage from his sudden fidgeting with his hat. He recovered quickly, though, assumed his best biggest-toad-in-the-puddle posture, and pinned her with a look of pure malice.

"I'm still mayor of this town, Miz McBride," he said. "Stringfellow answers to me, not to you. So you git yourself back over there to your little table and let him do his job."

There could be no better revenge, Kate thought, than winning the election.

At long last six o'clock rolled around, and Hardy Osborne declared the polls officially closed. A hush fell over the crowd. The townsfolk who hadn't gone home yet jammed themselves into the open doorway and spilled out onto the boardwalk and into the street.

Kate, along with the women on her ticket and their husbands, held prime spots near the doorway. Inside, Hardy unlocked the ballot box while Judge Warren and Obediah Stringfellow, who would serve as official witnesses, pulled two chairs up to the council table.

At first no one uttered a sound or even rustled a skirt as Hardy unfolded ballots and called out names. "Moffet . . . Moffet . . . McBride . . ."

"Why don't you just say 'men' and 'women'?" a man hollered.

"Yeah," someone else chimed in. "That's what this is all about, ain't it?"

Kate sincerely hoped not, but she feared that was exactly the way too many people perceived it. And if that were so, she and her all-female ticket didn't stand a snowball's chance in hell.

Once the silence was broken there was no regaining it. Conversations broke out, and some of the more inebriated men started singing a rousing ditty off-key. After a while Kate gave up on keeping a running tally in her head anyway. There were simply too many ballots.

Around seven, Hardy called for quiet. "We have ourselves a new mayor," he said, his voice sounding thin and tired.

"Well, who is it?" Mort demanded, pushing his way into the room.

"Miz McBride."

The breath left Kate's lungs in a whoosh and she swayed against Sally Myers. "We did it!" Sally squealed.

Mort's cheeks bloomed scarlet and his eyes bulged. "That's not possible!" he railed. "What was the count?"

The piece of paper in Hardy's hand rattled and his Adam's apple bobbed several times before he squeaked out, "McBride, two hundred fifteen. Moffet, two hundred twelve."

"Three votes!" Mort screeched. "She beat me by three votes! That's too close. I demand a recount."

"Well, we was sort of distracted," Hardy allowed, "what with all the noise and such."

"Damned straight!" Stringfellow bellowed. "The count prob'ly ain't right. Stuff 'em all back in the box, Hardy, and let's start over."

By this time Kate had recovered somewhat, enough to note that Ainsworth Warren looked miserable and seemed determined to stay out of the argument. "What do you think, Judge?" she asked. When he didn't answer and simply sat puffing on his pipe, she posed a more specific question. "Could there have been a mistake?"

"Possibly. It is awfully close. Let's do it again. But this time, behind closed doors. I'd like to go home sometime tonight."

Kate set the kettle back on the stove and glanced at the heavily carved—and heavily scarred—clock on the kitchen wall. Six minutes to eight.

Noting the time, she assured herself, was crucial to producing a palatable cup of tea and bore no relationship to the fact that almost an hour had passed since Judge Warren had shooed them all away and the recount had begun. Despite her best intentions, she'd counted every minute since, minutes that seemed to drag by at the pace of a bloated garden slug.

She tried to cling to hope, but as the minutes passed, the thread that bound her to the dream grew thinner and thinner. She'd had her moment of glory, she counseled herself. Forever, she would remember the look on Mort Moffet's face and hear Sally's squeals and feel her own heart fluttering in her chest. But to expect the count to hold up was unrealistic. She doubted any one of the three men who were doing the counting wanted her to win, and she wouldn't put it past a single one of them to fix the count.

Though good at heart, Hardy had worked for Mort Moffet for years and would probably feel uncomfortable with anyone else for a boss. The same held true for Stringfellow, and her defiance that afternoon hadn't helped endear her to him. As for Judge Warren, Kate had never known him to be anything but fair, and yet she didn't fully trust him to remain totally unbiased in this situation.

Then there was the possibility that an honest mistake had been made, that the three men had counted incorrectly.

Regardless of the reason, Kate anticipated a reversal when all was said and done.

And when they lost what would she do with her life? She couldn't quite imagine getting up every day with nowhere to go, nothing to do, no one to take care of.

If she and Arnold had only had a child . . . how different her life would be. A little girl, maybe, with hair the color of unripened strawberries and eyes as blue as a robin's egg. Or a boy, with black hair and dark brown eyes like his father . . .

"It's all your fault," Adelaide had said. "If you'd been a proper wife and produced a child, my son would still be alive. . . ."

Kate shivered and quickly returned to considering the course of her immediate future. Suddenly, everything had changed, and now she didn't want to leave Paradise, to move to Kansas City and work for the suffrage movement again. She supposed she could swallow her pride and ask John McCready for a job in his office. John was the only candidate and therefore certain to be the new Madison County registrar of deeds. But now that she'd had the whole pie, she didn't think a small piece of it would satisfy her.

Still, she couldn't stay at home every day or she'd go crazy as a betsy bug. As it was, surviving the lonely weekends consumed all her emotional strength. Alone in the quiet house, she heard strange, nonexistent noises—a baby crying, a child laughing . . .

Cuckoo. Cuckoo. Cuckoo. Cuckoo.

The sound jerked Kate out of her daze and drew her attention to the clock. From his perch atop the pie safe, Hobo crouched, his gray body trembling in expectation.

Cuckoo. Cuckoo. Cuckoo.

The cat's flanks stiffened, and he sprang at the little carved bird.

Cuckoo.

The bird retreated safely into its cubby and the tiny door swung shut before the cat reached the crest of his vault. Almost immediately, his right paw struck the door, adding another scratch to the dark walnut. The gray tabby hung poised in midair, then plummeted to the floor and landed with a resounding thump on a strategically placed braided rug. Kate might not mind so much about a clock that could easily be replaced, but she wasn't about to allow the cat to damage her hardwood floor.

Kate laughed, poured herself a cup of tea, and sat down at the kitchen table. "Come here, silly," she called, patting her lap. As was his habit, Hobo gave the clock a long, defiant stare before vacating the rug. When he had settled himself on Kate's thighs she ruffled the thick fur behind his head, then stroked his back until he relaxed.

How many times had she tried to do the same thing for Arnold? she wondered. How many times had he come home from work tense and angry with the world? How many times had she rubbed his neck and stroked his back, willing her strong hands and long fingers to grant him surcease?

Countless times. And not once had her ministrations proved effective. For eight long years, she had tried. She had given Arnold everything she had to give—every consideration, every regard; everything— except her love.

A lone tear escaped her eye and fell *plop* into her teacup, but Kate didn't see it or hear it or feel it anymore than she saw the polished tabletop or heard Hobo's contented purrs or felt the warmth of the thin china teacup against her palm. Instead, she saw Arnold's stern, unyielding face. She heard her mother-in-law accuse her of making Arnold miserable. And she felt a deep, abiding sadness at her inability to bear children, at her inability to love another human being.

Clanging cymbals, screeching trumpets, and the steady beat of a snare drum startled Kate from a troubled sleep. She shook her head, certain she'd been dreaming, but the *oom-pah-pah* of a tuba and the discordant note of a trumpet convinced her the sounds of the brass band were real.

And they were coming from right outside her front door.

Chapter Three

With trembling fingers, Kate dabbed at eyes swollen from sleep while her heart lurched within her chest. Was it possible? Had they won?

Though she could think of no other reason the Paradise Brass Band would be playing a rousing march on her front walk, she tempered her rising hope with enough mental ballast to keep her spirit earthbound. Slowly, she rose from the table, moving to lift the still-sleeping cat and place him on the chair without conscious thought. Slowly, almost in a daze, she patted her hair and smoothed her skirts. Slowly, she moved out of the kitchen and into the dining room.

The sudden beating upon her door and the whistles and shouts from outside sent her pulse racing through her veins and her feet running through the house and into the vestibule.

Long streamers of golden light beamed through the frosted glass, its etchings fracturing the light and spinning it out in obtuse angles, creating a wondrous array of light and shadow that begged for the soft strains of an orchestra and the nimble feet of fairies to dance upon the spun-gold threads. For a moment Kate stood mesmerized, certain the crashing and banging were but figments of her imagination, a dissonant counterpoint to the delicate beauty before her.

But there was no denying the sharp rap upon her door.

She shook off the illusion and snatched open the front door to find Dr. Myers standing on her porch, a wide smile and twinkling eyes setting his face aglow. Behind him, spilling down the steps and into the yard, stood a multitude of Paradise residents, many of them holding blazing torches high over their heads. Although the torches failed to illuminate their faces, Kate could feel their excitement so strongly, she thought if she but reached out, she could grasp it in her hand.

Her pounding heart matched the roll of the drum beat for beat. When a clash of the cymbals ended the energetic tune the crowd erupted in disjointed shouts of "Congratulations!" and "You won!"

The heat of the crowd's enthusiasm permeated her senses until she felt hot and liquid and so light-headed she was certain that if she let go of the heavy door, she would float away.

"Can it be?" she whispered, thinking surely she must still be asleep and dreaming.

Doc's lips twitched. "They did make a mistake, Kate."

"I knew it," she breathed, her chest suddenly tight.

"Hardy got confused about whose tally marks were whose," Wilbur Myers explained, "and gave some votes to Mort that belonged to you."

"So we won?"

"Yes. By *twenty-three* votes."

Kate laid an open palm between her breasts in an effort to control her pounding heart and made him repeat it. Even then, she wasn't sure she'd heard correctly. The doctor took her elbow and guided her away from the door and onto the porch.

A strange combination of joy and apprehension washed through her. "Do the others know yet?"

"Just the two of us so far," Sally said, stepping forward and taking Kate's other elbow. "Come on." She gave Kate a gentle tug. "Let's go tell them."

The following morning, while Kate and her new council awaited the official results, they met informally in Kate's dining room.

Kate dragged out the big pot she reserved for company and made coffee, and Julia brought an angel food cake, but Kate made it very clear that they had not gathered to socialize.

"We can't do anything official yet, of course," she clarified, "but we can assess the status quo and map out a plan of action."

"When will we receive official notice?" Sally asked.

"Probably not until tomorrow. Maybe even Thursday," Kate speculated. "The ordinance says they have two days, and I expect them to take every one of their forty-eight hours. And don't be surprised if it all gets turned around. But let's don't worry about that. My biggest concern right now is money. Last Friday Mort told Doc that there is only thirty-six cents in the treasury."

"Whew!" Liza groaned. "Old Mort didn't leave us with much, did he?"

"Probably a stack of outstanding bills," Julia speculated in a sour voice.

"I haven't seen the books yet, so I don't know what amounts we may owe," Kate replied.

"That's all right. We're homemakers," Stella said

brightly. "We know how to squeeze blood out of turnips."

You do better than the rest of us, Kate thought, but she suspected that the knowledge stemmed from necessity rather than talent, and she wasn't about to embarrass Stella by saying so.

"We'll manage the town finances far better than our predecessors," Kate said, "and taxes are due now, so we will have operating funds. But let's not worry about that today. Today, let's list the major problems and set some definite goals, both short- and long-term. Julia volunteered to record, but I think we all should take notes. Who wants to start?"

"There's the mud," Marty said.

"Now that's a problem," Sally agreed.

"We need a new sign on the way into town," Julia put in.

"That's not a big problem," Marty snapped.

Julia defended her recommendation. "I think it is."

Kate sensed an argument brewing. "For the time being let's simply list the problems. We'll categorize and prioritize them later."

Several more times during the course of the discussion Kate found herself serving as arbitrator between Marty and Julia. Never had she anticipated these two locking horns, but they seemed determined to disagree that day on every issue—except one.

And though Kate wholeheartedly agreed that there was only one course of action to be taken on that particular issue, she dreaded having to take that action herself. But she was the mayor now, with all the duties and responsibilities holding that office entailed. If one of those duties happened to be making Marshal Obediah Stringfellow toe the line, then so be it.

She'd have to be firm with him; let him know right up front that he answered to her and her council now, not Mort and his bunch. But she couldn't do anything until she received official notice that proclaimed her the new mayor of Paradise, Kansas.

The notice arrived just before ten the following morning, delivered by a nervous Hardy Osborne. If Kate hadn't been waiting, she might not have heard his timid knock. Hardy stood staring at the toes of shiny new shoes. Kate's gaze followed his. Had his feet always been so large? Or his legs so long? Funny, she thought; she'd never paid the man much attention, but if she was to work with him every day, they'd have to learn to be a bit more comfortable with each other.

He moved his gaze to the hem of her dress, cleared his throat, and sputtered, "This here's for you, ma'am."

As she waited for him to raise the envelope he clutched so tightly and offer it to her, her heart skipped a beat. What if Doc had been wrong about the election results? she wondered. Worse, what if he'd been right, but the folks at the town hall had seen fit to rearrange the numbers to suit themselves?

Hardy Osborne was disposed to nervousness, Kate reminded herself. There was no reason to worry. Not yet.

Slowly, almost painfully, Hardy raised the envelope, and though his chin came up, he fixed his gaze on the wide board Kate had tacked up over the shattered sidelight.

"Did somebody break your glass?" he asked.

"Not intentionally," Kate said, taking the envelope from Hardy's hand. Across the center someone had written her full, legal name. Without bothering to fetch her letter opener, she ripped at the flap. Discretion stayed her hand before she removed the single folded sheet. As clerk, Hardy more than likely knew the exact contents of the message, but she had no desire to share her reaction to those contents with him.

"Is there something else?" she asked.

He shuffled his big feet and moved his gaze to the potted boxwood beside the door. "No, ma'am."

"Well, then, I'll see you later at the town hall."

Hardy's response fell dully from lips that barely moved. "Yes, ma'am."

The second he turned his back and took a step toward the street, Kate closed the door and pulled the sheet from the envelope. Her eyes bypassed the salutation and went straight to the message:

> You are hereby notified that at an election held in the city of Paradise on Monday April 2/88, for the purpose of electing city officers, you were duly elected to the office of Mayor of our city. You will take due notice thereof and govern yourself accordingly.

The letter was signed by both Mort Moffet and Hardy Osborne, who had written his title as "Clerk Protem."

Poor Hardy! No wonder he'd been so nervous, signing his name to this frosty confirmation of her victory at the polls, a confirmation Mort had obviously penned since his signature matched the handwriting. And now Hardy depended on her for his job.

Kate jerked open her door and called to Hardy, who was climbing into his buggy. "I'd be proud to retain you as town clerk, Hardy, if you still want the job."

Hardy grinned, and his head bobbed enthusiastically. "Oh, yes, ma'am!"

The full weight of the mayor's responsibilities had yet to settle on Kate McBride's narrow shoulders.

Until that moment, she hadn't stopped to consider how many city employees fell under her jurisdiction.

But only one of those employees mattered to her that morning.

"Could I ride into town with you, Hardy?"

"I'll be happy to take you, Miz McBride, and bring you back whenever you're ready."

She returned the note to the envelope, tucked it into her reticule, and set off for the town hall.

Obediah Stringfellow took his own sweet time coming around to see Kate, who spent the intervening hours being sworn in by Judge Warren and then going through the pile of papers Mort had left on the mayor's desk. She sorted, filed, and made notes while she mentally practiced the speech she would deliver to the rude man—if he ever showed up.

Had she not been determined to talk to him on her own turf, she would have given up and gone to him. In fact, she was just about to do that very thing when Obediah strolled into her office. Without waiting to be asked, he plopped down in one of the two visitors' chairs. That, Kate thought, was bad enough, but then he folded his arms across his chest, propped his scuffed boots on her desk, and pinned her with an insolent grin.

"You wanted to see me?" he drawled.

Kate stared at the tips of his boots until he dropped his feet to the floor. Then she stared at the sweat-stained band of the felt hat that rode low on his forehead until he removed the offensive piece of headgear. Obediah wasn't going to make this easy.

She took a deep, fortifying breath. "There are some matters the two of us must come to an understanding on," she began.

"If you're talkin' about the time I spend away from the jail, you can save your breath," he interrupted. "It's bad enough havin' to live in that dump. I ain't about to stay there all the time. 'Sides, we ain't got no prisoners. Ain't had none in a while."

Unwittingly, Obediah's interruption led straight to the heart of the matter. Kate smiled sweetly and moved in for the attack. "Can you explain why that is true, Marshal Stringfellow?"

He lifted his shoulders indifferently. "I s'pose it's 'cause we ain't had no shoot-'em-ups in a spell. Ain't had no other serious crimes committed neither, not that I know about, anyways."

Obediah smiled then, obviously pleased with himself.

Kate smiled, too. She laid her forearms on the now clear desktop and leaned toward him, assuming a conspiratorial air. "If I'm not mistaken, Marshal, blatant disregard for state law constitutes a crime; a serious one."

That remark pulled his bushy eyebrows together. "I ain't followin' you, missy."

"Did you ever call Mort Moffet 'boy'?"

"Oh, no, ma'am, but it wouldn't abeen no crime iffen I had of."

"No," she agreed, "merely disrespect." Kate let that sink in. "Seven years ago," she resumed, "Kansas passed Prohibition. Have you forgotten?"

Obediah grinned. "Oh, no, ma'am. I ain't forgot. But nobody pays that law no mind. Never have. Never will."

"We will, Marshal Stringfellow."

"Now, Miz McBride, you can't honestly expect me to—"

"Yes, I do. And so does the town council."

Obediah sprang up from his chair and leaned

menacingly over her desk. Kate steeled herself against his foul breath and the glint of malice in his pale eyes.

"Well, I ain't gonna!" he declared, his nose practically in her face.

Though outwardly calm, inside Kate felt like her stomach was being run through a meat grinder. "Wouldn't you like to reconsider that stance, Marshal?"

"Hell, no!" he bellowed.

She held out her right hand, palm upward. "Then you offer me no other choice. Please surrender that badge."

Obediah Stringfellow stood up straight and pierced Kate with a look of pure meanness. "You kin ask all you like, *missy*. You ain't gettin' it. I'm the marshal in this town and you ain't man enough to change it."

Before she could protest further, Obediah turned on his heel and strode out of the office. Kate's first reaction was to chase after him, but there were better ways to deal with this situation.

"Lock up for me, Hardy, will you," she said on her way out the door. "I have to get to the telegraph office before Simon closes up for the day."

"How dare you!"

The words didn't fully penetrate, but the tone did.

"Remove your feet from the top of that desk. *Now!*"

Let her rant, Mitch thought. She was probably an old hag who'd been rode hard and put away wet by a man who'd left her for greener pastures, and now she had to work to feed her younguns. Elsewise, she wouldn't be here. Whoever she was, she wasn't important.

"How dare you ignore me!"

Fiesty thing. She liked that word—*dare*. Lazily, he

lifted a hand that had been stroking the calico cat in his lap, pointed the forefinger, and tipped his hat back a mite—just enough to uncover his eyes but far enough down on his forehead to show her who was in control.

The sight before him caught him completely unawares. She stood in the doorway, bathed in light. The early morning sunlight streaming through the window behind her danced on vibrant strands of reddish-blond hair and framed her tall, slender figure in a golden halo. She was one of the most beautiful women he'd ever laid eyes on . . . and one of the maddest.

He couldn't imagine what she had to be angry about. She couldn't possibly be saddle sore from four days of hard riding. She couldn't possibly be so hungry for a hot meal her insides were rubbing together. She couldn't possibly know what it was like to leave the town you grew up in, the house you'd called home for thirty-four years, and set out for some strange place you'd never heard of, and then arrive to find it a little town so pitifully ugly that only the funnel cloud of a tornado could fix it. *Paradise?* Not even close.

No, she couldn't possibly feel or understand these things.

But Mitch did. He narrowed his eyes at her and mumbled the vilest oath he could think of.

"Who *are* you?" the woman snapped.

Mitch grinned at the fire leaping from eyes as pale and pure a green as the new prairie grasses. This woman had spirit, that much was certain, but Mitch hurt too bad to garner any spirit himself. His voice matched his weariness and reflected the lackadaisical attitude he'd practiced so well he had it down pat. "Mitch Dawson. The mayor's expecting me. Would you please tell him I'm here."

The woman closed her eyes and took a deep breath.

Mitch liked the way it made her face go all soft and her bosom poke out. She didn't have much up top, but what she had looked awfully firm and round. Without his direction, Mitch's fingers curled into an empty grasp the same size as her breasts, and his hands squeezed thin air.

He wondered if she was married. Not likely. He didn't know a man who'd allow his wife to work in a government office. In fact, he didn't know a man who'd allow his wife to work outside their home. Period. Selling butter and eggs was one thing; working for a regular salary was something else entirely. He might have had the "old hag" part wrong, but he'd bet she had a passel of younguns to feed and no husband to provide for them.

Whatever misfortunes she might have suffered didn't give her the right to be rude, though. And that's what she was being, standing in the doorway with her arms crossed under her bosom and her toe tapping against the floor. How was he supposed to see if she was married with her hands tucked under her armpits?

Hell, it didn't matter. She might be pretty, but she wasn't his type. Too uppity, he decided. Let her and her younguns starve. They weren't none of his concern.

"Look, lady," he growled, "I've been ridin' for four days and I ain't in no mood for no female contrariness. All I want right now is to meet the mayor, get me some breakfast, and then go find a barbershop. If the mayor ain't around, just tell me and I'll come back later."

So this was the man she'd hired over the wire—this cowboy with a bearded stubble that had been collecting for days, long, scraggly hair so dirty she couldn't tell for sure what color it was, and mud splattered all over his chaps. This *chauvinist* who hadn't even risen from *her* chair when she'd walked into the room, let alone removed his hat or taken his spurred boot heels off her desk. At least Obediah Stringfellow had finally succumbed to a degree of deference. But not this fellow. This man hadn't even bothered to bathe and shave before coming to see her.

No wonder they'd fired him in Dry Creek.

Kate had a notion to send him on his merry way herself, but she'd promised him a three-month trial and she wasn't one to go back on her word. Besides, Paradise needed a marshal, and she was directly responsible for seeing that the town had one. Considering the circumstances, she'd expected a bit more trouble hiring an experienced man. This one not only had experience, he had also agreed to take the job. Most men would have run from, not *to,* a town that elected an all-female government, a "petticoat" government newspapers all over the country had dubbed it, taking their cue from Mort Moffet.

Suddenly, Kate smiled. Obviously, she knew more about Mitch Dawson than he knew about her. How he'd missed seeing a newspaper or hearing about the world-changing event in Paradise she couldn't imagine. But he didn't know. He'd said, "Would you please tell *him* I'm here."

Caution stayed the shrewish retort she wanted to hurl at him; caution and the tiniest bit of delight in this situation. Witnessing his reaction when he found out *she* was the mayor was going to be a pleasure. And then she'd see to it that Mitch Dawson learned some manners—if he stayed around long enough.

His staying around, even temporarily, constituted her first priority.

Kate pursed her lips and let her gaze roam leisurely over his long legs, up his buckskin vest, and across his wide shoulders, finally settling on a pair of the biggest, darkest brown eyes she'd ever seen. They were even darker than the battered, chocolate-brown Stetson that rode low on his brow. She'd been taken in by a pair of dark brown eyes before . . .

Kate shivered at the thought, then pushed it safely away into the lumber room of her memory and resolutely closed the door.

"So," she said, her voice low and mellow by design, "you're the new marshal."

The slow smile that lifted the corners of his wide mouth made her head reel. Kate mentally leaned against the door she'd just closed.

He rubbed his stubbled chin with fingers long and brown and lean. Aristocratic fingers. A pianist's fingers. Fingers that ended in square nails with broken cuticles, nails that were both dirty and too long. The inconsistency startled her while the slow stroking of his chin set her limbs to quivering.

"Yes, ma'am," he drawled. "And who might you be?"

"Kate," she said, and without thinking, she added, "McBride."

He nodded knowingly. "Ah, the mayor's wife."

"No."

"His sister?"

Kate shook her head and fought back a grin. "No."

"Daughter."

"No."

He swung his feet off the desk, planted them on the floor, and stood up, dislodging the cat, who promptly stretched out on the floor and resumed its nap. But Kate wasn't watching the cat. She was watching Mitch Dawson. She watched in unabashed fascination as his long, lean body unfolded until he towered over her.

Kate was tall for a woman. Height, as she well

knew, intimidated most people. This man might be uncouth, but at least he possessed the required degree of both arrogance and physical presence necessary to perform his duties.

"Well, you can't be his mother. I don't know how old you are, lady, but you can't possibly be old enough to have a son old enough to be the mayor of this town."

"My, my," she clucked, "that was a mouthful. The truth is, I don't have a son."

"Then how are you kin to the mayor?"

"I'm not." It wasn't a lie. Not really. How could you be kin to yourself? Kate reached for a diversion, anything to stall this line of questioning. She'd tell him who she was, but in her own good time, not his. She walked around the desk, opened a drawer, and removed a dull metal star she'd cut from the bottom of a tin can.

"What's this?" he asked when she offered him the star.

"Your badge."

He laughed—a deep, rumbling, mirthless laugh. "I'm not wearing that piece of trash."

"Not for long, I hope." She paused, relishing the hint of anxiety that slackened the arrogant set of his jaw. Oh, this man was hungry, no doubt about that. And that was good. Very good.

"Your first order of business," she continued, "will be to retrieve the official badge from your predecessor. He refuses to give it up."

"I can handle that," he said in a voice rife with unrestrained confidence. He accepted the proffered star, then promptly dropped it when one of its freshly cut edges sliced the pad of his thumb. Blood spurted out and plopped onto the blotter.

"Here," Kate said, pulling a rolled-edge hanky that

bore her initials from the waistband of her skirt. "Hold still while I tie this around your thumb."

"Never mind," he grumbled, turning away.

"But I do mind," she insisted, stepping around him and taking his hand in hers. "You're dripping all over the place."

"It's not my fault! Somebody should've taken a pair of pliers and tucked in those sharp edges."

"That somebody is me, and I don't think I own any pliers."

She made short work of bandaging the thumb with her white linen handkerchief, then picked up the tin star, slid it over the edge of his vest, and pressed its tab into the soft buckskin. Beneath her hand, his heart hammered against the hard wall of his chest. At the quickening of her own pulse, she hurriedly backed away.

"There now," she said, busying herself with straightening a stack of papers on her desk, "you're official."

"Isn't someone going to swear me in?"

"Judge Warren," she squeaked, wishing her sudden breathlessness would go away. Kate gulped air, drawing his male muskiness deep inside. His scent filled her head, making her dizzy, and her knees went all wobbly.

What was wrong with her? she wondered. A few months earlier she would have attributed the symptoms to a greatly desired pregnancy, despite Adelaide's insistence that she was barren, but too much time had passed now for that to be possible. Kate clutched at the remnants of her wits and continued in a somewhat stronger voice.

"He won't be here until court day. Until then, your verbal promise to perform your duties will be sufficient."

"When is court day?"

"Third Wednesday of the month." Careful to avoid looking at him, she glanced up at the large bank calendar on the wall. "That's nine days from now."

"Where will I find what's-his-name?"

"His name is Ainsworth Warren, and you'll find him at the courthouse, but not until next Wednesday. He's on his circuit."

"I'm not talking about the judge, Miz McBride. I meant the other marshal, the one who has the real badge."

Of course he did. Kate felt a crimson stain flush her cheeks. For a reason she couldn't fathom, Mitch Dawson's very presence stole both her composure and her ability to think clearly. She had to get him out of her office—now. She opened her mouth to speak, but nothing came out.

"Obediah Stringfellow," she managed finally. "He's probably at the jail, but he could be anywhere. Ask around."

Stringfellow wasn't at the jail, but all his stuff was still there.

Mitch came close to gagging on the sour odor that permeated the small sleeping room behind the outer office and adjacent to the single cell. If cleanliness was truly next to godliness, Stringfellow was bound straight for hell. Repelled, Mitch kicked at a crumpled pair of moldy denim britches on the floor and nearly lost his balance when they didn't move. He slipped the toe of his boot behind the waistband and tugged upward. The stiff upper portion rose a few inches, but the rumpled legs refused to budge. A mouse poked its head out of a pocket, then wiggled out, scurried across the floor, and disappeared under the bed.

Amazing, Mitch thought, what one man could learn about another simply from his habits. He'd willingly bet every dime to his name, which only came to about twenty dollars, that Stringfellow was shiftless, irresponsible, and unreliable. No reason to bet on either the former marshal's personal hygiene, or lack thereof, or his affinity for a bottle of whiskey. The condition of his quarters attested loudly to those facts.

No wonder Mayor McBride had fired the man!

Turning away from the smelly room, Mitch pondered his next move and decided to start with the boardinghouse he'd passed on the way into town. He needed a room, at least temporarily, and perhaps the owner could direct him to Stringfellow's favorite haunts.

At the boardinghouse Mrs. Jones assured him she ran a decent establishment. "No upstairs visitors allowed," she said as she led him down the second-floor hallway and into a small but immaculate room. "I serve breakfast at six in the morning and supper at six in the evening. You're on your own at noon."

"That's simple enough," he said.

"How long you planning on staying?"

"Just until the former marshal clears out his junk and cleans up the jailhouse."

Her thin lips crooked into a grin that said she knew something he didn't. "The fee's four bits a night or three dollars a week. Knowing Obediah the way I do, you might as well pay for the week."

Mitch dug a roll of greenbacks out of his hip pocket and peeled off one of them, ignoring Mrs. Jones's raised eyebrows when he handed her the single bill. "You know where I might find him?"

"Obediah? Try Mort Moffet's house. They're probably consoling each other," she said, still grinning slyly. "It'll be real interesting to see how you make out with our new mayor, young man. Yes, sir. That ought to prove the most interesting thing that's happened around here for a while."

She laughed then. Cackled was a better word, he supposed, glad he'd only obligated himself to two nights in the crazy woman's boardinghouse and thinking no more of her reaction until Max Smart, the barber, and Jethro Smith, the owner of a greasy café, laughed out loud, too, along with every customer in both establishments.

It was at the café that he found Stringfellow, who laughed the loudest of all.

Chapter Four

By the time Kate realized she'd never properly identified herself, Mitch Dawson had been gone for some time. Pressured by the imminence of that night's town council meeting, she'd spent the intervening hours talking to several residents who'd stopped by and trying to put together an agenda in between listening to their complaints, while Hardy worked at creating some order out of the chaos of paperwork Mort had left. She was hoping both of them finished in time for her to discuss the agenda with her council members before they finished cleaning up the council room and went home.

This would be the first time the new council would meet officially, and although she'd been making notes for a week, Kate wasn't the least bit certain she was ready for it. She still wasn't sure what shape the town was in, outside of the fact that Mort had left them with thirty-six cents in the treasury. The records Hardy was sorting should provide the information she needed to put together a budget.

And then, she thought, *if people will just stay away from my office for a while . . .*

They had been streaming in, with first one complaint or suggestion and then another, or lying in wait for her every time she walked out the door. Though she considered input important and needed to know exactly what the townsfolk wanted, their varying opinions were beginning to confuse and confound rather than enlighten her. She also needed an uninterrupted stretch of solitude to complete her report.

The vote of confidence Herman Stockley gave the petticoat government in Saturday's *Chronicle* served to boost her morale, and from time to time that morning Kate slipped the paper from beneath her stack of notes to gain strength from the article, which covered the entire front page.

Herman called them "bright, cheery, intelligent, womanly women with a large share of common sense. Not one of them is of the short-haired, speech-making, office-seeking sort, but rather they are mothers and housekeepers. If they can direct their individual households so well, can they not direct and guide the municipal affairs of this city? They will have to be awful failures as lawmakers and rulers if they cannot do better than their masculine predecessors."

Most of his article continued along a similar vein, but he also warned of skepticism. "Paradise will quickly become the focus of national interest," he claimed. "We will be like fish in a bowl, watched by the world. These women have assumed a huge responsibility, not only to the government of this city but to the fortune of the woman suffrage movement as well."

That last paragraph hit her harder than anything else Herman had written. He was absolutely right. One wrong move could wreak havoc for the female government and discredit the entire women's movement. Had she already damaged her integrity by not telling Mitch Dawson who she was?

Kate put her pen down and rose from her chair, intending to go after him and find him before he found

Obediah, who was certain to tell him about the election if someone else hadn't already.

The utter futility of her mission struck her about the same time her foot struck the calico cat, who let out a screeching yowl and bounded for the open doorway. The yowl brought Hardy Osborne running. Kate winced when his big shoe connected with the cat's rump. A second caterwaul pierced the air as the cat leapt onto the outer office counter and landed on a stack of documents Hardy had spent the morning organizing. The cat slipped on the slick paper, dug in its claws, and went sledding on top of one of the documents down the freshly polished counter, sending a metal holder full of pens and several inkwells soaring.

In the calico's wake, sheets of paper flew everywhere. Moaning and groaning, Hardy darted around the room, extending his big hands and trying to catch the featherlight papers as they floated around. He stumbled on one of the inkwells, then slipped on a pen. His big feet came up, his long arms flailed thin air, and his behind hit the floor with a resounding thump.

The spectacle was about as funny a thing as Kate had ever seen. It teased her first with a tiny grin, but soon the grin spread all over until uncontrollable laughter shook her frame and she clutched her waist with both arms. Her eyes were swimming so, she couldn't see clearly. She let go with one arm and swiped an open palm at the moisture.

Someone opened the outside door, a stranger whose long legs brought him right up to her side. His strong grip on her elbow took her by surprise, but her funny bone refused to stop twittering long enough for sobriety to get a firm hold. Even when he propelled her into her office and slammed the door she couldn't stop laughing.

"You're insane!" he bellowed. "This whole town's insane!"

Kate hiccupped and batted her eyelids rapidly in an effort to clear her vision.

The voice belonged to the new marshal, but the face and body didn't. Even through her tears, Kate could see this man's soft, shorn waves—still long, but neatly trimmed and now a shade of dark blond with golden streaks shot through it. His clean-shaven face revealed rugged planes and angles the stubble had obscured: prominent cheekbones and a firm, square jaw. She could see the form-fitting blue denim, faded but spotless, that encased his long, muscular legs. These shiny boots couldn't possibly be the same ones the arrogant newcomer had propped on her desk. There was, quite simply, no way Mitch Dawson could clean up this handsome.

But it was Mitch Dawson; Kate might not be able to believe her eyes, but she couldn't deny her ears.

"Stop that infernal laughing right now!" his brusque voice demanded. "It's bad enough that everyone else laughed at me without having you laugh at me, too."

Even if Kate had been able to explain, he didn't give her a chance.

"Why didn't you tell me who you are? I had to hear it from the whole town first. At the barbershop and the boardinghouse and the café, people looked at me and laughed out loud. I thought they were laughing at that ugly badge you made until I found Stringfellow. Do you have any idea how embarrassed I was when he asked me why I was wearing the mayor's handkerchief on my thumb? 'So, you're the one working for them petticoats,' Stringfellow says. 'I see Kate's already got you tagged good and proper, like the prize bird at a turkey shoot.'"

Mitch mimicked Obediah almost to perfection. Despite his strong hold on her upper arms, Kate was hard-pressed to keep a straight face.

" 'The mayor's handkerchief?' I say. 'Naw, this ain't *his* handkerchief. This one belongs to that purty little lady that works for him.' 'That pretty little lady,' Stringfellow says, *'is* the mayor!' "

The volume of Mitch Dawson's voice rose significantly. "You shoulda told me! You shoulda told me before I ever wasted my time coming here. And you sure as hell shouldn't of laughed at me, too."

He let go of Kate so suddenly she almost fell. She stumbled backwards until her posterior bumped against the desk.

"I'm sorry," she sputtered, unable to fully oust the mirth from her voice. "I intended to tell you, honestly I did. And I wasn't laughing at you just then . . ."

"Save it, lady," he said, his jaw clenched, "for the next dimwit who's fool enough to accept this job. And he'll have to be a dimwit. There ain't no man worth his salt who'll take orders from a woman." He ripped the official marshal's badge off his leather vest and tossed it on her desk.

Kate gulped and stared at the badge. "But you did accept, for a three-month probationary period, Mr. Dawson."

"Well, I'm unaccepting." He jerked the door open and stomped out.

Oh, my gosh! He's really quitting. The thought sent a shudder rippling through Kate; she pushed herself away from the desk and started after him. "Wait!" she called.

Kate breathed a sigh of relief when he turned around and took a step toward her, but then he marched to the end of the counter, picked up the calico cat, and stalked out the door. Almost immediately, the hard pounding of hooves rattled the window glass.

Hardy, who was down on all fours in the middle of the floor, stopped gathering up papers long enough to give Kate a long, hard glare. "You've done it now, Miz McBride," the clerk said. "That man was right. You shouldna oughtta laughed. First, you made fun of me, and then you made fun of him. Hurts a man's pride, that does. I'm tempted to quit myself."

Kate squatted down next to the clerk and began picking up papers. It would take hours to reorganize them, but the impending council meeting demanded that it be done. He was right. She shouldn't have laughed at him. He couldn't help having big, clumsy feet.

"Please forgive me, Hardy," she said, her voice contrite. "I never intended to make fun of you. It's been so long since I truly laughed . . . and it felt so good! Once I got started, I couldn't seem to stop. And you should have seen yourself—"

Laughter bubbled on her lips again. Kate held it at bay until Hardy snickered and broke into gleeful peals of laughter himself.

"That does feel good," Hardy choked out between chortles. "It's okay, Miz McBride. I ain't gonna quit. But I sure did want to a few minutes ago. Maybe Mr. Dawson will laugh it off and come back."

"Maybe," Kate said, but she didn't believe it. Not for a minute.

A brisk wind sailed across the prairie, catching tiny particles of dust from the road and flinging them into Mitch's bare face. For a while he ignored their choking, blinding sting, but when Little Booger, the calico cat, leapt from her basket and bounded off after a shrew, Mitch reined in the huge black gelding and fished his kerchief from his hip pocket. With the red bandanna came a scrap of white linen.

Mitch unfolded the crumpled, blood-smeared square and smoothed it out over his thigh. For the first time he noticed the airy drawnwork around the rolled hem and the tiny white letters embroidered in one corner: *K-G-M*, with the *M* centered and much larger. A dainty flowered vine wove itself among the curved letters, and the scent of flowers wafted upward from the hanky to tease and tantalize his senses.

For a moment Mitch sat mesmerized by the soiled hanky and the memory of the woman who owned it, the woman who was as fresh and delicately feminine as the primrose fragrance that permeated her handkerchief.

Kate McBride? Delicate? Feminine? Mitch questioned. *Are you crazy?*

She was a liar, that's what she was. A liar and a schemer. One of those women who spell disaster with a capital *D*. One of their kind near-bout broke his heart thirteen years ago. Two of their kind cost him his job in Dry Creek. And what had he gone and done? Hired himself out to another one of the disastrous bunch!

Mitch had almost forgotten about the three-month-trial stipulation, which he'd reluctantly agreed to via telegraph—until Kate reminded him. Before he arrived he hadn't liked it even a little bit. And then, when Stringfellow told him Kate McBride was the mayor . . . well, he just wasn't about to work for a woman of the third variety. No, sirree.

Yep, that Kate McBride was a liar and a schemer, sure as his name was Mitchell Everett Dawson, and he owed no allegiance to a liar and a schemer. Obviously, she'd found out about his little fiasco in Dry Creek and capitalized on the information. She'd investigated him behind his back, knew he was a lawman at heart, knew he was miserable operating the Western Union office. Probably she knew he was in danger of losing that job, too, thanks to Jabez Smiley's big mouth. If she knew that, then she also knew he needed her job the way a willow needs water. And she knew he'd never have accepted the position, even for a trial period, if he'd been aware that Mayor McBride was a woman.

Nevertheless, he had accepted it. He'd accepted the job because he wanted it desperately, because he did need it as much as a willow needs water. He needed it to survive—not physically nor financially, but emotionally.

He could move on, look for work elsewhere. He'd had a bath and a shave, he reminded himself, along with a hot meal. He could live on venison jerky for a few more days and he still had seventeen dollars and change in his pocket. But if Kate knew about him, so did everybody else. They'd know he'd lost one job and come close to losing another in less than six months. And now they'd know he'd quit this job before giving it a chance. He'd successfully squashed the opportunity for further employment. Through no fault of his own, Mitch hastily added. But would others see it his way?

He tugged a small canvas bag out of his shirt pocket and proceeded to roll himself a cigarette. He could go weeks on end without smoking, but there were times when he just plain wanted a cigarette. This was one of those times. He found a match, raked it across his belt buckle, and let the sulfur burn away before touching it to the end of the paper.

Now that he'd seen what he'd gotten himself into, he wondered if perhaps this trial might work more to his advantage than Kate's. If he did a good job, she'd have to give him a good recommendation. After three months he could say he just wasn't content and quietly resign. In the meantime he'd keep his eyes and ears open for another position in law enforcement and have something lined up to move on to. And then Kate and her petticoat government would play hell hiring another competent, experienced marshal, 'cause no man with good sense would deliberately accept this job—not when the whole world knew what had happened in Paradise, Kansas. And the whole world would know by that time. Mitch didn't doubt that at all.

Satan snorted his impatience and Little Booger vaulted onto Mitch's thigh, the shrew tightly clenched between its teeth.

"Oh, to hell with it!" Mitch muttered, smashing the end of the cigarette between his thumb and forefinger and then flipping what was left onto the ground. He transferred a lemon sour from his shirt pocket into his mouth, stuffed Kate's handkerchief back into his hip pocket, and then popped the bandanna good and hard, which sent the cat scurrying for the basket tied onto the back of the saddle. Folding the red kerchief across two corners to make a triangle, Mitch pulled it over his nose and mouth and tied it at the back of his head.

"You all settled back there, Little Booger?" he asked, twisting his head around to assure himself that the cat was all right. The calico mewed contentedly and tore into the furry flesh of the shrew.

"What I'm about to do," Mitch muttered, a note of self-contempt in his voice, "is as crazy as that town electing a bunch of petticoats to run their government. But I'm just crazy enough to do it."

He unlooped the reins from the saddle horn and turned Satan south. "Yes, sirree," he whooped, suddenly pleased with his decision. "I'm just crazy enough to do it."

Like a congregation of old women preparing for sleep, the long shadows of late afternoon slowly tumbled from loosened snoods and spread their gray tresses inch by inch across the muddy streets and alleyways of Paradise.

In the alley behind the town hall, a man crouched low against a wall bathed in swarthy twilight. Silently, he blessed the encroaching darkness while he cursed the lagging women who, he feared, might not leave the town hall before the meeting started. Many a time that afternoon he'd casually strolled by and seen them sweeping and mopping, polishing the window glass until it twinkled, rubbing lemon oil into the benches and chairs and tables, gabbing all the while.

Damn bunch of cackling hens. Would they never finish their infernal cleaning and go home? Didn't they have husbands and children to feed? Surely they didn't mean to attend the meeting garbed in aprons, their hair dribbling out of their kerchiefs and their faces smudged with grime.

A mere wagon-length to his left, the back door creaked open. The man cringed; he hadn't expected the women to exit through the alley. He pressed his back into the depths of the evening veil and held his breath. To his surprise, the open doorway regurgitated a cascade of dirty water that hit him a glancing blow. He swiped the stinking filth from his face and caught himself from verbalizing a vile oath just in the nick of time.

"That ought to do it."

The man grinned at the thread of weariness that

unraveled Julia Hudson's naturally sweet voice. Served her right for dousing him.

"Yep," Sally Myers agreed.

"I don't know how any of us are going to manage to stay awake tonight," Stella Carey grumbled. "I'm pooped!"

"Oh, we'll manage," Liza Ziegler said. "This ought to be one lively meeting."

You just don't know how lively, he thought, chuckling to himself and patting the wooden crate at his side. A chorus of squeaks erupted from within the box. *You just don't know. . . .*

Kate thought she knew what she'd undertaken, but the full weight of the huge responsibility didn't hit her until she walked into the town hall that night and surveyed the crowd of townsfolk who'd already gathered for the council meeting. And then it walloped her with the force of gale winds slamming across the open prairie.

In anticipation of a large turnout, the councilwomen stuffed as many chairs into the room as it would hold, leaving barely enough space between the rows for legs and feet. The arrangement put the front row too close to the council table for Kate's comfort, especially in light of the men who'd chosen the middle seats.

There sat Mort Moffet and his five ex-councilmen, right on the front row, their heads bent as they whispered and snickered among themselves. Behind and around them clustered other groups: Brother Sikes and his deacons; Max Smart, Al Youngblood, and several other Paradise merchants; gossip enthusiasts Simon Carlson from the telegraph office, postmistress Marietta Brown, and the Finks—Billy, with a splint on his leg, and his wife, Betsy—both known for wagging their tongues when it came to things that dissatisfied them, which included almost everything.

Adelaide and Horace perched stiffly on a bench set against the far wall, their mouths gelled in identical unyielding lines. In stark contrast, Obediah Stringfellow slouched lazily beside the bench, half standing, his scuffed boots crossed at the ankles, one shoulder hugging the wall, his slack mouth working in obvious amusement.

They're all amused, Kate thought, returning her attention to Mort and his band. Cold beads of perspiration broke out on her forehead and her heart skittered to an abrupt halt. She clutched the sheath of notes tighter and fought the urge to fan her face with the papers. Her gaze sought the long, narrow table everyone faced. From behind it stared five pairs of frightened eyes.

She must present the illusion of complete control, regardless of how sporadic her pulse or dry her mouth. She might be just as terrified as the women of her council, but she didn't dare show it. A quick glance back at the throng packed into the room assured her of a modicum of support: Doc Myers, Skip Hudson, the Dahlmers, Herman Stockley from the *Chronicle*.

Kate tried to imagine Arnold sitting there, smiling his confidence in her ability, but she failed miserably. Had he lived, she wouldn't be mayor of Paradise. Regardless, he wouldn't have smiled. Not Arnold. He would have taken great pleasure in her motherhood, but never in her mayorhood.

Suddenly Kate's throat tightened up. Why had she ever thought she could manage a town when she couldn't manage something as simple as a relationship? And now she had to tell these folks that the marshal she'd hired had already quit.

"Excuse me, Miz McBride." Hardy scooted around her and took his place at the clerk's desk.

Silently blessing his clumsy intrusion, Kate swallowed her trepidation and moved toward the one empty chair at the long, narrow table.

A deserted, forlorn air, abetted by the lack of street lamps and the fury of the wind, hung over the town. Even the meager light spilling out of the houses lacked warmth. The closer Mitch got to the hub of the business district, the more the light thinned out, until it was virtually nonexistent.

Somewhere in this godforsaken place there must be a saloon. Every town had at least one, and Mitch Dawson needed a beer to whet his dry whistle. He couldn't recall when he'd needed a beer quite so much. He was just thirsty, he argued with his conscience. He hadn't had a beer since he left Dry Creek almost five days ago. The dust-laden wind had sapped him. Could he help it if he preferred beer to water? His need for beer had nothing to do with fortifying himself before facing Kate McBride again. Nothing at all.

But in the depths of his soul, Mitch knew that wasn't quite true. There was something about her that scared the hell out of him. Since he'd met her that morning, disaster with a capital *D* had taken on a new meaning.

As Satan clopped along, Mitch listened closely for the merry tinkle of a piano while his gaze searched the darkness for a shaft of light. Though he saw no light, he did hear two male voices raised in argument. Mitch guided Satan toward the racket, which seemed to be coming from the rear of one of the businesses.

"I paid you for the finest whiskey you got," a whiny voice declared.

Impatience strained the answering voice. "That *is* the finest whiskey I've got."

"Cain't be. This here ain't nothin' but blackstrap! Tain't near as smooth as that last jug you sold me fer six bits less. You got any more of that?"

Ah! Mitch sighed. A saloon at last.

But why did the door open into an alley?

So intent was he on looking for the place, he rode past the voices and had to backtrack. This time he spotted the two men, who were standing in the open doorway of a dimly lit storeroom. One of them held a crockery jug. Mitch reined Satan to a halt and called out, "Excuse me, but I'm new in town. Could either of you tell me where I might find a saloon?"

"Ain't no saloons in Paradise, mister," the man with the whiny voice answered. "Don't you know Kansas is dry?"

How well I know, Mitch thought, intentionally misunderstanding the reference. *I'm carrying a pound of its dust in my throat.* "Gives a man a powerful thirst, don't it? You fellows don't happen to know where I might get a beer, do you?"

"I'm plum out," the other man said, "but I've got some mighty good whiskey here."

Mitch hesitated, sorely tempted even if it was blackstrap. "No, thanks," he said finally.

"Then you might try over to Mission's."

"Mission's?"

"Drugstore. Ned might still be open, if he ain't at the meetin'." He pointed down the alley. "Go back out the way you came and turn left, then right onto Main Street. It's over close to the town hall. You can't miss the hall. That's where the meetin's goin' on."

The two men snickered, then resumed their argument.

Mitch knew full well how to get to the town hall,

and he thought he recalled noticing a drugstore nearby. He didn't think a tinker's damn about any meeting, nor did he care. Only two things mattered to him at the moment: beer and bed, and in that order. Kate McBride could wait until tomorrow.

But both the front and back doors at Mission's Drugstore were locked tight and no light shone from within. Like it or not, he'd have to wait until morning for the beer. That left the bed. He'd skedaddled so fast, he hadn't bothered to go by the boardinghouse and tell Mrs. Jones he wouldn't be staying the night, so he ought to have a room there still. It was too late for supper, but he hoped she had some leftovers. If he couldn't have his beer, he damned sure wanted something to eat.

Mitch was about to remount Satan when the town hall erupted in peals of male laughter and squeals of female terror. Whatever could have caused such opposite reactions at the same time? he wondered, putting his foot in the stirrup. He might be curious, but not curious enough to hang around.

That's what he told himself, though he made no further move to mount the black.

The door flapped open and three women came running out, reaching for the moon and screaming so loud Mitch had no doubts as to their lung capacities. The open door allowed a narrow view of the townsfolk gathered within, but only enough to affirm that something had caused a general alarm among the women. Whatever it was, the men didn't appear to be affected beyond having their humors tickled.

Little Booger bounded out of her basket, hit the uneven boardwalk with a thump, dashed down the walk and into the building.

A rat . . . or maybe a snake, Mitch reasoned, grinning.

He hadn't planned to show his face to Kate McBride before morning. That was before the damned cat gave him away. Kate was bound to recognize Little Booger, and even if she didn't, Mitch wasn't going anywhere without the calico. He removed his foot from the stirrup and took a couple of steps toward the door, then stopped. Perhaps if he waited a few minutes, the cat would return on her own.

She didn't. Mitch could see her scurrying around inside, chasing a mouse. Two mice. No, three. With that many mice to occupy the cat's attention, she might never come out.

Grumbling, he tossed Satan's reins over the hitching post and headed inside.

Total bedlam knocked the wind out of him as effectively as a sharp jab to his stomach. Never in his life had he witnessed such chaos, and never would he have dreamed a few mice could cause so much commotion. By and large, the women stood in chairs, their wide-eyed gazes darting about the floor, their arms hugging their middles and their voices screeching, while the men's heads flopped back and their shoulders shook with wild, uncontrollable laughter.

All the men, that is, except Obediah Stringfellow. The erstwhile marshal leaned against the far wall, something closely akin to a sneer on his thin, grinning lips. The man shifted his weight from one foot to the other, a movement Mitch detected only from a swapping of shoulders against the wall since the first row of chairs obscured Obediah's legs and feet from view. Then, suddenly, Obediah bawled like a cow with a bellyful of pea vines, pushed away from the wall, and fumbled with the buttons in the fly below his pot belly, his shoulders twitching and his eyes wild.

Mitch stood on tiptoe to get a better view. In a flash, Obediah skimmed his khakis down and kicked his feet out of them, exposing heavily patched long underwear in a shade that matched the livid color of his face and neck. The moment his feet were clear, Obediah jumped up and down on his britches, screaming obscenities.

One less mouse for Little Booger, Mitch thought.

Obediah's ranting garnered the attention of some of the ladies, whose perches allowed them a better view. They pointed their fingers and tittered so, Mitch feared they might fall off their chairs. He knew the instant Stringfellow realized his state of undress by the look of horror that washed over the man's florid features. Without bothering to pick up his pants, Obediah took off running for the back door.

Amid all the hullabaloo, Kate shouted for order and banged her gavel on the table. Mitch couldn't help admiring her control anymore than he could prevent the laughter that bubbled from his throat and soon overtook his broad shoulders.

While the women screamed and the men laughed, Little Booger dashed in and out of the open door, leaving each time with a mouse in her jaws and returning within moments to renew her pursuit. In less than five minutes the cat cleared the room of every mouse that didn't get away, but no one other than Mitch seemed to notice. He moved to the back of the room, sat down in a vacant chair, and waited for the townsfolk to calm down.

Kate banged her gavel again and shouted, "They're gone now," until the last guffaw drifted away. Still snickering, the men assisted the women off their perches and back into their seats. At long last, a semblance of order returned.

"My," Kate said, holding a hand to her chest and shaking her head, "that certainly livened things up!" Her remark elicited smiles from some folks, sighs of relief from others.

Who would bring live mice to the meeting? Mitch wondered. Someone had. One mouse, maybe two, could be explained away. But a multitude of the furry little creatures? Mitch didn't think so.

"Where were we?" Kate said, looking to Hardy for an answer.

"Discussing the need for street lamps," he said.

"I couldn't agree more," Mitch muttered to himself, loud enough to draw the attention of three men sitting close to him.

"Who're you?" one of them hissed.

"Dawson," Mitch whispered back. That seemed to satisfy the man's curiosity, at least for the moment.

"Mayor—" Hardy's face turned red and he cleared his throat. "I mean *Mister* Moffet was speaking."

"Too damn much money," Mort declared, "for the good they'll do."

"Yeah," agreed James Larue, who'd served on Mort's council. A chorus of consensus burst from his other cohorts.

Kate banged her gavel. "Paradise will have gas street lamps before our terms are out," she announced. "However, our present lack of funds"—she pierced Mort with an accusing glare—"prohibits their purchase and installation at this time and renders pointless any further discussion tonight."

Kate recognized Mrs. Jones. "When do you think we'll get them?" the boardinghouse owner asked.

"We can't say for sure, but this is one of our priority items," Kate explained. She lifted a piece of paper from the table, gave it a brief perusal, and looked suddenly uncomfortable.

"There is one other item of business," she said, cutting her eyes to the spot Obediah had recently occupied and then letting her gaze come to rest on the newspaper editor, who was sitting near the front and scribbling notes on a pad. "As you are all probably aware, thanks to Mr. Stockley's reporting, the council and I discharged Marshal Stringfellow last week and replaced him with a well-experienced man. Mr. Dawson arrived today and, after brief consideration, decided he—"

Without stopping to think about what he was doing, Mitch jumped to his feet. "Definitely wants the job," he finished for her.

Mitch felt every eye in the room focused on him, but he set his gaze on Kate McBride's face. Her mouth dropped open, then immediately snapped shut. He waited for the shock, which he'd expected, to change to approval. Instead, she surprised him by narrowing her pale green eyes and skewering him with a look that clearly expressed her displeasure. Mitch glared back, refusing to flinch when every ounce of his self-esteem shrank in the face of her scowl.

What the hell was wrong with her? he wondered, wishing he'd kept still. But it was too late.

"This is Mitchell Dawson," Kate said, extending a hand in his general direction—as if all those seated folks couldn't see him standing there, Mitch thought.

"He comes to us from Dry Creek, Nebraska, where he served as town marshal for seven years." Hell, she sounded just like a minister in a pulpit introducing a revival preacher.

"Mr. Dawson and I have agreed that he will serve a probationary period of three months, during which time he can get to know us and we'll get to know him, and then we'll mutually decide whether he will stay on permanently. Let's all welcome Mr. Dawson and offer him our full cooperation."

Her gavel hit the table one last time and she declared the meeting adjourned. People pressed close, offering him handshakes and friendly greetings. Mitch responded absently, his attention following Kate's movements as she gathered up papers and left the hall.

She might *look* like a lady of the first order, but she wasn't one. No, sirree. She was one of those third kind, one of those ax-grinding preacherwomen he'd sworn to forever avoid.

He might have to tolerate her for a spell, but three months were sure to pass quickly enough. Come early July he'd take Satan and Little Booger and what money he'd managed to save and vamoose—to God knew where. Anywhere was all right with Mitch. Anywhere that wasn't another Paradise, Kansas.

Chapter Five

"What good will it do to investigate? There's no law against collecting live mice or letting 'em loose."

Kate set her jaw and willed her racing pulse to slow down. It was his defiance, registered in the cool tilt of his wide mouth and the imperious lift of a heavy eyebrow, that put her on edge, she assured herself, not his jutting hip and long legs, and certainly not the sparkle in his chocolate-brown eyes or the gleam of his white teeth behind curled lips.

Unbidden, the heartsinking feeling she'd experienced when he'd stormed out of her office the day before returned. Kate hadn't imagined that anything could hurt quite as bad, especially when failure was no stranger to her. And that was all it had been, she'd tried to convince herself. Failure at her job. Failure to satisfactorily complete the first required task. Mitch Dawson the man had nothing to do with it. Her interest centered solely on Mitch Dawson the marshal.

Then why, her inner voice niggled, had she been so upset when he'd returned last night? She should have been thrilled to see him, thrilled to hear him say he wanted the job. Yet something deep inside told her this man symbolized trouble, that if she intended to retain control of her life, she'd send him packing without further ado.

She pushed the thought aside and concentrated on the matter at hand. Never had she wanted to succeed at anything quite so much as this. She might never have planned to serve as mayor of Paradise, but once the opportunity had been dropped in her lap, everything else—motherhood, the women's suffrage movement, social acceptance—paled in significance.

Though her election might have been serendipitous, she knew she couldn't continue to count on good fortune to see her through. In the short run her success might depend on keeping Mitch Dawson around, at least until she could hire a suitable replacement, but her long-term success hinged on her own strength. If she backed down now, even to ensure Dawson's stay in Paradise, she'd never regain the upper hand.

Kate mentally reached for her bootstraps and unclenched her jaw. "Let's get one thing straight right now, Marshal Dawson. You answer to me and me alone. You *will* investigate this incident because I told you to do it. Regardless of whatever laws may or may not be on the books, I will not condone a prankster bent on disrupting town council meetings. You will attempt to find this prankster and put the fear of God in him, if not the fear of the law. Is that clear?"

"Definitely a number three," he muttered.

What in heaven's name was he talking about? "Pardon?"

"Yes, ma'am," he drawled, lifting the other eyebrow so that his forehead wore a matched pair. "You've made yourself quite clear. How d'you suggest I proceed?"

Was the man daft? she wondered, exasperation coloring her reply. "Surely this is not the first time you've ever been required to conduct an investigation."

"Aw, no, ma'am," he drawled. "It's just the first time I ever went looking for a mouse bandit."

Kate took a deep breath in an attempt to quell her exasperation. "Ask questions. Someone had to see something."

"And if they didn't?"

"Then we won't have anything to go on, will we, marshal?"

"Maybe it *was* a coincidence."

"You don't believe that any more than I do. You said you counted nine mice in your cat's basket. Obediah stomped another one to death, and surely a few got away," she said. "That makes at least a dozen in all—far too many to lay to coincidence."

"Don't you think you're making a mountain out of a mousehill?"

"Very funny!" Kate said, seething but trying to keep her anger under control. "People have been getting away with far too much in this town. That's all about to change."

She chewed her bottom lip and swallowed hard. She wasn't the least bit certain she liked Mitch Dawson, yet she would ardently resist losing her new town marshal. But her primary concern, she reminded herself, centered only in the future of Paradise. As mayor, she owed her council, the town, and the state her fealty. If that meant having to fire another marshal—or accept his resignation—then so be it.

"There's one other thing," she said.

"Yes?"

"You do know why I dismissed Mr. Stringfellow."

"He says it was 'cause he refused to kowtow to a woman."

Kate thought she detected the merest trace of mischief in Mitch Dawson's rough baritone. Oh, the nerve of the man! But at least he hadn't argued with her about who was boss or told her again that he wasn't about to take orders from a woman. In fact, he seemed almost cooperative today. Perhaps his ride out onto the prairie had helped him sort out his priorities.

"He refused to enforce Prohibition."

Mitch nodded. "That's what the newspaper said."

"That's what *I* say. I'm the one who fired him."

"You gonna fire me if I refuse?"

"Yes, Mr. Dawson, I am."

God! How those words hurt to say! Their utterance left her throat parched and her mouth so dry it burned. Kate glanced at the pitcher of water on her desk and fought the urge to expose her nervousness by filling up the empty glass and downing its full measure without pausing to breathe.

She needn't have concerned herself. Mitch filled the glass for her.

"You're thirsty, ain't you, Miz McBride?" he asked, holding the glass up and gazing into the clear, sparkling liquid. "What if someone came along and made the consumption of water illegal? What would you think about that?"

"How ludicrous!" she gasped, her thirst growing stronger by the second. "Water is necessary for physical survival."

His gaze didn't leave the glass. "And liquor ain't? Is that what you're saying?"

Kate gulped hard. "Yes."

He pushed the glass closer to her, taunting her with its contents. "Me, I don't never drink water if I can have a beer instead. I done seen too many animals and people die from drinking foul water, but I ain't never known of no one to die from drinking beer."

"Well, I have!"

The words tore from her sore throat and moisture glazed her vision as the image of her father's bloated face swam before her eyes. For years she'd watched Tom Gillis consume mug after mug of beer, watched his middle thicken, his jowls swell, his eyes grow puffier, his nose redden. She'd watched him stumble and listened to his slurred speech. Many a night she'd lain in her bed, cringing, while her father hollered at her mother in the next room, and then she'd cried herself to sleep. For all the good it had done, she'd wished upon every evening star that her father would quit drinking and prayed until she was certain God tired of hearing her.

Yes, she'd seen beer eat at a man from the inside out until there was no future but the grave.

When her vision cleared Mitch Dawson was gone.

Without waiting to be dismissed, without waiting for further instructions, he'd walked out.

And he'd left the issue of enforcing Prohibition unresolved.

Oh, the nerve of the man!

Enforce Prohibition? Was she crazy?

Next, she'd have him enforcing the ridiculous blue law or involved in some other such nonsense.

Every instinct screeched at Mitch to forget his promise, forget honor, hightail it out of Paradise, and go back to Dry Creek or anyplace else where convention reigned, which was virtually everywhere except Paradise, Kansas. The people here were lunatics. Downright insane, that's what they were. They had to be, or else they would never have elected a petticoat government. Didn't they know what they were getting themselves into? Didn't they know women didn't think like men? Didn't they know about women with causes?

Apparently not. They'd gone and elected a suffragist and temperance woman as their mayor. Someone ought to turn the entire town into an asylum. And he had no business hanging around until that happened. He'd never planned to spend the rest of his life living among a bunch of idiots, and he damned sure didn't plan to start now.

Nor had he ever planned to work for a bunch of women with causes. These women defined deviousness to a fault, which at least one Paradise resident saw right through. Hadn't Herman Stockley written in the *Chronicle* that not one of them was of "the short-haired, speech-making, office-seeking sort"? Just because they were homemakers who didn't cut their hair didn't mean they didn't belong to Mitch's third class of women—the same kind who'd broken his heart, the same kind who'd ruined his career in Dry Creek, the same kind who'd nearly ruined his life twice.

And then what had he done? Jumped from the frying pan into the fire, jumped out, and then right back in. He'd told Little Booger he was crazy to come back here. And he was. Crazy as the people in this town.

Mitch had about half-convinced himself to leave again and not come back this time, when it dawned on him that there were some people who hadn't voted for Kate and her gang. Not everyone in this town was nuts. If he just bided his time, sought out the sane folks and made them his friends, he just might be able to tolerate the probationary period.

He assured himself that he had other choices concerning his future as a lawman. Obviously he'd been wrong when he told Earl Woody that no one would ever hire him again. His new position in Paradise proved him wrong. But quitting now would destroy his integrity, destroy any chance of securing another position in a normal town. He'd given his word to stay for three months, and three months it would be.

But that was it. Not one day longer than three months. And during that time he'd follow orders, or try to, even so far as enforcing Prohibition, no matter how much that particular chore stuck in his craw.

Thus resolved, Mitch headed toward Mission's Drugstore.

Dammit, his throat ached already for a tall mug of foaming beer.

It was going to be a long, dry three months.

Kate was sorting through paperwork, trying to prepare a budget, when Mitch sauntered into her office the next morning, removed a folded piece of paper from his back pocket, and laid it on her desk.

As though it were a rattlesnake, she jerked upright in her chair, clasped her throat with an open hand, and gawked at the wrinkled, dirt-smeared paper.

"What's that?" she breathed, terrified that it was his resignation. Her pulse throbbed against her palm.

"A bill for my room and board at Mrs. Jones's," he replied, a hint of perplexity in his voice.

Her frown echoed his confusion. "Why are you giving it to me?"

"Because I expect to get paid back. Or have you forgotten that a place to live was part of this deal?"

"No, I haven't forgotten," she said, pleased to hear the evenness in her voice, to feel her pulse returning to normal. She pushed the folded paper back toward him. "We never agreed to pay for your meals, and you have a room at the jail."

"Have you seen that place? I'm not staying there. It's filthy."

"Then clean it up."

His voice rose. "I didn't make the mess!"

"You're bigger than Obediah Stringfellow. Make him clean it up."

"And if he won't?"

"You borrow more trouble—"

"I'm closing the mousehill investigation," he announced.

She blinked. "You're doing *what?*"

"No one saw anything, so I'm closing the investigation."

Refusing to allow his arrogant presumptuousness and rude interruption to rile her, she went back to shuffling papers. "I find it hard to believe that no one saw anything. Someone has to know something, Marshal Dawson."

Kate heard the shrewish tone in her voice and made a mental note to practice speaking firmly without sounding like a fishwife.

"Well, ma'am, if they do, they ain't saying nothing," Mitch said, his tone as casual as the way he slouched in the chair on the opposite side of her desk. Kate wanted to tell him to sit up straight and employ proper grammar, which she knew he was perfectly capable of doing, but she didn't. Apparently slouching, swearing, and murdering the English language came with marshaling, and she figured she'd better get used to all three.

"The way I got it figured," he continued, "those who know something are the very ones I offended when I shut off their liquor supply. They ain't gonna cooperate, Miz McBride. You might as well forget it."

"I'm not going to forget it, Marshal, and neither are you." *That was better. Firm but not too shrewish. Just a little more work and I'll have it down pat.* "Let's examine the evidence again."

"What evidence? Little Booger done ate it all up."

Kate cringed inside and fought to keep her temper

under control. "I'm not referring to the dead mice, Marshal. Even were they alive, they couldn't tell us anything. I'm talking about motivation."

Mitch rolled his eyes upward, which sent her blood pressure into orbit. Kate clenched her fists in her lap and swallowed the tongue-lashing she wanted to give him.

"That's your department," Mitch said. "I don't know these people well enough to divine motivation."

Kate did a double take. Had he honestly used *divine* as a verb? And spoken two sentences without butchering a single word?

She cataloged those observations and covered her sudden bewilderment by taking up pen and paper. "My first suspect would be Mort Moffet." She wrote his name. "Though I suppose he could have been the instigator, he was sitting right in front of me and didn't have any mice on him, so scratch him." She marked through his name and chewed on the end of her pen for a moment. "In fact, almost everyone who might have wanted to disrupt that meeting was sitting right up front . . . except . . . Have you talked to my mother-in-law?"

The instant she mentioned Adelaide, Kate knew she'd made a grievous error. Once Mitch talked to her, he'd know everything there was to know about Kate— from Adelaide's point of view—and then she could forget his ever respecting her.

Mitch didn't allow her time to ponder further, however. He reacted as though she'd pulled a peacemaker and aimed it at his heart, sitting straight up and pinning her with a look of total disbelief. "You think your *mother-in-law* is responsible?"

"I wouldn't put it past her, though I can't quite imagine Adelaide collecting live mice."

"She could have had an accomplice."

"Possibly. However, I was thinking about Obediah Stringfellow."

Mitch shook his head. "I don't understand the connection."

"He was standing beside my in-laws, next to Adelaide. Now that I think about it, he didn't seem the least bit surprised by what was happening."

Trying not to stare but unable to stop herself, Kate watched his chiseled lips gather into a crinkled purse, then widen into a half smile. "You're right. He was just standing there grinning during all the bedlam—until the mouse ran up his leg. 'Course, he'll never admit anything himself. I'll go talk to your mother-in-law. But don't go getting your hopes up."

Kate sighed. "Where Adelaide is concerned, I never do."

All the way to the McBrides' house, Mitch pondered Kate's parting words. Twice now she'd revealed a tiny bit of her inner self to him: She had a personal reason for wanting Prohibition enforced and she didn't get along with her mother-in-law. Mitch wasn't at all certain he liked being privy to such information. Knowing such things tended to make her human, and that was the last way Mitch wanted to think of Kate McBride. Having a woman for a boss was bad enough, but he reckoned he could tolerate it if he could keep his distance from her.

The fact that she was married helped. Not for the first time Mitch caught himself constructing a mental image of Kate's husband. When would he meet the fellow? he wondered. He'd been in town for three days, been in and out of all the stores, all the professional and government offices, but not once had he run into the man nor even heard his name mentioned. That left only a couple of viable occupations for Mr. McBride, but try as he might Mitch couldn't see him as either a farmer or a rancher. Farmers and ranchers were *men* through and through, strong and tough, like lawmen. Such men didn't marry women like Kate.

Only weak men married women like Kate.

Maybe her husband was old and decrepit, or an invalid. Or maybe he was the one who'd died from drinking too much. Someone close to Kate had, Mitch was sure of that. But, damn! If that was the case, then she was a widow. That would make her available. And that wouldn't do at all.

Mitch consciously buried the notion and concentrated on following the directions Hardy had given him. He was glad Kate had sent him to see her mother-in-law. Despite his aversion to knowing any more about Kate than was absolutely necessary, Mitch wanted desperately to meet her husband, to see firsthand what sort of man would tie himself to a woman like Kate McBride. Not that it really mattered to him, Mitch assured himself. He had no personal interest in the woman whatsoever. He was merely curious.

Though he didn't actually expect to meet Mr. McBride that morning, at least he ought to be able to find out something about the man. Who better to enlighten him than the man's mother?

And Lord help me—the thought came unbidden as he turned up the walk—*if he's six feet under.*

For the first time in nine months Kate wished Arnold were still alive. She might not have been happy married to him, but at least their union had provided a convenient emotional barrier. The man in front of her seemed bent on destroying whatever remnants of that barrier were left.

Mitch leaned over her desk, his fingers folded into his palms and his knuckles supporting the weight of his torso. His face was so close to hers, his warm, lemon-scented breath lifted the unruly locks at her temples that refused confinement to the bun pinned on her crown no matter how much pomade she applied.

Until that moment Kate had always despised being stuck with the twin cowlicks. Now she found herself relishing the tickle of Mitch's breath upon the recalcitrant strands as she stared at his lips—wide and firm but slightly reddened and chapped, baring teeth that were astonishingly white, though the two lower ones in the center had grown in crooked, one overlapping the other. Without thinking, she raised her finger, wanting to touch those dry lips and trace the angle in his teeth.

But the lips curled in contempt so potent it burned clear through to her soul.

"You're one scheming little piece of work, ain't you, lady?"

She dropped her hand and stared. "What are you talking about?"

"Preening like you was born with a silver spoon in your mouth. Actin' so high and mighty, gritting your teeth at the way I talk, and looking down your nose at me when you was raised up in a saloon and probably didn't have more'n one pair o' stockings and two dresses to your name till you married poor old Arnold."

"Adelaide."

Though her voice barely rose above a whisper, she knew Mitch couldn't help hearing her, especially when he hunched even closer to her. Instinctively, Kate pushed her chair back and stood up, then realized how defensive the gesture seemed.

"If she hadn't told me, someone else would have. Eventually."

"What difference can my roots possibly make?" Kate asked, unconvinced herself yet determined to keep her insecurities safely locked away. "What's important is the present. I'm perfectly capable of running this town, Mr. Dawson."

"That remains to be seen, doesn't it?"

He straightened his spine, settled his dark brown Stetson back on his head, and turned on a booted heel.

"Where are you going?"

He whirled back to her. "To make my rounds. Or would you rather I hid away in my office like Stringfellow did?"

His gaze swept her office, from the botanical prints on the walls to the neatly stacked papers on her desk, his eyes accusing her of closeting herself away from the world, away from reality. She couldn't let him get away with turning the tables on her.

"Stringfellow didn't hide away in his office."

"That's right," he said, snapping his fingers. "He surely didn't. Even *he* couldn't stay in that pigsty for long, and I can assure you I'm not staying there *at all*! Not until something is done about it."

"I told you—"

"And I told you *I'm* not cleaning it up. If you and your council want to foot my bill at the boardinghouse, that's fine with me. But I'm not paying for my room there any longer. Mrs. Jones will be sending the bill to your office. And if she kicks me out, then I'm gone. You can find yourself another marshal to push around. Is that clear?"

"Perfectly," she said, resisting the urge to bite her lower lip, drawing herself up to her full height of five and a half feet and still having to tilt her head back to look into Mitch Dawson's eyes. He offered her a curt nod, reached for the brim of his hat, and almost tipped

it before he stiffened in defiance, then walked purpose-
fully away.

He was everything she detested in a man: arrogant,
cocky, stubborn . . . yet, something about him drew
her to him, made her want to be the one to peel back
the offending layers and discover the tender, generous
man she suspected existed deep down inside. A man as
tough as Mitch pretended to be wouldn't keep a cat for
a pet; he'd have a wolf or a mountain lion trailing at
his heels.

Kate plopped down in her chair and rested her brow
on an open palm, her mind awash with conflicting
emotions that at once pricked her heart and rekindled
her resolve. She had no business feeling anything for
Mitch Dawson, no business allowing his barbed words
to wound her, no business wanting anything to be
different in her life.

She had what she wanted, didn't she? The freedom
to do as she pleased, the opportunity to make a difference in her world, the knowledge and skills to accomplish anything she set out to do. She was the mayor of
Paradise, a worthy achievement for a girl who'd grown
up over a saloon. She needed to focus on her duties
and not think so much about the new marshal she'd
hired.

Her gaze followed in reverse the path Mitch Dawson's had so recently made, from the neatly stacked
papers on her desk to the botanical prints on the walls.
Perhaps she did need to get out of her office more,
circulate about town and talk to people, find out what
the populace wanted for Paradise instead of concen-
trating so hard on what she wanted for herself.
Though many of the townsfolk had sought her out,
there were many, many more she'd yet to talk to.

Kate settled her own hat—a small navy straw with
a turned-up brim and a wide band of green-and-white-

striped silk that matched her day gown—on her head, adjusted the hat pin to secure it to her bun, and told Hardy she didn't know when she'd be back.

By supper time that night Kate had collected a list of complaints so long, she feared she and her council would never find the time or the finances to address them all.

Folks who'd been too shy to come to her—or too scared of Mort Moffet to initiate criticism at the council meeting—spoke to her openly when she approached them personally, and those who hadn't hesitated to voice their grievances elaborated further on them. It would take hours to sort them all out, but Kate dove right into the task when she got home, stopping only long enough to remove her shoes, peel off her stockings, and shimmy out of the five heavy petticoats she wore. Supper could wait.

A part of her knew that much of her enthusiasm stemmed from the escapist quality of the activity, that she embraced the work because it took her mind off Mitch Dawson's accusations. Escaping reality through mental activity wasn't new to her. She'd learned quite well the soothing powers of such work during her eight years of marriage to Arnold McBride. It was like smearing salve on a wound that refused to heal, but it was the only momentary cure Kate found effective. As far as she knew, no permanent cure existed.

She began by reading through the notes she'd taken from her informal survey, jotting down recurring complaints, keeping a running tally of the number who had concurred with each, and then ranking them accordingly.

As she worked, dusk turned into candle lighting and

then into darkness, and with the night came erratic soft breezes that billowed the kitchen curtains and teased her nose with the promise of rain. The air grew heavy and warm, and though thunder rumbled occasionally, it remained low and distant. Kate unfastened the buttons at her neck, considered changing into a dressing gown, and then decided that could wait until she'd written a few more notes. Time flew by and the rain finally arrived, but she paid neither any mind until the cuckoo popped out to chirp the hour of ten.

The little wooden bird made it to eight before Hobo pounced from the top of the piesafe, caught its head in his mouth, gave it a vicious yank, and pulled the bird loose from its mooring. Cat and bird fell to the floor. Hobo looked up at Kate, triumph shining in his gray-banded blue eyes as he trotted proudly toward her, the bird clutched firmly between his teeth.

Thunder clapped directly overhead and a torrent of rain pelted the tin roof. Behind the cat, the clock teetered precariously, slipped off its nail, plummeted to the floor, and crashed, its veneered case splintering into hundreds of pieces. Hobo dropped the wooden bird and bolted out of the kitchen.

Kate laughed so hard, she had to hold her sides and tears gathered in her eyes. When she calmed a bit she went looking for Hobo and found him meowing loudly and scratching at the front door. She bent down and rubbed his back, and though his meows gave way to purrs, he scratched on the panel again.

"All right, old boy," she said, trying to keep her voice level although laughter continued to bubble in her throat, "I'll let you out."

She partially rose from her crouched position, just enough to slide the bolt and open the door, her hand still stroking Hobo's back. The cat's tail slipped through her palm and she started to stand up when her gaze fell on the scuffed toe of a man's boot mere inches from the threshold. Kate's breath caught in her throat and her heart beat rapidly in her chest. She threw her shoulder against the door, breathed again when she heard the click of the latch, then fumbled in the dark for the bolt.

Immediately, a trio of knocks resounded over her head, sending her pulse pounding so hard in her ears that some time passed before she heard a half familiar voice calling her name. Shaking uncontrollably, Kate peeked through the frosted glass, trying to discern the identity of the man who stood on the other side, which would have been almost impossible even in broad daylight. A fortuitous streak of lightning ripped through the darkness, outlining a muscular frame and long, lean legs.

Mitch Dawson.

What in heaven's name was he doing at her house this late? A series of possible crises clambered for attention while her pulse, which had momentarily slowed, rushed ahead again as she acknowledged each one. The town was on fire. A rabid dog was on the loose. A crazed gunman was shooting people.

"Are you okay, Miz McBride? It's me, Mitch Dawson. Would you please open the door?"

A herd of cattle had stampeded. Lightning had struck the Episcopal church bell tower. A wild boar had gored a child.

Kate couldn't find the breath to answer and barely garnered enough strength to move the bolt. Before she could drive it completely open he pushed against the door, firmly jamming the lock. He pushed again, jiggling the knob and rattling the frosted glass.

"Answer me, Miz McBride, or I'll break this door in!" he demanded.

Kate found her voice in an instant. "Don't you dare!"

"Then let me in!"

"I can't. The bolt's stuck."

A slight pause ensued, and then he ordered loudly, "Meet me at the back door."

Somehow, Kate forced her wobbly legs to work, though not very well. He was already at the back door, banging away on the frame, when she got to the kitchen.

"I'm coming!" she called, his beating and the rolling thunder drowning out her voice. The moment she turned the key in the lock and opened the door, he stepped into her kitchen, pushed past her, snatched the kerosene lamp off the table, and headed for the dining room.

For a moment Kate stood in the open doorway, her astonished gaze following the trail of water and the muddy footprints Mitch's purposeful strides left behind. A violent shiver racked her frame. She attributed the sudden quaking to fright until she realized that the rain, whipping under the narrow overhang that protected the kitchen stoop, was drenching her back. She shivered again, then closed the door and followed Mitch.

Chapter Six

What was he up to? she wondered, anger beginning to displace alarm. There was only one way to find out.

She dogged his wet trail, wincing when the mud he'd left behind squished between her bare toes, then screeching in pain when a sharp splinter from the destroyed clock case pierced her right heel. Her shriek brought Mitch running back into the kitchen. He stopped just inside the doorway.

"Where is he?" the new marshal demanded.

Kate was in too much pain to pay any mind to Mitch Dawson's irrational question. She hopped to the table, sat down hard in one of the Windsor chairs, and folded her right leg over her left, resting her ankle on her knee. Mindless of the view of calves and ankles she exposed to this man who was almost a stranger, she pulled up her skirt and bent low over her foot.

"Bring my lamp over here," she said, mashing on her heel with her thumb and forefinger. "I can't see."

"Well, I can, lady," Mitch said, his mellow, appreciative tone snagging her attention. A swell of pride laved her discomfort, but the low, dragged-out whistle that followed rekindled her anger at his intrusion, which she decided to postpone dealing with until after she got the splinter out. The whistle also reminded her that ladies never exposed their legs. Indeed, proper Victorian ladies and gentlemen never referred to them as legs at all; to the socially correct, legs were "limbs."

Kate didn't set much store by convention, but she did find Mitch Dawson's leering eyes and grin embarrassing. Hastily, she pulled her skirt around her legs, covering both of them as best she could, tucking the fabric behind her left leg and beneath her right and hoping it stayed put.

He set the lamp on the table, squatted down in front of her, and took her hands in his. Kate stiffened and tried to snatch her hands away, but his grip held them tightly.

"Let go!" she hissed.

He raised his head and gazed up at her with dark brown eyes that exuded a warmth and tenderness she'd never seen in Arnold's dark brown eyes . . . a mesmerizing warmth that penetrated her senses deep down inside and radiated upward and outward, weakening her resolve yet filling her with an inner strength unlike any she'd ever experienced.

"You're making it worse," he explained, his voice as warm and tender as his gaze. "Let me get it out for you."

Without conscious thought, Kate quit struggling. He retrieved the dishrag from the sink, wet it, then returned to squat in front of her chair and scrub away the grime from the bottom of her foot.

The task complete, he half stood up. Fascinated, she watched his thigh muscles ripple beneath the tight, faded denim that snugly encased his legs. He dug into a front pocket, pulling the coarse fabric tautly over his flat stomach and hauling it upward so that it tightened over his crotch.

Her gaze riveted on the bulge and she gasped.

"I'm not going to stab you," he said, diverting her

attention to the pocket knife he'd fished from his jeans and providing, thankfully, an excuse for her sudden breathlessness.

Squatting again, Mitch wrapped long fingers around her ankle and gently pulled her foot toward him, turning it on its side and laying it on his thigh. The rough fabric tickled her bare skin and the heat from his leg took a long, slow journey from her foot to her stomach. Kate felt faint.

"I can do it," she said, tugging each word past her throat and clinging to the hope that he would ignore her.

He did.

"Be still. This won't take but a minute."

She closed her eyes and basked in the feel of his hands on her foot, oblivious to the storm that raged without, ignoring the sharp pain and wishing with all her heart that his ministrations took forever. Each punch and probe with the point of the knife pierced the core of her femininity until she was hot and weak with longing.

Never with Arnold had she felt this way. A part of Kate's consciousness, the part that wanted it to go on forever, accepted this acknowledgment. The rational part of her, the part that knew a relationship with Mitch Dawson was impossible, attempted entrance to her thoughts, but Kate firmly pushed that part away. Not one to live in or for the moment, Kate nonetheless embraced this moment with every ounce of her being.

He used his fingers to grasp the end of the splinter and pull it out, then pressed hard on the wound until an ooze of warm blood trickled down her heel, but in her mind it was not her foot that bled but her entire being. It was a cleansing, soothing bleeding that momentarily washed away spiritual pain and left her feeling alive and whole and delightfully giddy. He crushed his handkerchief against the puncture, and she reveled in the texture of the soft cloth and the tenderness with which he applied the pressure.

"There, now," he said, sliding her foot down his thigh and rising slightly so that his eyes were level with hers. "Hold still for a minute. I'll be right back."

He disappeared into the dining room, then returned carrying an unlit lamp. He removed the globe, unscrewed the wick casing, and poured kerosene directly from the base onto her heel.

"Y-a-a-ouch!" she screeched, her jaw dropping and her eyebrows stretching in reaction.

"You don't want lockjaw," he said, mopping up the spilled coal oil with the dishrag he'd used to wipe her foot. "Watch for festering. I think I got it all, but there might be some tiny bits left in there. I wouldn't recommend putting any weight on that heel for a few days. It's gonna be sore."

Kate nodded, disoriented, her heart and mind and soul suddenly empty, drained of the unaccustomed luxury of emotion that had filled her almost to overflowing. She came crashing back to reality. The throbbing pain in her heel reminded her that his action stemmed only from ordinary concern, his ministrations nothing more than first aid.

As if awakening from a dream, she heard the thunder rattling the windowpanes and the rain beating a tattoo on the tin roof. Had the storm abated for a while, or had her senses been so keenly attuned to Mitch that they had blocked out everything else?

She blinked several times and swallowed hard, attempting to regain her voice. "Thank you."

The words rang hollow in her ears, mere language incapable of expressing her innermost thoughts.

"You're welcome."

He made no attempt to stand, but continued to stare

steadily into her eyes, which she was having difficulty focusing. Realizing they were awash with tears, she lifted a shaking hand and swiped at the moisture.

"I didn't mean to hurt you," he said.

She shivered. "You didn't."

"You're cold."

"Yes."

He grasped her upper arms and rose to his full height, bringing her with him. "No wonder you're cold," he said. "Your back's all wet."

She shivered again, so fiercely this time it set her teeth to chattering. "I should change."

"You need a warm bath."

Kate nodded, reluctant to pull away from him. Never would she have believed that being held by a man—any man, but certainly not *this* man—could feel so right.

He hadn't come to hold her. He'd been looking for someone . . . frantically looking for someone . . .

"Why did you come?" she asked.

"Oh," he said, dropping his hands from her arms, shoving them into his jeans pockets, and backing up a step. "I was chasing Stringfellow, which wasn't easy in both the dark and the rain. This town needs street lamps."

She nodded. "I know. We're working on it. Why were you chasing Mr. Stringfellow?"

"I caught him lurking around the town hall, and when I asked him what he was doing he took off running. I lost him a short piece down the street and figured this was where he was headed."

"Why would he come here?"

Mitch shrugged. "You're not on his list of favorite people, Miz McBride."

"Still, he's harmless. I'm sure of that."

"Harmless? Maybe. But he's a prankster. I'm certain of that."

"You think Stringfellow brought the mice to the council meeting?"

"Yep."

"Did Adelaide see—"

"Nope. Or if she did, she's not talking."

Just thinking about her mother-in-law brought another tremble to her limbs. Kate hobbled to the stove, picked up the kettle, and started toward the sink. Mitch stopped her.

"Let me do that."

She leaned against the table and watched him pump water into the kettle, captivated once more by his muscular physique. She tried to imagine Arnold standing in front of the sink, his flaccid arms working the lever, and failed. He'd considered such labor menial and, thus, beneath him. Even when they'd had the spigot, he'd only drawn water on rare occasions, when neither she nor Adelaide had been there to do it for him. Never would he have taken the kettle from her, however. Never would he even have offered to help, no matter what infirmity might have disabled her. He'd been so thoughtless, so callous, almost mean at times.

The memories hurt, but this acknowledgment of the spiritual pain she'd lived with for eight long years was more than Kate could bear. The tears that had only threatened earlier now flowed uncontrollably.

She had to get out of the room, away from this stranger who would never understand, away before he turned around and caught her crying. She turned to flee—and hiccupped.

She was crying. Although Mitch couldn't see her face, he'd bet on it.

He stopped pumping water and turned around. The wet fabric of her shirtwaist and skirt clung to her straight back and molded itself against her hips. Another hiccup jerked at her head and trunk, but she quickly recovered, squaring her shoulders and taking another step away from him.

"Wait!" he called, going after her. She ignored him, but her limp slowed her pace. In a few long strides he caught up with her and draped his left arm across her shoulders.

"I did hurt you. I'm sorry. I didn't mean to. Let me help you to your room."

"No . . . no," she said, her voice scratchy. "I'm fine. Or rather, my heel is."

He frowned in confusion. "Then why—"

"I was thinking about my husband."

Her confession walloped him in the gut. Her husband. He'd almost forgotten she ever had one. She missed her husband. She wished Arnold McBride had been there to tend her foot, to hold her and comfort her. Like one burned, Mitch dropped his arm from her shoulders and moved back to the sink. Kate didn't move at all.

Mitch went back to pumping with a vengeance. When the kettle was full he turned his attention to shoving sticks of stove wood into the firebox as hard as he could chunk them. "It's going to take awhile to get this water hot," he said, his voice tight. "You shouldn't let those wet clothes dry on you in the meantime. You'll catch cold for sure."

He listened to her bare feet pad across the wood floor, her steps slow and erratic, her earlier question echoing in his head.

Why had he come? Hadn't he promised himself the minute he'd learned Kate was a widow that he'd keep his distance? Hadn't every one of his instincts warned him to stay away?

Why had he panicked at the thought of Stringfellow being inside Kate's house? She was more than likely right: The man was probably harmless. Regardless, she was one of the third kind of women, the kind who didn't need a man's protection. The kind who could take care of themselves. A woman like Jennie Clark.

Then why had he insisted on tending her heel? And why had she let him? Why had she cried? Her kind weren't ever supposed to cry. Jennie would never have cried. Why had his heart surged at her tears? Why had the blood rushed to his groin at the feel of her bare foot in his palm? Why had the sight of her collarbone and the pulse beating at the base of her throat turned his insides out?

And those legs! Ah, those legs! So long and firm, with delicately turned ankles and shapely calves. He'd seen legs before, lots of times. Hadn't he frequented every brothel and saloon he'd come to when he was scouting for the Army? Hell, every whore and dance-hall girl from St. Louis to San Francisco advertised her wares with black fishnet stockings and short skirts. But none of them had legs quite like Kate McBride's. What would it feel like, he wondered, to run his palms up her calves, over her knees, and . . .

Mitch caught himself in mid-dream and hastily turned his thoughts elsewhere.

What had Stringfellow been up to, lurking around the town hall? Did Kate keep cash there? Mitch didn't think so, but he knew her office was cram-packed with records. Why would Stringfellow want municipal records? Or did the man have another prank up his sleeve? More mice, perhaps? Why had he run toward Kate's house when Mitch surprised him? Was Stringfellow even now skulking around outside Kate's house?

Taking the lamp with him, Mitch walked through the dining room and into the front hall. She'd jammed the front door but good. Mitch was wrestling with the bolt when she came out of her room.

"Can you get it free?" she asked, no trace of tears left in her voice.

"I'm trying," he said through clenched teeth as he pushed his shoulder against the door and worked the bolt at the same time.

"Just please don't break any more glass," she cautioned.

"I didn't break your glass in the first place, ma'am." He heard the impatience in his voice and attempted to smooth things over a mite. "But I'll try to keep from breaking any more of it. It shore is pretty, this glass is."

"I think so, too. I've ordered another panel from Baltimore, but I'm afraid it won't match."

"You ought to put in some plain glass in the meantime. You're awful isolated, you know, here at the end of the street with no other houses close by."

His back was to her. Mitch thought it safer to keep it that way, for as long as possible, anyway. Eventually he'd have to face her, have to see her in her dressing robe, have to view her tall slenderness encased in silk. He knew it was silk from the swishing noises he'd heard as she approached. What color would it be? he wondered, imagining it was the same shade of green as her eyes. And what did she have on underneath it? Maybe nothing at all . . . He felt himself grow stiff and hot with longing.

"There!" he crowed. "I think I've got it." He slipped the bolt back and opened the door. Cool, damp air hit him in the face, its blast somewhat cooling his burning desire. He had to get away from Kate McBride, and the sooner the better. He'd make sure her doors were locked and then skedaddle back to the boardinghouse.

Thinking about the boardinghouse raised another subject, and Mitch supposed now was as good a time as any to bring it up again. He closed the door and slipped the bolt home, but he didn't turn around.

"Have you thought any more about my room at the jail?"

"Why?"

"Because I meant what I said. I'm not staying there until somebody cleans it up. I'm not cleaning it up myself. That wasn't part of our bargain."

"We have a temporary shortage of funds, Mr. Dawson. We can't pay for your room at the boardinghouse right now."

Her lack of concern infuriated him. He whirled on her. "Well, I refuse to continue paying for it myself, and I'm sure as hell not sleeping in that vermin-infested room, so what do you suggest we do?"

Her shoulders slumped, and though the light from the lamp he'd set on the floor failed to illuminate her face, it caught the green glitter of her eyes, eyes he'd like to drown himself in.

"I don't know," she said, "but I'll think of something."

"You better make it soon, lady," he snapped, jerking the bolt loose and opening the door wide.

He was halfway back to the boardinghouse before he realized that he'd been right about the color of her robe. And he was right about everything else concerning Kate McBride, too.

Wasn't he?

*   *   *

"Why don't we just set a match to the place?" Sally suggested.

"I'm going back home to get my shovel," Marty declared.

Wearing her oldest shoes and most serviceable clothes, Kate had set out shortly after sunrise that morning. On the buggy seat beside her sat a laundry basket overflowing with rags and cleaning supplies. On the way to the square she stopped by Sally's house long enough to tell the councilwoman of her plan and to ask that she pass the word. Now, she, Sally, Julia, and Marty stood surveying the unholy mess Obediah Stringfellow had left behind. No wonder Mitch refused to stay there!

"This gives me a headache," Kate said, nervously watching a fat roach skitter across the floor. Her head already ached from lack of sleep, which the sight and smell of Stringfellow's old room intensified.

"It turns my stomach," Julia put in. "I think something's living under the bed. I keep hearing little noises over here."

"Oh, pooh!" Marty scoffed. "Stop being such a child."

Sally quickly intervened. "If we're not going to burn it down, then we need to get to work." A born organizer, she divided up tasks among the group, and by the time Mitch Dawson arrived, which was close to ten, they had made remarkable headway.

"There was a mouse nest under the bed," Julia said, shivering.

"I trust you've taken care of it," Mitch said.

"*I* took care of it," Marty said from her perch on the floor, her hands busy scraping at the pile of clothes. "Thank goodness, I'm not as skittish as that one." She stopped scraping and pointed her trowel at Julia, then leaned back on the flats of her hands to get a better look at the new marshal. "I thought I was strong," she continued, "and I s'pose I am for a woman, but I need your muscle."

Mitch threw up his hands. "Oh, no. I'm not getting involved in this. Go find Stringfellow. Make him do it."

"That useless critter! Shucks, he ain't nearly as strong as I am," Marty allowed. "But you, now, you've got muscle. I can see those biceps bulging underneath your shirtsleeves. Just help me with this one little thing and I promise I won't ask you to do nothing else."

What man in his right mind wouldn't succumb to such flattery? Certainly not Mitch Dawson. He saw right through Marty's scheme, but hell, he thought, why not? The sooner they got the room clean, the better. And at least he wasn't having to do it all himself.

While Marty remained true to her word, no one else had promised not to ask for his assistance. Before Mitch knew what was happening, he'd helped Sally get the window unstuck and hauled bucketful upon bucketful of water for Julia. Kate struggled with some of her tasks, but not once did she request his aid. And not once did he offer it, though from time to time he caught her grimacing when she put her weight on her right foot.

I can be just as stubborn as you, Mitch thought, all the while watching her far more closely than he intended. Despite her puffy face and the dark circles under her eyes, despite the faded calico dress and the dishtowel tied over her hair, she looked quite fetching. In fact, she was just about the most fetching woman he'd ever seen.

He hated to see her work so hard, but he balked at

feeling guilty about refusing to clean up the mess himself. By rights, he supposed, Stringfellow should have been made to do it, but there was no law that said he had to—and how did you *make* someone do something, anyway? Mitch figured Stringfellow would choose to spend a couple of days in the jail's lone cell rather than clean up his old room. And heaven only knew what mess the man would leave in the cell.

By noon they were all tired and hungry. When Julia suggested they break for lunch no one objected. She'd brought a picnic basket jammed with food: freshly baked bread, thick slices of smoked ham, boiled eggs, peach pickles, and her famous angel food cake. They moved into the outer office and laid the food out on Mitch's desk.

"You must give me the recipe for this cake," Sally mumbled around a mouthful of the light confection.

"Me, too," Kate said, "although I'll never be able to make one this good. Baking and I don't mix too well."

"It takes more elbow grease than talent," Julia insisted. "My right arm used to ache for days after I made one, but I'm used to it now."

"Humph!" Marty snorted. "If you'd get out in the garden and do some hoeing everyday, you'd—"

"Well, well. What do we have here?" a familiar voice sneered. In unison, the group looked up to see Obediah Stringfellow lounging in the open doorway. "Our petticoat government. More concerned about how to bake a cake than run this town."

"So good to see you, Mr. Stringfellow," Kate said, her voice dripping with syrupy sarcasm. "High time you showed up." She dusted cake crumbs off her hands and stood up. "You left some unfinished business here, particularly the filth you left in your room, which by now, thanks to our grueling labor, has been greatly diminished. Nonetheless, there's plenty of work left. If you'll follow me, please—"

Stringfellow blanched, worked his mouth, and stared at Kate in utter disbelief.

"Let's go, old man," Mitch chimed in. "I have just the chore for you. . . ."

Amid a chorus of chuckles and cackles, Stringfellow took off running down the boardwalk.

"And good riddance," Sally said.

The cleaning party broke up around midafternoon. Sally needed to be home when her children arrived from school and Julia said she had to start supper. Marty started packing up supplies and carrying out dirty water and Kate walked down to the mercantile to purchase sheets, a pillow, and a blanket for the bed. When she got back the jail was deserted.

She stood for a moment just inside the room and basked in self-warranted pride. Never had she imagined the room would clean up so well. It smelled pleasantly of lemon oil and beeswax. The painted wood floor and walls sparkled, the furnishings gleamed, and the window glass and small square mirror glistened. Sally had hung new muslin curtains at the single window; Marty had brought a used but clean hooked rug for the floor; Julia had contributed a bowl and pitcher. Though too busy with their families that day to help out, Stella and Liza had sent over a selection of towels and washcloths.

Mitch Dawson should be pleased. Or he would be, once she'd made up the bed.

They'd pulled the bed out in the middle of the floor to clean under it and behind it, and no one had thought to put it back. All her beds at home were on casters; if this bed had ever been so outfitted, someone had removed the rollers. Kate stared at the tall, black walnut headboard and the thick, square legs and wondered how she'd ever manage the heavy monstrosity by herself. She considered leaving it where it was, but she didn't want to give Mitch Dawson something else to gripe about.

She laid the package on the bed, from which they'd removed the top two ticks, then positioned herself behind the footboard and began to push. She pushed and pushed. Sweat broke out on her brow and her limbs trembled from the unaccustomed exertion, but the bed wouldn't budge.

Kate moved around to the headboard and pulled on first one side of it and then the other. Little by little, she scooted the bed toward the wall, but hardly enough to make an appreciable difference. She moved back to the footboard and pushed again. After almost half an hour of backbreaking labor, she'd moved it a grand total of six inches—and completely exhausted herself in the process.

Maybe, she thought, if she rested a few minutes, she could get her strength back and try again. . . .

In the alley behind the jailhouse, Mitch watched the flames die down. Whatever vermin Stringfellow had left in the room were now either burned to a crisp or drowning in ammonia water.

And good riddance, Mitch thought. Sally Myers had that part right. Though he hated to admit it, he found himself liking Sally and Julia and Marty. Of them all, Marty came the closest of them all to fitting his mental image of a feminist. He'd been taken aback by her overalls and brogans, but he had to give the woman credit. She could work rings around most men.

As they'd worked, Marty and Sally had talked about their families. He'd been amazed to learn that Marty was a widow with five children. Somehow, he couldn't quite see her in bed with a man, but she certainly hadn't conceived those children by herself. Perhaps Herman Stockley was right: Maybe these women weren't of the speech-making, office-seeking sort. They seemed pretty normal to him. Almost lady-like.

Naw! It wasn't possible. No lady would ever run for public office. Such a thing would be beneath her dignity.

He dumped a pail of dirty water over the smoldering bits of cotton ticks and denim britches, then went inside to get himself a drink of water before going over to the boardinghouse to collect his duds and tell Mrs. Jones he wouldn't be needing his room anymore. On his way past the cell, he paused to give his new sleeping quarters one last critical survey and stopped cold at the sight of a woman in his bed.

"What the Sam Hill?" he whispered, tiptoeing across the floor to take a better look.

Kate McBride! What was she doing in his bed? From the looks of her, she was plum tuckered out—they all were, but why hadn't she gone home to rest?

Mitch leaned closer, so close his breath lifted a loose strand of hair from over her ear. He planted his open palms on the mattress, one on either side of her, and blew harder on the strand. She twitched in her sleep, then rolled over on her back and smiled.

I should have known, he thought. *You're no lady. Ladies don't get raised in a saloon.* He'd aroused her by simply blowing in her ear. What would she do if he kissed her?

The thought started his blood racing and his imagination spinning with possibilities, all kinds of possibilities, all of them involving a lustful response on her part. Already, he could feel her long legs wrapping around him, could hear her sighs of pleasure, could taste the honeyed sweetness of her mouth.

There was only one way to find out if he was right. And he was damned sure going to give it a whirl.

Chapter Seven

"Let me show you how to tuck the corners," she said, and she laughed, relishing the sound of the merry tinkle and the way it refreshed her spirit.

This is what life ought to be like, she thought. *Two people working together in peace and harmony and love.*

While she folded and tucked, he held up the corner of the mattress, and when he set it down their hands touched. The contact set her nerves to tingling and filled her being with the sweetest combination of warmth and desire. Slowly, she raised her head to gaze into liquid brown eyes that mirrored the passion sweeping through her.

He leaned into her, gently pushing her backward until they fell together onto the partially made bed. He was going to kiss her. She could feel it in her bones and see it in his eyes, those big, dark, long-lashed eyes so much like Arnold's they still terrified her.

As much as she longed for his kiss, she turned her head away from his mouth. She couldn't let him see the panic that twisted her face, couldn't let him see her mind's refusal to accept him for who he was and not a carbon copy of her deceased husband.

For the briefest of moments he hesitated, but it was long enough to scare her far more than the similarity of his eyes ever could. What if he never kissed her? What if she had ruined everything and never experienced the delicate mystery of his lips touching hers, the masculine perfection of his mouth, the roughness of his tongue or the taste of his breath mingling with her own? In that briefest of moments a part of her slipped away, slipped toward the finality of death, leaving a dark void in her soul.

But then she felt his breath in her ear, felt his lips nibble at her earlobe, felt whole and alive in a way she'd never felt before. His caress snatched the dying portion of her back from the grave, filling her entire being with warmth and love and belonging.

She didn't think her soul could hold any more sweetness, but his low moan proved to her it could. He wanted her, this man did; wanted her despite the fierceness of her independent spirit, wanted her despite her inability to return his love, wanted her despite the barrenness of her womb.

And she wanted him. Lord, how she wanted him!

His lips trailed across her cheek, laving and nibbling, searing into the core of her womanhood and melting her bones into liquid fire. No longer afraid, she lifted her cheek from the pillowy feather mattress, turning her mouth into his, molding her lips to fit his, shivering in utter delight.

Her arms felt like the gossamer wings of a butterfly as they left her sides to float upwards and fold over the hard musculature of his shoulders. When his tongue raked the seam of her lips she opened up to him, exalting in the thrust of his tongue and flicking tentatively with her own until the two joined in a wondrous mating dance.

Never had she dreamed passion could be like this.

Never had a dream seemed so real.

Never had she wanted a dream to last forever.

* * *

Never had Mitch imagined a mere kiss could turn into something as bright and bold and adventurous as this.

He felt as though he'd been panning unfruitful waters all these years and now, suddenly, he'd struck the mother lode. The acknowledgment hit him hard in the gut, yet he couldn't tear himself away from the waves of pleasure that crashed over him, around him, and through him. Kissing Kate McBride, he assured himself, *enjoying* kissing Kate McBride and wanting to do far more than that had nothing to do with commitment and everything to do with fulfilling his starved carnality.

And she liked kissing him, too. He could tell by the low, guttural moans that escaped her throat into his open mouth, by the tightness of her hold on his back, by the thrust of her bosom against his chest.

He gathered her against him and rolled to his side to allow for better access to her breasts. He slid his open palm over her shoulder and down her arm until his hand grazed the side of her breast. With painstaking slowness, heeding an inner voice that warned him to proceed with caution, he continued the journey until his hand reached the dip of her waistline. Up and over her ribs he moved, savoring each ridge of delicate bone and gasping when his hard, callused hand met the warm, throbbing mound.

He'd known her breasts were small, but he'd never imagined how delightful small breasts could be. Hers fit perfectly into the palm of his large hand, changing shape, pushing against his touch, begging for the feel of flesh against flesh, for the wet heat of his mouth upon the hardening crest. In answer, his hand slipped over her breast, beneath her arm, and around her back until his fingers encountered the row of hooks lying against her spine.

One slipped loose, and then another. The third hook snagged on a thread and refused to budge. Mitch was fighting with it when heavy footfalls rained across the planked floor of the office and a male voice hollered, "Marshal, come quick! All hell's broke loose out here!"

Mitch tore his mouth away and swore quietly. Before he could remove himself from the bed, the man burst into the room. Mitch took one last, long look at Kate McBride's swollen lips and watched their sweet smile dissolve into a pout. Then, with more difficulty than he would have thought possible, he turned to face the intruder.

It was Hardy Osborne.

"Sorry," Hardy said, looking down at his big feet. "I didn't mean to interrupt nothing . . ."

Behind him, Kate moaned and rolled over. Mitch swallowed hard. "It doesn't matter."

Now that his attention had been turned elsewhere, he could hear the peal of boisterous male laughter, the shrill cries of female voices, and a pounding so loud he wondered how he'd ever been deaf to the cacophony. He reached for his gun belt, which he'd hung on a nail beside the bureau earlier that day. "What's all the commotion?"

"Tain't nothing but some stray livestock," Hardy said, his tone apologetic and his face red with embarrassment.

"Sounds worse than that to me," Mitch said, ushering Hardy into the walkway that ran beside the cell and opened on the back end to the alley and the front end to the office. He pulled the door closed behind him.

"Don't worry, Marshal Dawson. I won't say nothing about what I saw."

"Thank you, Hardy," Mitch said, walking toward the office. " 'Cause what you saw ain't what you *think* you saw."

"How's that?" Hardy asked, his voice rife with confusion.

"What you saw was a man taking advantage of a sleeping woman."

"Oh," Hardy said, obviously still confused. "Wasn't that Mayor McBride?"

"Yep."

"What was she doing in your bed?"

"Hell if I know. She's probably bone tired. I know I am."

They reached the front door. Mitch stepped out onto the boardwalk, mere inches from a raging sea of stampeding cattle, pigs, and goats. Among the fray, squawking chickens and quacking ducks darted and flew about, some of them landing on the backs of the stampeding animals, feathers flying everywhere. Mitch jumped back inside so fast he almost knocked Hardy down.

"Damn! Does this happen very often?"

Hardy nodded vigorously.

"How come?"

" 'Cause no one makes folks keep their livestock penned up. One horse or steer gets spooked, and wham! We got ourselves a stampede."

"I've never seen pigs stampede before," Mitch said.

"They ain't really stampeding," Hardy said, "just trying to get out of the way before they get crushed."

"What do folks usually do about this?" Mitch asked, tossing his useless gun belt at the desk and scratching his head.

"Turn it into a rodeo. You're gonna need some rope."

Kate awoke to whoops and hollers, animals bawling and squalling, and the pounding of what sounded like hundreds of hooves. Her mind assembled all this rather slowly, for she had been deeply asleep.

She dragged herself off the bed, feeling an unaccustomed languor that sapped her of physical strength even while it filled her with wonder and delight. She felt as though she'd taken some powerful drug and understood, at least partially, why some folks sought out opium dens to escape their spiritual bonds.

On the other hand, Kate abhorred losing control of even the tiniest portion of her life. She fought then to regain that control, beginning with pouring out water from the pitcher into the basin and splashing some onto her face. She used one of the towels Stella had sent over to pat off the clinging drops, then checked her appearance in the small rectangular mirror hanging on the wall.

Gone were the dark circles that had shadowed her eyes. Gone was the pallor that had suffused her complexion. Gone were the lines of fatigue that had wreathed her mouth.

Amazing, she thought, what one short nap could do for one's appearance. She leaned closer to the mirror, examining her face from different angles, somehow unconvinced that what she saw was actually real. But there was no denying the bright sparkle in her green eyes, the healthy bloom upon her cheeks, or the swollen fullness of her lips.

She couldn't recall her lips ever looking quite so full. She lifted a finger and pressed its pad against the middle of her lower lip and winced at its soreness.

Why would her lips be sore? she wondered, suddenly reliving her dream in graphic detail. It was almost as though the dream had been real. But it couldn't have been. Could it?

Kate closed her eyes and wallowed in the sensuality of remembrance. An errant breeze sailed through the open window and onto her neck, its breath cool and soothing. It lifted a loose strand of hair and whipped it over her earlobe, and in her mind she felt not the breeze but Mitch Dawson's warm breath and his soft lips nipping at her responsive flesh.

The noise from outside rudely intruded upon her fantasy, and Kate willed strength back into her legs, forcing herself to put the daydream aside and attend to her duties as mayor. This sounded like another stampede. Whatever it was, chaos ran rampant, and something had to be done about it. She pushed the wayward strands of hair back under the tea towel she'd tied over her head and smoothed the flats of her hands over her bodice and skirt to remove some of the wrinkles.

As she bent down to shake out a recalcitrant pleat from the bottom of her skirt, a gust of wind far stronger than its predecessor blustered its way across the room, its force flailing her skirt and petticoat against her legs, ripping at the towel on her head and cutting like the cold blade of a knife into a spot of bare skin in the middle of her back.

Oh, my God! she thought, shooting up straight and catching her horror-stricken gaze in the mirror. It *was* real. She hadn't dreamed it.

Slowly, she pivoted toward the door. The closed door. She'd left it open. She knew she had.

The cad! He'd come in and found her asleep and . . .

Memories flooded in, staining her neck and face a

deep, dark pink. With trembling fingers, she refastened the two loose hooks, her mind busily dredging up elusive details of what she had thought was nothing more than a pleasant dream but what she now realized was a very disturbing reality.

Whatever had she been thinking of? Certainly not her reputation. She had been asleep, for Christ's sake! She hadn't been thinking at all.

Just reacting.

And Lord, how she'd reacted. Shamelessly reacted.

Mitch Dawson had kissed her—and she'd responded like a brazen hussy. If it hadn't been for the trouble outside, she would probably even now be wrapped in his embrace, her naked body writhing beneath his . . . and in broad daylight!

To her chagrin, the noise outside began to abate. Mitch and the townsmen must be getting the livestock under control, which meant he'd be back soon. Kate couldn't face him, not now. Not until she'd sorted out the emotions that raged through her.

She escaped through the alley, holding up her calico skirt and heavy cotton petticoats and walking as quickly as she could through the thick mud. Choosing a route that skirted storefronts, she wove her way through backstreets and alleys until, at last, she came to Elm Street and then, all the way at the end of the street, the refuge of her house.

It was not until she'd had a bath and eaten a light supper that she realized she'd left her buggy in town.

She had to do something about this situation—and fast!

These situations, Kate corrected herself. She was losing control of both situations, which in turn was leading her straight to disaster and failure.

First, there was the town. But how could she and her council do anything without revenue? The sum total of the taxes due for collection, she'd discovered, would barely pay the salaries of the municipal employees for the coming year. If her government was to provide drainage, pave streets, and put in gas lamps, they were going to have to look elsewhere for the funds.

Then, there was Mitch Dawson—the arrogant, self-serving, conniving so-and-so who seemed determined to disturb her carefully guarded emotions. In her dream state, she'd believed he wanted her despite her inability to love him, despite her barrenness. She realized now that he didn't know those things about her. No, the naked truth was that he wanted her because she was available. And, given time or another opportunity, she would surrender. They were like opposite poles of a magnet, inexorably drawn to each other and yet destined to live apart if they were to retain their separate identities.

Though she dreaded it, she had to talk to him, tell him he was never to kiss her again. Perhaps practicing her speech would make talking to him easier—and more effective.

She was in the middle of giving him a mental what-for when he showed up on her doorstep.

"What do you want now?" she snapped, sounding like a fishwife again and not caring one whit this time.

"Well, pardon me for breathing!" he drawled, his slow speech carrying far more annoyance than her sharp voice. He dropped her laundry basket, which was heaped with dirty rags, onto the porch, then pivoted away from her and set his long legs to walking toward the street. There, next to the picket fence, stood her horse and buggy.

"Wait!" she called, swallowing her anger and moving swiftly toward him. "Thanks for bringing my things home."

"I can't imagine why I bothered," he said without turning around—and without slowing his pace. "For some idiotic reason, I figured you'd want to talk about this afternoon."

"Oh, I want to talk about this afternoon, all right, but I'm surprised you do."

Ignoring her, he opened the gate, walked through, and latched it before looking her in the eye. For a moment she met his hardened gaze. He seemed intent on staring her down, and she was equally intent on keeping up with him. She might have succeeded had a bumblebee not chosen that moment to swoop down out of nowhere and fly right into her face.

At least, that's what it looked like it was going to do. Kate gasped and threw up a protective hand just as the bee pulled up, banked to the right, and buzzed past her ear. When she looked back at Mitch she found herself staring not at his face but at his whitened knuckles, where his hands gripped two of the pickets.

"Is there supposed to be some significance to that gate?" she asked.

He blinked. "To what?"

"Oh, never mind," she said on a sigh, thinking he understood perfectly well that she referred to his throwing up a barrier between them. If that was what he wanted, then so be it. It was better that way. Wasn't it?

"About this afternoon," he said.

Kate flinched inwardly, then braced herself and waited for the shoe to fall. When it did she couldn't believe what she was hearing.

"You have to do something about the stray live-stock. Hardy says this happens a lot, but I think our prankster started this stampede and I think it's going to happen again and again if you don't fix it so it can't."

She was still trying to recover from this reversal of expectation. Here she was, all ready to blast him for taking unfair advantage of her, and he was talking about stray livestock. "Fix it? How?"

"You're the mayor. That's your department. If you can't fix something as simple as this, lady, then you had no business running for office."

With that, he turned and sauntered away, but his words rang in her ears until he disappeared from her sight—and then some.

So much for the speech she'd planned to give him. Oh well, she thought, perhaps it was best to let sleeping dogs lie. Besides, what if she was wrong? What if she *had* dreamed the whole thing? She supposed there might be a logical explanation for her loosened hooks and swollen lips, though she couldn't imagine what it could be. Nevertheless, Mitch Dawson's nonchalance gave her ample reason to doubt that he'd actually kissed her.

And what if—heaven forbid!—she had been kissed, but by someone else. What if it had really happened and she'd only *dreamed* it was Mitch?

No, she wouldn't even think about that. She wouldn't waste any more time thinking about it at all. Instead, she turned her mental energies toward ways to improve Paradise.

Kate arrived for the council meeting on Monday night with her confidence high, but her soaring spirits received a thorough dousing the moment she walked into the town hall. She'd momentarily forgotten about the swarm of newspaper reporters from all over the Midwest who'd poured into town over the weekend.

They sat now with pens poised, ready, she was sure, to tear the petticoat government to shreds.

And they weren't the only ones. Mort Moffet and his cohorts were there, and so were Adelaide and Horace, Obediah Stringfellow, the Finks, and many others who voiced loudly and often their objections to the female leadership.

Kate silently thanked Mitch Dawson for shaking her up. As much as she hated to admit it, he was right. If she couldn't fix a problem as simple as stray livestock, she had no business being mayor. But she was about to show him and everyone else that she *could* fix that problem, and a whole heap more besides.

At least she hoped she could. A great deal of her success depended on the individual achievements of her council, to whom she'd assigned various tasks upon which her entire plan hinged. She'd thought she would get around to each of them that afternoon to discuss their progress, but the reporters had kept her tied up all day.

Luckily, she'd managed to evade most of their questions. It wouldn't do to give too much away before she and her council announced their plans that night. The last thing they needed was an informed crowd who *arrived* irate. She fully expected them to leave that way.

Late that afternoon, dark clouds had rolled in and the air hung heavy and close. Kate had hurried home from her office, bathed herself with cool water, and doused herself all over with talcum powder. She chose a lightweight linen dress over the heavier silk suit she had planned to wear, dressed her hair so that it was completely off her face, and hoped she wouldn't perspire too profusely.

When loud thunder promised an imminent downpour Kate hurried to the town hall, arriving thirty minutes early and before any of the councilwomen got there. Already, there were so many people in the room, she wondered how there was going to be enough oxygen for them all to breathe. Folks filled every available chair and occupied every available inch of wall space, while even more spilled into the exterior doorways or stood outside the windows, which had been opened in an attempt to provide additional ventilation. The women fanned their faces and the men who were in close enough proximity leaned close to the women, none too subtly, in an attempt to receive a bit of the stirred air.

Although lightning popped and thunder continued to rumble, the rain held off. Kate wasn't the least bit certain she didn't want it to rain. Maybe it would cool things off.

The minutes ticked by and still not one of the councilwomen showed up. From time to time, Kate stole a surreptitious peek at the pendant watch hanging from a gold chain around her neck. She tried not to panic, but when she glanced at her watch at five minutes to seven, her heart started beating so hard, she figured folks could surely see it, and she couldn't seem to inhale deeply enough to keep from panting. Sweat broke out on her brow, which she supposed was natural enough in the motionless, humid air, but she didn't think the mugginess had anything to do with it.

She was scared. More frightened than she'd ever been in her life.

Where were they? Had something gone wrong? Had *everything* gone wrong? Had they deserted her, left her alone to deal with the reporters and what was certain to turn into an angry mob?

That thought caught in her throat. An angry mob. Oh, God! Why hadn't she warned Mitch Dawson?

Perhaps she had time now, before the women arrived and they started the meeting. . . .

She was just about to seek him out when, one by one, the councilwomen came in, each nodding and smiling at Kate as they took their seats. She allowed herself an internal sigh, patted her brow with her handkerchief, and fortified herself with a long swallow of water.

This time, she made no pretense of checking her watch. It was precisely seven o'clock. Kate rose, banged her gavel on the table, and called the meeting to order. A hush fell over the crowd and all faces turned expectantly toward the council table.

"Last week," she said, "we discussed the deplorable conditions of this town and the changes we all want to see initiated at the earliest possible time. We also discussed the critical lack of municipal funds available for any project, no matter how small. I would like to reiterate that this council started with thirty-six cents in the treasury. Within the last week, we collected almost a hundred and eighty dollars in taxes, and an additional eight hundred or so is due by the end of the month. This may sound like a great deal of money, but traditionally taxes have been our major source of income. Most of this revenue, therefore, must be held in reserve to pay salaries and maintenance costs throughout the year."

She paused, taking a sip of water and allowing time for the townspeople to absorb the information and the reporters to record it before continuing.

"This doesn't mean that we don't intend to move forward with such projects as gas lighting, drainage ditches, new boardwalks, and paved streets. In the short time we've been in office, your council and I have been working diligently toward those ends." She looked down the table at Marty and gave her a reassuring smile. "I turn the floor over to Mrs. Pence."

Kate sat down and Marty stood up, but before she could say anything, Sally popped up. "Excuse me for interrupting, Mayor McBride," she said, "but I'd like to be recognized first. This won't take long," she added.

Kate had no idea what Sally was doing, but she trusted her implicitly. She gave Sally permission to speak.

"I move that noncouncil-member discussion of each motion, proposal, or issue brought before this council be limited to five minutes."

Hooray! Kate silently crowed, glad Sally had thought of this. She knew they could completely close discussion from the townspeople; Sally's compromise, however, would set better with everyone without bogging down the proceedings.

"Second!" Julia piped.

"Call for a vote," Liza said.

Without further ado, the motion passed. Kate assigned Sally to keep time, then Marty started her speech. For a moment, Kate wished she were sitting directly in front of Marty so that she could visibly lend her support, but Marty's voice quickly lost its nervous quiver as she warmed to the subject of laying gas lines.

"Eventually, of course," Marty said, "we'll need to construct our own gas plant, but in the meantime we can make acetylene and pipe it from Tully Patterson's old storage shed on Gardner Road. I spoke to Tully this morning, and he's willing to let us have it for two dollars a month. I move that we accept his offer."

As they had all expected, the townsfolk quickly started voicing questions and opinions immediately following Liza's second. At the end of five minutes Sally called time, and the motion passed unanimously.

"I propose that, beginning tomorrow," Marty continued, "Hardy start accepting orders for residential and business connections. I further propose that the required deposit be five dollars for residences and eight dollars for businesses."

Mort Moffet, who owned and leased out half a dozen commercial buildings, jumped to his feet and hollered, "That's outrageous! There's no way I can afford—"

Kate rose to her feet, but before she could call him down for not waiting to be recognized, Marty said, "Then don't. No one's twisting your arm, Mort. Those who want gas bad enough will pay it. But heed my warning. If you wait until the lines are laid to pay the connection fee, it'll be even higher."

A low murmur broke out among the spectators, and the reporters scribbled notes so fast, Kate wondered how they'd ever manage to read them later. She banged her gavel and called for silence.

Marty further proposed that all males between the ages of fifteen and forty-five be required to provide four days' street service per year, which included ditch digging and maintenance. The tenure would be cut to two days for any man who provided a team of horses. Those who failed to comply by year's end, either partially or fully, would spend the number of days equal to the unfulfilled service in jail. In this way, she explained, the connection fees could be used for the purchase of lead pipe, street lamps, and the calcium carbide they needed to make acetylene, instead of paying salaries to a street crew.

Again, the crowd moaned in protest.

"You women ain't doin' nothin' but pickin' on us men!" Stringfellow hollered without waiting to be recognized. "First you take away our booze, and now you're makin' us work for free. It ain't fair."

Kate started to rise, but Marty quickly responded. "The state of Kansas took away your booze, Obediah, and most towns require their men to perform street work."

The crowd settled down again, and Marty concluded by recommending that advertisements be mailed to Kansas City, Lawrence, and Topeka newspapers for the purpose of seeking a qualified engineer to supervise construction and run the plant.

"No need to mail any ads!" a reporter shouted. "We'll take 'em home with us!"

For a minute laughter reigned. Since it relieved much of the tension in the room, at least for the moment, Kate allowed it to die down on its own.

The vote was called and the council accepted Marty's proposals without discussion or dissension. Kate checked off the first item on her list. Before she could introduce the next topic, however, a crash of thunder resounded through the room and the anticipated downpour commenced with such ferocious swiftness that those hanging around outside were drenched to the skin before they could gain shelter. People standing in front of the windows quickly turned and yanked them down, while the ones standing in the alley and on the front boardwalk squeezed themselves inside and closed the doors.

"There's no better time than in the middle of a thunderstorm," Kate said, raising her voice to be heard over the booming and crashing from without, "to discuss our drainage problem, but we're saving it for another meeting." Another low drone of discontent rippled through the crowd. "Instead, we're going to address the problem of stray livestock roaming our streets. The chair recognizes Mrs. Zeigler."

* * *

This ought to be interesting, Mitch thought. For three days he'd wondered what Kate would decide to do about this particular problem. Now he wondered if the ideas Liza Zeigler voiced were her own or Kate's. He'd bet they were Kate's. Having her council members make these proposals showed intelligent forethought, keeping the townsfolk from thinking she was trying to ramrod everything herself. He listened with pleasantly tense curiosity.

Liza proposed that a corral and a coop be built on a small plot of town-owned land just off the square and that the town hire someone to catch stray livestock and pen it up in the corral. Fines would be assessed, the amounts depending on the size and general disposition of the stock.

"Catching a docile cow is one thing," she explained. "Catching a billy goat is something else entirely."

"Especially Obediah's goat!" James Larue thundered.

The crowd sniggered. Stringfellow's face flushed scarlet. "Y'all better stop pickin' on me," he threatened.

There would be an additional feed and boarding bill, prorated according to the type of animal and the length of time it was incarcerated before the owner came to claim it. The catcher would be paid a percentage of the fines instead of receiving a regular salary. The entire cost of the project would come out of fines and fees collected. Any excess would go into the general operating fund.

Liza barely got to the end of her proposal before the entire crowd, or that's the way it appeared, exploded. People shook their fists and stomped their feet and everyone started talking at once. Kate rapped her gavel repeatedly, but no one paid it any mind.

Mitch couldn't believe his eyes and ears. Didn't

these people see the problem? Didn't they know they had to assume some responsibility if they ever wanted conditions in Paradise to improve? There was so much racket, Mitch had a difficult time picking out specific objections, but he did catch a few.

"It ain't that big a problem!"

"You're gonna make me take time out from my regular job to work on the streets, and now you say I have to pen up my livestock? This'll cost me a fortune!"

"Let's rid ourselves of this damned petticoat government!"

"Right! I demand a recall!"

These people could be vicious. Mitch was sure of it now. He shoved his hands in his jeans pockets and closed his fingers around a folded-up piece of paper Hardy had given him last Friday, the day the women had cleaned his room. Hardy had found it tied to a rock someone had sailed through a window at the town hall. Stringfellow, most likely. That would explain why he'd been lurking around there the night before. The note contained a warning: "Quit or die." He'd been meaning to show it to Kate, and didn't know why he hadn't. He guessed he hadn't wanted to scare her, but he wished now that he had.

Mitch watched Kate closely, and saw the merest hint of fear pinch her brow and widen her green eyes. Her hand gripped the gavel tightly and her arm raised and lowered it with increasing rapidity, but he couldn't even hear its taps any more over the bedlam.

Someone had to calm this crowd before the townspeople turned into a bloodthirsty mob. Why didn't somebody do something?

Kate's gaze found his. Her silent appeal was so strong it walloped him right between the eyes. Hell, he was the marshal! He was the someone who was supposed to be doing something.

But what? In all the years he'd been Dry Creek's marshal, he'd never faced a similar situation. Panic grabbed his heart and froze his limbs, leaving him as worthless as the granite statue of James Madison that stood in front of the courthouse.

He might not be able to breathe properly, but there was nothing wrong with his vision. He watched in horror as a wave of men left their places and moved toward the council table, waving their arms and shaking their fists and crying their outrage.

And through it all, Kate McBride stood her ground.

But her eyes remained locked with his. The appeal he'd read in them moments before shifted to accusation.

"Coward!" they cried.

Coward. Coward. Coward.

Chapter Eight

Coward! Kate's soul screamed. *How can you stand there and do nothing?*

She tore her gaze from Mitch Dawson's rigid stance and gasped when she saw the wave of men surging toward her, their eyes reflecting anger and malice. Of them all, Obediah Stringfellow's eyes burned the hottest. He pulled his six-shooter from its holster and pointed the barrel right at her heart.

Oh, my God! she thought. *He's going to shoot me!*

Kate felt as though she were frozen in time and space. With her gaze fixed on the peacemaker, she sensed rather than saw the five councilwomen stand up and move closer to her side and silently blessed their loyalty. But what could six women do to hold off a swarm of angry men?

Nothing.

A shot rang out. The loud bang jarred her through and through, ripping away conscious thought and physical pain. Her body recoiled from the impact, her head spun out of control, and her soul, suddenly no longer a part of her body, danced weightless and radiant before her eyes, which were quickly glazing over.

So, this was how it felt to die. It wasn't so bad, and yet . . . Yet, there was so much she had wanted to do first, so much she had wanted to feel deep down inside, so many things she had wanted to see and touch and taste and smell and hear.

Those things fought for control of the fragment of consciousness she clung to with all the inner strength she could muster. Folks said that when you knew you were dying your life flashed before your eyes. Now it wasn't the life she'd lived but rather the one she hadn't that burst across her soul. In that moment of transcension she saw herself completing a successful year as mayor of Paradise. She felt her heart fairly split wide open with love for a faceless man. She heard a baby cry, smoothed her fingers across the soft down covering his head, and reveled in the tug of his tiny mouth upon her breast as he suckled the nourishment her body provided.

Another shot rang out, and though Kate flinched this time, the second impact paled in comparison to the first. In a moment it would all be over. She would sink to the floor and Doc Myers would rush forward and hover over her, pushing Sally and Julia out of the way, pressing his handkerchief against her chest, shaking his head in despair. She would die, and her twenty-eight years on this earth would have counted for nothing. She would leave behind no one who truly loved her, no heirs, no mourners, no one. In a few years no one would be able to remember her face; in a few more they would forget her name.

Her name . . . her name . . . Someone was calling her name. . . .

"Kate! Kate! It's over!"

The voice sounded hollow. The words echoed through her head as though she were in a well. Falling into a well, falling . . . falling . . . Her life was over. The voice said so.

A hand grasped her upper arm and squeezed hard,

pulling her out of the well, out of the darkness and back into the light. Light. Full, sparkling, glorious light, blinding in its brilliance. Streets of gold. They said heaven's streets were paved with gold, and now she knew that they were, indeed. She blinked, closed her eyes tightly, then blinked again.

But this wasn't heaven. This was the town hall. A deathly quiet town hall. The only noises were the patter of rain against the windowpanes and a slight shuffling of feet as people returned to their places. The reporters, most of whom sat directly in front of her, scribbled notes on their pads. One of them—Kate thought he was the one from the Kansas City *Star*—stopped writing long enough to glance up at the ceiling.

Kate's gaze followed the reporter's. Powdery bits of plaster hovered beneath two large, gaping holes.

She squeezed her eyes shut, took a deep breath, then chanced a peek at her linen bodice. Light bounced off the gold pendant watch, momentarily blinding her. She blinked and looked again.

No blood. There was no blood. The pale blue linen was as crisp and clean as when she'd put it on that afternoon.

A familiar male voice and a commotion at the door snagged her attention.

"Come on, you. *Move!*"

Though Mitch prodded Obediah Stringfellow with his gun, the ex-marshal dragged his feet.

"You'll never make the charges stick!" Stringfellow bellowed.

Mitch poked him with the barrel of the gun again. "You better be glad you didn't pull that trigger," Mitch said, "or they'd be carrying your dead body out of here. Now walk!"

She turned her gaze to the ceiling again, and suddenly she knew what had happened. Mitch had fired the shots, and now there were two holes in the plaster instead of two holes in her chest. He'd probably saved her life.

How odd, she mused, to think you were dying, to feel your life slipping away, to know with every living cell in your body that you'd never see another sunrise or hear another bird sing or lie with another man. And then to have it all given back to you, to realize your life had been preserved, at least for the present. Kate took another deep breath. It was over—and she had escaped unscathed. Mitch had come through for her after all.

"I think we're ready to take a vote on my proposal," Liza said, pulling Kate back to the business at hand.

"Yes, I suppose we are," Kate agreed.

Somehow she made it through the rest of the meeting, though she had difficulty keeping her mind on the agenda. The instant she announced the meeting adjourned, a crowd gathered around her. One after another of the townspeople offered their complete support of her program, thanked her for taking the bull by the horns, and assured her that if Obediah Stringfellow or anyone else so much as harmed a hair on her head, they'd kill him. For the first time in a long time—maybe ever—Kate felt the warm glow only friendship can bring.

There were plenty more who found fault with her program and told her so in no uncertain terms, but the overwhelming support she'd been offered far outweighed the criticism.

No one, however, seemed to understand how terribly shaken up she still was. No matter that Stringfellow was in jail. The last thing she wanted to do was go home by herself and then be alone in her house all night. But she couldn't ask any of the councilwomen to stay with her. They all had husbands or children who needed them at home. She decided to ask Hardy to see her safely home, but when she approached him, he gave her the strangest look, then gathered his papers and almost ran out of the building.

Whatever had gotten into him? she wondered. A tug at her elbow curtailed further reflection on the matter.

"Pardon me, Mrs. McBride," one of the reporters said. "I was wondering if I could get a picture of you and your petticoat government for my paper. Maybe here? Tomorrow? Say ten-ish?"

Without fully absorbing his words she gave him a weak nod, her thoughts lingering on Hardy's odd behavior.

Doc and Sally stayed around to help her turn out the lamps and lock up.

"You're doing a good job," Doc said. "No, better than good. Great. I knew you girls could do it. No one's going to recognize this town a year from now."

"I don't know, Doc," she said. "I don't think I can handle many more nights like this one."

"You did fine, Kate. And there won't be any more nights like this one."

She wanted to believe him. Oh, how she wanted to believe him. But even he didn't believe it himself. She'd heard the skepticism in his voice. It was just a hint, but that was enough.

Still feeling uneasy, she was about to ask them to follow her home in their buggy when she realized her own buggy was parked just outside the door—and Mitch Dawson held the reins.

A part of her rebelled. This was worse than being alone. Alone, she was safe from the emotional turmoil being with Mitch Dawson inevitably stirred up. . . .

"Are you getting in or not?"

"Pardon?"

The orange tip of his cigarette glowed brighter for a second, then arched through the air when he flipped it away. She hadn't known he smoked. What else didn't she know about Mitch Dawson? she wondered, then answered herself, *Plenty.*

"Do you need help, Miz McBride?"

"No," she said, her voice thin. "No," she repeated, louder, firmer. To herself, she ran the word through and through her brain. *No. All I have to do is tell him no. If he touches me. If he tries to kiss me again, the answer is no. No. No.*

But the more she mentally repeated the negative, the more she felt herself weakening. Telling Mitch Dawson no was tantamount to being ravenously hungry and refusing the offer of food. She needed him; needed to hear his comforting voice, needed to fold herself into the shelter of his arms. But this need would pass, she assured herself. She had her reputation to think of, her social and political position in Paradise. Those things were far more important to her than a few moments of pleasure in this man's arms.

This man who had, she was certain, taken unfair advantage of her. This man who'd caught her dreaming of him, dreaming of his arms around her and his mouth on hers. This man who'd plied her with his caresses, eliciting responses from her she'd never imagined possible. . . .

The memory shot flames of mortification into her cheeks, and she covered them with her palms in an effort to cool them off. Fortunately, the night, made even darker by the clouds banking the moon and the fog of steady drizzle, cloaked her embarrassment.

She wasn't going to think about it. She'd promised herself she wouldn't. But with Mitch so close and the night so dark . . .

The buggy stopped moving. How had they arrived

at her house so quickly? She wasn't ready to deal with this situation. *No,* she repeated. *No. No.*

Before he could dismount and come around to assist her Kate jumped down from the buggy and hurried up the walk.

"Hold on!" he called.

She ignored him.

His feet pounded the bricks behind her. In seconds he caught up with her and caught her around the waist with one of his long arms, matching his stride to her own. He held her gently enough, but Kate resented his holding her at all. She felt herself weakening again and rebelled with every ounce of determination she could muster.

"Unhand me!" she yelped.

"And let you get away from me? No way, lady. You aren't going in that house by yourself. Not after the way that crowd came at you tonight. I'm the marshal of this town, remember? It's my duty to protect the citizens. And I don't shirk my duty."

They reached the porch. Kate jerked herself from his grasp and stood panting, her face raised to his, her anger as sharp and clear as the shard of frosted glass that had convinced her to run for mayor.

"Don't shirk your duty! Maybe not, but it surely took you long enough tonight to decide what your duty was, Marshal Dawson! Obediah Stringfellow could have killed me while you stood there gaping."

He took her upper arms in his big hands and pulled her toward him. Kate searched the thick blackness for his face, desperate for some indication of his reaction to her indictment. Part of her wanted to hurt him, to make him pay for his delayed response when Stringfellow had pointed the gun at her, to make him suffer the way she'd suffered. But another part of her longed to hear his apology, longed to feel his tender caress, longed to believe this man was different.

His hot breath, redolent of lemon sours and tobacco, lifted the unruly hair at her temple and tickled the end of her nose. With every breath she took she drew his masculine essence deep inside. He was standing so close to her. . . .

Despite her resolve she felt herself wilt against his chest, felt herself go weak with longing.

She heard his sharp intake of breath and winced when his grip tightened on her arms.

"I did my job, Miz McBride," he said, his voice hard. "Neither you nor anyone else in that room was harmed and there's a man in jail. I did my job and don't you never forget it. Now if you'll be so kind as to hand over the key, I'll just go on in and make sure there ain't no one in there that ain't supposed to be."

"The door isn't locked," she said, choking on the words.

"Isn't locked!" he railed, shaking her hard.

"Stop! You're hurting me!"

He quit shaking her, but he didn't let go of her arms.

"Listen to me, lady." The title came out sounding derogatory. "You've put yourself in a dangerous position in this town. Don't you *ever* go off and leave your doors unlocked again. And get that glass replaced. Pronto!"

He pushed her away from him and stormed into her house. Kate swayed and grabbed the porch railing for support, her head reeling with a confusion of guilt, fear, self-doubt, and righteous indignation.

The indignation finally gained a strong enough foothold to shove the other emotions to the back of her mind. How dare he manhandle her! How dare he talk to her so contemptuously! How dare he not offer her the emotional and physical support she so desperately needed!

But by the time she found the courage and the words to ream him out, he'd pronounced her house safe for occupation and disappeared into the dark, misty night.

"Hey! Let me out of here!" Stringfellow hollered, rattling the bars. "You can't do this to me! I'm an officer of the law. Let me out of here!"

Mitch buried his head beneath the pillow, but it didn't help. Even if the son of a bitch would shut up and go to sleep, Mitch wasn't sure *he'd* be able to, but at least he could do his thinking in peace.

What was wrong with him all of a sudden?

Six months ago he wouldn't a-ever froze up like that. Why, his Colt would have been out of his holster and pointed at the ceiling faster than he could say "Jack Sprat." But nothing had ever scared the bejeezus out of him like seeing Stringfellow's gun pointed at Kate McBride's chest. Not even when he'd tracked down the Conn Gang all by his lonesome, then busted into their camp and arrested all five of 'em without getting himself shot to smithereens.

That, he supposed, had been nothing short of a miracle. And so was Kate surviving tonight.

If she'd died—and she surely would have if he hadn't done something when he did—it woulda been all his fault.

Next time, he promised himself, he wouldn't be caught off guard.

But there wasn't gonna be a next time. He was gonna make sure of that.

* * *

When Kate arrived at her office the next morning she couldn't get to the door for the long line of people that snaked out onto the boardwalk and curled around the corner. That put the tail out into the cold, gray drizzle, and folks at that end were grumbling considerably. In fact, Kate realized, she didn't see one single smile among the entire group.

She cringed inwardly, horrified at the very idea of having to deal with so many disgruntled people so early in the morning, especially after she'd slept little more than a wink all night. Despite her best efforts, she hadn't been able to stop reliving the horror of having a gun pointed at her chest, hearing the two shots so close in succession, and knowing, simply *knowing* she was dying.

It wasn't that she was ungrateful about being alive; it was that she hadn't yet fully acknowledged how grateful she actually was. Instead, she kept thinking that no one should have to go through what she'd been through the night before.

The visiting reporters, all seven of them, moved along the line, firing questions and jotting down responses, feeding on the discontent like vultures tearing at a bloody carcass.

Given a choice, Kate would have turned around and gone back home. And, she supposed, she still could. During the sleepless night, she'd certainly questioned often enough the wisdom of remaining mayor. She'd seriously considered resigning. But that would be the coward's way out, and she refused to concede defeat so easily. She'd jumped off a cliff and there was no sense looking for a soft spot to land. She pushed on toward the door.

"Morning, Miz McBride," Gabby Dahlmer greeted her, tipping his weathered straw hat.

The warm smile that spread across his wrinkled face

stopped her cold. "Good morning to you, Mr. Dahlmer."

"Good thing I got here early," he said. "This here's 'bout as long a line as I care to stand in." He twisted his head around so he could see the street. "And it's gittin' longer by the minute. Folks're sure anxious to sign up for that there gas line y'all are puttin' in."

So! That was why people had crowded into the town hall. But if that were the case, why did they all seem so out of sorts? She supposed the cold, gray drizzle frazzled nerves the same way it kinked her hair. Yes, the weather was surely to blame. Folks weren't angry with her; they wanted gas lights. They wanted them bad enough to stand out in a cold drizzle to get them. Kate couldn't contain her relief—or her wide smile. She forgot all about being tired.

"I expect Hardy could use some assistance," she said.

"Yes'm," Gabby allowed, "but I was wonderin' iffen I could talk to you 'bout that there job."

"What job is that?"

"The one that rounds up the stray animals."

"Certainly," she said, wondering how well the elderly man would hold up in such a physically taxing position but willing to grant him an interview. "Why don't we wait until the end of the week?" she suggested, nodding at the growing line. She bade Gabby Dahlmer good-day and scurried inside, her step as light as her heart.

Between filling out applications, writing receipts, dealing with the reporters, and getting her council together for the photograph, Kate barely had time to breathe, let alone eat lunch or think about her scrape with death or consider her mounting frustration with Mitch Dawson. Later, however, at home and alone again, Kate found her thoughts turning to him no matter in which direction she tried to point them.

When she removed her shoes and massaged her sore heel, which was healing nicely, she thought of Mitch, and her feelings toward him softened a bit. When she rubbed Hobo's back she thought of Little Booger and remembered the calico settled into Mitch's lap, remembered his long fingers gently stroking the cat. She couldn't recall ever having known a man who kept a cat for a pet. Dogs, yes, but not cats. Her heart thawed a tiny bit more.

When she prepared her bath she thought of Mitch, standing at her sink, pumping water—for her. He'd treated her far more kindly than she supposed she deserved. Most of her pent-up anger and frustration dissipated in the face of his recollected thoughtfulness.

And when she fell into her bed, pleasantly exhausted, she thought of Mitch, remembered the softness of his lips pressed to hers, felt his hand graze her breast, and knew in her woman's heart that he had kissed her. It hadn't been a dream. It was as real as the wanton desire that surged through her every time she was near him. She wished she'd been able to feel as much passion with Arnold. Perhaps, then, things would have been different. . . .

She fell asleep hearing Adelaide's accusation scurry back and forth in her head: "This is all your fault. If you'd been a proper wife and produced a child, my son would still be alive. He just gave up. My son, my only son, had nothing to live for anymore. Now he's dead, and it's your fault."

Bright and early Wednesday morning, Mitch marched Obediah Stringfellow over to the courthouse. He was a mite worried about the judge being some kind of friend of Stringfellow, both of them being from the same place and knowing each other for a long time. But he had to do his duty. Like he'd told Kate, he didn't shirk his duty. This was one time, though, when he wished he could. He wished he could just leave Stringfellow to rot in the cell.

He found Judge Warren, introduced himself, and started right in, explaining why he'd arrested the ex-marshal.

Judge Warren frowned and held up a restraining hand. "I reckon I ought to swear you in, young fellow, before we see about these charges here."

Rattled, Mitch raised his right hand and promised in an uneven voice to uphold the law in Paradise for as long as he wore the marshal's badge.

The judge looked at the handcuffs linking Stringfellow's wrists together—and smiled. In fact, his watery blue eyes fairly twinkled in what could only be amusement with the situation. It appeared the judge knew Stringfellow for what he was.

"Now, I'll listen to your story, Marshal Dawson."

Mitch relaxed. When he'd finished telling him everything, Mitch said, "There were more than a hundred witnesses, judge. I'll be happy to go fetch a few of them if you need substantiation."

Ainsworth Warren waved an indifferent hand. "That won't be necessary. I've already heard the same story from at least fifteen or twenty people. You're to be commended, young fellow, on your efficient handling of the situation." He assumed a dignified pose and pierced Obediah Stringfellow with a stern gaze. "What do you suggest we charge this rat with?"

"Take that back!" Stringfellow barked, his face livid. "No one calls me a rat, Ainsworth, not even you."

The judge pursed his wrinkled lips and his gaze

hardened. "I'd be careful about what I said to me if I was you, Obediah."

Stringfellow clamped his jaw shut but he matched Judge Warren's withering gaze with one of his own. The problem was, he couldn't seem to decide which of the two men he'd rather have receive his glare. Since he couldn't bestow it upon both Mitch and the judge at the same time, he bounced the glower back and forth between them, which totally destroyed the intended effect.

Mitch grinned despite himself.

"The charge?" Judge Warren repeated.

"How about two charges?" Mitch suggested. "Inciting a riot and attempted manslaughter."

"What!" Stringfellow hollered. "I never even fired my gun!"

"And it's a good thing you didn't or we'd be charging you with murder," Judge Warren said.

"I demand a trial!"

"And you'll get one. In the meantime, I'm going to have Marshal Dawson here hold you without bail."

Mitch escorted Stringfellow, who was ranting and raving, outside and down the street to Jethro Smith's café. He'd rather have taken this meal at the Madison House, but Stringfellow's friends gathered at the café, and Mitch wanted them all to see what happened to people when they disobeyed the law. He ordered breakfast only for himself.

"Ain't you gonna feed me?" Stringfellow whined.

"No," Mitch said, cutting into a half-burned steak. "You're gonna feed yourself. Back at the jail."

"That ain't fair!"

Mitch shrugged and salted his runny eggs. "What you did to Kate McBride the other night wasn't fair, either." He made a show of cutting and chewing, murmuring, "Mmm-mmm," around each bite and moving his head from side to side. Watching Stringfellow's eyes bug and his tongue rake his lips made the mediocre food taste almost as good as Mitch pretended it did.

"Tell you what," Mitch said, laying his knife and fork aside and wiping his mouth with the red-checkered napkin he'd tucked into his collar. "You admit to letting those mice loose at last week's town council meeting and I'll see what I can do about getting the judge to set bail."

Stringfellow grinned, exposing brown-edged teeth.

I've got him, Mitch thought. *He fell right in.*

"Nothin' doin'. You'd just trump up another charge against me."

"So you did do it."

"I didn't say nothin' of the sort."

"You might as well have," Mitch said. "You sure didn't deny it. What about the stampede?"

"What about it?"

"Did you start that?"

Stringfellow clamped his lips shut and glared.

"Well, did you?"

"I ain't sayin' nothin' else, Dawson, until you feed me."

Mitch ordered another breakfast, minus the steak, and had it put on a tray to take back to the jail. He pumped Stringfellow all day, but the man refused to admit to any of the mischief Mitch accused him of perpetrating. Mitch supposed it didn't really matter. They had him on the other charges. All that remained was convincing a jury to sentence Stringfellow to the full penalty allowed by law.

And that ought to be for the majority of Obediah Stringfellow's remaining days.

* * *

By late Wednesday afternoon the crowd at the town hall finally thinned out and then dwindled away. In two days Kate and Hardy had signed up some three dozen business customers and over two hundred residential customers for the new gas lines.

Kate slipped the last application into its appropriate alphabetical spot and turned to Hardy, who was counting money.

"My goodness!" she exclaimed. "We thought it would take several weeks to collect enough money to start this project, but you're holding enough to buy all the pipe and have it laid. There may even be enough there to buy several street lamps."

She paused, waiting for the clerk to comment, but all she heard was a muffled, "Yes, ma'am."

"You've been acting awfully strange for the past couple of days, Hardy," she said. He didn't look up. "Are you not feeling well?"

He ran his finger along the inside of his collar, stretched his neck, and went back to sorting a pile of dimes into neat stacks. "I'm fine, Miz McBride."

"Why won't you look at me?"

For the first time in two days he turned his face to her, but he couldn't quite meet her gaze with his own. A stab of regret pricked her heart. For a while they'd gotten along so well. . . .

"You know, we're going to need a clerk for the Paradise Gas Company. Perhaps you'd like that job better than this one."

Hardy frowned, genuinely perplexed. "Ma'am?"

"For the time being we'll use the council room for the gas company office. All we need is a desk and a filing cabinet, which shouldn't be in the way too much when we have meetings. What do you think?"

Kate steeled herself for his reply. Hardy had been a

great help to her. She would hate to lose him, but she hated to see him so miserable, too.

"I think that's a good idea, but you'll have to hire someone else for the job. I'm not interested. If you don't want me working with you anymore, I'll go to work for Al Youngblood. He's been begging me to for years."

It was Kate's turn to be confused. "Of course I want you to stay, Hardy, but you seem so . . . uncomfortable here all of a sudden."

"I, uh, I'm okay. Really and truly, I am. It's just that, well—"

"Is it because I'm a woman?"

A hint of a smile lifted the corners of his mouth. "I guess that's what it is, ma'am. But I'll get used to it in time."

Though she wasn't completely satisfied with his answer, Kate wasn't about to pursue the subject any further. For the moment having Hardy stay on was sufficient. Perhaps, one day, he'd feel comfortable enough to confide in her. Already he seemed much more relaxed than he'd been moments before. And in time . . . well, in time everything would work itself out.

Everything—including her attraction to Mitch Dawson.

As she tidied up her office, Kate gave herself a good talking-to about that attraction. Nothing good could come of it. If it could . . .

But it couldn't. If she could have children . . . if she was capable of sustaining a loving relationship . . . if Mitch Dawson was the type to settle down. But he wasn't.

It's all a matter of mind over body, she assured herself. *Think about something else when he's around and he'll fade into the background. Think of him as just*

another man and that's what he'll become in your eyes.
She had almost convinced herself that she could think him clean away when Mitch walked through the door.

Chapter Nine

Kate willed her heart to stop fluttering, but it refused to obey. *He's just a man,* she assured herself. *Think of him as just another man.*

It didn't work.

"Stringfellow's trial is set for Monday," Mitch announced.

"Monday?" Kate repeated, mentally cringing at the inanity yet knowing it bought her a tiny bit of time—enough, she hoped, to regain her equilibrium. It was crazy to allow a man, any man, to upset her emotional balance so completely.

Monday. What was significant about Monday? Oh, yes.

"That should draw a crowd," she said, "especially since Court Week starts on Monday."

"That's what Judge Warren said. I think he wants a crowd there."

"Why? I'd think he'd want to get it out of the way now, before he's bombarded with civil cases."

Mitch shrugged. "Maybe to set an example before as many witnesses as possible. None of us want another mob scene like we had the other night."

Kate certainly agreed with that, but a word of caution was necessary. "Even at the courthouse, a crowd is liable to get out of hand."

"I know. That's one thing I wanted to talk to you about. I'd like to hire a part-time deputy."

He might as well have hit her with a brick. A deputy? How would they ever pay another salary when they were already scraping the bottom of the barrel? "We're not budgeted for a deputy," she said.

"Most towns this size have one."

"That's not a good enough reason for me to propose the expense."

His dark eyes fairly shot sparks. "What is a good enough reason, Miz McBride? We have a serious problem here. I don't see how you and your council think I can continue to handle angry crowds all by myself."

"You've only been here ten days," she argued, grasping at straws, "scarcely long enough to determine whether you actually need a deputy. Besides, Obediah Stringfellow handled your job all by himself for a number of years."

He shrugged. "If you want me to perform my duties with the same sense of disregard as Stringfellow, then you're right, I don't need a deputy."

Mitch turned on his heel and started for the door.

"I'll discuss this with the council," Kate called, telling herself she was making the offer to placate him and not the least bit eager to stall his departure.

He stopped walking, but he didn't turn around. "The council doesn't meet again before the trial. I want another man wearing a badge in that courthouse on Monday."

"Do you have anyone in mind?"

"Not really. I don't know that many folks yet."

Kate drummed her fingers on her desktop, thinking. "What about Skip Hudson? He ought to be able to spare the time—if he doesn't have a big order to get out right now. And I expect he and Julia would appreciate the extra money. Just temporarily, until the trial's over," she added hastily. "Then we'll see what we can do about a permanent part-time deputy."

"I'll ask him."

"You said there was something else?"

He turned sideways and leaned lazily against the doorjamb. "If you want me to enforce the law, I'm gonna need a copy of all the town ordinances."

"There's a copy in your desk drawer."

"No, there ain't. Stringfellow didn't leave nothing in that desk. It's the only thing he cleaned out."

Kate noted his sudden reversion to incorrect grammar and wondered what prompted it. "Hardy will give you one, and I'll see that you get regular updates."

"Thank you, ma'am," he drawled, pushing his back away from the frame and nodding his head in farewell.

Kate sat for a long time, staring at the space he'd occupied and pondering the wealth of emotions his very presence stirred within her bosom.

There wasn't any reason a woman should rattle him the way Kate McBride did.

He'd gone into her office with a memorized speech in his head, and what had he gone and done? Taken one look at her sitting there so calm and collected and downright beautiful that he'd promptly forgotten almost everything he'd planned to say.

Did she ever lose control of a situation? he wondered. Even when she'd had a gun pointed at her heart, she'd stood her ground. And what had he done? Frozen up. Here he was, not just a man, but a man of the law, a protector of the innocent, and he'd frozen solid.

It wasn't natural for a woman to be like her. Even

those two temperance women had fallen to pieces
when he'd shoved them in the cell and locked the door.
They'd bawled like babies for a spell, then hollered
and threatened and thrown the tin cups of water he
brought them right back in his face. If they'd just told
him who they were to begin with, he probably
wouldn't a-ever locked 'em up.

He'd bet Kate would have told him. Naw, she
wouldn't of, but she wouldn't a-bawled or hollered
like those other two. She woulda sat right down on the
cot and taken her knitting out of her purse and not
uttered another word except to count stitches. She
woulda driven him crazy with silence.

And she was gonna drive him crazy before July
rolled around and he could bow out of this job.

Damn! He'd been in town only ten days. Ten days!
That left eighty to go. How in Sam Hill was he gonna
make it through eighty more days of dealing with Miss
Cool-as-a-North-Wind McBride?

Mitch smiled then, recalling a moment when she
hadn't been in control. His touch had broken through
her icy exterior. Maybe it was because she was asleep.
But maybe, just maybe, she would respond with equal
passion if she was wide awake.

He let that idea roll around in his head, let his
imagination run wild with the contemplation of doing
wicked things to her—until Stringfellow's bellyaching
destroyed his daydream.

"It will be a thankless job," Kate told Gabby
Dahlmer. "Folks don't like the idea already. Once you
start penning up their livestock, they're going to raise
Cain. You'll have to stand firm on the fines and fees
schedule. No one slides."

He bobbed his bald head and grinned. "I can do it, Miz McBride, iffen you'll give me the chance."

"Fifty percent of the collected fines may not add up to much income," she cautioned.

"I reckon it pays more'n I'm makin' right now, which is exactly nothing. Aw, I have my garden and my chickens, trade enough eggs at Al's store to keep me and Eb supplied with flour and such, but Eb, he does most of the work on the farm. We git by. But I need me sompin' more to do. I been roundin' up livestock all my life. Figure I ought to be able to do it for you."

"All right, Mr. Dahlmer," Kate said, offering him her hand in a firm shake. "The job is yours. You can start tomorrow with building the corral and chicken coop. Get what supplies you need from Moffet's Lumber yard and have them send me the bill."

"Yes'm," Gabby said, squeezing and pumping her hand hard. "You won't be sorry, ma'am. I promise you won't."

Kate was sorry. Not for hiring Gabby Dahlmer, but for sending him to Mort Moffet's lumberyard. Not that she had any real choice. It was the only lumberyard in town.

Mort's bill arrived late Friday afternoon, minutes before time to lock up and go home. In fact, Kate passed the delivery boy on her way out the door. Before she got to the end of the boardwalk Hardy hollered at her to come back.

His naturally pale face was blanched pure white.

"Whatever is the matter?" she asked.

"Look at this," he whispered, shoving the statement at her.

As her gaze skimmed over the handwritten page,

Kate felt the color drain from her face, too. "Fifty dollars? He charged us *fifty dollars* for a few boards, some fence posts, and a roll of chicken wire?"

She backed into the counter and leaned hard against it while she read over the bill again. "There must be some mistake."

"Yeah," Hardy said, his voice firmer, angrier. "There was a mistake, all right. Trusting Mort Moffet to be honest was the mistake."

Kate folded the bill twice without bothering to crease it and shoved it into her purse.

"What are you going to do?" Hardy asked.

She started for the door. "Stop Gabby from using any more material than he already has and go see Mr. Moffet."

"It won't do no good," Hardy predicted.

"Maybe not, but I won't be able to sleep a wink until I give that man a piece of my mind. Just hope Gabby's slow at carpentry work."

Without stopping by the livery to collect her rig, she hurried over to the corral site, which was in the opposite direction. To her dismay, Gabby had finished the chicken coop and cut all the rails for the corral. She was sure Mort would refuse to take back cut lumber. Gabby was nowhere in sight.

Kate backtracked to the livery, paid Everett for the week, got in her rig, and drove to Mort's lumberyard, which sat on the outskirts of town. The gate was locked and the place looked deserted.

"I won't be outdone," she mumbled, turning the rig around and heading back to town, straight to Mort's house.

"He ain't here," Mrs. Moffet said through a crack in the door. "He went over to Bagdad. Don't know when he'll be back."

Though Kate wasn't the least bit certain Mort

wasn't at home right then, she saw no point in arguing. He'd show his face in Paradise eventually, and she'd be ready for him when he did.

Kate spent all day Saturday in town, looking for Mort Moffet and asking folks if they'd seen him, but no one had since midday Friday. From the story Kate pieced together, the scoundrel had left town about that time and hadn't come back.

She talked privately with Gabby Dahlmer, who assured her he'd been completely unaware of the charges for the materials he purchased. "Let me see," he said, scratching his head, "that little bit of stuff shoulda come to no more'n ten, twelve dollars."

"Who do I need to see at the lumberyard to get this statement adjusted?" she asked.

"There ain't no one. Not when Mort hisself makes out the bill. And this one came directly from him. See"—he pointed to a pair of *M*s—"them's his initials. You'll have to see Mort."

Unconvinced, Kate went to the lumberyard and demanded to see the foreman, a big, burly man named Tinker Sikes whom Kate had never met before.

"Cain't help you, ma'am," Sikes said, shaking his head. "Mr. Moffet charges some folks more, others less, depending on their ability to pay."

"He ought to know—" Kate bit back the remainder of the sentence. There was no reason to air her problems to the foreman when he had no authority to alter the charges.

On Sunday she went to the Methodist church for services instead of the Episcopal one, where she was a member. Mort was Methodist and never missed a service. But he missed that one.

Late Sunday afternoon she went back to see Mrs.

Moffet, whose first name Kate had never heard. Again the woman denied that her husband was home and insisted she didn't know when he'd be back.

Kate figured the ex-mayor was certain to show up at Stringfellow's trial on Monday, but cornering him there might cause problems. The last thing she wanted—or her petticoat government needed—was a public argument between her and Mort. Thus far the transition had gone smoothly enough, with no thanks to anyone from the former administration. Kate intended to keep everything on as even a keel as possible.

The more she thought about his inflated bill, the madder she got. The more she thought about Mort conveniently disappearing for the weekend, the madder she got. By Monday morning she was about as mad as a woman of her disposition could get, and that was mad.

She'd promised the townsfolk to be a good steward with their money, and right off the bat she'd put them in debt. They'd be a long time recouping this investment, if they ever did. Even if she managed to find Mort now and confront him, she was convinced he wouldn't budge. Unless she thought of something fast, this situation would prove an embarrassment to both her and her council, and would serve to damage their integrity.

But what could she do today, she wondered, when she was the primary witness and required in court?

On her way to the courthouse Kate stopped by Sally's house and filled her in.

"Do you trust me?" Sally asked.

"Implicitly," Kate averred.

"Good. Then leave this to me. Come back here for lunch. Your office isn't private enough."

"But you're a witness, too," Kate argued. "You were standing right beside me."

"You forget, Tully Patterson is my brother-in-law."

Though he worked primarily as a bookkeeper, Tully sometimes practiced law. Judge Warren had asked Tully to prosecute this case.

"We'll get Mort for this," Sally promised.

Equipped with two sections of long wooden pews, the almost square courtroom comfortably held about fifty observers. A rail in front of the pews cordoned off two tables for the attorneys, the judge's bench, the witness stand, and the jury box. Long windows, dressed with wooden blinds, lined the two outside walls, which faced the sides of the pews. Someone had opened the windows to allow for cross-ventilation and adjusted the blinds to provide enough light to see. Already heat was building in the room, as much, Mitch figured, from tempers as from the weather, which was actually a bit on the cool side.

Trouble was brewing; Mitch could feel it in his bones.

Mitch counted as people came in, then closed and locked the doors after number fifty-two. A sign on the vestibule side of the doors announced that the room was full.

He stood in the back of the courtroom, next to the closed double doors, listening to the disgruntled crowd in the vestibule and familiarizing himself with the disbursement of the assembly. For the most part the spectators were curious townsfolk, many of whom were certain to be called as witnesses. The seven out-of-town reporters arrived en masse and positioned themselves as close to the front as they could get.

As he'd expected, the hecklers arrived in small groups of three or four and sat together in knots. There were three distinct clusters of them sitting in three different spots. It would have been smarter, in his estimation, to scatter throughout the courtroom, making it difficult for the two officers of the law to keep up with who was sitting where and who was doing what. Luckily, he was smarter than they were.

Deputizing Skip Hudson had been a good idea. Mitch had feared the young fellow would resist direction, but thus far Skip had proved to be very cooperative. He stood near the front, pencil and paper in hand, jotting down the names of those in each group of potential rabble-rousers. Mitch knew most of these men only by face. He wanted their names recorded, just in case.

However, the likelihood of a riot scared Mitch far less than his being questioned on the witness stand. Giving trial evidence came second nature to him, and if that was all he had to do today, everything would be fine. It was possible questions from James Larue, who was representing Stringfellow, that had Mitch worried.

At precisely nine o'clock Judge Warren came out of his chambers, which were behind the courtroom on the left side, and took his place on the bench. Skip opened another door on the opposite side, and the twelve jurors filed in from the jury room and took their places in the jury box. The members of the jury had been selected and agreed upon in advance by the two legal representatives in counsel with Judge Warren.

Ainsworth Warren banged his gavel and called the proceedings to order.

Tully Patterson's opening speech impressed Mitch. As he continued, Tully exhibited a talent for manipulating a jury. He called two of the councilwomen to the stand, then several people who'd clearly witnessed Stringfellow's deed. Each one told basically the same story: Stringfellow flew off the handle, advanced on the council table, pulled his gun, and pointed it straight at Mayor McBride. No, he hadn't been provoked. And yes, they were all certain at the time that he intended the mayor bodily harm if not sure death.

When James Larue chose not to cross-examine any of these witnesses Mitch breathed easier.

Next, Tully called Mitch to the stand.

"And what did you do, Marshal?"

I froze. Mitch cleared his throat. "I drew my pistol and shot at the ceiling to get everyone's attention."

"And was that effective?"

"No," Mitch said. "I had to pull the trigger again."

"And after the second time, the crowd calmed down?"

"Yes. I then arrested Mr. Stringfellow."

Tully sat down and Mitch stood up.

"Just a minute, Marshal Dawson," James Larue said. "I have a few questions for you."

Mitch settled himself back down and drew a deep breath. He'd known it was coming, but knowing didn't make enduring it any easier.

Larue stood right in front of the witness box and rested an arm on the railing. He smiled rather friendly-like. Like a snake, Mitch thought. He sat up straight, poised for the strike.

"You're an experienced officer of the law. Is that right?"

"Yes, sir."

"The several witnesses Mr. Patterson called all testified that Mr. Stringfellow advanced on the council table." Larue pushed away from the railing and walked back toward his table. "Was he alone?"

"No, sir."

The attorney whirled around. "Speak up, please, Mr. Dawson, so the jury can hear you."

"No, sir, he wasn't," Mitch said, louder. He thought

about the dirty slip of paper Hardy had given him, the one that had been tied around a rock, the one that said, "Quit or die." He wished he could prove Stringfellow had written it.

"In your opinion, did any of the other men pose a threat to the mayor or her council?"

Mitch mentally squirmed, but he didn't think his nervousness showed. "Possibly. That's hard to say. You see, Stringfellow was the only one—"

"Just answer 'yes' or 'no,' Mr. Dawson."

"—who had his pistol drawn," Mitch finished.

Larue leaned casually against the table and crossed his ankles. "You came here two weeks ago from Dry Creek, Nebraska, where you had served as marshal for seven years. Is that right?"

Here it comes, Mitch thought, nodding his head in answer to the defense counsel's question.

"Were you employed by the town of Dry Creek when you accepted the position here?"

"No."

James Larue frowned and turned to face the jury. "You were, in fact, employed by Western Union at the time, weren't you?" Before Mitch could respond, Larue said, "The Dry Creek Town Council dismissed you last November, didn't they?"

"Yes." Mitch choked on the word.

Larue twirled toward Mitch. "What was that?"

"Yes," Mitch repeated, somewhat louder, recrossing his legs. *Calm down,* he told himself, *and don't squirm. You made a mistake. Don't let this son of a bitch turn it into a crime.*

He'd been dismissed?

The courtroom spun in front of Kate's eyes, and she thought she would surely faint. She mentally shook herself, forcing her mind to absorb and assimilate this new information while her heart denied that Mitch could ever be dishonest with her.

Somehow Mitch made it through the barbed and often sarcastic interrogation without raising his voice or hanging his head or making a single defensive statement. But then the son of a bitch questioned his character.

"I'm a good lawman," Mitch said, looking at the jury instead of the lawyer. "Until last November I'd never even been reprimanded. I'm not proud of what I did, but I'm not ashamed of it, either. It was an honest mistake."

"We're happy to hear you admit your error, Mr. Dawson," Larue sneered. "Couldn't your arresting Mr. Stringfellow have been an honest mistake, too?"

"No," Mitch said, but Larue stepped on the response, effectively drowning it out by hollering, "I have nothing else for this witness."

Mitch refused to let it lie. "It wasn't a mistake."

"Thank you, Marshal," Ainsworth Warren said. "You may step down now."

It took every ounce of dignity Mitch could muster to hold his head up and walk all the way up the aisle to his position at the vestibule doors. Along the way he felt folks staring at him and heard them muttering about the mistake he'd made in Dry Creek. These people would be no more forgiving and forgetting than Dry Creek folks. He'd lost their respect—if he'd ever had it. He was done in, and he might as well get his bags packed, 'cause Kate was sure to let him go.

The judge picked up a gold pocket watch from his bench and flipped open the case. "Do you have any more witnesses, Mr. Patterson?"

"One, sir. Mayor McBride."

Judge Warren snapped the case closed. The click reverberated through the courtroom. "Since it's almost noon, we'll break for lunch and reconvene at one."

Kate's gaze followed Mitch as he walked away from the witness chair and down the aisle as far as her row. He held his head high and stared straight ahead, but a pulsing tick in his temple told her his teeth were clenched. And well they should be. James Larue had been merciless.

Mitch's testimony shocked her to the core. It wasn't what he'd said that bothered her as much as the fact that she hadn't known anything about it. She'd never had any reason to believe he wasn't serving as Dry Creek's marshal when he accepted the position she offered. She fussed at herself for not questioning his desire to leave his home and come to Paradise. She should have known something had happened. Why hadn't she asked him?

She hadn't even asked for references. She'd been in such a hurry to hire a new marshal, she'd taken him sight unseen, background unknown. And now there were folks in town who were bound to blame her for her haste.

Part of her wanted to blame Mitch for not volunteering the information, but her sense of justice wouldn't allow it. If she'd been in his shoes, she would have kept her mouth shut, too. He hadn't shot anyone or put anyone's life in danger. He'd made a simple error in judgment; not a very serious error at all, yet one most people would have difficulty understanding, especially a female mayor. Or so it would seem to Mitch.

Having to tell a courtroom packed with people about it couldn't have been easy. It must have really hurt his pride to be forced to expose his mistake that way, but he'd handled his testimony with remarkable composure.

When Tully called her name her heart jumped into her throat and refused to budge. She'd known she would be called, figured she'd be Tully's last witness. Regardless, she hadn't been prepared. She wondered if anyone ever was. She hoped she could remain as calm as Mitch had but she had her doubts. Serious doubts. Even thinking about Obediah Stringfellow made her head pound and her heart race. Talking about him was going to be difficult, indeed.

She hurried to Sally's house, which was only a few blocks from the courthouse. Sally's wide grin and twinkling blue eyes took Kate's mind right off her worries about her testimony.

"Whatever have you done?" Kate asked.

"Something."

"Something thoroughly devilish, by the look on your face. Tell me."

"Over lunch," Sally said. "All this thinking's made me powerfully hungry." She led the way into the dining room, where two places had already been set. Sally disappeared into the kitchen and returned with a large bowl of chicken salad and a loaf of freshly baked bread.

"Now tell me," Kate insisted, barely waiting for Sally to sit down.

"Have you talked to Mort?"

Kate shook her head. "He was in the courtroom, but there was no opportunity to speak to him privately."

"It doesn't matter. He won't change his mind. But we need to give him the opportunity." Sally cut her sandwich in half, then pointed with her knife to a stack of papers on the sideboard. "I took the liberty of writing him a letter, which is all ready for your signature. We'll have Hardy deliver it to him personally this afternoon."

"What does the letter say?"

"I suggested that he rethink the situation and adjust the bill before tonight's council meeting."

"And if he doesn't?"

"We move in for the kill, but I didn't warn him. We want to catch him completely unawares."

Kate wanted to hear Sally's plan so much, she thought she was going to pop, but she allowed Sally a minute to chew before begging her to reveal all.

"It's really quite simple," Sally said. "First we pass an ordinance requiring all merchants to put in boardwalks where they don't exist and to repair the ones that do."

Kate nodded.

"Then," Sally continued, "we pass an ordinance forbidding anyone to purchase the materials from Mort Moffet."

"How can we do that when there's no one else to buy lumber from?"

Sally smiled and winked. "There is now. I talked to Al Youngblood this morning. He's decided to add lumber in limited dimensions to his general store."

"The sizes used for boardwalks?"

"Exactly. It will be here Thursday."

Kate wiped her mouth with her napkin and giggled. "Mort will be furious. But can we do this?"

"I don't know why we can't. We're the government in Paradise. We can do anything we want to. Now tell me about this morning," Sally said, and Kate complied.

Sally laid a comforting hand over Kate's. "Don't

fret over what folks are gonna say about your hiring Mitch," she said, "but don't let on that you didn't know about it all along. He's already proved himself worthy of the badge."

You weren't facing the barrel of Stringfellow's pistol, Kate thought, angry at Mitch again for taking what had seemed like an eternity to gain control of the situation. But there was no point in pursuing the subject. Sally would think her ungrateful—and maybe she was.

Kate sighed. "I'm much more concerned right now about my own testimony."

"You'll do just fine. And now that I've worked out our Mort Moffet problem, I can sit in on the proceedings."

Later, while they were drinking coffee and eating apple pie, Sally broached another subject. "I've been thinking about the occasional stampedes. Our new animal control measures should help, but we're always going to have a problem with mares as long as we allow the stabling of stallions within the town limits."

"But no one in town has a stallion—"

"Except Mort Moffet!" they said in unison.

"I never knew you could be so mean!" Kate said.

"Me, either. Nor did I know that meanness could be this much fun."

They laughed again, and for the first time since she'd moved to Paradise Kate felt as though she had a friend.

"We'd better hurry," Sally said, rising and taking her dishes to the kitchen, "or we'll be late for court."

"I worried for nothing," Kate told Sally as soon as the jury went out. "Tully only asked a couple of questions, and I still can't believe James Larue didn't cross-examine me."

"I can. He didn't dare give you the opportunity to expound on your dealings with Stringfellow—or to voice your suspicions that he's turned into a real troublemaker."

"We have no proof," Kate reminded her.

"Maybe not," Sally allowed, "but once something is mentioned the jury can't forget it. I'm disappointed in Tully for not bringing it all up himself."

"How long do you think the jury will be out?"

"Not long. The man's guilty as sin on both counts. Surely they can see that."

"Yes, surely they can," Kate agreed, but her voice lacked conviction. "James Larue did a good job of representing Stringfellow."

"Larue's a snake if I ever saw one. Those men on the jury are smart. They saw right through his tactics."

"I hope you're right," Kate said, thinking about the Garden of Eden and the serpent persuading Eve to taste of the forbidden fruit. Snakes knew well how to sneak up on unsuspecting folks and then strike before people knew what had hit them. Suddenly Kate wanted to get out of the courtroom.

"It's stifling in here," she said. "Let's walk over to the Madison House and get some lemonade. We'll ask Skip to send someone to get us when the jury comes back in."

It seemed almost everyone else had the same idea. The hotel restaurant was as packed as the courtroom had been earlier. Kate and Sally drank their lemonade standing up.

Thirty minutes passed, and then an hour, and still no one brought news from the courthouse. The longer they waited, the more nervous Kate became. When the crowd at the Madison House began to thin out Kate and Sally decided to return to the courtroom before someone claimed their seats.

Mort was waiting for them in the vestibule, his hands twisting rolled-up paper. The second they walked in the door he pounced.

"What are you trying to prove, Kate?" he bellowed, shaking the contorted roll in her face.

"Prove? Why, absolutely nothing," she replied, forcing a sugary sweetness into her voice, while all the while her knees were quaking beneath her five petticoats.

He acted as though he hadn't heard her. " 'Cause if you're trying to prove you've got more power than me, you've got a rude awakening coming."

It won't be my rude awakening, Kate wanted to say, but she held her tongue. With lightning speed she ran the contents of the letter through her head, trying to recall anything Sally had written that would have given Mort the idea that that was exactly what she intended to prove. The last thing she and Sally wanted to do was tip their hand, and she didn't think they had. But they had scared him, and that was good. *Let him squirm.*

"You know your prices are outrageous," she accused, repeating the contents of the letter almost verbatim. "Neither I nor the Council appreciate your taking such an unfair advantage. We simply thought you might want to reconsider before everyone hears about it."

"No," he said. "The charges stand."

"So be it."

His eyes bugged. "You aren't going to argue about it?"

Kate moved toward the door. "Why debate an issue

you can't win?" she asked, casually throwing the question over her shoulder.

When they were seated Sally put her hand over her mouth to stifle a snicker.

"What's so funny?" Kate whispered.

"You! You let Mort think he's won. Lord, is he in for a surprise!"

"Sh-h-h!" Kate warned. "Let's make sure it is one."

Candlelighting came and went, and the jury didn't return. Doc Myers, who had been called out to deliver a baby and, therefore, missed the trial, squeezed in beside his wife and asked how things were going.

"We've been waiting since a little after four," Sally said. "I'll bet they're having trouble agreeing on the recommended sentence. I wish they'd hurry up. The council meeting starts in twenty minutes."

"If they don't reach a decision soon," Doc said, "Judge Warren will send them home until tomorrow." He surveyed the courtroom. "I'm glad to see you gals hired Skip to help Mitch. We're liable to have some trouble here in a minute."

He nodded toward the chamber door, through which Ainsworth Warren came. Almost immediately the back door opened and the jury walked in. Ned Mission, the jury foreman, nodded at James Larue and smiled.

Kate's heart sank to her knees and her breath left her in a *whoosh*. Spots swam before her eyes and her ears rang so loudly she barely heard Ned say, "Not guilty on either count."

Chapter Ten

Immediately the courtroom erupted in whoops and shouts of triumph and victory—and moans and groans of disappointment and indignation. Fortunately, those who mumbled in dissatisfaction were not the kind to express their emotions physically.

At his post in the back of the courtroom, Mitch shook his head in a combination of shock and despair. Ned Mission's words rang in his ears like a death knell: "Not guilty on either count." In his estimation this decision condemned his future in Paradise as surely as it freed Obediah Stringfellow. Despite the exposure of his grievous mistake in Dry Creek, a guilty verdict might have earned him a modicum of respect as a lawman and, therefore, bought him enough time to prove himself.

But now . . . now that hope vamoosed right out the door along with the grumbling townsfolk. As people filed past him, Mitch watched closely for Kate McBride. He figured she must be as disappointed as he was—disappointed in him as well as in the verdict.

Funny, he thought, how much he'd come to care for her in the two weeks he'd been in Paradise. Not romantically, of course, he hastily corrected, but as a person. Only fools who didn't mind losing control of their lives believed in love and romance, but not men like him. He'd lost control once—and with a woman much like Kate—but never again. He could admire Kate McBride all he wanted, even if she did infuriate him beyond belief at times. And he might even kiss her again sometime, just for the sake of finding out if her passion burned as hot as he suspected. But love her? Never.

It was only admiration and respect that made him care how she felt right now, he mentally affirmed. It was only admiration and respect that made him seek her face in the crowd. It was only admiration and respect that caused him to worry about her reaction to the verdict.

At long last his troubled gaze found her. She hadn't moved, but sat stiff as a corpse without a whiff of movement to indicate whether she continued to breathe. Mitch worked his way down the aisle, his gaze never leaving her erect back.

Cry, dammit! his mind screamed at her. *Kick, scream, cuss . . . let it out, Kate, whatever it takes. Just don't hold it inside. It'll kill you to hold it inside.*

People sidled past her to get out of the pew, most of them mumbling and grumbling under their breath about the injustice. Stringfellow pushed his way through the throng in the aisle; the rabble-rousers gathered around him, slapping him on the back and congratulating him. And through it all, Kate sat, still as a whipping post, only vaguely aware of what was going on around her, her eyes seeing a pistol barrel pointed at her, her ears hearing Ned's gravelly voice declaring the verdict, her heart thundering in her chest.

Slowly she regained full consciousness, as one coming out of a deep sleep. She heard her name and turned her face toward the soft female voice.

"Are you going to be all right?" Sally asked.

"I—I think so. I'm just so . . . shocked."

"We all are," Doc said.

"I wish you could go home and rest," Sally said. "You shouldn't have to conduct a council meeting immediately after this."

Kate swallowed hard, grasped the back of the pew in front of her, and stood up. For a moment she held on to the curved back, waiting for the strength to return to her legs, waiting for her head to stop throbbing, and wondering why right had not prevailed.

She felt a hand, strong and sure, take her elbow, and she looked up into warm dark eyes that said, *I'm here to protect you from harm.* His voice, though, came cold and unyielding. "Come, Miz McBride. I'll escort you to the town hall."

She couldn't blame him. She herself felt all cold and unyielding inside. Her head understood, but that didn't stop her heart from wanting him to take her in his arms and hold her close. She needed his warmth, his reassurance, his tenderness, as she'd never needed anything or anyone before. She couldn't recall ever feeling so devastatingly empty.

It wasn't fair. The jury shouldn't have let Stringfellow go. He was dangerous.

But they had released him, and she was certain he'd march himself right over to the town hall and take his place among the hecklers. He'd be wearing his gun again. And when the council introduced Sally's boardwalk ordinance he was certain to come after her again. Only this time she might not be so lucky. . . .

"I sent Skip on over to the town hall," Mitch said, "with instructions to collect peacemakers and Arkansas toothpicks and all other weapons from every man who walks in the door. We may have some problems, but they won't be the same problems we had last week."

"Thank you," she said.

"Are you ladies planning on passing any more laws tonight that are liable to cause trouble?" Mitch asked.

"Yes." The word echoed in her head. For a moment she closed her eyes to the world and looked deep inside her soul for the strength needed to continue her crusade to clean up Paradise. When she found it she took a long breath and continued. "And next week, and the week after that, and the week after that. We were elected to clean up this town, Marshal Dawson. That means change. And change doesn't set well with some folks."

"You're right about that," he said, his voice suddenly so dry it almost cracked. "Sorry I won't be here to witness all that change."

"Pardon?"

"Come next Monday I'll be gone."

"Why?" she asked, her head snapping up, her mind seeking an explanation even as she anxiously awaited his reply.

He looked away from her. "Surely you don't plan to keep me. Not after today."

Was that all it was? Kate wanted to laugh in utter relief. "I don't like what happened today either, Marshal, but I do believe in our system of justice. You did your part when you arrested Mr. Stringfellow. I can't blame you because a jury of his peers saw fit to acquit the man."

"You mean you're not dismissing me?"

"Of course not. What a silly thing to suggest."

"But now everyone in town knows I arrested the Nebraska governor's wife on grounds of prostitution." Defeat riddled his voice.

"So?" Kate said, her own voice merry. Somehow, talking this out with Mitch erased her worries and renewed her hope. "From what I hear about that particular *lady,* you were probably not far off the truth."

He laughed, and his hand left her elbow and moved around to ride the small of her back. "We should have had this discussion a long time ago," he said. Then he leaned over and whispered in her ear, "What *do* you know about the esteemed governor's wife?"

"Enough to know she's no lady," Kate said, deliberately cryptic. Actually, she'd heard very little, and that had been vague. Nevertheless, the rumors flew, and where there was smoke, there was usually fire.

"I sensed that much," Mitch said, wanting to tell her his theory about there being three kinds of women, but catching himself in time. Kate might not appreciate being classified with the likes of the Nebraska governor's wife.

Kate sensed that he wanted to say something else, but she didn't push him. Besides, time had run out for them. They had reached the town hall.

They separated at the council room door. Though his hand no longer rode her back, the warmth it left there burned still. Kate moved to her place behind the table, more confident than she would have ever dreamed possible given the circumstances. She harbored no doubt that folks would rant and rave. Mort Moffet would raise holy hell, and the reporters would have a field day. Someone might even threaten her life again. She was living on the edge of danger, yet she'd never felt more alive.

Still, something was missing, something warm and vital, something necessary to life, something she'd never possessed but always wanted. . . .

She looked directly into Mitch Dawson's dark brown eyes and saw his firm chin dip in a nod of assurance. At once she felt both safe and vulnerable. She knew in the depths of her soul that as long as he was around, no physical harm would befall her. Yet she couldn't be in the same room with him without her heart tripping all over itself, begging that she relinquish her hold on self-control and allow herself to think of him as something far more than the town marshal doing his job.

Could she afford to give her heart to a man again? Would she want to give it to a man like Mitch Dawson? A man who constantly challenged her at every turn? A man so thoroughly independent and completely sure of himself?

Why, a man like Mitch would take her heart, smash it to smithereens, and then eat it for breakfast.

No. She could live with the cold, dark void in her soul. She always had. Perhaps, somewhere out there, there might be a man for her, a man who would love her and lend her the emotional support she craved. But he wouldn't be a man like Mitch Dawson.

"Listen to this, Hardy!" Kate called, not waiting for him to answer before starting to read from the Kansas City *Star*. " 'The first business transacted was to promptly and unanimously snow under a motion to limit debate to five minutes. Time was divided between a discussion of controlling wayward livestock and a new recipe for making angel food cake.' "

"Of all the gall!" Hardy allowed, coming into Kate's office, his mouth hanging open and his eyes bulging.

"My sentiments exactly," Kate said. "We never discussed angel food cake at all."

"Or anything else that wasn't strictly town business, for that matter. Let me see that." She passed him the paper. "Nice picture," he said, thumping the photograph of Kate and her council with his forefinger.

"Yes," she mumbled, "if you like sourpusses. Do I always look so stern?"

"Oh, no, ma'am. And you were real happy that day. I remember. He must've caught you off guard or something."

While Hardy read the article, a vague recollection of having discussed making angel food cake niggled at her memory.

"The day we cleaned the jail!" she said, jumping to her feet.

"Ma'am?"

"Julia brought one of her angel food cakes and we were talking about how she made it when Obediah Stringfellow walked in. Of all the gall is right. That was no more an official council meeting than our present conversation is. That reporter must have talked to Stringfellow, but why he would believe an accused felon is beyond—"

"You'd better read the rest of this," Hardy broke in, his voice deathly soft. The clerk doubled the page and passed the newspaper back to Kate. "There, just below the fold."

" 'If there is truly trouble in Paradise,' " she read aloud, " 'it is not in the Madison County court system. Last week a jury acquitted former town marshal Obediah Stringfellow of the dual charges of inciting a riot and attempted manslaughter, which were trumped up by Mayor Katherine McBride after Mr. Stringfellow quietly voiced his objections to the council's proposed animal control measures.' "

Kate gasped.

"It gets worse," Hardy said.

"I don't know how."

"Read on."

She blinked back hot tears born of supreme frustration. "I don't think I can. You read it." She passed the newspaper back to Hardy, wanting more than anything to take the newsprint and tear it into little shreds.

" 'In an effort to milk additional revenue from an already much depressed economy,' " Hardy read, " 'the unified petticoat government passed an ordinance requiring Paradise residents to pen up their docile livestock, consisting for the most part of cows, chickens, geese, and ducks, which have always been allowed to run loose in such country towns. The fines exacted to retrieve a captured animal are often more than the creature is worth. An examination of the ordinance proved that Mayor McBride and her female cohorts are as corrupt as any male politician. Both cats and dogs, which are the only animals owned by the mayor and four of the councilwomen, are omitted from the list.' "

"What!" Kate cried, bolting upright.

" 'It should also be noted,' " Hardy continued, " 'that the new town marshal also owns a cat.' "

"Cats and dogs are not livestock!"

"We know that, Miz McBride, and so does this reporter. He was deliberately trying to make you look bad. All reporters do that nowadays. Don't let it bother you none."

It wasn't the irresponsible reporting that bothered Kate so much as it was the fact that the man had obviously listened to Stringfellow and believed his lies. And, perhaps, Mort Moffet was behind the article as well. He'd promised her a rude awakening. Was this what he'd meant?

"Oh," she said on a sigh, "I suppose I knew all along the press would have a field day with this situation. I might as well get used to it. But they won't stop me." Her voice grew stronger. "No, sir, they won't stop me from doing my job. I mean it, Hardy. There may come a time when you'll have to remind me I said that, but I do mean it with all my heart. The townspeople elected us to turn things around, and that's exactly what we're going to do."

"I'm behind you," he said, "a hunnerd percent. And so are a slew of other folks. We're all proud of the way you handled Mort Moffet at the council meeting the other night. What are you planning to do next?"

Kate grinned wickedly and laughter bubbled on her lips. "You're just gonna have to wait and see, Hardy. But the wait will be worth it, I assure you."

Sitting behind his desk at the end of a long, hot day, Mitch licked his lips, swallowed the modicum of saliva in his mouth, and groaned so loud the cat in his lap jerked her head up.

"Sorry, old gal," he said, running the flat of his hand down the long yellow fur on Little Booger's back until she settled back down.

He wanted a beer so bad he could feel the foam on his lips and taste the sharp tang of malt on his tongue.

Damn Kate McBride! And damn the state of Kansas for making the confounded law in the first place.

All he had to do to wet his whistle the way he wanted to wet it was to ride over to Bagdad, which was only an hour or so away on horseback. And maybe while he was over there where no one knew him from Adam, he'd satisfy another thirst that kept gnawing at a different part of his anatomy. He'd been trying to get out of town for a week, just for an afternoon. That was one reason—oh, hell, who was he trying to fool? That was the *main* reason he'd asked her to hire a deputy. If he had a deputy, he could take an afternoon off every once in a while.

Kate and her council said they'd take the matter under consideration, but they insisted the town couldn't afford even a part-time deputy's salary now. For the time being Skip could fill in when it was absolutely necessary. Otherwise, Mitch was on his own.

The way things were going, he'd never get over to Bagdad for a beer and a woman.

At first, keeping an eye on Stringfellow prevented his going, then the trial, and now his increased duties, thanks to Kate's new ordinances. She'd told him in no uncertain terms that she expected him to oversee Gabby Dahlmer, hound the merchants to begin boardwalk construction and repairs, and then make sure no one bought any of the materials from Mort Moffet.

Despite his thirst, Mitch grinned at the memory of Kate introducing the boardwalk proposal at the last council meeting. She'd maintained the proper decorum, but he could see how much she wanted to smile, maybe even laugh out loud, especially when Mort's cheeks looked like they were going to explode.

In a sweet, ladylike tone, Kate offered Mort the opportunity to challenge her measures, then sat calmly while the former mayor pranced across the narrow space between the council table and front row of chairs and vented his outrage in a less than gentlemanly manner. At the end of five minutes Sally said, "Time's up." A low rumble of displeasure from the audience met Mort's sputtered objection. In a fit of what appeared to be extreme frustration at the lack of support from the townspeople, he clamped his mouth shut, stomped back to his seat, and sat down.

Since Mort had used up the audience's five minutes of discussion and no one on the council offered a comment, Kate called for a vote and the proposal passed with six yeas. Although Kate didn't usually vote, she said she wanted her wholehearted approval on record.

"I've got to hand it to 'em," Mitch said to the cat, his long fingers pushing deep into the fur on Little Booger's back. "They may be a bunch of scheming women, but they know how to pull together. And they sure as hell know how to turn things around. I wouldn't want to be Mort Moffet right now. I know what it's like to be the laughingstock of a whole town, and I don't ever intend to be there again."

He reached for the thick document Hardy had given him and slid it across the desk. "Reading all these ordinances is gonna take awhile. I reckon I ought to get started."

Kate gave Mort and his bunch of malcontents till the end of the week to lick their wounds before she reloaded her cannon. She'd never meant to start a war, but since she had, she figured she might as well learn how to play the game. In the interim she read up on Napoleon and Washington, who were, in her opinion, two of the greatest military strategists in recent history. She'd decided to employ one of their oft-used maneuvers: Lay low, lull the enemy into complacency, and then strike when they least expected it. No one expected a battle on Sunday.

Directly following service, Kate went to see Mitch at the jail.

"You want me to do *what?*" he bellowed.

She put a finger to her lips. "Sh-h-h!" she hissed, tossing her head toward the open window, in front of which folks were passing by on their way home from church. "You'll destroy the element of surprise."

"Oh, they'll be surprised, all right," he barked, though in a slightly lower voice. "For the most part these are good folks, Miz McBride. Why do you want to go and make 'em mad again?"

"I have no desire to rile them, Marshal Dawson. My council and I merely wish to see all the laws on the books enforced. That includes the blue law."

"But folks've been ignoring that law since it was enacted," Mitch argued.

"Just like they ignored Prohibition."

The reminder made him thirsty for a beer all over again. "Some laws are just plain stupid, Miz McBride. Why can't you just ignore 'em like everybody else?"

Kate pulled herself up to her full height and pinned him with what she hoped was a defiant glare. "You're not in the business of ignoring the law, Mr. Dawson, but rather enforcing it. If you prefer to put yourself on the other side of that badge, then perhaps you'd better give it back to me."

Mitch glared right back, and there was something in his glittering brown eyes that told her she'd best not push him too far.

"Yes, ma'am," he said. "I'll enforce your blue law."

There wasn't an ounce of respect in his voice. His cynical tone cut her to the quick, but she was right about this. Wasn't she?

"I suppose you want me to start today?" he asked.

"That would be nice," Kate said, suddenly feeling like she'd picked up a snake. "Since they had no warning I suppose we can allow the merchants to stay open this afternoon, but I insist that all businesses be closed next Sunday. Is that compromising enough for you?"

"Yes, ma'am."

For a moment she fully expected him to snap to attention and salute her.

I won this skirmish, she thought, *but have I lost the war?*

* * *

"I hate to be the one to tell you this," Mitch said to Al Youngblood, who was straightening a stack of feed sacks, "but I'm under orders from the mayor."

Although it was the truth, Mitch winced inside. He hated passing the blame, but he couldn't allow folks to think this had been his idea.

Damn her hide, but Kate McBride seemed bound and determined to turn him into a pesky mosquito, making him go 'round nipping at folks just a little at a time until they were so covered up with welts they couldn't think about nothing but what put 'em there. When folks got to itching they started reaching for their swatters. And when that happened he hoped they remembered it was Kate and her petticoat government that bred the pest.

With Prohibition, he'd only had to make three store owners mad. 'Course, there was a slew of menfolks a mite miffed, but they could still buy booze if they didn't mind riding over to Bagdad. But this time . . . This time Mitch wished he could turn himself into a no-see-um, as the Indians called biting midges.

Oh, well, he'd better get this over with so he could go bite another merchant.

"You'll have to close your store next Sunday."

Al shrugged. "What's going on next Sunday?"

"Nothing I know of."

"Then why do I have to close the store?"

"The blue law."

Al laughed so loud three customers standing nearby stopped looking at merchandise and stepped closer to the pair at the feed sacks.

"I'm serious," Mitch said.

"Close my store on Sunday?" Al asked, his jaw agape. "Why, 'cept Saturday, Sunday's my best day. I get almost a fourth of my business on Sunday. Lots of folks from out in the country pick up stuff 'tween services. I ain't about to close up on one of my best days."

"You don't have a choice, Al," Mitch said, suddenly hating Kate McBride. "The law's on the books, and the mayor says we have to obey it. That means you and every other store owner in Paradise."

"Nobody ever pays that law no mind," Al argued, hefting a burlap bag of grain onto his shoulder.

"You'll have to take that up with the mayor," Mitch said. "I already tried."

"And if I open my store next Sunday? What're you gonna do about it?" Al dropped the sack onto the floor and reached for another one.

"Don't make me have to arrest you, Al," Mitch pleaded.

Al dropped his hands from the feed sack and whirled around. "You can't be serious."

"I already told you I am. It's my job to enforce the law. And I will."

But only 'cause I need this job until July. Come July, I'm hightailing it out of this crazy place. I'm heading out to parts west, where folks ain't quite so citified—and where there ain't no number-three women mucking everything up. I'm gonna put as much distance 'tween me and Paradise as I can and still be on this side of the Rockies. But 'fore then, I'm gonna get me another kiss from Kate McBride. Hell, she owes me that much and more for what she's put me through already.

And once I'm outta here, I ain't never working for no woman again!

Kate arrived at her office the next morning to find a contingency of store owners waiting for her. There were so many of them crowded into her small office, she couldn't see her desk. They all started talking at once.

"You can't make us close up on Sunday!"

"The economy is bad enough, Kate, without having you pulling a stunt like this."

"You're making me sorry I voted for you."

"Hold on!" Kate cried, throwing up a hand in an attempt to bridle their tongues. "Please. Now, one at a time."

She might as well have told a pack of wild dogs to stop howling. She let them go for a few minutes, then attempted to shush them again. When she failed the second time she turned to Hardy, who was standing beside her. A deep frown wrinkled his wide brow.

"Whatever's the matter with them?" he asked.

"They don't want to obey the blue law," she said, then had to repeat herself to be heard above the din.

"You better find some money somewhere," Hardy shouted.

"Why?"

"Our jail's not big enough."

Kate backed out of her office and closed the door. None of the merchants seemed to notice.

"What're you gonna do?" Hardy asked.

"Go to the post office and then go talk to Gabby; see how many animals he's caught in the past couple of days. And then"—she glanced at the closed door—"and then I'll probably go back home for a spell. In the meantime, maybe they'll realize I'm not here anymore and go on back to work."

"I mean, what are you gonna do about them?"

"Nothing."

"You have to do something, Miz McBride."

"I *am* doing something," Kate insisted. "I'm trying

to make this town a cleaner, more hospitable place to live and raise a family. Can't they see that?"

"What they see is that you're being unreasonable. Those men ain't criminals. They're solid, hard-working citizens. Most of them voted for you. They want a clean town, too, but they have to make a living."

"What do you suggest I do?"

"Forget this business about the blue law."

Kate looked him straight in the eye and sighed inwardly at the disapproval she read in his face. "I can't, Hardy. It's the law. If we start deciding which laws we will and won't obey, we'll have chaos."

"Then at least visit them at their stores. Talk to them one at a time."

"I'm not a politician, Hardy."

"Maybe not," he allowed, "but you owe them the courtesy of an explanation."

Kate talked to the merchants individually, as Hardy had suggested, and tried to explain, but they bucked her on every point.

She said it was state law. They said the state had no right to dictate to them when it came to earning a living. Was the state going to feed their families or put a roof over their heads? Not likely.

She said the enforcement wouldn't affect their income, not in the long run. People couldn't manage without certain items. They would get used to stores being closed on Sunday and make their purchases on other days. The blue law supported God's law. Folks were supposed to rest on Sunday.

Rest? the merchants asked. Did she call getting six or eight or more children ready for church, packing a picnic lunch, hitching up a team of horses, and then driving an hour or more to get to God's house restful?

That's what the country folk had to do every Sunday. Why not allow them the privilege of doing a bit of shopping while they were in town? Otherwise, many of them wouldn't be able to rest later in the week if they had to make the trip again.

They said the law was crazy. That was why hardly anyone paid it any mind. They'd been ignoring it for years. Why couldn't they just go right on ignoring it? Why was she so hell-bent on enforcing such a stupid law when the state government—and they were the ones who'd passed it—couldn't care less?

They argued so persuasively, Kate almost recanted. But, she told them, she'd promised to see that every law and ordinance on the books was enforced. That included the blue law. If they thought the law was crazy, then they needed to petition the state legislature to repeal it. In the meantime, any merchant who opened his store for business on Sunday would be fined. Repeated offenses, she reminded them, would result in jail sentences.

All week long she debated the issue with the diffident merchants. On Sunday a few defiant storekeepers opened for business as usual. Mitch ordered their doors closed and reported the offenses. The collected fines increased the meager town coffer.

"Don't you feel just the least bit guilty about this?" Mitch asked.

"No," she firmly replied. "They all knew the consequences. It's not my fault they didn't listen."

Though a niggling inner voice told her she should, Kate refused to consider the wisdom of her endeavor to see that all laws were enforced. She was right. She knew she was. At present, people couldn't see the proverbial forest for the trees, but eventually the townsfolk would grow accustomed to the changes and everyone would come to view things her way. They would see that order had grown out of chaos, and they would thank her and her council for providing such excellent leadership.

"Mort hasn't moved his stallion," Mitch said.

"Did you cite him?"

"Yes."

"How many times?"

"Once."

"What?" Kate gasped out.

"How many times did you want me to cite him?"

"Once a day until he moves the horse out of town."

Mitch looked at her as though she'd lost her mind. "But, Miz McBride," he said, "the fine's twenty-five dollars a pop."

"Exactly. Keep citing him and he'll move the horse."

He didn't say anything, just gave her a mulish glare.

"Think of it this way, Marshal," she said, "the more citations you write, the more fines we collect. The more fines we collect, the better we can afford to add items to the budget. As in a part-time deputy's salary."

"That's blackmail," he accused, his thick eyebrows glowering at her.

"No, that's good business. I'm not going to fire you over some silly misunderstanding, and I don't expect us ever to see eye-to-eye on everything, but come July eighth I'll have to make a decision on whether or not you keep this job. That decision will be based on your overall performance. Am I making myself perfectly clear?"

"Oh, yes, ma'am," he drawled, tipping his hat and backing toward the door. "Perfectly clear."

Chapter Eleven

When Mitch handed Mort the second citation the former mayor laughed and tore the paper into shreds.

Mitch watched the pieces flutter down and collect into a little pile on the top of Mort's desk. "Now what did you go do that for, Mr. Moffet? I'm just gonna have to write you another one."

"I'll tear the next one up, too. I paid one fine, Marshal," Mort said, his voice brooking no argument. "I ain't paying another."

Mitch scratched his head. "I don't want to have to arrest you."

"And I don't want to go to jail." Mort dug a wad of bills out of his pocket and removed the engraved gold clip that held them together. "How much is this gonna cost me?"

"Twenty-five dollars, same as before. But you don't pay me. You should know that. You take your citation over to the town hall and pay Hardy."

Mort nodded at the empty chair next to Mitch. "Why don't you sit down, son, and we'll discuss this."

Mitch ignored the offer. "There isn't anything to discuss."

"I think maybe there is." Mort counted out a hundred dollars and shoved the bills across his desk.

Mitch frowned in confusion even while his fingers itched to snatch up the money and shove it into his pocket. It was more than he'd seen at one time since before his mother died and left a heap of debts. Eventually he'd paid them all off, except the house, which the bank had been kind enough to rent to him after they'd foreclosed. Why, with a hundred dollars in his pocket, he could go anywhere, start over . . .

"Let's just call it payment for cooperation," Mort said.

Mitch looked down and saw how close his right hand had come to picking up the greenbacks. He snatched it away and shoved it into his front pocket, where it couldn't get him into trouble. "Cooperation?" he echoed. "I get paid by the town, and my cooperation is with the government, not with a lawbreaker."

Mort rolled his eyes ceilingward. "Come on now, son. Name your price. Everyone has a price."

Mitch clenched his left hand into a tight fist. "Not everyone, Mr. Moffet."

"Oh, yes. Everyone. Even you." Mort grinned, a sly, almost evil grin that twitched the nostrils of his hawk's nose, reminding Mitch of a pit viper. "How'd you like that article in the *Star?*"

This sudden change of topics threw Mitch for a minute, and then the light dawned bright and clear. "You were the one who fed that reporter all those lies!"

Mort's bushy gray eyebrows shot to mid-forehead. "Lies? That's a strong accusation. The way I've got it figured, you're obliged to me for keeping that little fiasco you had in Dry Creek out of the papers."

Mitch's heart skipped a beat, but he wasn't about to let Mort Moffet know it bothered him at all, so he tried to shrug it off. "Everyone knows about that now, so what difference does it make?"

"A lot, if you're thinking about ever leaving this town and looking for a job somewhere else. Maybe a lot if you're planning to stay."

Without consciously thinking about what he was doing, Mitch lowered himself into the chair. He was growing tired of Mort Moffet's veiled threats, but he couldn't just walk out without some knowledge of Mort's plans. He supposed the man could truly ruin him if he set his mind to it.

"Why don't you explain it to me," Mitch said.

Mort rested his lower arms on the desk and leaned forward. "It's really quite simple. I go down to the telegraph office and send a message to the *Star*. Next week your face and a complete biography appear in that newspaper, which, I should remind you, has a rather large circulation."

Mitch nodded. "Go on."

"Reporters love raking muck. Other papers pick up the story, and before long the entire country knows everything there is to tell about one Mitchell Dawson, town marshal. No one would ever give you a job as a lawman again."

"Maybe. Maybe not. It doesn't matter if I choose to stay here."

Mort leaned back and grinned again. "That's where you're wrong, son. I can ruin you just as surely right here in this town. The people here trust me. If I stir up a big enough stink, they will demand that Kate dismiss you, and then where will you be? Besides, there's no way she'll get reelected, assuming she manages to make it through a year without being recalled. Who do you think will be mayor then?"

"You?"

"Damn straight, me!" He shoved the bills closer to

Mitch. "You're better off just taking my money and looking the other way."

Mitch's gaze followed Mort's liver-spotted hand as it pushed the bills. He was tempted. Sorely tempted. Everything Mort said made sense. Kate had certainly stirred up a hornet's nest in Paradise, and she didn't seem the least bit content at stopping there. He owed his first loyalty to himself, not to her, not to this town. . . .

"Join up with me, son, and I can get you friends. Lots of friends. You don't have any, you know. Not really. And I can get you women and beer. I can get you all the women you want and all the beer you can drink."

Mitch swallowed hard. He missed close male companionship almost as much as he missed women and beer. He reached for the money again, but when the pads of his fingers touched the bills, sparks of sudden, acute distaste—for himself and for Mort Moffet—surged into his hand and up his arm.

Kate was right. He wasn't in the business of ignoring the law, but he'd almost allowed himself to forget on which side of the badge he stood.

"No," he said, hating the hesitation in his voice. "No," he repeated, more confidently this time. "If I did, I'd be obliged to you, as you put it, from now on out."

Mort scooped up the greenbacks and waved them in front of Mitch's face. "You're gonna be sorry, son."

The money smelled of stale bay rum, cold sweat, and corruption. Sickened, Mitch stood up and turned toward the door.

"You can't win," Mort said.

"I'll take my chances." Mitch paused, his hand on the doorknob. He turned back to Mort and nodded at the pile of shredded paper. "You don't really need that copy, you know. It's on Hardy's record. You have ten days to pay the fine, but if you haven't moved that stallion outside the town limits by noon tomorrow, I'll be back with another citation."

He snatched open the door, then turned to look at Mort one more time. "And don't ever call me son again."

Much to Mitch's relief, Mort paid the fine and moved the stallion. Maybe the former mayor's threats held no more promise of fulfillment than heat lightning. And if they were real, well, Mitch would deal with the situation when he had to. In the meantime he wasn't about to lose any sleep over it. He couldn't stop Mort Moffet or anyone else from digging into and publicizing his past any more than he could go back and relive it.

He did relive his conversation with Mort in a dream. He dreamed he'd accepted Mort's money, not only the first time, but again and again afterwards, until he'd stashed away a considerable nest egg, enough to purchase a small farm. In his dream he resigned as marshal, moved into the farmhouse, and began caring for chickens and pigs and cows and putting in a vegetable patch. That was when his dream turned into a nightmare. The livestock wouldn't eat, the crops wouldn't grow, the creek dried up, and the bank foreclosed.

Mitch woke up in a cold sweat. He couldn't recall ever wanting to be a farmer or anything else besides a marshal or a sheriff. Nor could he recall a single time in his life when he'd traded honor for avarice, but that didn't mean he couldn't go a little bit crazy and step over the edge at some point in his life. He regarded the dream as a reinforcement of his values and a lesson for the future.

As the weekend approached, the weather grew hotter and stickier. Though clouds gathered at night and breezes cooled the early morning hours, by noon each day the sun burned off most of the cloud cover and not even a breath of wind stirred the sultry air. Occasionally thunder rumbled in the distance, promising rain but never producing so much as a drizzle.

Tension as heavy as the humidity hung over the town. Tempers flared at the slightest provocation. Mitch found himself moving from one quarrel or fistfight to another. Even small children fell prey to the conditions. And while folks mumbled about the desperate need for a storm to blow through and take the mugginess with it, they silently questioned Nature's ability to dispel the heavy atmosphere.

Finally, late Friday afternoon, the storm hit, but it was one created by people, not by rain clouds. Mitch was sweeping out the jailhouse when James Larue blustered in, dragging Marty Pence with him, his elbow locked around hers.

"Help me!" Marty screeched. She jerked and kicked and probably would have walloped the attorney if her hands hadn't been tied behind her back.

"Let go of her," Mitch said.

Larue ignored him. "I'm making a citizen's arrest, Marshal."

Mitch frowned. "A citizen's arrest? What did she do?"

"Nothing!" Marty bellowed. "Get me loose so's I can tie his hands up and drag him around by his elbow. Let him see how it feels."

"She's wearing trousers," Larue said, seemingly unperturbed.

"So?"

"It's against the law."

Mitch felt the corners of his mouth tug upward.

"Then I suppose I'd better arrest you and all the other men in this town."

"Don't be a cussed fool, Dawson."

"Is there a law says you can't wear a skirt?" Marty asked her captor.

"Well, no . . ." Larue hedged.

"Then there shouldn't be no law says I can't wear trousers," she insisted.

"But there is a law," Larue told Mitch, "and I want her locked up."

Mitch knew such a law existed. He thought it was about as idiotic as Prohibition and the blue law. "Be reasonable, Larue."

Marty wrenched her body sideways so hard she and Larue both tumbled to the floor, right into the pile of dirt Mitch had just swept up. The lawyer loosened his hold on Marty, got up, and brushed himself off. Marty stayed on the floor.

"You've been going around town telling everybody your job is to enforce the law," Larue said. "All laws. I want to see you enforce this one."

That was the last thing Mitch wanted to do. In the first place he liked Marty; in the second, he was getting purty doggone tired of folks making him enforce crazy laws. In desperation he searched his memory for the exact wording of the ordinance. "This isn't a jailing offense."

"I ain't paying no fine," Marty declared from the floor. "And I ain't wearing no dresses, neither."

Mitch cringed. If Marty would just keep her mouth shut and cooperate . . .

"See, Marshal?" Larue crowed. "Lock her up. The law says offenders must pay a two-dollar fine or spend one day in jail."

"Pay the fine, Miz Pence," Mitch advised.

When Marty struggled to get to her feet without the

use of her hands Mitch realized why she'd stayed on the floor. He helped her up, then untied the rope.

"Thank you, Marshal," she said, smiling at him and rubbing her reddened wrists. She threw Larue a narrow-eyed glare, then marched herself back to the cell and sat down on a bunk. A smirk of pure pleasure at Marty's expense twisted Larue's thin lips.

"You've done your bad deed for the day," Mitch told him. "Now get out of here."

"You better make sure she does her time or pays her fine," Larue said.

"That's for Judge Warren to decide," Mitch countered.

When James Larue left, Mitch tried to talk Marty into going home and putting on a skirt, but she staunchly refused. "I'll just spend the night here," she said. "My younguns can take care of themselves until tomorrow, I reckon."

Mitch threw up his hands in defeat. "I'm going to get me some supper. I'll bring you a plate back."

He put on his hat and headed for the door. "Aren't you going to lock me up?" Marty hollered.

"Nope. I'm hoping you'll come to your senses and go on back home."

"No, thank you," Marty said. "I ain't gonna get arrested tomorrow for breaking out of jail."

"I'm not going to arrest you, Miz Pence," Mitch assured her. "I can't even hold you on a misdemeanor without an order from Judge Warren."

"Don't matter," she said. "I'm staying."

Half an hour later Mitch returned to find Stella Carey in the cell with Marty. "What are you doing here?" he asked.

"Tinker Sikes arrested me," she said.

"Why?"

"For hanging my underwear on the clothesline in

my backyard. Tinker says there's an ordinance that requires some sort of screen around clotheslines to hide women's underwear from view. Mine's wide open."

This was quickly going from the ridiculous to the absurd. "Why didn't you just take it down?"

" 'Cause it wasn't dry."

"Look," he said, addressing himself to Marty as well, "neither of you have been convicted of anything, and Judge Warren won't be back until next week. Why don't you just go on home and we'll see about all this when he gets back?"

"Can you get me a plate of that food?" Stella asked, pointing at Marty's supper. "I'm hungry."

Mitch swore under his breath and put his hat back on, but before he got out the door, Ned Mission walked in—with Liza Ziegler in tow.

"Arrest this woman, Marshal!" the pharmacist bawled.

The method of Mort Moffet's madness was rapidly becoming clear to Mitch. "What has she done?"

"What has she done?" Ned echoed. "Why, Marshal, this woman is guilty of the most heinous of crimes. She—"

"I'm perfectly capable of speaking for myself!" Liza exclaimed, her hazel eyes flashing. "I'll tell you what I did. I simply opened my parasol in the presence of Mr. Mission's horse. He says there's a law against it."

Mitch sighed. "There is."

"Oh, hello, Stella, Marty," Liza said. "What are you two doing here?"

In some amazement, Mitch watched her stroll toward the cell. These women were as loony as the ordinances they had broken.

"I suppose you're hungry, too," he said.

"I haven't had my supper, if that's what you mean,"

Liza replied. "Would you be a dear and bring me something to eat?"

At this rate he was going to use up his entire annual budget in one night. He figured he'd best go tell Kate what was going on.

He didn't get any farther than the nearest corner before Kate came to him, via Billy Fink's decrepit cart, pulled by a contrary old mule.

"I'm bringing an outlaw to justice!" Billy piped.

People stopped walking and stared at Billy, the cart, and Kate, who sat with her back ramrod straight and her gaze fixed on the horizon. She was wearing the same tailored skirt and jacket bodice Mitch had seen her in earlier that day, and atop her head sat a high-crowned, narrow-brimmed hat.

"And what law, pray tell, has Miz McBride violated?" Mitch asked.

Billy grinned, exposing brown-edged teeth. "She's wearing on her head a . . . a . . ." He frowned so hard his eyes squinched closed.

Mort picked the wrong stooge for this particular task, Mitch thought. Poor Billy couldn't recall the charge.

"A device capable of lacerating the flesh!" the shrimp finished, grinning again and pointing to the oversized pin in Kate's hat.

Laughter erupted from the small crowd that had gathered on the boardwalk. Folks shook their heads and stood out of the way as Mitch helped Kate down from the cart and escorted her into the marshal's office. Through it all, Kate maintained a stoic silence.

"Better take that penknife out of your pocket, Billy!" someone hollered. "It's capable of lacerating the flesh, too."

"I ain't wearing it on my head," Billy sneered. "The law says you can't wear it on your head."

Within the next thirty minutes Jethro Smith filed charges against Julia Hudson for owning more than five cats, the maximum allowed by an old town ordinance, and Simon Carlson brought Sally Myers in for lifting her skirt more than six inches while dodging a mud puddle.

"I'm glad all you ladies are here," Mitch told them as the final batch ate their suppers. "When you're finished with those plates I'd appreciate you joining me out in the office. We have a lot to talk about."

"What do you think's going on?" Liza whispered as she forked a fat butter bean swimming in bacon grease.

"Whatever it is," Marty said, "we can't blame the marshal. He tried his best to talk mean old James Larue into dropping the charges, and then later he tried to get me to go home."

Everyone else nodded in agreement.

"It's Mort Moffet and Obediah Stringfellow," Kate said with conviction.

"How do you figure that?" Stella asked. "Neither of them was involved in the arrests."

"They're just trying to make it *look* like they're not involved, but believe me, they masterminded the entire operation."

"I don't know," Sally said. "Whoever did this had to know the law backwards and forwards, and that's what's got me buffaloed." She twirled her fork in a mound of mashed potatoes topped with congealed brown gravy. "I don't think there's anyone in town who's bothered to memorize all those obscure ordinances we're accused of violating. And we have all the copies of the town ordinances."

"No, we don't," Kate said. "Mitch had to ask me

for a copy because the one that was supposed to be in his desk was missing."

"Stringfellow!" Julia alleged.

Kate smiled. "But we all know he isn't capable of creating such an elaborate plan."

"Which leads us to Mort Moffet," Liza concluded. "Okay. Now that we know who was responsible, what do we do about it?"

"Before we make any plans," Kate said, "let's see what the marshal has to say."

They set their trays aside and filed into Mitch's office, hauling four chairs with them since there were only two besides his in the office area. Mitch had lighted all the lamps, pulled the shades down over the windows, and locked the door. The room was stifling.

As they sat down, Mitch handed each of them one of the seven neat stacks of printed sheets on his desk, explaining that they were portions of the book of town ordinances.

With a mischievous grin on his face, Mitch sat down on the top of his desk. Kate watched him swing his feet and thought anybody that happy ought to be whistling. He let his gaze settle on each woman individually before he started talking.

"I heard you ladies talking back there, and I'm glad you figured this out on your own, 'cause now we can dispense with the discussion and get down to work. Before we begin, does anyone need to go home anytime soon?"

Kate doubted anyone would own up to such a need—not since he'd piqued their interest. Whatever did he have in mind?

"I think I can speak for the group," Sally said. "Our families know where we are, and they can fend for themselves awhile. Tell us what you want us to do."

Mitch nodded. "Two days ago Mort Moffet offered me a bribe in exchange for my cooperation."

The women—every last one of them—gasped and said *"What?"*

"I guess we all knew he was crooked," Stella said, "but we didn't expect that."

"When I refused his offer," Mitch continued, "he promised he'd make me sorry. Although he wasn't targeting me with this little effort, I hope you ladies will remember my assistance on your behalf whenever he does decide to come after me."

"What do you think he's trying to prove?" Liza asked.

"That he has more power than anyone else in this town," Julia said. "Even us."

Mitch agreed. "The way I've got it figured, Moffet and Stringfellow sat down with this book of ordinances and found various obscure laws none of you had ever paid any attention to, even if you knew about them. They made a list of the ones they thought they could catch you ladies violating, then passed out the lists to the group of men who arrested you all."

"So now we're criminals," Marty snarled.

"No, you aren't," Mitch said. "None of you has been convicted, and even if you are, the violations are all minor. You won't have criminal records, but you all need to appear before Judge Warren next Wednesday morning."

"But tomorrow they can arrest us again on different charges," Julia said.

The impish grin returned to Mitch's face. "Exactly. That's why we're fixing to go through these ordinances with a fine-toothed comb and make our own lists."

Mitch wiggled off the desk. "Here are pencils and blank paper, and there's a fresh pot of coffee on the stove. I suggest you each find some place you can work comfortably. When we're all finished we'll meet back here and exchange notes."

"And then we'll go out and arrest Mort and his bunch on other obscure violations," Marty said, beaming.

"No," Mitch said with a shake of his head. "You're going to do better than that. You're going to make sure you don't do anything else that's against the law."

"Does that mean I have to wear a skirt?" Marty asked.

"Until Tuesday," Mitch said, "because come Monday night at the council meeting you're going to repeal all the unreasonable ordinances on the books that have long since been forgotten. After that you're safe. You can wear trousers and open parasols and lift your skirts without worry."

"And in the meantime," Liza observed, "you want us all to keep quiet, right? That's why you locked the door and pulled the shades. Because you want to keep what we're doing a secret."

"It won't matter if word gets out," Mitch said, "but it'll be a whole lot more fun Monday night if we surprise the scalawags."

Kate felt her own mischievous grin tease her lips. She couldn't have devised a better plan herself.

No one said a word, even to their families.

Following Mitch's plan, the council started the meeting with regular business. When Stella, whom the council had elected financial director, finished giving her report, Liza popped up and asked that an old ordinance requiring mules to wear hats during the month of August be repealed. The townspeople just raised their eyebrows. The council voted to repeal the ordinance, and Kate moved on to Marty's report on the progress of her Public Works department. Next, Sally raised her hand and suggested they repeal an old ordinance that made it illegal for men to carry bees around in their hats. This time, laughter broke out among the crowd, while Mort frowned and recrossed his legs.

Good, Kate thought. *We've got him wondering what we're up to. Just keep your mouth shut for a few more minutes, Mort, and then you can make a complete fool of yourself.*

The bee ordinance was repealed, and the council moved on to a proposal from Julia to require all businesses to repaint their exteriors, which created a stir and some discussion. Although the buildings needed painting and the council approved the recommendation, the real purpose in the proposal was to create a distraction, which it did.

Throughout the meeting, the members of the council interrupted the normal flow to repeal forgotten ordinances. Since many of the old laws applied solely to men, Mort and his bunch kept quiet. By the time the council got around to the six ordinances the women had been arrested for violating, most folks were grinning.

"Now, wait a minute!" Mort thundered when Sally asked for the repeal of the ordinance limiting the number of inches a woman could raise her skirt while dodging a mud puddle. "I wrote that ordinance myself, and with good reason."

Kate smiled at him. "And what was that, Mr. Moffet?"

He fell right into her trap. "We had a woman in this town once who exposed her limbs up to her knees every time she dodged a puddle. Men couldn't do their work for following her around like she was a bitch in heat just so's they could see her lower limbs."

"Sounds to me like that was the men's problem," Kate allowed. "Maybe we should revise this ordinance and make it illegal for men to watch women dodge mud puddles."

Everyone laughed. Mort huffed a mite, but he offered no further objection. The council made short work of repealing that ordinance along with all the others, and Kate went home thinking Mitch Dawson was far more clever than she'd ever imagined. She didn't for one minute think Mort and his cronies had given up, but hopefully it would take them awhile to regroup.

Chapter Twelve

Dragged down by a combination of the clammy air—which a rainstorm earlier in the week had only briefly suspended—the constant battle of trying to pacify the citizens, and dealing with Mort's antics, Kate desperately needed a day of undisturbed rest. Planning just that, she took her Saturday morning coffee out to the gazebo in her backyard, hoping any visitors she might have wouldn't think to look for her there.

She settled down on a wicker chaise and breathed deeply of the delicate fragrance wafting from the Lady Banks rose that twined its smooth vines over the back side of the gazebo. It was in full bloom now, a veritable explosion of tiny yellow flowers clustered along its branches. For a long time she gazed up at the fragile blossoms, then she closed her eyes and luxuriated for a moment in the ruffle of a soft breeze that lifted the short, curly hair at her temples until the mournful call of a dove to its mate dredged up the deep, abiding sadness in her heart.

Despite her attempts to shoo the sadness away, her heart sang its own mournful tune. Her chest tightened and a lump rose in her throat. She blinked back the threat of tears, took a sip of coffee, and almost choked trying to swallow it.

Why, oh why, couldn't she manage to spend a quiet day at home without feeling so empty inside? Without hearing the sweet voices of little children at play? Without desperately wanting to experience the joys of motherhood?

Melancholy solved nothing, and Kate wasn't about to have her day ruined by a fit of depression. Her body might need rest, but her mind needed occupation more. Over the years Kate had learned that she could lose herself in physical labor far more easily than in mental tasks. She'd start with the garden while it was still cool outside; then she'd clean her house until it sparkled.

And maybe . . . just maybe, she could go one whole day at home without hearing the cry of a baby she'd never have.

Mitch stopped dead in his tracks and stared at the picture she made, sitting on the grass with her pale yellow skirt billowing around her, a wide-brimmed straw hat perched on her head, and her hair streaming down her back. In sharp contrast to the dark shadow of her face, the sunlight spun the red-gold strands into molten copper.

Did she ever rest? he wondered, watching her gloved fingers pluck dead blossoms off red petunias massed around the base of a white latticed gazebo near the far end of the yard. He considered asking her, but talking to her would shatter the picture, and he wasn't quite ready to let it go.

Quietly, he moved into the thick shade of a half-mature elm, stooping to avoid brushing against branches lower than his head and then squatting beneath the tree. He'd just sit for a spell and soak in the tranquil beauty of the scene. If she didn't need to rest, he did.

As one minute bled into another, Mitch's legs started to cramp and his knees got sore from squatting. He figured he might as well expose himself, state his business, and get on back to the marshal's office. But then Kate began to hum a soulful tune in a minor key, and Mitch found himself entranced all over again. He sat down on the grass, leaned his back against the tree trunk, and let her deep, mellow alto wash through him.

He was almost asleep when a sharp female voice splintered the air. His head popped up and his heart skipped a beat until he realized the voice, which belonged to Adelaide McBride, was directed at Kate.

"There you are!" Adelaide snarled. "I knocked on your front door so long I wore the skin off my knuckles."

The brim of Kate's hat tipped upward, but not enough to allow sunlight on her face. Mitch wished he could see her expression. He'd watched something akin to fear skitter across her face that day she'd sent him to talk to Adelaide about the mice. He'd bet Adelaide scared the drawers off her. If so, she was the only person in town who frightened Kate McBride.

"Oh?" Kate said, her voice slick as glass. "Is something wrong with the bell?"

Bully for you, Mitch silently cheered, biting on the knuckle of his forefinger to keep from laughing out loud. So he'd been wrong. Well, maybe not completely wrong, he amended when Kate stood up and shook out her full skirts. If she was truly unafraid of her mother-in-law, she wouldn't have bothered to stand. The way he had it figured, Kate couldn't possibly hold any real regard for the woman. Who could?

"I came to try to talk some sense into you," Adelaide said, hefting herself up the gazebo steps and plopping down on a wicker chair that didn't look sturdy enough to support her considerable weight. "My, it's hot! Get me a glass of water, will you?"

Mitch didn't doubt Adelaide's discomfort, considering she wore a dark blue silk dress with a high, tight collar, long sleeves, bustle, and voluminous skirts, with multiple layers of undergarments and petticoats beneath, he was certain. Why did women insist on dressing so ridiculously?

"There's a pitcher on the table there," Kate said, bending down to capture a faded blossom she'd missed.

"But there's only one glass and it's obviously yours."

"I wasn't expecting company."

He could hear Kate's exasperation in the swish-swishing of her skirt. She walked past him so fast, her toes kicked up the yellow hem and exposed a single grass-stained petticoat.

Only one petticoat? he questioned. Everyone knew ladies wore at least five at a time. With any fewer, the skirt fabric might mold itself against the hips and show a man something he wasn't supposed to see.

The skirt swished back toward the gazebo. This time, she walked a bit more sedately, probably to keep the tinkling glasses on the tray she carried from toppling to the ground.

He shifted his position so he could appreciate her attire better, but the lattices obscured much of his view. If he could see her better, he could appreciate it even more.

In the midst of his appreciation, his conscience pricked him for spying on Kate and then eavesdropping on her conversation with Adelaide. Mitch bucked at that accusation. After all, he was sitting there in plain sight. It wasn't his fault neither woman bothered to look his way. Besides, he hadn't set out to spy. He'd just come by to discuss a matter with the mayor, decided to take advantage of a bit of shade first, and then got himself stuck. By not calling attention to himself, he mentally argued, he was saving Kate from certain censure by Adelaide. There was no telling what the old bag would think if he announced himself now—and she would surely spread her conclusions all over town.

Adelaide took a dainty sip of water. "You must listen to me, Kate. You must stop this insanity *immediately.*"

"What insanity?"

"You know quite well what I mean! I begged you not to run for mayor, but did you listen to me? Of course not. And then, as if the disgrace to our name and our son's memory wasn't enough, you started right in pushing people around." Adelaide popped open a large, ornate fan and fluttered it in front of her round face. "Now Horace and I aren't being invited to parties, and people we've known all our lives avoid us on the street. Last week at church the Youngbloods got up and moved to another pew when we sat down next to them. It's a sin and a disgrace, I tell you, and it has to stop!"

Kate's voice came so low Mitch had to strain to hear it. "What do you suggest I do?"

"Resign!" Adelaide thundered.

"I can't do that."

"Can't—or *won't?*"

Kate sounded exasperated. "All right, then; I won't. And even if I did, I expect it wouldn't undo the damage that's already been done to your relationship with the townsfolk."

Mitch smiled at her double-edged reply, which, he was sure, was lost on Adelaide.

"You could leave town," Adelaide said.

"Leave?"

"Yes. Sell the house. Go back to Kansas City. You don't have anything holding you here. You have no friends, no blood kin, and since you were unable to give us any grandchildren . . ."

Though she let her voice trail off, Mitch had no trouble finishing Adelaide's sentence—and he didn't reckon Kate had any trouble adding the words either. *Since you were unable to give us any grandchildren, we don't care what happens to you.* Or, *we don't care if we ever see you again.* They meant the same thing.

"I'm sorry if my actions have caused you problems," Kate said, surprising Mitch with the dignity she maintained. If he was in her shoes, he'd be itching to slap the old biddy. "It certainly wasn't intentional."

"If you're truly sorry," Adelaide sniveled, "you'll agree to resign."

"Then I don't suppose, at least in your eyes, that I'm truly sorry."

Adelaide rose, almost tipping over the fragile chair, and thrust out her rather large bosom so far the side seams of her tight bodice threatened to pop. "Is that your final word?"

"Yes."

"Well!" she huffed. "Of all the unmitigated gall!"

You have it, Mitch wanted to hear Kate respond, but she merely rose along with her mother-in-law and said, "Shall I walk you to the gate?"

The moment the two vacated the backyard, Mitch removed himself from beneath the tree and walked over to the gazebo. When Kate came back he was reclining on a wicker chaise and drinking a glass of water.

"Where did you come from?" she asked.

"Downtown," he said, twisting his head in an effort to see her hipline better as she turned slightly to adjust a cushion before she sat down on one of the wicker chairs. Damn, if she wasn't slender as a sapling!

She shook her head and smiled. "That isn't what I meant, but never mind. Did you want anything in particular, or were you just looking for a place to park your feet?"

"I think I did want something, but I can't recall what it was at present. This shade's really nice and this chair thing's really comfortable. I think I'll just stay right here for a while."

She chuckled. "Rather presumptuous, wouldn't you say?"

"Why?" He grinned. "You're not going anywhere."

Kate's heart lurched and her blood spiraled through her. What was it about his smile that made her come so close to losing control? He could make her angry enough to want to wallop him, but all he had to do was lift his chiseled lips into that lazy grin and she melted.

She swallowed hard. "And what makes you think I'm not going anywhere?"

He narrowed his eyes and gave her a long, cool assessment before answering. "For one thing, you're as dirty as a street urchin. You really do need a bath, Kate."

She'd thought she had her emotions under rein again, and she supposed she had—until he called her Kate. It was the first time he'd used her given name, and she liked the way it rolled off his tongue. In fact, she liked it so much, it sent gooseflesh prickling down her arms.

"I'd planned to take one . . . later. I have a mountain of work left."

"Ah, yes!" he said. "Work. Tell me something, Kate. Do you ever stop?"

She frowned. "Stop? What do you mean?"

He leaned forward, snatched up a plump cushion from the settee, and stuffed it behind his back. "You know, sit back and relax and watch the world go by."

Mitch demonstrated as he talked, throwing his arms up and making a cushion for his head with his open palms, and then wiggling his bottom deeper into the chaise. He sighed contentedly and let his eyelids slither down to half-mast.

"Sometimes," she said.

"I don't believe it."

"I sleep just like everyone else," she piped up defensively.

"That's not what I'm getting at and you know it," he drawled, his voice as languid as his posture. "I'm talking about just being downright lazy every once in a while."

"That's what I was going to do today—" She bit her lip and wished she'd held her tongue.

"What's stopping you?"

She lifted one shoulder in a noncommittal gesture. "Weeds."

"They'll be here tomorrow."

"Tomorrow is Sunday."

His eyes fell closed and he sighed loudly. "I almost forgot. It's against your religion to work on Sunday. Maybe I need to come back tomorrow and watch you work at being downright lazy. That ought to prove real interesting."

Kate winced at the sarcasm in his voice. "You're welcome here anytime, Marshal."

"Well, ma'am, I'll try. But don't go making no cakes or nothing, 'cause you see, I've got to work tomorrow. Since I don't sell nothing, that blue law don't apply to me."

"One would think, Marshal Dawson," she snapped, as outdone at his slide into poor grammar as at his attitude, "that a man of the law such as yourself would want to ensure that the law, *every* law, be upheld. I suppose I misread your intentions before."

"Please, Miz McBride," he said, his tone a cross between chagrin and frustration, "let's don't discuss the law today. There's no sense working up a sweat over something so insignificant when the heat's bad enough—"

"Insignificant!" she railed. "You're calling the law insignificant? I don't believe my ears."

"Well, maybe not exactly insignificant . . ." He sat up, shifted his legs off the chaise, and planted his booted feet on the floor. "Look, I didn't come over here to argue with you. I came to talk about having to be on duty all the time. But now that you've gone and gotten yourself all worked up, I don't suppose you're in too favorable a mood, so I'll just come back another time."

He stood up and reached for his hat, which was on the table, and Kate's heart sank to her stomach. When he left, she'd be all alone again . . . all alone with her insecurities, all alone with her emptiness, all alone . . .

"Who said you had to be on duty all the time?"

"Well, nobody," he said, twirling his hat.

Kate wished he'd put it down and stretch out on the chaise again. Bantering with him was far more enjoyable than being alone.

"It just sorta comes with the territory when you don't have a deputy."

"Sit down and let's talk about it."

He obliged her, but he held on to his hat. "Talk's cheap, ma'am. I'm listening."

Kate chewed the inside of her mouth. "What if I could arrange for you to have a morning off once a week?"

"Make it an afternoon."

She nodded. "Okay. An afternoon. Does it matter which one?"

"You gonna hire Skip?"

"If he wants the job."

"Then you'd better ask him which day's most convenient. Me, I don't care so long as someone's covering for me."

She rested her elbows on her thighs. "Good. I'm glad that's settled. Could I get you a glass of lemonade? I have some cooling in the well house."

He stood up again, and this time she followed suit. "No, thanks. I need to get back to the jail. Someone may be looking for me."

For a long time after he was gone Kate lay on the chaise, feeling incredibly at peace with herself.

From time to time that day Kate marveled over the tranquility of her usually troubled soul, but never for long. She feared that should she dwell on the extraordinary feeling, it would dissipate and she might never be able to recapture it. Therefore, she refused to analyze it, refused to listen when logic demanded a reason for its existence.

Instead, she listened to the wind sough through the branches of the trees in her backyard. She listened to the warble of the birds and the whir of a dragonfly's wings and the harmonic chorus of crickets and locusts and grasshoppers. She couldn't recall ever sitting still long enough before to hear the glorious clamor of nature.

And while she was listening to nature, her heart spoke to her. Like a hinge grown rusty from disuse, it barely managed to squeak out its message at first, but her newfound affinity with her natural surroundings gently oiled its strings throughout the day. Slowly, the voice gained in strength and volume, so that by the time the sun dipped low in the western sky its message pulsed through her veins.

Accept yourself for what you are.

What am I? she asked, and answered sadly, *a childless widow. A barren woman, useless to any man.*

No, her heart argued. *That is only a small part of what you are, a mere ripple on the surface. Explore the width and breadth and depth of the pond until you discover who you really are.*

Oh, God, she silently cried, terrified at what she might find in the murky bowels of her soul. *I can't do that!*

Yes, you can, her heart replied. *You can. You must. And you will.*

Her peace shattered, Kate struggled with her heart's commands until long into the night, when the sudden roar of angry voices and the dull thuds of something hitting the walls of her house abruptly halted thoughts of everything . . . except survival.

Where in the Sam Hill had Little Booger gotten off to? Mitch wondered. It was nearly midnight, and he hadn't seen the cat since he'd let her out that morning.

Oh, well, she was a cat. Cats liked to roam sometimes, especially at night. Nothing to get upset over. She'd come home when she got good and ready.

That's what Mitch told himself, but he didn't believe a word of it. Little Booger wasn't like most cats. She never went off by herself. Never. Since he'd found her half dead and nursed her back to health when she was just a kitten, she'd clung to him like a fly on fresh manure.

She must have followed him that morning when he started his rounds, and no telling where he'd lost her— or she'd lost him. She must have gotten in a fight or been struck by a hoof. Whatever, something was wrong with her or she'd be back by now. It was pure-dee silly to think so highly of a damned cat, he fussed. It wasn't like she was his kid. Hell, she was just a cat.

Mitch lay in his bed at the jail, listening for her meows until he couldn't stand it anymore. He didn't care if it was late. He'd never go to sleep until he found Little Booger, so he might as well go looking for her as lie in bed and worry.

Kate sat straight up in bed. Her heart pounded hard against her chest wall and she laid an open palm on her breast in a vain attempt to slow its runaway pace. Cold sweat broke out on her upper lip and a stream of quick shivers raced down her spine. Two questions fought for domination of the little mental faculty she could muster. *Who is out there? What are they doing?*

They sounded like a bunch of wild Indians, whooping and hollering and shooting arrows at her house. Kate gasped for air. That's what it was. Indians. But how? Indians hadn't caused any trouble in eastern Kansas in years. She knew she ought to get off the bed and take a peek out of the window, but she couldn't move. Her legs were like chunks of lead. So were her arms, which kept her from lighting a lamp. As long as she didn't light a lamp, they shouldn't be able to see her, but she'd never craved light quite so much as she did at that moment.

The arrows went *thump, thump* against her house, and her heart went *thump, thump* in her chest, and all the while she tried not to listen, tried to force her legs to move, tried with every ounce of strength she could summon to push her fear aside. If they set fire to her house, she had to get out. She had to be able to run like the wind. But first she had to get out of bed.

One foot struck the floor and then the other. Her knees wobbled and the muscles in her calves quaked. She gathered the bottom sheet in her hands, slid her hips to the edge of the mattress, and put her weight on her legs a little at a time, all the while clutching the sheet in her fists.

The nearest window was a mere three or four feet away, yet the distance seemed like a mile as she inched her way along the side of the bed, holding on to the sheet as she walked to keep her legs from buckling under her. At long last she reached the window. She lifted a shaking hand, caught the drapery fabric, and pulled it aside.

Something hit the pane with a *splat.* Something yellow and slimy. The slime dripped down the glass, carrying with it shards of thin white shell.

Egg.

Well, she could throw eggs, too, by God!

The acknowledgment quickly restored life to her limbs. She let go of the drape, hightailed it to the kitchen, and snatched up her egg basket. Out of the back door she went, running around the house toward the shouts of glee. A three-quarter moon lit her way and exposed one of the miscreants in her front yard. Kate sailed off an egg. It landed just shy of the dark-clothed man, whose hat completely eclipsed his face.

She reared back and let fly with another one, and

then another. One struck the man on his shoulder, the other on his boot. He yelped so loud, a body would have thought he'd been shot; then he looked over at Kate and bolted toward the far side of the house, hollering, "She caught us! Let's go!"

Kate dashed behind a lilac bush and waited for them to come around the corner. As they ran past, she pelted them with her eggs. Most times, her eggs landed right on target. She could see them splatter in the moonlight and was amazed at how wide an area they covered, especially when she lifted her leg as she pulled back her arm. That gave the eggs greater velocity. The harder she threw them, the louder they yelped.

If she'd had a hand free, she would have used it to squelch the laughter that bubbled in her throat as the men darted first one way and then another in an attempt to avoid her flying eggs. Because she didn't have a free hand, she let her merriment flow until she fairly cackled from behind the bush.

"What the hell—"

Mitch snatched his pistol from its holster and took aim at one of the darting figures. Before he could pull the trigger, the dark-garbed man disappeared around a corner of Kate's house. But there was another shadowy form right behind him. And another. And another.

He couldn't believe his eyes when Kate stepped out from behind a bush, the moonlight making her white nightdress shimmer. She hurled a small white ball at one of the darting figures. The man screamed, "Ouch!" and disappeared. Kate scooted back behind the bush.

While Mitch was trying to figure out what was going on, something hit the side of his head, just above his left ear. Whatever it was, it hurt like hell. No wonder the man had screeched so. Something warm and slick slithered down his hair, behind his earlobe, and onto his neck. Part of it landed on the front of his shirt. Mitch swiped at it with his free hand and cursed under his breath. Egg!

Mitch pointed the barrel at the sky and squeezed off a shot.

One of the men hollered, "Marshal!" and they all took off running down the street. Mitch chased them a short distance before the night swallowed them, and then he tore back to Kate's house, his heart in his throat. If they hadn't done anything except throw eggs, she was all right, but he had to be sure.

Kate was still giggling when she deposited the basket on the kitchen table and groped along the wall until her hand connected with the match holder.

A fist beat upon her door. If that was Mitch, he was back too soon. He couldn't possibly have caught the rascals. She wanted the culprits under the jail, but she supposed she'd given them tit for tat. Whoever they were, they couldn't have expected her to throw eggs back. She had had them on the run when Mitch showed up and fired off his six-gun. Maybe Mitch was chasing them yet and one of her neighbors had come over to check on her.

She called out, "I'm coming." The match flamed and the acrid smell of sulfur filled her nostrils. She pulled a lamp toward her, fumbled with the globe, turned the knob to run up the wick, and let out a long breath when light filled the space around her.

The fist stopped beating and her bell started ringing.

"I'm coming," she called again, louder that time, her spirits soaring. It had to be Mitch. No one else was quite so impatient. She replaced the globe, and her feet fairly sailed down the hall.

"What took you so long?" Mitch barked when she opened the front door.

His harsh tone smashed her exuberance. "Did you catch any of them?" she asked, her own tone business-like.

"No. They all got away. There were six or eight of them. It's too dark out there to say for sure." He wiped a hand across his neck and showed her the orange-streaked slime. "Do you think I might be able to wash this mess off?"

"Be my guest." She stepped backward, waved her free arm toward the kitchen, and followed him. "Why did they do it?"

"That's an asinine question, Kate, and you know it. You've made yourself very unpopular with a lot of folks. It's only human nature to fight back."

"There are other ways to fight back," she said, "legal ways."

"There's no ordinance against throwing eggs," he argued, unbuttoning his shirt, "at least none that I saw when I read through them."

"There will be, come Monday night." She opened a cupboard and removed a clean cloth.

"They'll always be one step ahead of you, Kate," he said, shrugging out of his shirt. Kate's breath caught in her throat and she swallowed hard.

Oblivious to the way his bare chest affected her, he laid the shirt out on the table with the messy side up, then wet and soaped the cloth and began to scrub off the gooey egg. He rubbed his head, ear, and neck before starting on the shirt. "You can pass all the ordinances you want to, but they'll always think of something you haven't outlawed yet."

"Well, I refuse to let them frighten me," she vowed. "I can throw eggs, too."

His eyebrows shot up, his hand stopped moving the washcloth, and his gaze found the almost empty egg basket on the table. "You didn't."

She puffed out her chest. "Yes, I did."

"That was really stupid," he scoffed. "What if one of them had shot you?"

"They didn't."

"You can't live alone anymore," he said, "unless you give up the mayor's post."

"I'm not quitting," she averred.

"And I'm not always going to be here to prevent something bad from happening to you," he growled. "You've been extremely lucky . . . so far. If I were you, I'd be worrying about how long my luck was going to hold out."

"Well, you're not me!" she snapped. "And I don't need you to protect me, either."

"Oh, really? What are you planning to do? Go out and sweet talk an angry mob into leaving? I don't think so."

"They were just throwing eggs."

"This time. Next time, it might be flaming arrows."

His suggestion hit too close to her earlier theory and she shivered.

"I'm glad to see something frightens you," he sneered. "Go pack a bag."

Kate frowned in confusion. "Pardon?"

"Go pack a bag. You're going to Mrs. Jones's for tonight."

She stiffened her back and threw him a look she hoped registered the defiance in her heart. "I will not. This is my home, and I'm not about to let a few hateful men run me out of it."

"Don't make me have to arrest you, Kate," he threatened, his voice low and menacing.

"On what grounds?" she hurled. "I haven't done anything wrong. I'm not leaving here—and you can't make me!"

Two long strides brought him so close, she could feel the heat of his breath on her eyelids. He hurled the wet cloth toward the sink, wrapped his big hands around the soft flesh of her upper arms, and pulled her even closer. His hands were as hot as his breath, his fingers searing brands against her flesh. She'd been in such a dither to throw her own eggs and then answer the door, she hadn't thought to slip on a robe, and now she stood before him with nothing but a thin cotton nightdress to shield her from his scalding, naked gaze.

"Then, by God," he breathed, his mouth edging ever nearer to hers, "I'm staying here with you."

Chapter Thirteen

What in the Sam Hill was he saying? Stay with her? Was he crazy?

Yes, he supposed he was. As crazy as the voters who'd elected a woman to run their town. If he knew what was good for him, he'd tuck tail and run, right now, before it was too late.

But damn, she smelled good, like a meadow in spring. The heady fragrance beckoned, inviting him to linger, guilelessly suggesting he ignore sanity.

The dim light from the coal oil lamp shone like the early morning sun, rising behind her, burnishing her red-gold curls, creating a golden halo of light that hovered at her crown and cast her curves in delicate shadows. Without mental direction his gaze wandered downward, absorbing the capering light upon the shimmering fabric of her nightdress and the play of shadow beneath the sheer cloth.

He felt like a butterfly, gliding through the dawn light, surveying the wildflowers before dipping to drink from first one and then another of the delicate blossoms.

He groaned and pulled her closer, slipping his arms around her back and crushing the length of his body against hers.

She moaned and shivered and whispered, "Oh, Mitch!"

That was his undoing. He covered her mouth with his, moved his lips upon the softness of hers, and skimmed his tongue along her lips until he gained access to the honeyed sweetness within the recesses of her mouth. *Just a sip,* he thought, but a sip wasn't enough. The deeper he drank of the nectar, the more his appetite begged for sustenance.

He set his hands upon a sensuous journey, grazing the heath of her back, traversing the rivulet of her spine, and settling upon the hillocks of her derriere. His palms cupped the twin cheeks and pulled her upward until the soft mound of her womanhood rested against the ever-growing bulge in his jeans. And still he yearned for more.

Never had he wanted a woman as much as he wanted Kate McBride. He wanted to bury himself deep inside her and live there for the rest of his life.

. . .

Kate swam in an eddy of sensuality that pulled her deeper and deeper into the vortex of no return. Never had she imagined drowning could be so blissful.

She reveled in the heat of his hard, callused hands holding her buttocks, in the pressure of his midsection against hers, in the coarseness of his tongue as it dipped and tasted and flickered inside her mouth. His initial touch set off a fire in the core of her womanhood, and his caresses fanned the flames until they threatened to consume her.

Was it possible? she wondered. Did he feel as lost and yet as at home as she? Could he want her as much as she wanted him?

She knew almost nothing about Mitch Dawson, and yet she knew everything.

Tentatively, she moved her hands along his ribs, upward over the firm muscles of his chest, and onward until she held the thick column of his neck between her palms. Her fingers found the shells of his ears, toyed with their crevices, and then drove into his hair.

A long shudder rippled through him, lending her confidence. She pulled his head closer and mated her tongue with his in the ritualistic lovers' dance.

When he dragged his mouth from hers she thought for an instant that she would die from lack of nourishment, but then he suckled gently at one corner of her mouth and trailed his tongue along her jawbone and across her cheek, raining tiny kisses all over her face and finally returning to sup again upon her mouth. All the while his hands tugged gently on the fabric of her nightdress. The lace around its hem tickled the backs of her legs as it slipped ever upward.

She knew she should stop him before it was too late, and yet . . . and yet she longed to explore the deep-seated carnality his caresses revealed. She longed to learn everything his touch could teach her. She longed to discover the sensual woman she hadn't known existed.

Her quivering skin beneath his open palm sent rivers of ecstasy coursing through him. She made him feel hot and cold, soft and hard, weak and powerful . . . all at the same time. No other woman had ever made him feel this way.

He loved the way she kissed him back, loved the way her hands held his head, loved the way her body fit so perfectly against his. She was every bit as passionate as he'd imagined. Even more passionate than he'd imagined . . . more passionate than he'd ever dreamed a woman could be. . . .

He found a breast and felt it mold to fit the shape and size of his hand, felt its hard nib thrust against the heart of his palm, felt all his blood, all his energy, all his power rush to his groin.

His hand left her breast to capture her legs, and he scooped her up into his arms. He made it halfway across the dining room before she pulled her mouth from his and began to struggle out of his embrace.

God, it hurt!

Without realizing it, she'd been a barren desert. And then Mitch Dawson had come into her life, tempting her with tiny raindrops, seeping into her defenses, germinating the seeds of passion and desire, and she'd almost given in.

Almost.

But without the promise of continued sustenance, the new growth would shrivel and die, and she'd go right back to being an arid desert. That was going to be difficult enough. But to allow the plants to mature, to allow the fruit to ripen, and then to have the bountiful garden snatched away would be even more painful.

Yet, she questioned, how could anything hurt more than this did?

"You can stop fighting now," Mitch said, his voice ragged. "I'm not holding you anymore."

His words brought her abruptly back to reality. She watched her fist hit his chest again and wondered how many times she'd pummeled him. If the throb in her hand was any indication, several.

"I'm sorry," she whispered around the knot in her throat.

"You didn't hurt me," he said, his pain-filled tone belying his words. "Are you going to be okay?"

Kate tried to swallow the knot, but it wouldn't go away. "I think so."

He nodded. "Go on back to bed. If you need me, I'll be outside."

"Outside? Why?"

Exasperation, or something closely akin to it, riddled his voice. "I told you I wasn't leaving you here alone. I'll sleep in the gazebo. That chair thing is pretty comfortable."

"It's called a chaise," she said.

"I know, but I never liked that word. It sounds so erudite." He turned away from her and headed back toward the kitchen.

"Good night!" she called, her voice squeaking.

"Good night."

The back door creaked open, and the lump in her throat swelled.

"Thank you," she said, but she didn't think he heard her. She barely heard the words herself.

A door rattled shut, but Kate wasn't sure which door she heard: her back door or the door to her heart.

Kate awoke from a fitful sleep to the soft splashing of water against the side of her house. For a while she lay in bed with her eyes closed, letting the tranquil sound permeate her senses while her inner eye replayed the awakening of her passion.

Though Mitch's hands and lips danced dreamlike upon her now, she knew the recollection was founded in reality. Mitch had truly kissed her. She hadn't dreamed it, nor did she think now that she'd dreamed it before. He'd kissed her that afternoon at the jail as surely as he had last night. If she allowed it, he would most likely kiss her again. He seemed to like kissing her. And she liked kissing him.

Too much.

Mitch dove his head into the rain barrel and came up shaking out his hair like a wet dog.

She was his boss, for Christ's sake!

That fact alone should have stopped him from pawing her and slobbering all over her like an adolescent boy. How could he have forgotten who she was and what she represented? Hell, he was well on the way to the bedroom when she stopped him.

And she had stopped him. Eventually. When she jerked away from him and wriggled to the floor something deep inside refused to let her go. He pulled her back into his arms and kissed her again. Or tried to. The strength in Kate's slender arms amazed him still.

He dried his face with a piece of linen towel he'd found in the potting shed and thought about spending the remainder of the night tossing and turning upon the wicker chaise, longing to go back into Kate's house and rekindle the fire he'd started, but knowing that it would be madness. More than once he got up and started toward her house. Each time he turned around and went back to the gazebo. She didn't want him. She'd made that perfectly clear.

So had Jennie Clark. The similarities between the two women astounded him. Both were independent to a fault. Both were driven by dedication to a cause. Both were passionate. And neither one wanted him.

He rolled a cigarette, lit it, and took a long drag.

Neither one wanted him . . .

Twice in his thirty-four years he'd found a woman who touched his soul, and neither one wanted him.
. . .

He found a tin bucket and a stack of clean rags in the potting shed and a bar of soap next to the rain barrel. Mitch filled the bucket with water, dumped in a handful of rags and the soap, and picked a spot to start scrubbing.

It was funny, he thought, how for almost fourteen years he'd managed to repress so much of the hurt Jennie had inflicted. But he remembered it now, remembered every word of every conversation, remembered how just looking at Jennie had inflamed his passion, remembered how devastated he'd been when she had refused his proposal of marriage.

"What?" Jennie had said. "Marry you? Why, I couldn't possibly degrade a man by marrying him. I couldn't possibly allow you to tie yourself to a political outcast and pariah. No, Mitch. It's better this way."

It was better this way, he told himself. Better that he forget the feelings Kate stirred deep within his soul. Better that he do his job for the next seven weeks and let her be. . . .

Grateful to have something to take his mind off Kate McBride, he fished a rag out of the bucket, squeezed it out, and attacked the stinking yellow mess on the clapboard siding.

For a full half hour he managed to put her completely from his mind. He'd just about convinced himself the task was easy when she came around the corner of her house, wearing a lightweight day gown and carrying a cup of coffee. When he saw her like this he forgot all about her role as mayor.

"Good morning," she said, her voice low and husky. "Did you sleep well?"

"Great," he lied, trying to push back the sudden surge of longing threatening to suffuse him. "How about you?"

"Wonderful," she said, but the dark circles under

her eyes bore evidence to the contrary. She handed him the cup, then made a show of stretching and yawning. She didn't fool him. Not for a minute. But she sure as hell made him want to kiss her again, and that he wasn't about to do. No, sirree. He'd learned his lesson the hard way, and he wasn't foolish enough to make the same mistake twice. If Kate were only a woman of the first variety . . .

There was no sense wishing for something that couldn't be. He dragged his gaze away from the sight of her breasts straining against the bodice of her un-adorned dress, took too big a swallow of the hot coffee, and choked.

"Are you all right?" she asked.

"Fine," he said when he could talk again. "This is a mess." He heard the inanity of the words and tried to convince himself he didn't care one whit whether he impressed her with intelligent conversation.

"Yes, it is," she agreed, wrinkling her nose as the breeze carried the sulfuric odor of rotten eggs to her nostrils. She squatted beside the bucket and took out one of the rags. "You don't have to do this."

He sipped his coffee and watched her rub the cloth against a board. "I know," he said, "but you'll be all day scrubbing this off by yourself."

"We shouldn't have to do this," she said gruffly.

If she expected him to apologize for not doing his job, she had another thing coming. He couldn't be everywhere at once. Besides, if she would just step off her soapbox—

"What day is this?" she asked.

"Sunday." Mitch set his cup down and resumed scrubbing.

"I don't suppose I'll make it to church."

If she expected him to volunteer to finish this by

himself, she was wrong about that, too. He bit back those very words and scrubbed harder.

"You know, I can't remember when I've missed church. I don't think I've ever missed, unless I was sick."

She seemed bound and determined to make him talk. And he was equally bound and determined not to.

"I don't suppose it'll matter if I miss today."

Mitch threw down his rag. "Look, lady, I may be in the town's employ, but that doesn't make me your slave."

Kate threw down her rag. It landed with a plop next to his. "I never meant to imply you were! Nobody asked you to do this. If you'd rather not, then you're free to go."

She stood up and stalked into the backyard.

Mitch followed her. His legs were longer, so he could walk faster. He caught up with her at the bed of red petunias and seized her elbow. "Where do you think you're going?"

She jerked away and marched up the gazebo steps. "This is my house and my yard. I can go anywhere I want to in it."

Her swaying hips made his mouth go dry. "You don't have to be so fractious—"

Kate whirled around. "Fractious? Me? You're accusing me of being fractious? Isn't that like the pot calling the kettle black?"

How dare she accuse him, when he'd gone out of his way to be nice to her! He heard his boot heels clank against the wooden steps and told himself to calm down. "I haven't been fractious."

"Oh, no?" She plopped down on the chaise. "Then what do you call it? Argumentative is too mild a word. How about insufferable?"

Get up, Kate, his mind screamed. *Get up before I make both of us sorry you chose that chair thing to sit on.*

"Or perhaps vexatious?" she taunted, her normally pale green eyes darkening to a rich emerald.

Mitch took another step toward her, advancing on her with slow, deliberate strides.

"Oh, I've got it!" she declared, snapping her fingers. "Obnoxious. That's what you've been."

He raised his thick eyebrows a mite. "Obnoxious, Kate? You wouldn't know obnoxious if it came up and bit you on the behind—what little behind you have, which ain't much."

"So now you're going to deride my figure."

Kate's voice caught in her throat. Suddenly his face loomed a hairbreadth from hers, and the sharp, clean scent of a lemon sour drenched her senses. She leaned back on the chaise, trying to get away from him. When her effort put no space between them Kate knew she was in trouble.

His hands dropped, one on either side of her, and his voice came low and seductive. "Deriding your figure isn't what I have in mind at all."

"About last night . . ." she said, hoping to divert his attention.

"Yes," he breathed, pulling back an inch or two. "This is about last night. You see, I always finish what I start."

"You can't!" she croaked, panic-stricken. "Not here, in the gazebo. Someone's liable—"

His mouth covered hers, and Kate forgot anyone else existed but the two of them. He plied her with nips and fondles, teasing and tasting, toying with her senses until she thought she would explode with aching.

Both knew where his kiss was leading, but for the moment neither cared.

And then two furry creatures jumped up on the chaise with them. One nuzzled Mitch's neck and the other licked Kate's cheek.

"What the—"

"Our cats, Mitch," Kate said, at once grateful and yet annoyed by the interruption. She removed her arm from his shoulder and looped it around Hobo's stomach. "Where have you been?" she asked the tabby.

"With Little Booger," Mitch said on a groan. "Look, they're both covered with beggar-lice." He scooted off the chaise and dragged his fingers through his hair. "I, um, I suppose I ought to get back to the jail."

Kate sat up and pulled Hobo onto her lap. "And I suppose I ought to get ready for church," she said, her voice unsteady.

"What are you going to do about the egg?" Mitch asked.

"The egg? Oh, I forgot. Clean it up, I guess."

He scuffed the toe of his boot on the planked floor and looked off toward the picket fence that surrounded her yard. "I could come back this afternoon and help."

She shook her head. "Thanks, but I don't think that would be a good idea."

"I'll ask around. Maybe somebody got a good look at those men."

"I'd appreciate that."

"You didn't by chance recognize any of them? Or their voices?" he asked hopefully.

"No. One of them sounded an awful lot like Ned Mission, but I couldn't swear to it."

"If I find them, I'll make them clean up the mess they made." He shifted his gaze from the fence to a gardenia bush.

Given other circumstances, Kate might have

laughed out loud at the very idea of Mitch Dawson being nervous. Instead, her heart went out to him. Yet an inner voice warned her not to encourage their relationship by showing her compassion. Nothing could come of it, the voice said. Nothing but heartbreak—for both of them. As desperately as she wanted to plumb the depths of the passion his touch awakened in her, she knew that wouldn't be enough for either of them. And for the moment passion seemed to be all either had to give.

"There's a baseball game at three this afternoon," he said.

"Yes, I know. Are you planning to go?"

"I thought I might. I play a mean first base."

"Perhaps I'll come to watch."

A hint of a smile lifted one corner of his mouth. "I'll look for you."

Mitch scooped up Little Booger, who meowed loudly at being separated from Hobo, and left.

Kate leaned back on the cushions and watched him go through eyes bleary with memories and regrets.

Once, she'd married for money and prestige. Oh, at the time she'd thought it was for love, but she'd been wrong. She hadn't known what love meant, wasn't sure she did even now. She'd looked at Arnold's suave exterior, at his tailored suits and his fine horse and carriage, and fallen head over heels in love with an ideal. Later, when reality set in, it had been too late—for both of them.

Even if Mitch fell in love with her, even if he pledged his undying commitment, she couldn't do to Mitch what she'd done to Arnold. She couldn't allow him to love her when she couldn't love him in return, when she couldn't even bear his children. She couldn't be responsible for making another human being miserable.

* * *

"Strike one!" Josiah Keane's voice rang out.

Jethro Smith, who was wearing a blue shirt like the rest of his team, scratched his head and frowned at the sand-filled croaker sack that represented home plate. "Aw, Josiah, that warn't no strike. The ball didn't even come close to the plate."

"Yeah," one of the spectators called, "you need to go back to cleaning out stalls, Josiah, and let someone else call this game."

"He's doing all right," someone else said. "We've had worse umpires."

"Str-r-r-ike two!"

"No sense in arguing over that one," Skip Hudson, who was catching for the White Shirts, said. "It came right over."

"Yeah," Jethro agreed, "but it was low. I'm glad Max trims hair better'n he pitches."

"You better hit the next one," Skip teased. "You've got one man on second and two outs. You're their only hope."

Max Smart let another ball go and Jethro whacked it hard.

From his position at first base Mitch watched the spiraling, grass-stained ball fly right over Max's head, then over Hardy at second base. It looked like a goner, but he wasn't about to take his foot off the bag until Jethro cleared it—just in case.

In center field, Ebenezer Dahlmer backed up, his glove held high, his gaze riveted on the ball. He was going to catch it. Mitch relaxed just a mite.

And then the ball came out of its arc and fell several yards in front of Eb, who rushed forward and snatched it off the ground. Mitch's heart leapt into his throat. He'd done some mighty big boasting to con-

vince these men he could play first base better than any
one of them. This was his chance to prove it—and to
show off for Kate McBride.

Eb threw the ball hard right at Mitch. Out of the
corner of his left eye Mitch could see Jethro fast ap-
proaching first base. Trying to ignore the runner, he
held his glove in front of his chest, and every muscle in
him strained toward the ball.

Ker-plunk! The ball hit his glove. A split second later
flying sand engulfed him and a foot struck his ankle,
throwing him off balance. He staggered and dropped
the ball, immediately righted himself, scooped his
glove down, and recaptured the ball before it hit the
ground.

"He's out!" Josiah hollered.

"Cain't be!" Simon Carlson, who ran the telegraph
office and was the next man up to bat, argued.

Jethro picked himself up and dusted off his trousers.
"I was safe," he claimed. "Mitch dropped the ball."

Josiah shook his head. "It didn't never hit the
ground."

"But his foot left the bag. I saw it," Jethro con-
tended.

"I couldn't see nothing but flying dirt," Josiah said.
"I'm the umpire and I say you're out."

A discordant chorus of cheers and boos went up
from the crowd. Jethro trudged back to the bench,
grumbling all the way. Inordinately pleased with himself, Mitch imagined Kate smiling and waving at him,
and his heart filled with contentment. He turned his
gaze to the left side of the field, where he'd seen Kate
sitting on a quilt, holding a light green parasol over her
head.

The contentment shattered.

She was still sitting there, but she wasn't watching
him anymore. She wasn't watching the game at all. She

was talking to a large woman swathed in mauve-colored satin and sporting a huge straw hat with one side of the brim turned up and the other side covered in silk flowers. Even though the shade from the hat obscured most of her face, the woman looked awfully familiar. And yet he didn't think she lived in Paradise. Nor had she been at the game earlier. He would have remembered that hat.

"You coming?" Max called.

Mitch glanced around and realized he was the only man still at his post. He set out for the bench at a steady jog, his gaze darting back and forth between the baseline he was running and Kate. She and the woman in the hat stood up. Kate picked up the quilt, shook it out, and started toward her buggy. She never even looked up.

"I don't know, Jennie," Kate said. "I believe in the suffrage movement and I'd like to help, but my duties here consume all my time and energy."

Jennie Clark, president of the Kansas Woman Suffrage Association, laid a white-gloved hand on Kate's arm. "You and your councilwomen made a great stride for the suffrage movement when you ran for office, an even greater stride when you six were elected. We appreciate what you're doing here."

"But it isn't enough. Isn't that what you're saying?"

Kate watched Jennie's face closely and thought she detected a slight softening around the woman's piercing black eyes. They were only one of Jennie's features that served to intimidate even the staunchest heart.

"Not exactly," Jennie said, the pitch of her voice even lower and more gravelly than Kate remembered it. It was Jennie's impassioned speech, given at a university women's rally back in '77, that had inspired

Kate to support the movement. Jennie had been much smaller then, but if anything, the weight she'd gained made her even more formidable.

"Then what, exactly, do you want me to do that I'm not doing already?" Kate asked, determined not to let Jennie snow her into a commitment she had neither the time nor the resources to fulfill.

Cheers and boos erupted all around them. People jumped up, some raising their arms in triumph, others shaking their fists at the umpire, but all of them noisy.

"Perhaps," Jennie said, raising her voice to be heard over the din, "we should retire elsewhere." She glanced at the diamond for the first time since she'd arrived at the field and a look of acute shock—or was it merely irritation?—washed over her face.

Kate nodded and rose. "My buggy is right over there."

Though the field lay within a half mile of Kate's house, she took the long way home driving back into town. When they reached the square, Kate waved an arm at the new boardwalks.

"We have been derisively tagged the 'petticoat government,'" she said, "but you can see what we're doing to improve conditions in Paradise—and you can see what remains to be accomplished here. The former administration left us with a whopping thirty-six cents to work with. In less than two months we have increased our operating revenue to a comfortable level and established various accounts to fund additional improvements."

"That's all well and good," Jennie snorted, "but I don't see those improvements furthering our cause."

Kate bit back a snide retort concerning the suffragist's poor vision and pointed to the muddy street they were traversing. She wasn't about to allow Jennie to sidetrack her. "This week a crew will begin digging ditches and laying lead pipe, under the supervision of the engineer our public works director hired last week."

"You hired a director of public works?" Jennie asked in a horrified tone. "I'm disappointed in you, Kate. I'd thought you would stick quite strictly to female supervision."

Lord save me from such short-sighted bigotry, Kate thought, making a mental note not to ever let herself fall into thinking only women possessed intelligence.

"The engineer is male," Kate explained. "The director is a member of our council, a woman named Martine Pence who could, in all likelihood, perform most of the tasks required, were she two people. But neither Marty nor anyone else in town knows much about acetylene gas, which can be deadly in inexperienced hands."

She breathed deeply and continued. "Once the pipe is laid, the posts and lamps installed, and the gas plant fully operational, our residents will no longer be forced to endure dark streets at night. We're hoping the lights will reduce the rash of petty crimes we've been plagued with recently."

Kate slowed the horse in front of her house and turned into the drive.

"From the looks of your house," Jennie sneered, "your government has a long way to go in terminating crime."

Kate shrugged off the egg stains. Her difficulties with a few discontented men were none of Jennie's concern. "Probably just bored youths. That's another problem we have to address."

"There are bigger problems, you know," Jennie said, alighting from the buggy. "The movement needs women like you, women with intelligence, vigor, and nerve. You appear to possess all the necessary qualities."

Kate led the way to the back door. *And money,* she mentally added; *you forgot to mention money.* Financing the movement had always been a major concern a decade ago; Kate didn't believe that had changed.

"At least allow me to elaborate on our current program. Perhaps you will find some area in which you can be of specific service to the movement."

Kate turned the key in the lock and frowned. The tumbler didn't turn.

"I know I locked this door," she said, as much to herself as to the suffragist at her side. She pushed the door inward and gasped at the sight before her eyes.

Chapter Fourteen

Sunlight from the open door magnified a haze of drifting wheat flour and filtered through the floating cream-colored particles to reveal overturned canisters and upturned chairs, broken dishes and glassware, piles of coffee, tea, salt, cornmeal, and sugar . . . in short, the biggest mess Kate could ever remember beholding. And there was no telling how much of it she couldn't see because of the haze.

Jennie Clark shouldered her way past Kate and into the room. "We've vowed to take women out of the kitchen," she said, "but don't you think this is taking things a bit to the extreme?"

Kate opened her mouth, then promptly closed it. She wasn't about to dignify Jennie's caustic remark.

"More bored youths?" Jennie asked on a snicker. The woman seemed determined to twist the knife.

"Obviously," Kate said, "I have work to do here. Why don't I take you over to the boardinghouse? Perhaps we could continue our discussion tomorrow at my office."

"Oh! I'd thought to stay here, with you."

Of all the gall! Kate thought. The woman irritated her more every minute. Could she stand her as a houseguest? And for how long? For all Kate knew, the suffragist "thought to stay" a week or two. She hadn't planned for an unexpected—and uninvited—guest and wasn't certain when she'd last put fresh sheets on the spare bed. And now, when someone had invaded her domain and wrecked her kitchen, she was supposed to play the ingratiating hostess and entertain this woman, who probably expected to be waited on hand and foot. Kate didn't think so.

"Only if you're willing to get your hands dirty," she said, letting her gaze wander across the chaos and then back to Jennie.

Jennie's jaw dropped, and Kate found herself staring impolitely at a long dark hair growing out of a brown mole on Jennie Clark's dimpled chin. "Well, I never!" Jennie huffed.

"You've never gotten your hands dirty?" Kate asked with wide-eyed innocence. "How can you possibly relate to the women who populate small towns like Paradise?"

"Of course I soil my hands from time to time," Jennie cried self-righteously.

Kate could plunge her own knife. And she did. "But the truth is, you have servants who do all your dirty work at home, don't you?"

"I—I—well, of course I have a *few,"* Jennie sputtered. "I'm very busy. I don't have time for mundane chores."

Suddenly Kate saw through Jennie Clark as clearly as if she were a stem of the finest lead crystal. "And the further truth is, you browbeat people like me into doing your dirty work in the field."

Jennie's dark eyes popped. Kate wondered if, perhaps, she hadn't been the first person ever to render this woman speechless.

"I can well afford to hire servants," Kate said, hoping she didn't sound too smug, "but I prefer to do my own housework. And my own yard work. Physical labor is good for the soul. And getting your hands dirty, really dirty, on occasion brings everything into perspective."

Jennie stood perfectly still and stared, her thin lips set in a straight line and a multitude of wrinkles gathering up her brow, but Kate refused to back down. She might be wrong about a lot of things, but she was right about this. All of it. She knew she was.

Finally the suffragist walked past Kate into the dining room and came back sans purse, parasol, gloves, and hat. It was Kate's turn to stare as Jennie unbuttoned her narrow sleeves at the wrist and rolled up the mauve satin.

"Well," Jennie said, "what are you waiting for? I need an apron."

"Who do you reckon that was with the mayor?" Skip asked Mitch as they were leaving the field.

"Hell if I know." Well, he reasoned, he didn't know. Just because she looked a little bit like someone he'd known years ago didn't mean a thing. Then he dug himself even deeper. "I never saw that woman before in my life."

She couldn't be Jennie Clark. Naw. It wasn't possible. Jennie couldn't have let herself get so big. The woman simply reminded him of Jennie. That was all it was. Whoever she was, Kate's visitor was a number-three variety. Mitch would bet his life on it. A Jersey cow in a herd of Texas longhorns. Disaster with a capital *D*.

"We don't get many folks here from big cities," Skip said. "I don't know if you noticed, but those reporters caused a big stir in town. And I guarantee that by tomorrow morning everyone'll know who she is and why she's here."

"You're probably right," Mitch said, his mind elsewhere. "I gotta make my rounds, Skip."

"Yeah, Julia's waiting for me." He slapped Mitch on the back. "Thanks for playing on our team, old man. We wouldn't have won if it hadn't been for you getting Jethro out. You playing next week?"

"I suppose."

"Guess I'll see you Wednesday noon."

Mitch frowned. "Wednesday?"

"Your afternoon off. Remember?"

"Oh, yeah. See you then."

How could he have forgotten Wednesday? Wednesday meant getting out of this crazy place and spending some time in Bagdad with a mug of beer and a loose woman.

Wasn't that what he wanted?

Mitch wasn't so sure anymore.

Kate was amazed at how well she liked the woman Jennie Clark became the moment she took off her hat and put on an apron.

The two talked as they worked and then well into the night, exchanging ideas, expounding ideologies, debating current political issues. Despite their differences they agreed wholeheartedly that it was high time men recognized women as their intellectual and political equals and allowed them all the requisite privileges on both counts.

"I came here to ask you to organize the women of Paradise," Jennie said. "And if I have to, I'll browbeat you into doing it. Our movement needs leaders like you."

Kate's eyebrows rose. "Me? A leader?"

"Of course. You're a natural."

Kate shook her head. "Not me."

"Why not?"

"Leaders have followers. You don't see anyone following me, Jennie. You see people egging my house and trashing my kitchen."

Jennie waved Kate's statement aside. "Oh, that's just a few shortsighted men, probably of the old political regime in this town. They're set in their ways and angry because you're showing them up." She laid a hand on Kate's shoulder. "And you *are* showing them up, Kate. I've been keeping a close watch on you these last six weeks. The whole world has been keeping a close watch on you. People out there are cheering for you and your petticoat government."

"But that doesn't mean I'm a leader," Kate argued. "All that means is that I happen to be the political head of five bright, capable women, any one of whom could do a better job as mayor than I."

"No, Kate. You are a leader. And you have followers. Your followers put you in office. Your followers are keeping you there. If you didn't have followers, lots of followers, someone would have initiated a recall petition by this time."

Kate sighed in mock defeat, her wide smile evidence of her renewed enthusiasm for the women's cause. "Did you ever have me fooled!"

"How's that?"

"I fully expected to be manipulated, but through intimidation, not flattery."

"Compliments, Kate. I meant every word. And as for intimidation, no one has mastered that quality quite as well as you."

Kate flicked her fingers across Jennie's sleeve, dusting a cloud of flour into the air. "I promise not to tell anyone that you got down on your knees and scrubbed my kitchen floor."

"And I promise not to tell anyone that you ever doubted your leadership abilities. That is, if—"

"All right." Kate laughed. "Tell me what you want me to do."

The next few days flew by for Kate while they dragged for Mitch.

She and Jennie became fast friends. They never stopped talking, except during the hour or so of the council meeting Monday night, during which Kate initiated another ordinance certain to be unpopular among the men. This one prohibited spitting on the boardwalk.

Mitch desperately wanted to talk to Kate, though for what reason exactly he couldn't decide. After the council meeting, however, he had a reason. An excellent reason. This new ordinance wouldn't do at all. There was no way he was ever going to catch every man who spit on the boardwalk. Not when he had to be on constant lookout for a thousand other infractions.

There were other ways to handle such things, ways he wanted to discuss with her. He wished she'd talk to him about things like this first, before she went flying off the handle and wrote some ridiculous piece of legislation her petticoat government was certain to pass unanimously without even questioning the repercussions. Talk about shortsighted—those women truly couldn't see the forest for the trees.

But he couldn't talk to Kate—or *wouldn't*—so long as she entertained Jennie Clark. Even in his thoughts her name stuck in his craw.

Mitch couldn't believe it really was Jennie. Every

fiber of his being tried to deny that this Jennie Clark was the same woman he'd fallen in love with fourteen years ago, but just as Skip predicted, Monday morning everyone in town was buzzing with news about suffragist Jennie Clark. Everything they said pointed to the indisputable truth that the two women were one and the same.

What had happened to her? he wondered. The Jennie Clark he remembered looked nothing like this one. His Jennie had been svelte of figure, a beautiful woman who was meticulous about her appearance. Somewhere along the way she'd let herself go to seed. Then why did seeing her again make him feel like an old wound had been reopened?

For almost fourteen years Mitch had carried around the image of Jennie Clark at age nineteen, had anguished because she had rejected him, had allowed himself to become embittered by it all. He knew all of this, yet he refused to face the truth, refused to acknowledge that his bitterness had kept the wound from healing, refused to hear her say that it was her love for him that prevented her from marrying him. It was too easy—and not nearly so painful—to recall her saying she wasn't his political equal, which made him feel as though *he* was beneath her. After all, she knew all about politics, while he couldn't have cared less.

Since the townsfolk didn't know much about Jennie Clark, speculation prevailed. Mitch could've told them the important facts: She was a rich spinster with too much education for a woman and too much time on her hands. She was one of the third variety, a woman with a cause, a dangerous woman who could get you in more trouble than you ever bargained for— trouble you didn't even ask for. He knew, better than most. He'd keep his distance and his mouth shut tight—and hope Jennie didn't approach him or the townsfolk didn't ever find out that, once upon a time, he'd slept with the woman. More than once. And when she was gone, assuming she ever left, he'd try once again to close the wound.

Finally Wednesday rolled around, and Mitch got his afternoon off. He was sitting atop Satan when Skip showed up.

"Man, you're anxious to go somewhere," Skip teased.

"Nowhere in particular," Mitch lied, jerking on the reins to hold the gelding still. "Satan's ready to chase some prairie dogs. And me, I'm just ready to get away from this job for a few hours. You know the routine. Make your rounds and cite the violators. With this latest ordinance, they'll be plenty."

"Yeah," Skip said, "at the rate they're collecting fines, the council ought to be able to hire a full-time deputy soon."

Mitch liked Skip. He wasn't Earl Woody, but Mitch didn't suppose he could expect Skip or anyone else to fill that man's shoes. Mitch figured he could walk away from this job six weeks from now a helluva lot easier if Skip was ready to step right in and take over. "You want the job?"

Skip scratched his head. "I kinda like it. But I like making harnesses, too. I don't rightly see how I could manage both."

"Think about it."

"I will. Hey, you'd better get out of here if you're going. You don't want to spend your one free afternoon gabbing with me."

Kate and Jennie were on their way to the Madison House for lunch when Mitch rode Satan down the street.

"My, what a beautiful horse," Jennie said.

"That's our town marshal."

"You have a horse for a marshal?"

Kate laughed. "You know what I meant."

"Yes, I do." Jennie paused, turning her head and watching until horse and rider disappeared in a cloud of dust. She blinked away a sudden gathering of moisture in her black eyes.

"The dust will do it to you every time," Kate said. "When this street isn't dusty it's muddy. But this time next year, our streets will be paved."

"What color is the marshal's horse?"

Her offhanded question caught Kate completely by surprise. "Why?"

"Just tell me, Kate. What color is his horse?"

"Chestnut?"

Jennie swiped at the moisture dripping from her eyes and pasted a watery grin on her chubby face. "Wrong."

"Roan?"

"Wrong again. I'll tell you. Black."

"What difference does it make?"

"None," Jennie said, "except that it's obvious to me you have eyes only for the rider. And he watches you, too."

Suddenly Kate felt uncomfortably warm. "What do you mean?"

"He watches you. He was watching you at the ball game Sunday, and at the council meeting Monday night, and just now as he rode past. That man watches you. And he likes what he sees."

"You must be mistaken."

"No, I'm not. My work requires acute observation, and I've spent years training my senses accordingly."

Kate opened the restaurant door. "I'm his boss, for goodness sake."

"And you're a woman, Kate, through and through. Granted, you're different from most women, but you're still a woman. That man sees the woman in you, but he also sees you as a threat to his masculinity. Go easy with him," Jennie advised. "Listen to him. Don't overexert your authority with him."

Kate led the way to a corner table and ordered plate lunches for both of them. She didn't quite know what to make of Jennie's observations and advice. "You make it sound like you know Mitch."

Jennie shrugged. "He's a man," she said, as though that explained everything.

"But I don't need a man in my life right now," Kate argued.

"That's your head talking, not your heart."

"How do I tell the difference?"

"You have to learn to trust your intuition," Jennie said. "Promise me you'll be careful before you make any rash decisions, Kate. Sometimes opportunity knocks but once." Her eyes mirrors of regret, Jennie snapped her napkin open and laid it in her lap. "If you slam the door in its face, it may not be there when you decide to invite it in."

Bagdad looked about the same as Paradise—a bustling little prairie town with stores and houses and barns and corrals—with one major difference. Bagdad folks not only ignored Prohibition, they actually flaunted their rebellion against the ridiculous act.

Mitch stopped in front of the Red Dog Saloon and sat for a minute, closing his eyes and letting the sights and sounds wash over him. Damn, he'd missed hearing the tinkle of a piano and raucous laughter and the clink of glass against a wood counter. He'd missed seeing girls in short skirts, missed seeing their dyed hair reflected in mirrors hung over the bar. He'd missed the smell of spirits. And he'd sure as hell missed the tang of beer on his tongue and the warm glow it put in his belly.

But now, once a week, he could enjoy the privileges of sipping on a few mugs of brew, pinching a few female posteriors, and maybe even taking one of the girls upstairs for a fling.

So what was he waiting for?

He unclipped his badge and shoved it in his pocket before dismounting. No sense causing himself any problems. To these people he'd just be another drifter, a cowpoke stopping to wet his whistle. He pushed open the swinging doors and swaggered inside, then blinked at the sudden darkness. He'd forgotten how dark saloons were in the daytime.

Maybe that was why he'd misjudged those temperance women back in Dry Creek: 'cause he couldn't see 'em worth a damn. Yeah, he thought, that was it! He couldn't see 'em worth a damn. Shorty was hollering at them about not allowing no whores in his place and Mitch couldn't see 'em well enough to know they wasn't what Shorty called 'em. It wasn't his fault. Not at all.

God! That felt good. Like he'd been carrying around this real heavy load and now it was gone. Vamoosed right into thin air!

When his eyes adjusted to the dimness he walked over to the bar, propped his boot on the brass rail, and ordered a beer.

"You new to these parts?" the man next to him asked.

Mitch glanced at the owner of the friendly voice. He was a little man wearing a brown derby and sporting a well-waxed handlebar mustache that dripped below his jawline. The mustache looked incongruous on such a small face, and it endeared Mitch to the man immediately.

"Everett," Mitch said, using his middle name on a whim.

The little man stuck out a hand. Each stubby finger bore a heavy gold ring. "Welcome to the Red Dog, Mr. Everett. My name's Jenson. Melvin Jenson. I own this place."

"Pleased to meet you, Mr. Jenson." The strength in the little man's hand amazed Mitch. He took a sip of beer and then another, and then said, "To hell with it," and downed the entire contents of the mug in one long swallow.

"That's a mighty thirst you have there, Mr. Everett." Jenson smiled, and the corners of his lips disappeared into the mustache. "Bartender! Bring this man another beer."

Mitch dug in his pocket for change.

"No need," Jenson said. "This one's on the house."

"Thank you." Mitch sipped the beer, vowing to take his time and enjoy this one.

"Glad to oblige. Glad to oblige." Jenson looked Mitch up and down, scrutinizing him so closely, Mitch felt like a prize bull at a cattle auction. "You planning on staying around here?"

"Naw. Just stopping by."

"I've got a spare room upstairs," Jenson said, nodding at someone behind Mitch. "Be happy to rent it to you for the night."

"Won't be staying that long, but much obliged anyway."

Jenson grinned. "Just let me know if you change your mind."

The little man moved away from the bar and a tall, buxom floozy with hair the color of spun silver sidled into the vacant spot and laid a palm on Mitch's upper arm.

"Whatcha know good, cowboy?" Her voice flowed thick and rich, as intoxicating as warm brandy on a cold day.

"Not a thing," Mitch drawled, lifting his mug and drinking in the sight of full white breasts rising above a red satin bodice. For an instant the breasts shriveled in size and hid their dusky crests behind thin white cotton. He shook his head to erase the memory and said, "Can I buy you a drink?"

"Sure can. Make it a whiskey."

They took their drinks to a small table near the stairs.

"My name's Silver, cowboy," she said. "Now tell me all about yourself."

That was the last thing Mitch intended to do, but he supposed he could talk about his days as an army scout without giving himself away. He wasn't sure why he felt so uncomfortable being straightforward with these people. His name and present occupation shouldn't make a damn bit of difference. He had no authority in this town and he sure as hell wasn't gonna go ratting to nobody about an illegal saloon. Hell, everybody who mattered probably knew anyway. It was like he'd told Kate: Everybody outside of Paradise ignored Prohibition.

And yet he held back.

He was on his fifth beer and up to the time he'd found himself surrounded by a band of Sioux warriors when Silver suggested they take a little stroll.

"But I haven't finished my story," Mitch protested, "and I want another beer."

Silver got up from her chair and sat down on his lap. She ran her long, red-lacquered nails through his hair and cooed. "I've got a nice soft bed upstairs. You can bring your beer and talk all you want in my room."

Mitch gagged on her cheap perfume and leaned back in his chair in an effort to put some distance between them.

It didn't help. She leaned into him and rubbed her powdered nose against his. "What's wrong, baby?"

Why had he thought he could find pleasure with a whore? How he ever had before was beyond his comprehension at the moment. He might need a woman in the worst way, but not this woman.

He craned his neck, looking over the top of Silver's head at another saloon girl moving among the tables near their corner. The haze of smoke and dust softened the carrot-top's angular features, but not so much that he couldn't see the lines of sadness and discontent her occupation had drawn.

In sudden and complete disgust, he pushed Silver off his lap. She landed on her bottom, and her rouged lips crimped into a childish pout. Before she could say anything, he scraped his chair back, threw some silver on the table, and stomped out.

Without looking back, he pushed Satan hard. When Bagdad and the Red Dog Saloon lay several miles behind him he reined in, jerking the big black to a bone-jarring halt out in the middle of the prairie. The horse snorted and waggled his head.

"Easy, there, boy," Mitch said, patting Satan's neck and wishing he had someone to soothe him.

Since his affair with Jennie Clark, he'd slaked his lust on first one woman and then another. Not one of them had ever meant anything to him beyond satisfying his sexual appetite. And not once had cheap perfume or rouged lips or powdered noses repulsed him.

Until now.

* * *

"I hate to see you go," Kate cried, hugging Jennie tightly. The unaccustomed demonstration of such affection for another woman felt good, and Kate hugged her harder. If Arnold were alive, he'd be horrified, and if Adelaide could see her, she would be, too. But neither McBride was capable of feeling affection, much less showing it.

The realization stunned Kate, and she pulled back.

"Duty calls," Jennie said philosophically. "I'll be watching the post for your letters."

"Yes." The response fell automatically from Kate's lips while her circling thoughts chased each other inside her head. She was only marginally aware of Jennie hefting her tapestry bag, climbing aboard the coach, and hanging her head out the window.

"And I'll write to you, too. Thanks for having me as your guest, Kate. I truly enjoyed my visit."

The driver slapped the reins and called to the team. With a mighty shudder the heavily laden stage pulled out, sending up a cloud of thick dust behind it.

"Come back sometime!" Kate called, frantically waving her right arm. But it was too late. Jennie Clark was gone.

Kate felt temporarily lost and yet wonderfully full. She dreaded going back to an empty house, to lonely, quiet stretches devoid of human companionship. Yet as much as she liked Jennie, as much as she needed female friends, she knew deep down inside that no woman could ever fill the void in her heart. Nor was she the least bit sure that a man could. He would have to be a very special man. A man who could accept her without reservation. A man who loved her, and whom she loved in return.

She'd come a long way toward learning to listen

with her heart, thanks to Jennie, a long way toward understanding her hopes and dreams, her drive and ambitions—all those things that made her uniquely herself. And with understanding would come her own personal acceptance.

The day her heart spoke to her in the gazebo she'd been ready to listen, ready to learn. She recalled something her philosophy professor had said: "When the student is ready, the teacher will come." Jennie Clark had been that teacher.

All these years she'd blamed herself for her miserable relationship with Arnold. All these years she'd thought herself incapable of loving. But that wasn't true. She knew that now. She knew it the moment she hugged Jennie good-bye. A great burden had been lifted from her heart, leaving it wide open, ready to be filled with love.

God had sent her a teacher. And he would send her a man, the right man. Perhaps he already had.

She turned away from the station house and fairly skipped back to her office.

Mitch passed the stage on his way back into town. Normally he wouldn't have given it more than a cursory glance. He wouldn't have paid it any real attention that day had Jennie not stuck her monstrous hat out the window and hollered, " 'Bye, Mitch! Take care of Kate."

He came close to turning Satan around and going after the stage to ask Jennie what had happened to Kate while he'd been gone. But he'd managed to avoid the woman for three days; there was no sense chasing after her now. Nevertheless, a multitude of possibilities bombarded him as he spurred the horse forward, leaning low over Satan's neck and racing like the wind into Paradise. Part of him wished he had chased down the stage and asked Jennie about Kate.

Damn her anyway! he thought. No woman had any business getting herself into as many scrapes as Kate McBride did. He could understand, and even forgive, a minor altercation or problem every once in a blue moon, but with Kate, it was virtually every day. He should have known better than to think he could leave town for an afternoon and come back to find everything the way he'd left it.

Where in the hell should he look for her first? he wondered. At her house or at the office? At five o'clock in the afternoon one guess was as good as the other. The best guess, he supposed, was Doc Myers's office, but since it was next to the town hall, he'd try there first. He jumped off Satan and bounded through the door like a wild man.

"Where is she? Where's Kate?" he bellowed at Hardy, who merely pointed with his head toward Kate's office door.

Mitch never broke his stride. He threw Kate's door open and almost ran into her desk before he could stop himself.

She was working at her desk, as hearty and hale as he'd ever seen her.

"You're going to be the death of me yet," he wheezed between big gulps of air. "And if I ever see the Hat Woman again, I'm going to wring her thick neck."

Kate couldn't help smiling at him. Part of her wanted to tell him she wasn't a little girl anymore while another part reveled in his protective attitude. Yet she didn't think she'd ever known anyone who jumped to erroneous conclusions as often—and as drastically—as Mitch Dawson did, and she wasn't about to accept the blame for this particular incorrect deduction, whatever it was.

She supposed she might as well ask him and get it over with. "And what, pray tell, did Miss Clark do or say that brought you so close to apoplexy?"

"She—" Mitch clamped his mouth shut, and deep furrows ridged his forehead. "Uh, I passed the coach on its way out of town and she said I needed to take care of you. I thought she meant something had happened to you."

His frown dissolved into a menacing glare, but somewhere in the exchange of one crotchety face for another Kate thought she detected a look of pure sheepishness. She was forming an appropriate expression of her gratitude for his concern when he belched, and the stale smell of beer on his breath hit her in the face.

Suddenly a vision of her father's red nose and bloated face replaced Mitch's, and she exploded.

Chapter Fifteen

"Beer!" she screeched, jumping up and backing away from him. "You've been drinking beer!"

He waggled his thick eyebrows and licked his lips. "Yes, ma'am, I have."

His ready admission caught her off guard. "But . . . why?"

"Because I like it."

"That's not what I meant to ask," she said, quickly regaining the offensive. "*Where* did you get it?"

"Bagdad. It's legal over there."

"It is not," she snapped.

"Well, pardon me," he snapped back, "for misspeaking myself. I suppose you're the only person in the world who has the right to do that. What I *meant* to say is that the folks in Bagdad ain't quite so narrow-minded as you are."

She gasped at his accusation, then pushed it from her mind as best she could. There was another, more important issue here. "Your conduct is unbecoming of a town marshal, Mr. Dawson."

"Excuse me all to hell and back," he sneered, "but I ain't on duty right now. Skip is."

"And it's time you relieved him. You aren't going

back on duty in your present condition, Mr. Dawson, I can assure you of that."

"Oh, yes, I am!" He turned on his heel, staggered just a bit, and headed for the door.

Kate knew she ought to stop him, but what could she do? Physically wrangle him down and hog-tie him? Not likely. Threaten to dismiss him? If she did, then she'd better be ready to follow through, and where would that leave her?

He'd been in town almost six weeks, and this was the first time, as far as she knew, that he'd had a swallow of liquor. Otherwise, he'd followed her orders and carried out his duties. The townspeople were beginning to take a shine to him. If she fired him now, she'd not only be without a marshal, she'd also incur the displeasure of even more of the Paradise residents than she already had.

No, the best she could hope for at the moment was that he went back to the jail and slept it off. Tomorrow would be soon enough to pursue the subject with him.

She propped her elbows on her desk and rested her forehead on tightly clenched fists. She might as well admit it. She didn't want to lose Mitch Dawson for any reason. She couldn't stand the thought of him getting on his horse and riding out of town and never coming back.

But she couldn't stand the thought of dealing with a man who drank beer, either.

What was she going to do?

Thursday morning, Mitch woke up with his mouth full of cotton, his eyes full of sand, and his head full of rocks. He dragged himself out of bed and wondered how he got there in the first place. The last thing he remembered . . . the last thing he remembered . . .

Trying to remember inflicted entirely too much pain. He shuffled toward the washstand, where he caught a glimpse of himself in the little square mirror. Mitch squeezed his eyes shut, opened them, and looked again. He didn't look a bit more alive this time than the last.

And he felt like he was dying, or wished he could. He tried to wash the sand out of his eyes and brush the bad taste out of his mouth, but his efforts were futile. He rubbed his eyes and raked his tongue over his teeth. Shuddering, he hauled his suspenders up from where they hung around his hips, popped them over his shoulders, and winced. Everything hurt. He thought about changing his clothes, then quickly put that notion aside. Later, when his head cleared.

He should have eaten lunch. He wouldn't have gotten so drunk if he'd eaten lunch. Not so fast, anyway. That stuff Jenson sold must be home brew. Home brew got to you faster.

Never again, he swore. If he couldn't stop after one or two beers, then he'd quit drinking altogether.

He was outside in the alley, laboriously pumping water for coffee, when something bit him on the rear.

"What the Sam Hill!" Though his bellowing jarred the rocks around in his head, that part of him didn't hurt nearly so bad anymore as his posterior did. He turned slowly, so as not to disturb the rocks too much, and found himself glaring at a billy goat whose mobile mouth was chomping on a piece of his trousers.

"Get out of here, you mangy rascal," he ordered, consciously keeping his voice low but trying to make it firm and threatening. When the billy goat didn't budge Mitch shooed at him with his arms. "Go on. Get out of here."

That time, he screeched at the animal. The goat didn't flinch, didn't look up, didn't stir beyond making the bell around its neck jingle as it chewed away on the ragged blue denim.

"Where's Gabby when you need him?" Mitch muttered, taking his pitcher of water and starting back inside. The goat followed him, nipping at the seat of his pants again. Mitch whirled around and slung the water out of the pitcher and onto the goat. He slammed the door in the goat's face and the rocks crashed against each other in his head.

The damned goat had ruined a perfectly good pair of jeans. He supposed now he'd have to change clothes whether he wanted to or not. And to hell with making coffee. If he was going through the agony of changing clothes, then he'd get some at the Madison House. Besides, he was out of fresh water, and he wasn't about to go back out to the pump. Not as long as the goat was there. He had to find Gabby.

Surely, he thought, the day couldn't get any worse than it started out.

He was wrong.

Kate found him at the Madison House, sitting at a table all by himself and grimacing every time he took a sip of coffee, which couldn't have been very hot since it wasn't even steaming. He seemed so miserable that she had a hard time holding on to her exasperation with him. She'd come to ream him out but wanted to soothe and coddle him instead, which would never do. Mitch Dawson was a grown man. A supposedly responsible man. The town marshal, for pity's sake—not a sick child who needed comforting. If he was ill, it was his own fault. She sat down across from him.

"Would you care to sit with me?" he asked with a sneer, squinting his eyes at her and then screwing up his nose as though the very sight of her nauseated him.

"Your shenanigans aren't about to put me off my purpose," she said, waving at Sadie and raising an imaginary cup.

"Heaven forbid that anything should accomplish that feat!"

She smiled. "My, my, aren't we testy this morning. How about another beer?"

He made another face at her, one that said she'd drop the subject if she knew what was good for her. "If it'll make you go away, I'll promise not to ever touch another drop of beer in my life."

Sadie came back with a brimming cup of steaming coffee, to which Kate added sugar and cream.

"I accept your pledge," Kate said, stirring her coffee, "but if it's all the same to you, I'll have my coffee before I leave."

He snorted. "All right. Just hurry."

For a moment neither spoke. Then Mitch said, "Since you already think I'm being disagreeable, there is a matter I want to discuss with you."

She raised her eyebrows. "Yes?"

Mitch groaned, dragged his fingers through his unkempt hair, and turned his gaze to the window. Outside, shovels punched the ground and cart wheels creaked as the ditch-digging crew worked in front of the Madison House.

"Your spitting-on-the-boardwalk ordinance."

Kate stirred her coffee again. Every time the spoon clanked against the cup, Mitch flinched. She knew she shouldn't, but she took perverse pleasure in watching him cringe. "Actually, it wasn't my idea. It was Liza's. She said it was ridiculous to allow the new boardwalks to be ruined with nasty tobacco juice. I just happened to agree with her."

Mitch's reply took her by surprise. "I agree with her, too. As a matter of fact, I like most of the new ordinances, especially the one that prohibits stray live-stock from roaming the streets."

"Thank you," she said, smiling.

"But about this new one." He rubbed the pad of his thumb along the cup handle.

"You just said you agreed—"

"In its purpose," he corrected, "not in the ordinance."

Kate frowned. "I don't understand."

"Did anyone ever tell you that you have a penchant for controlling people?"

She didn't think she liked the direction this conversation was taking. "No."

"Well, you do. Or at least that's the way it looks to folks." He paused, taking a long swallow of coffee and nodding to Sadie to pour him another cup. "The point I'm trying to make is there's more than one way to skin a cat."

"You've lost me," she said.

"You don't want men spitting their nasty tobacco juice on the boardwalks."

"Right."

"So, why not put out some spittoons and ask the men to use them?"

"They wouldn't."

"How do you know? Have you ever tried it?"

"No, but—"

"Then how can you know what they will do? Try it, Kate. What can it hurt?"

Though she didn't believe men walking down the boardwalk would bother to aim their spittle so precisely, she supposed he made a valid case. "All right," she said, scraping her chair back. "I'll order some from Al today."

"And put a notice in the newspaper," Mitch advised. "They'll use them. You'll see."

On her way back to the town hall, Kate stopped at both the general store and the newspaper office and was surprised at how receptive both Al and Herman were to Mitch's idea. Maybe, she reflected, she was going about some things the wrong way. Was Mitch right about other things? Did she honestly attempt to control people? Or was Mitch the only one who saw her that way?

She decided to ask Hardy.

"Gosh, ma'am," he stammered, shuffling his big feet, "I don't know."

"We've been working together for over six weeks now," she reminded him, "and I think it's high time we started being honest with each other, don't you?"

"You really want me to be honest?" he asked in some amazement.

"Of course I do."

"Well, you seem to like being in control. 'Course, you're the mayor. You're supposed to be in control."

That didn't completely satisfy her, but Hardy seemed reluctant to comment further. Kate decided this was a good time to pursue another, perhaps related subject that had been on her mind.

"A while back you were standoffish around me. Did my controlling nature have anything to do with that?"

Hardy's pale cheeks bloomed a deep pink. "No, ma'am. I thought—" He coughed. "I was wrong about something, Miz McBride, but I know better now."

Kate chewed the inside of her lip. She wanted to ask him to elaborate, but that didn't seem to be a good idea. "Promise me you'll tell me if you think I step out of line."

He smiled, obviously relieved. "Yes, ma'am, I'll do that."

Hardy's opinion mattered to her, but not so much

as Mitch Dawson's. As she attempted to map out an organizational plan for the Paradise Women's Suffrage Association, Mitch's words replayed themselves over and over in her head.

An hour later Mitch sat at his desk, holding his head in his hands and thinking about what a total idiot he was. He should have known better than to get drunk. He should have known better than to bust in on Kate and let her know he was drunk. He should have known better than to tell her she was too dominating. He'd put his job in jeopardy. He supposed he'd put their relationship in jeopardy, too.

What relationship? So he'd kissed her a couple of times. That didn't mean they had a relationship. Did it? He didn't want to think about it right now. Thinking made his head hurt worse. He was telling himself he absolutely, positively, was *not* going to think about it when Gabby Dahlmer charged through the door, then leaned over and panted heavily. The old man's face was beet red and sweat dripped off his chin.

Mitch rose from his chair and started around his desk. "What's wrong?"

"Stringfellow's billy goat," Gabby wheezed. "He's done bit three people this morning."

"Four," Mitch corrected.

"I cain't ketch him by myself."

Mitch shoved his hat on and buckled his gun belt.

Gabby's watery blue eyes bugged. "You ain't gonna shoot him?"

"I will if I have to. Where is the critter?"

"All over. You name it, he's been there."

Mitch and Gabby chased the goat, which Gabby called "Billy," up Main Street, down Oak, and across First. Every footfall jarred Mitch from his toes to his pounding head and made him increasingly remorseful about drinking so much beer the day before. And all the while, the goat's bell jingled, jingled, jingled as the animal bellowed, "Neigh-hay-hay, neigh-hay-hay, neigh-hay-hay." It was enough to drive a man to drink—even a man who'd just sworn off liquor.

Billy zigzagged across First Street, dashed toward Josiah Keane's livery stable, and ran right smack into the wall.

"Grab him!" Mitch yelled to Gabby, who was closer than he was.

Gabby dove at the stunned goat, missed, and landed on his stomach in the dirt. Before he could get up Billy ducked his head and bit the back of Gabby's hand.

"Damn you!" Gabby yelped, righting himself and then rubbing his hand.

Oblivious to the pain it had inflicted, the goat backed up and headed into the stable. By the time Mitch and Gabby ran in the goat was heading out the back.

"Let's split up," Mitch said. "I'll try to steer him back this way. Maybe we can corner him."

Wheezing and coughing, Gabby leaned against the doorjamb and nodded.

"See if Josiah will help," Mitch hollered over his shoulder.

Mitch sprinted the length of the stable and came out into bright, blinding sunlight. He didn't see the goat anywhere. He looked to the right, where he could see clear to the end of the alley. No goat. Since Josiah's livery stood on a corner, buildings obstructed the view to the left. If he were the goat, Mitch thought, he'd go that way.

He rounded the corner and stopped to look for the goat. Almost immediately something bit into his rump again. Mitch whirled around, and there stood Billy grinning up at him. *Damn!* he thought. *Goats don't grin.* But Billy sure as hell looked like he was grinning.

"That makes two pair today!" Mitch hollered, madder than he'd been in a long time. He whipped out his pistol and took aim, but the infernal goat catapulted out of the alley like an arrow from a bow, darting and jumping around so fast, Mitch couldn't get a clear shot. More determined than ever to catch the beast, he holstered his gun and took off after Billy again.

The goat led him on such a merry chase that Mitch soon lost track of where he was. Before he knew it he was back on Main Street, in front of his office, and heading right into the ditch-digging crew. Mitch snatched a shovel out of a man's hand and flailed it above his head as he ran.

"I'm gonna get you, you son-of-a-bitch heathen goat!" he hollered.

The ditch-digging crew leaned on their shovels and howled their laughter. A few egged Mitch on with shouts of "Get him, Marshal," and "Don't let Billy outsmart you," and all the while Billy was doing just that. The blasted goat seemed to have more moves than a sidewinder. When Billy's back hooves hit the dirt his front ones twisted off to one side or the other.

Finally Mitch gave up zigging since Billy invariably zagged about that time. He decided the best way to catch the critter was to stay on a straight path. As soon as he changed his tactics, so did Billy. Damn, the goat could run fast! And Mitch was beginning to run out of steam.

He jogged to a halt and leaned against the side of a building, thinking he'd stop there only long enough to catch his breath. He watched Billy turn the corner behind Al Youngblood's general store. And then, quite abruptly, the goat's bell quit tinkling.

The hateful creature was waiting for him!

"Don't let Billy outsmart you," the ditchdiggers had yelled. Well, he'd show that billy goat . . .

Taking the shovel with him, Mitch ambled across the street and walked straight through Youngblood's all the way to the back and into the storeroom.

"Hey! Where you going?" Al called. Mitch ignored him.

A small, dusty window faced the alley. Mitch sneaked around to the window, stood against the wall next to it, and chanced a peek. Billy was there, all right, watching the entrance to the alley. Mitch grinned.

With slow and careful steps, Mitch made his way around stacks of boxes to the back door, eased up the bar, and winced when the hinges creaked. Fully expecting the goat to have resumed the chase, he poked his head out the crack. To his amazement, Billy hadn't moved.

Mitch squeezed out the door, holding the shovel well off the steps and then lifting it over his shoulder as he cautiously approached the goat.

Something happened to him when his foot struck the ground. Something wild and wonderful. Something that defied logic and transcended the bounds of propriety.

He let loose with a savage whoop, propelled himself at the goat, and brought the scoop of the shovel down hard on Billy's head right between his stubby horns. The goat's back sagged and his legs twitched, and Mitch stood poised, ready to wallop the critter again if need be. Finally Billy stopped quivering and collapsed.

"Stringfellow's gonna be furious."

Mitch turned around. Al Youngblood stood on the top step, staring at the lifeless goat.

"I don't care," Mitch said. "He oughta keep his

goat penned up." He looked at Billy again and wondered if maybe he hadn't killed him. But he wasn't about to take any more chances with the rascally goat.

"Get me some rope, Al."

"Whatcha gonna do?"

"Tie this goat to your steps and then go tell Gabby to come get him."

Mitch didn't know where to find Gabby, but he figured the livery was as good a place to start as any. He arrived there to find a group of men huddled near the door. Mitch shouldered his way through the clustering men and came up short. Doc Myers was on his knees, bending over a prone figure.

Gabby.

"What happened?"

Doc looked up, his face grim. "His heart gave out."

Mitch swallowed hard. "He's not—"

"I'm afraid he is. Go find Eb, will you? We'll get Gabby to the undertaker's."

With the exception of Obediah Stringfellow and maybe a few of his cronies, the entire town mourned Gabby Dahlmer's passing.

They laid him out in the front parlor of the Dahlmer farmhouse. Eb said this was the first time anyone had been in the room, outside of routine dusting, since his mother passed away three years before, and he supposed the next time would be when he passed on.

They left Gabby there for three days, might have left him longer had the heat not been so bad. Eb worried about burying his daddy alive. What if he was just sleeping? he asked. Doc Myers shook his head sadly, and in a gentle but firm voice insisted that the old man's heart had stopped beating and it wasn't going to start up again, no matter how much Eb wanted it to.

But if it would make him feel better, Doc said, they'd put a spade in the coffin with Gabby's body. Just in case.

Kate saw Mitch at the funeral on Sunday afternoon. He sat on the front pew of the Methodist church with the other pallbearers, looking straight ahead. It was the first time she'd seen him other than in passing since late Thursday morning, when he'd come to tell her about Gabby's heart giving out.

In the meantime, she'd been rocked with guilt over ever hiring Gabby Dahlmer as animal catcher in the first place. Although no one else blamed her outright, she knew everyone was thinking Gabby would still be alive if she'd never been elected mayor. She could tell by the accusing stares people threw her way. And they were right. It was all her fault.

At the cemetery she stood off by herself and watched the pallbearers tote the coffin to the grave site. She felt as though her dreams were being lowered into the ground right along with Gabby's body.

She couldn't allow this to happen again, couldn't be responsible for another tragedy. *At the council meeting tomorrow night,* she decided, *I'll resign.* It was the only way. Someone else could take over. Sally would be good, or maybe—

"Isn't it hot?" Sally whispered in Kate's ear, abruptly halting her deliberations.

Kate hadn't realized she was no longer alone. "Yes, it is," she agreed, keeping her voice respectfully low. "Wearing black doesn't help."

"We're going down to the creek to soak our feet. You want to come?"

"Who's 'we'?" Kate asked.

"Oh, just some of us girls. We figured we could use a good cooling off."

Kate nodded absently and followed Sally to the

cluster of buggies parked just off the road. "Can we take yours?" Sally asked, climbing aboard and taking the reins without waiting for Kate's approval. Within minutes she stopped the team behind another buggy and set the brake. "Come on, Kate," she said. "You need this more than we do."

Frowning in more than a little confusion, Kate looked over at Sally's uncomfortable-looking shoes and then kicked her feet out from under her skirts and stared at her own shoes. "I don't know why my feet would be any tireder or hotter than yours," she said.

Sally laughed lightly. "I'm not talking about feet, Kate. I'm talking about letting go."

"I don't understand."

"You will."

As Sally led the way through a line of willows, Kate thought she heard female laughter beyond the low-hanging branches. They came out of the undergrowth and onto the creek bank, and there, up to midshin in water, stood Marty, Julia, Stella, and Liza with their hems tucked into their belts. Their petticoats were strewn across willow branches and bushes growing along the bank, and their stockings and shoes had been tossed hither and yon. Liza scooped up a handful of water and tossed it at Julia, who giggled when it glanced off her neck. Kate couldn't remember ever seeing grown women having so much fun. She smiled, then caught herself.

"But—we just buried Gabby!" she protested.

"So? None of us was related to him." Sally squatted down and began to unfasten her shoes. Kate didn't move.

"He was a sweet old man, Kate," Sally said, peeling off her stockings, "but he was an old man. Wilbur says Gabby's heart had been giving him trouble for years."

Kate closed her eyes and shivered. "Then I truly am responsible for his death."

"No, you aren't. You didn't know that. And you didn't beg Gabby to take that job. Remember, he came to you. Wilbur tried to talk him out of it later, but Gabby stood firm. He said he was doing what he wanted to do."

"But—"

"No more recriminations, Kate," Sally proclaimed, "and I mean it." She shimmied out of her petticoats and flung them at a bush. "Are you coming in with us or not?"

Kate looked back at the four women playing in the water and smiled. "Yes," she said, her head suddenly light and her spirit frivolous. "Yes, I'm coming in!"

Candlelighting turned into moonlighting, and still Kate didn't come home.

Where in tarnation was she? Mitch wondered. He'd been lying on the chaise in the gazebo, waiting for her for nigh on to two hours. He took out his pouch of tobacco and papers and rolled a cigarette. If she wasn't back by the time he finished smoking, he reckoned he'd have to go looking for her.

He was flipping his butt into the grass when she drove up. He started to get up, then stretched back out. Why get in a hurry? She was home now. He watched a light come on in the carriage house and heard her talking to the horses. A few minutes later the light went out. Now why wouldn't she carry the lantern with her to the house? he pondered, sitting up straight. The carriage house sat in a back corner of the lot, which was a long way from the house. Even with plenty of moon glow to light the path, traversing it without a lantern was pure-dee foolish, what with it being the season for snakes. Surely she knew that.

There was no way to figure women.

Mitch stood up with the intention of intercepting her, then froze, mesmerized, when he spied her leaving the carriage house and tripping down the path. Moonlight glistened in her reddish-blond hair and cast a soft blush on her complexion, but it was the illumination of her long, shapely legs and bare feet that held him spellbound. Without moving a muscle, he watched without questioning her state of undress until she reached the back stoop and fidgeted with the key in the dark.

Like a flash, he leapt down the gazebo steps and ran toward her.

"What are you doing?" he hissed.

Kate jumped back and dropped the key. "I was trying to get in my house," she snapped, "until you scared the tar out of me. What are you doing here?"

"You didn't answer my question."

She stooped down and ran her open palm along the wooden step. "Yes, I did."

"No, you didn't. Where are your clothes?"

"There it is!" She stood up and poked the key in the lock. "In the carriage house."

The tumbler clicked and she pushed the door open. Mitch followed her into the pitch-black kitchen.

"Did I invite you in?"

Mitch ignored her. "Why are your clothes in the carriage house?"

"Because they're wet. And I suppose your next question is, 'Why are they wet?' "

"Good guess."

She giggled. "Because I've been wading in the creek."

"Wading in the creek! And you called my behavior unseemly?"

"I'm not drunk."

"You could have fooled me."

"I learned something today, Mr. Dawson." He marveled at the childlike quality of her voice. "I learned that water cleans the soul and play revives it. Did you know that?"

"You are drunk."

"No, I'm not. I'm deliriously happy. Have you ever been deliriously happy, Mr. Dawson?"

He wished she'd stop calling him "Mr. Dawson." And he wished he could see her face. Although his eyes were adjusting to the darkness, all he could see was the palest outline of her form. "Are you going to light a lamp?"

"Not until you leave, Mr. Dawson. As you obviously noted, I'm not decently covered."

Her admission made him forget every promise he'd made to himself about getting involved with another woman with a cause. In two long strides he closed the distance between them and pulled her into his arms.

"It's 'Mitch,' " he said, his voice suddenly full of gravel.

He could feel her breath on his chin, hot and sweet, and he dipped his mouth to hers.

"Don't ever call me 'Mr. Dawson' again."

Chapter Sixteen

"Mitch," she said into his open mouth.

He groaned and crushed his lips against hers. God! How had he thought he could ever touch another woman after he'd held Kate? He set his tongue on an exploratory path that quickly evolved into the most sensuous journey he'd ever imagined.

She trembled in his embrace, and he pulled her tighter against him. When she rose on her tiptoes and wrapped her arms around his shoulders, he slipped his hand down her back and over the thin cotton fabric that covered her slender hips. As he'd thought, she wore only a camisole and drawers. The image of her sprinting through the moonlight, bare-legged and barefooted, flittered across his inner eye.

He released her mouth and placed a trail of nipping kisses along her jawline to the delicate shell of her ear. "I want you," he whispered.

"Yes," she said, her voice deep and husky.

He lifted his arms and drove his fingers into her loose hair, then gently tugged on her head until he'd put a small space between them. In the darkness his gaze searched for hers.

"I mean, I *want* you, Kate. In every way. And I have to see your face. I have to see your acceptance."

Kate's heart surged. He wanted her. Mitch Dawson wanted her. And she wanted him.

She loosened her hold on his shoulders and reached along the wall behind her until she located the match holder. The sulfur stick flared against the metal, and she slowly moved the tiny torch toward her face.

"You don't have to say anything," he said. "I can see your answer."

He took the match from her and snuffed it out. Kate's fingers tingled where he'd touched them. She leaned into him, every cell in her body straining toward him, yearning for him to take her in his arms again.

"You'll have to guide me," he said. "I don't want to stumble over your furniture in the dark."

Thankful that he didn't demand the aid of a lamp, Kate took his hand. For some reason she couldn't fathom she didn't want a light.

She heard the contrast of the pad of her bare feet and the click of his boots on the wood floor, and for the briefest of moments the reality of her agreement sliced through her. But in the deepest recesses of her soul she knew beyond the shadow of a doubt that this was what she wanted. This was what she'd longed for, what she'd waited for, what she'd dreamed of all her life. Somehow she'd known the first time he'd touched her—no, the first time she'd seen him, sitting behind her desk with his boots up and his hat down.

This afternoon, she'd learned what it meant to let go. Tonight she'd learn what it meant to feel. The student was ready; the teacher had come.

Her foot struck the thick Oriental carpet that covered her bedroom floor and his hand tightened over hers. Her thigh bumped against the bed and he drew up against her back. He didn't let go of her hand.

With her free hand she tossed decorative pillows

across the room and listened to them land with little thuds. His breath tickled the top of her head and his masculine essence teased her nose. Amazing, she thought, how alive she felt, how much in harmony with herself and her world.

She folded back the covers and turned into his embrace.

Never in his life had he felt such perfect peace as he did in Kate's arms, and yet, somehow, he recognized the peace as a fragile, almost ethereal entity that must be guarded with prudence.

Ever so tenderly he picked her up and laid her on the bed, then smoothed his hands over her face, over her hair, over her breasts, until her skin quivered beneath his touch and she moaned deep in her throat.

He sat down on the edge of the bed and tugged off his boots. She trailed a finger up his arched spine and slid her hand into his hair. He shivered and twisted toward her, and she pulled his head down until his lips met hers. At first he kissed her lightly, toying with her but teasing himself as well. He felt her fingers on his shirt, loosening the buttons one by one until it fell open to his waist. She slipped her hands inside his shirt and ran her open palms over his ribs and upward until her thumbs found his nipples. He shivered again.

He pulled back and snatched his shirt from his jeans. "I'm sorry," he said. "I can't wait any longer."

"I don't want you to."

They came together in a frenzy of passion, in a fury of satisfying two lifetimes of want and need that quickly built to a fevered pitch and exploded and exploded and exploded until they gasped for breath and clung to each other as if neither ever wanted to let go.

And in that moment Mitch knew that he would do

whatever it took to make Kate McBride his for all eternity.

Kate wanted the physical gratification of their love-making so much, she didn't stop to think about not hearing the word *love* spoken between them. But well into the wee hours, while she lay awake in Mitch's arms and listened to him breathe, she found herself yearning for something more between them.

She couldn't fault his lovemaking, nor take exception to her responses. He'd made her feel like a virgin all over again, and she supposed she had been before tonight. Not in the physical sense, but emotionally. Though she'd spent many a night lying thusly in Arnold's embrace, never had her husband made her feel so special, so beautiful, so loved.

And yet neither she nor Mitch had uttered the word *love*. Kate wanted to. With all her heart, she wanted to wake him up and rain kisses on his face and declare her love to him for always and forever. But she was afraid to. She was afraid such a declaration would drive him away, not only from her bed but from her life.

Intentionally or not, she supposed she'd always reached for the future, always lived and breathed for some far-off, intangible dream . . . until now. Now that dream lay beside her, a living, breathing man with whom she had nothing—and everything—in common, a man whose caresses heated her blood and humbled her heart, a man who'd just given himself to her wholly and completely and asked for nothing in return. She wasn't about to jeopardize this wonderful gift.

Her heart had never felt so full. She snuggled closer and cried softly into his shoulder.

* * *

A crowing rooster jolted Mitch from a deep, peaceful sleep. For an instant he was disoriented and confused, and then the memories flooded in and he sighed with more contentment than he'd ever known. The sigh caught in his throat and he hugged Kate tighter.

God! Nothing had ever felt so good. Or so right.

He'd never wanted anything so much as he wanted Kate. And he was going to have her.

A nagging voice whispered a warning: *She's one of the third kind, Mitch.* Disaster with a capital *D.*

Kate's different, he argued. *She has room in her heart for me.*

But are you willing to share her? the voice questioned.

I won't have to. She loves me. I know she does. And I love her. When I tell her she'll give up this nonsense of being mayor and devote herself to me and our children.

Oh, Lord. Children. How could he have forgotten?

"Since you were unable to give us grandchildren . . ." Adelaide had said.

Kate couldn't have children.

He hadn't come to Paradise looking for a wife, hadn't ever given much serious thought to settling down and becoming a father, but now that he'd found Kate, now that he wanted her the way he did, he wanted their children, too. He wanted a daughter with Kate's hair and a son with her eyes. He wanted to see their children grow up and find mates and have their own children.

He couldn't have that with Kate.

Tenderly, he moved the arm she had wrapped around his ribs and placed it by her side. She made a soft snuffling sound and rolled over. He slipped out of bed and made his way through the dark to the bathroom without bumping into anything.

But he already had more with Kate than he'd dared to hope for since Jennie. Maybe children weren't that important. It wasn't as though he'd built a dynasty. What did he have to give a child other than himself?

He fumbled through the items on a washstand until he located a small lamp and a match. The soft glow illuminated the space around him, and suddenly he felt oddly out of place in Kate's well-appointed bathroom, with its white porcelain commode and claw-footed tub. He couldn't recall ever being in a room that had both. In fact, he didn't think he'd ever seen a real working commode before. Such things were true oddities west of the Mississippi.

The contraption snagged his interest. He looked at it long and hard while he was swishing some Dr. Tichenor's around in his mouth. He had to see how the thing worked, so he lifted the highly varnished walnut lid and peered into the crystal-clear water in the bowl. Over his head, a chain hung from a white porcelain box mounted on the wall. Mitch spit the Dr. Tichenor's into the water, then reached up and pulled the chain. The water disappeared with a loud *whoosh.*

He waited for a minute, but nothing happened. Wasn't the thing supposed to fill back up? What if he'd broken it? There was no telling what another one cost or how long it would take to get one from back East. Sweat broke out on his brow and his stomach tied itself in knots.

"Good morning."

The soft, husky voice jarred him, and he swallowed hard. There he was, standing in front of her broken commode without a stitch of clothing on. Self-consciously, he turned away from Kate and scratched the back of his neck.

"I think I broke it," he mumbled.

"I doubt it," she said. "I expect you merely flushed the water out and all we have to do is put some more in."

He heard the grind of a pump handle and the splash of water from behind him, but he didn't turn around.

"You're going to have to move out of the way," she said, laughter in her voice.

Mitch stepped back and watched her empty a pitcher of water into the bowl.

"There now," she said. "It's all ready to use again."

Though Kate wore the same green silk robe he'd seen her in before, she seemed oblivious to his nakedness as she casually replaced the pitcher and walked out of the bathroom. When Mitch peeked into the hall a few minutes later he heard her moving around in the kitchen, clanging pots and pans and working the pump. The aroma of dripping coffee teased his senses, and he hurried into the bedroom to retrieve his jeans.

"I don't understand," he said when he joined her in the kitchen, "why you have bathroom fixtures without running water. Isn't that putting the cart before the horse?"

"Oh, we had running water, once upon a time. Arnold insisted on it when he built this house eight years ago." She broke an egg into a muffin tin and shook her head. "Now that I think about it, I suppose he would have been considered terribly eccentric by most folks. Anyway, he had a cistern put in, but the pipes between the cistern and the ground kept freezing in the winter."

"So?"

She picked up a hunk of dark yellow cheese and began to grate it. "So they invariably broke when they thawed out. The trouble wasn't worth the convenience. When Arnold died last year I had the cistern removed, a well dug, and pumps put in." She sprinkled the grated cheese over the eggs. "Without running water the flush box can't fill, so I have to put water in the commode every time it's flushed."

"That must get awfully tiresome."

She looked up at him and smiled, and he thought about how lucky he was to be sitting in her kitchen watching her cook. He'd never thought about whether or not she could cook, but she appeared quite at ease with the task.

"Not really," she said. "It's better than most alternatives I can think of."

Mitch nodded in agreement. He'd hauled out slop jars and braved freezing rain to get to an outhouse often enough in his life. He started to ask her if the sewage ever stopped up, then decided that would take this particular topic of conversation far beyond the conventions of decorum. Most women would faint dead away at the mention of a commode, let alone discuss one. But Kate was different. He'd known that all along. He smiled.

She opened the oven door, held her hand out to test the heat, then shoved in the muffin tin. From the parlor, a clock chimed four times.

"Why are you cooking so early?"

"Because I'm hungry. Aren't you hungry?"

In answer, his stomach growled loud enough for the neighbors to hear. He grinned. "I guess I am."

Kate poured out two cups of coffee and brought them to the table. For a while they sat in silence, drinking their coffee, fidgeting with their spoons, not looking at each other.

The longer the silence dragged out, the more uncomfortable Mitch became. He wanted to talk about their lovemaking, their relationship, their future together. And then again, he didn't. He was afraid to.

This thing between them was still too fragile, like a newborn kitten that hadn't yet opened its eyes.

He remembered how tiny and helpless Little Booger had been when he'd found her abandoned on the street, how gently he'd picked her up and how lovingly he'd cared for her. Folks in Dry Creek had laughed at him, told him he was a fool to think he could play wet nurse to a newborn kitten, but he'd committed himself to the cause of saving the kitten, and he had been prepared to do whatever was required.

Last night he'd committed himself to Kate, and he wanted to tell her that, but he fretted over her reaction, her possible lack of commitment. No, it was better to be still for the moment, to play wet nurse to the relationship until the eyes opened and the danger of imminent death had passed.

But one of them needed to break the tense silence, so he asked, "What are you doing with the eggs? They smell wonderful."

She raised her chin and looked at him with eyes that were a misty, almost smoky green.

His breath caught in his throat. Suddenly, filling his empty stomach was the last thing on Mitch's mind.

"Baking them," she said, blinking rapidly and then quickly rising and moving to the oven to check the eggs.

Was it his imagination, or was she crying? He watched her reach for a mitt and slide it on. She hiccupped. In an instant he was behind her, folding his arms around her waist and hugging her tightly.

"What's wrong, Kate?"

She shivered, and he wondered if it was from pleasure or anxiety.

"Nothing," she said, setting the pan on a cold burner and closing the oven door.

"Something is," he insisted.

She removed the mitt and hung it on its hook, then turned and buried her head in his shoulder. Deep, heartrending sobs racked her slender frame, and Mitch felt his own heart breaking in two. He rubbed her back and whispered, "I'm sorry."

"You didn't do anything," she sputtered between sniffles. "Arnold did."

"I don't understand."

"Oh, Mitch," she said, raising her head and putting her hands on either side of his head, "I didn't know it could be like this."

He eased away an escaping tear with the pad of his thumb, and his voice was low and seductive. "I didn't either."

He only meant to kiss away her tears, but when she wrapped her arms around his neck and moaned deep in her throat he scooped her up and carried her to the bedroom. This time she didn't protest the light.

When they finally ate breakfast the eggs were cold and the cheese was rubbery, but neither noticed. Their greater hunger had been appeased, at least for the moment.

"I fell asleep at my desk twice today," Kate told Mitch on Monday night. They were in her kitchen, having a midnight snack of buttermilk and corn bread.

"Yeah, me, too," he admitted sheepishly.

"Funny. I'm not the least bit sleepy now."

"Me either." He winked at her, and she felt herself go weak all over. "But I *am* hungry."

Her eyes widened in disbelief. "I don't know how. You ate a huge supper, and now you're eating again."

"You know what I mean, Kate," he said. And she did.

They were up again at four. Kate made biscuits

while Mitch heated water and hauled it to the claw-footed tub. They drank their coffee amid a froth of bubbles, and when their cups were empty they set them aside and took turns scrubbing each other's back. By the time they made it back to the kitchen the biscuits had turned into charcoal. They laughed and went back to bed.

They fell into a routine. Mitch ended his evening rounds at her house, arriving between ten-thirty and eleven. He stayed until minutes before the sun crested the horizon.

Sometimes they talked. Mitch regaled her with stories about fighting Indians and tracking outlaws. Kate told him about growing up in Topeka. They discovered that neither had living relatives beyond a cousin or two. But they avoided all sensitive areas. Kate didn't mention her father's drinking problem or her barrenness; Mitch omitted any reference to Jennie Clark. They both sensed that a delicate bubble surrounded their relationship, and each took extreme care to preserve it.

Wednesday afternoon they met at the creek. Mitch tied Satan to the back of Kate's buggy and they drove downstream until they were several miles out of town. Kate had packed a picnic lunch, which they completely ignored. They made love on the creek bank and played in the water, and then made love again. That evening Kate languished while Mitch made his rounds. She couldn't seem to get enough of him, or he of her. That night he found a note on her door that said, "The gazebo." He found her lying on the chaise, her arms open and ready for him.

Kate had never been so happy. When she was with Mitch she felt whole and complete. It was as though she'd been only half a person by herself, a shell waiting for the tide to come in and fill her up. She realized that never once had she felt whole with Arnold. All these years she'd thought a child would fill out her life. She understood now that only the gift of a man's love could do that, but she found herself yearning for children—Mitch's children—more desperately than ever. Eventually, she knew, she was going to have to tell him that she was barren, but not now. Not yet.

Mitch had never been so happy. Not in all the years he'd roamed the West, not in the seven years he'd served as a town marshal. Not even during his affair with Jennie Clark. In fact, his relationship with the suffragist paled in comparison. He realized he'd never understood what love was all about before. He wasn't sure he understood now, but he was learning. Eventually, he knew, he was going to have to tell Kate that he couldn't marry a woman of the third variety, but he wasn't completely convinced anymore that Kate fit the mold. In time she'd see things his way and give up this silliness of playing at politics. But he wasn't ready to broach that subject with her. Not yet.

For a week they existed on love without ever giving voice to the word. They simply accepted—without question, without explanation, without judgment. They knew that their relationship required nurturing and that their cautious avoidance of painful subjects stymied the growth process, yet they continued to shy away from anything that might break the gossamer thread that bound them together.

Kate said they were being discreet. Mitch said they were sneaking around.

Mitch said he couldn't keep staying at her house all night, every night. There would come a time when someone needed him in the middle of the night, and people would start questioning where he was. Kate said staying at the jailhouse was too risky. They were certain to be found out there.

"Eventually someone's going to catch on anyway," Mitch said.

They'd had the same discussion three nights' running, and each time they reached this point, Kate steered the conversation elsewhere. It was now Saturday night and time, she supposed, to let the subject take its natural course, wherever that might lead. She took a deep breath and hoped she wasn't making a big mistake.

"What do you suggest we do?" she asked, twisting sideways on the bed and propping her cheek on an open palm.

Mitch was lying on his back with two pillows under his head and shoulders, his arms folded and his head resting on his hands. The soft light from the lamp behind her played across the planes and angles of his face. She watched his chest rise and fall several times, watched his eyelids blink in an unsteady rhythm, watched his mouth twist from one side to the other as though he was chewing on the insides of his lips.

"Go public."

That was the *last* thing she'd expected him to say. "Oh, Mitch," she said, laying her free hand on her forehead and gaping at him, "we can't."

"Why not?"

"It would be political suicide for me."

That was the last thing he'd expected *her* to say. He trailed his tongue across his front teeth and looked at the ceiling. "Which is more important to you, Kate?"

A small lump obstructed her throat. "What do you mean? Are you saying I have to make a choice?"

Slowly he lowered his chin and turned his head. In his eyes she saw a strange, almost opaque glaze. "Yes, I suppose I am."

Her own eyes widened and she raised her voice. "You're telling me I have to choose between you and my job as mayor of this town?"

She sounded like a fishwife again, but this time she made no effort to temper the shrillness.

"No," he said, and she knew a moment of relief. "I'm saying you have to choose between *us* and your job."

"That isn't fair."

"I think it is."

Kate closed her eyes and sighed. Perhaps this conversation could be salvaged yet. "I don't want to argue with you, Mitch."

"Fine!" he snapped, rolling out of bed so fast he fell to the floor.

"Are you all right?" Kate asked. She sat up and raised the wick until the coal oil lamp burned as bright as a torch.

"I don't need that damned light! I've adapted quite well to getting dressed in the dark."

The lump in her throat increased to the size of a goose egg. "Where are you going?" she whispered.

"Home!"

"Mitch, please—"

He jerked on his shirt and stuffed it into his jeans without bothering to button it. "It's no good, Kate. It was fun while it lasted, but I won't be tied to a woman who cares more about causes than she does about me. I made that mistake once."

Through eyes stinging with unshed tears, Kate watched him scramble around on the floor, looking for his boots. One was wedged between the bureau and the wall, and the other was under the bed. He plopped down on the chair and yanked them on. She swallowed hard, trying to dislodge the lump, but it wouldn't go away.

This wasn't happening, she told herself. She was only dreaming. She'd wake up in a few minutes and find Mitch softly snoring at her side. She'd smooth a palm over his hair and say a prayer of thanksgiving. Tomorrow she'd tell him about her nightmare, and they would laugh together over the whole thing. But first she had to finish dreaming so she could wake up.

"You've been married before?" she squeaked.

"No, thank God." He snatched his hat off the bureau and picked up his gun belt from the chair. He was leaving. He was actually leaving. And he wasn't coming back.

The realization hit her hard. Kate threw the covers back and swung her legs off the bed, but the hard, flinty glare in his dark brown eyes stopped her cold.

"That's one mistake I haven't made yet."

She couldn't have understood him correctly. "What did you say?"

"You heard me, Kate. I've made a lot of mistakes in my life. Marrying you won't be one of them."

She didn't move, couldn't move. The lump in her throat plummeted to her stomach and her chest constricted, cutting off her breath. For a moment she thought her heart had surely stopped beating.

His footfalls echoed through the house as his parting words echoed through her head. . . . *I've made a lot of mistakes . . . marrying you won't be one of them.*

The back door slammed into its frame so hard the entire house vibrated. Kate looked at the other side of the bed—the empty side of the bed. One of his socks was draped across the footboard, and the lightweight blanket she favored and he hated was twisted into a heap near the end of the mattress. Her gaze traveled upward, across the wrinkles on the sheet and to the stack of pillows lying against the headboard. The top one still carried the impression of his head.

Slowly, methodically, she reached for the pillow and brought it to her face. She closed her eyes and breathed deeply of his essence, which lingered on the white linen case.

And then she fell forward on the bed, buried her head in the pillow, and cried until she had no more tears to shed.

Chapter Seventeen

It started raining the morning after Mitch walked out and didn't stop for a week. Kate wasn't the least bit sure the sky dropped a single tear more than her heart shed.

Using a summer cold as her excuse, she didn't go to church on Sunday, to the council meeting on Monday night, or to her office all week, except for a brief time Monday morning to check in with Hardy and pick up some files she could work on at home.

"Goodness gracious, Miz McBride," Hardy said, "you look plum awful!"

Kate wasn't the least bit offended. "I feel plum awful."

And she did. A misery of the soul, she was learning, was far worse than any physical malady she could have contracted. With most bodily ailments you could see the light at the end of the tunnel. You knew that, at some point, you were either going to get well or die. Kate perceived no light, not even a glimmer.

From time to time Kate tried to tell herself that this misery stemmed from self-pity, which she could cure in short order. But she knew it didn't. It was a misery born of conflicting values, values that formed the bases of what made her and Mitch individually unique. It was a misery born of sincere regret for what might have been.

She spent most of the week searching her soul, trying to find a solution, but all solutions involved compromising the self she had so recently discovered existed. With discovery had come acceptance, which in turn had opened her heart, enabling her for the first time in her life to give and receive love. Though she knew the Golden Rule by heart, now she understood that Jesus was also saying that self-love was a prerequisite to loving others.

Because she had learned to love herself, she could love Mitch. If she forced herself to deny the most important precepts of her soul, she couldn't love herself anymore. That brought her to an impasse.

It was a vicious circle, this path her soul-searching made, and circles had no end. The only hope for resolution was to break the circle and stretch out its line toward eternity. And though Kate searched through every link of the chain, she could not find a portion she could successfully sever.

The loss of hope brought grief, the deepest, most heartrending grief she could imagine.

Mitch dreaded seeing Kate at the council meeting. When Sally Myers announced Kate's illness and presided in her stead Mitch found himself both relieved and disappointed. Dammit! He wanted to see her, desperately wanted to see her, yet he couldn't afford to. The minute she turned those jade-green eyes his way, he'd melt. He'd forget everything he'd ever promised himself about women like Kate and go running to her and tell her he was sorry.

And would he be sorry. For the rest of his life, he'd be sorry.

He began counting down the days remaining in his probationary period, marking them off on his office calendar and trying to take sustenance from the thick, black *X*s.

Somehow he had to manage to stay away from Kate as much as possible during the next five weeks. Somehow he had to last that long.

Summer came, bringing with it hot, dusty days and warm, balmy nights.

The street crew finished digging ditches and started laying pipe. Since Monroe Terrell, the engineer Marty had hired to supervise the acetylene gas plant, needed a temporary base of operations near the center of town, Kate gladly gave him her office. It gave her a good excuse to stay home, which was the only place she felt truly comfortable these days.

How strange, she thought, to want to stay at home, but for the first time in years the house seemed to welcome her. From time to time she still heard a baby cry, and though her heart quivered with each imaginary whimper, the flutter was now one of hope rather than despair.

Kate could no more explain her new attitude than she could define the source of her hope, but she clung to both with every ounce of emotional energy she could muster. She'd come through the week of her grief feeling drained but somewhat renewed. The grief brought her to terms with herself, the only acceptable terms available to her. She loved Mitch with all the emotion she had to give and she wanted him in her life, but not at the expense of her soul. She thought of him often, replaying the times they'd spent together and wishing things could be different between them.

Fortunately, she supposed, town business occupied

much of her time. To compensate for not being accessible at the town hall, she called informal council and committee meetings and hosted them at her house, and she delegated more responsibilities to her council members. Julia hired a young man to replace Gabby and took on the job of supervising his duties. Liza became public spokeswoman for the group, and Sally prepared all proposals and reports. Stella retained custody of the town's finances, while Marty, of course, had her hands full with the various public works projects.

Thankfully, Marty and Julia no longer jumped down each other's throats at every turn, and Kate didn't question their silent truce. They were all working together as a team, moving things along with the efficiency of a well-oiled machine. The townsfolk saw this. They saw as well the progress and change, and fewer of them grumbled. Kate took the general acceptance of her program coupled with the cessation of harassment she had suffered as a sign that all was well in Paradise.

All was not well in Paradise.

Mitch couldn't put his finger on it, but he knew something was wrong.

"Don't you sense it?" he asked Skip.

"Naw, can't say as I do. What is it, you reckon?"

Mitch scratched his head and felt like a fool for bringing it up. "I don't know. But things are too quiet. Entirely too quiet. No one's made any threats or bothered the mayor now for several weeks. Something's wrong."

"Just be thankful everyone's quieted down," Skip said.

"Maybe you're right," Mitch allowed, "but keep a

close watch out anyway, will you? I don't trust those scoundrels, whoever they are."

And I don't want anything to happen to Kate, he added mentally.

Lord, how his heart hurt every time he thought of her! Why did he always fall for a woman with a cause? Why, just once, couldn't he be content with a woman who fit his image of a proper lady?

Jennie and Kate corresponded on a weekly basis.

"Patience and persistence must be our twin virtues," Jennie wrote. "We will overcome."

Kate kept Jennie informed of the activities of the Paradise Woman Suffrage Association, which within three weeks boasted a membership of thirty-seven and was growing rapidly. At Jennie's direction, the Paradise group sent regular messages to state legislators, asking that they grant women the right to participate in both county and state elections, and several enthusiastic women were drafting articles for the state association's newspaper.

Although her letters were official communications from the Kansas Woman Suffrage Association and typed by a secretary, Jennie often penned personal notes to Kate at the bottom. "How are things between you and the marshal?" she wrote, and, "Don't close that door." Kate knew Jennie would eventually demand a response, but for the time being she couldn't supply one.

One morning in mid-June, Kate woke up with a queasy stomach, which she attributed to the greasy pork chop she'd eaten for supper the night before. She wouldn't have thought anything else of it had she not been bothered the following morning with the same complaint. The second time sent her flying to the calendar.

Kate's heart fluttered in her chest and her knees wobbled. Was it possible that she wasn't barren after all? Could she be carrying Mitch's child?

For a moment her spirits soared, then Kate, as practical as ever, forced herself to settle down and face reality. There were other possibilities to consider. Although her monthly times had always occurred with unfailing regularity, she'd heard that age could affect a woman's cycles. She *was* twenty-eight, she reminded herself. And the stomach ailment could be as easily explained away. After all, she'd eaten so sparsely the week of her grief, she'd probably knocked her system all out of whack.

She refused to allow herself to become overly excited about something that would, in all likelihood, turn out to be nothing. Despite her resolve, she didn't attempt to control the lilt in her voice or the spriteliness in her step. And with each successive waking to an uneasy stomach her hope grew.

A week later, she pulled out her patterns and began knitting a pair of booties.

Mitch crossed out the block on his calendar that represented Saturday, June 23. By his calculations, he had fifteen days left as the marshal of Paradise.

Fifteen days. He had a whopping fifteen days to settle his account with Kate McBride once and for all.

He hadn't heard a word from her in four weeks. Four weeks! For twenty-eight days he'd waited for her to come crawling to him. He reckoned he could wait twenty-eight years and she'd still be holding tight to her belief that she was his equal.

And that was what all this was about. She'd never

said so, but that was what she thought. He'd heard the speech enough from Jennie, who just happened to be a bit more articulate and a hell of a lot more militant about this equality crap.

Hell, Kate had been elected mayor of a pretty good-sized town. She was only the second female mayor ever, and the first to head an all-female government. Why couldn't she be happy with those accomplishments? Why couldn't she just quietly bow out and let someone else step in and run the town? He'd bet Sally could do it, and Doc Myers wouldn't mind. Doc believed in this equality crap.

Mitch chewed on the end of his pencil and thought about that for a minute. Yep, he'd be willing to bet Kate would back down in a heartbeat if the right person put it to her the right way. And then they could be married and live happily ever after, just like in the fairy tales.

All this time he'd been waiting when what he should've been doing was taking the bull by the horns and setting a plan in motion. He was the man; it was up to him. From what he understood, Doc had started the whole thing. Maybe Doc was the man to end it.

He pulled out his pocket watch and checked the time: nine o'clock. He'd just mosey on over to Oak Street and see if there was a light on in the Myers's parlor.

"You must be joking!" Doc said, his expression registering his disbelief. "Why would I, or anyone else for that matter, want to talk Kate into resigning? She's the best thing that's happened to this town in years. Maybe ever."

"Because . . . because . . ." Mitch searched for a reason that didn't involve wanting to make her Mrs.

Mitchell Dawson. "Because she's in physical danger."

That ought to do it! Mitch grinned at this flash of ingenuity.

"What makes you say that?"

Mitch found himself searching again. "Well, there was the incident with Obediah Stringfellow."

Doc waved a hand in dismissal. "That was weeks ago. No one has posed a threat since. Have they?"

"Someone tied a death-threat message around a rock and tossed it through one of the windows at the town hall."

Doc frowned. "Was that before or after Stringfellow's trial?"

Mitch rubbed his chin while he thought back. "Before, I think."

"Anything else?"

"You know some men egged Kate's house one night. Then somebody dumped out all her canisters and made a mess in her kitchen."

Doc smiled and shook his head. "Neither qualifies as physical danger, Mitch. And if anyone seriously intended to carry out that anonymous death threat, they would have tried it already." He paused long enough to light his pipe. "All this is nothing more than a few disgruntled folks lashing back the only way they know how. People are happier now that they can see the evidence of Kate's enterprise."

He puffed for a moment, his brow furrowed in thought. Mitch couldn't fault Doc's logic, but now he wondered if perhaps the physician wasn't considering the problem from a different angle. He might be able to salvage this yet.

Doc blew a smoke ring at the ceiling and grinned. "Are you sure there isn't another, maybe more personal reason you want Kate out of her position?"

God! Was his motive that transparent? Mitch felt

his cheeks flame and figured it was time to take his leave. Obviously Doc wasn't going to help him.

"I'm just worried about her," Mitch said. "Thanks anyway, Dr. Myers."

On his way back to the jailhouse he shooed home three adolescent boys who were loitering on a corner and checked the doors of businesses along the way to make sure they were locked.

Everything was quiet. Entirely too quiet for a Saturday night. Hell, most of the stores had closed less than an hour earlier. On a normal Saturday night a host of men would be sitting on the edges of boardwalks and leaning against wagons, smoking and swapping yarns. But now that he'd run the three boys home there was no one else in sight. His observation to Skip reverberated in his head: "Something's wrong. Don't you sense it?"

Skip Hudson and Doc Myers might not be worried, but Mitch was. He took his time making his rounds and came to the conclusion that if anyone was up to any mischief that night, it wasn't in Paradise.

Puzzled, he leaned against a picket fence, took out his pouch of tobacco, and rolled a cigarette. He smoked it down to a nub before he realized the fence at his back belonged to Kate McBride. Without conscious direction, he ended his rounds every night at her house. Just habit, he told himself, a habit he needed to break.

Oh, well, in a little over two weeks he'd be gone anyway. Today's *Chronicle* had carried three advertisements for deputies and one for a policeman in Kansas City. He'd been watching the paper and the bulletin boards in the post and telegraph offices for weeks now, hoping to see a notice for a town marshal, but all the law enforcement announcements were for subordinate positions. Mitch didn't know how well he could handle a job where he wasn't in command, but he supposed he didn't have much of a choice anymore. Come Monday, he'd answer the advertisements and maybe send letters to the U.S. Marshal and the Texas Rangers. Hell, he didn't care where he went so long as he could find another job as a lawman.

He flipped the glowing butt into the street and headed down her driveway. What the hell; he might as well follow habit for another night. After all, he'd spent almost every night for the last four weeks sleeping on the chaise in her gazebo. If his instincts were right, if some person or persons were planning to harm Kate, he needed to be close enough to stop them—and, hopefully, to catch the scoundrels this time.

And that was the only reason he tortured himself every night. He was just doing his duty.

He knew better, but that's what he told himself anyway. Like taking a pill with a tablespoon of buttermilk, it made the truth easier to swallow.

Mitch leaned back on the chaise, laid his head on his open palms, and gazed at the dark windows on the back side of Kate's house. For a long time he lay awake, fighting the desire to march himself up to her back door and beat upon its frame until she let him in.

The sun rose early in a cloudless sky, bringing with it the promise of another hot day. It was the relentless heat, finally, that disturbed Kate's slumber.

She stretched and yawned and resisted getting up. Though she was, by nature, an early riser, of late she'd let dawn slip well past her rising more often than not. Another sign that life grew within her? she wondered, smiling broadly at the prospect.

If that was the case—and every day she became

more firmly convinced that it was, indeed—she had some planning to do.

Her major concern lay with the child. While she had no great desire to align herself permanently with Mitch Dawson, she couldn't allow her child to suffer the stigma of illegitimacy. Of course, she couldn't swear she actually was in the family way, but if she was, her body would confirm it within a few months. That bought her some time. And if it was true, she would swallow her pride and talk to Mitch. She'd tell him all she wanted was his name. After the baby was born they could seek a quiet divorce and he could go his merry way.

Kate counted up the months on her fingers. The baby would be due in late February. Not quite eight months away, but ample time to prepare herself; ample time to acquire another name.

To acquire another name . . .

Kate sat up and piled pillows at her back. What was she thinking? She didn't need to acquire another name! She was a widow, for heaven's sake! All she had to do was pack up and move to a big city and tell folks there that she was a widow; they would naturally assume that the child belonged to her late husband.

But would that be fair to Mitch? her conscience niggled. Didn't she owe him the privilege of learning that he was to be a father? Didn't she owe him the right to give his name to his own child?

She heaved a huge sigh, dragged herself out of bed, and headed for the bathroom. She didn't have to consider all the alternatives right now, she told herself. She didn't even know for sure that she carried a child in her womb. Time was on her side. Mitch wasn't going anywhere . . .

"Oh, my!" she mumbled through the foam on her toothbrush, glancing up at the mirror and seeing the dismay that knifed through her written all over her face. She'd forgotten all about his probationary term, which was up—she did some fast calculating—in two weeks!

That wasn't enough time. If she shared her suspicions with him now, he'd marry her immediately. She knew he would. Mitch Dawson might be narrow-minded, but he was honorable.

But what if she was wrong? What if she wasn't pregnant? Did she dare take the risk of waiting to see?

She groaned in pure frustration, rinsed her mouth, and vowed to have a talk with Mitch whether she wanted to or not. But it could wait, she decided, for another week. Maybe he'd come to her in the meantime.

Time was quickly running out. When Kate closed her eyes she could see the sand spilling into the base of the glass, but she held to her resolve to give him a week.

Sunday arrived again, and Kate went looking for the marshal. He wasn't at church—not that she'd expected to see him there. When she didn't find him at his office she thought maybe she'd catch him at the café. He wasn't there, either. Kate sat down with Skip and Julia and ordered a plate lunch. She had to eat somewhere, she supposed, and this gave her an excuse to stay downtown awhile longer.

"Are you coming to the game?" Skip asked over dessert.

"What game?"

"The baseball game this afternoon," he explained between bites of juicy apple pie.

"I hadn't really thought about it," she said.

"You can sit with me," Julia offered.

"You have to come," Skip insisted. "This is going to be one exciting game. We're three up with the Blue Shirts. Whoever loses this game has to host the Fourth of July barbecue next week."

Kate recalled the last baseball game she'd attended—the day Jennie Clark had come to town. Mitch was playing first base that day . . .

"I haven't been to a game in weeks," Kate said, attempting to sound nonchalant. "Do you still have the same players?"

"Every one of them," Skip replied, grinning. Then he lowered his voice and said, "Confidentially, they're all great, except Max. Something's happened to his pitching arm. Most of the time he still gets the ball over the plate, but he just can't seem to throw 'em as hard as he used to. The Blue Shirts have been getting hit after hit off Max's pitching."

"Don't you have a relief pitcher?" Kate asked.

"We don't have a single extra player, but the Blue Shirts have five."

Kate's interest was piqued. "Why?"

Skip hung his head sheepishly. "We're known as the mayor's team. Some of the guys who would be playing with us don't have the backbone to take the ribbing."

"The *mayor's* team?" Kate's brow ruffled in warranted confusion. "I don't recall sanctioning one team over the other."

"You didn't. But most of us are either in the town's employ or husbands of the councilwomen."

Kate ran a list of the White Shirts' team members through her head and realized Skip was right.

"You will come?" Julia asked hopefully.

"Of course," Kate said, smiling. "How can I miss seeing my own team play in such an important game?"

Besides, she thought, Mitch would be there. And afterwards she'd ask him if he planned to stay on in

Paradise. As long as he said, "Yes," everything would be all right. But if he said, "No" . . .

There was no sense in crossing bridges before one got to them. She turned her attention to her pie and coffee and concentrated on holding up her end of the conversation. But all the while her heart beat an erratic rhythm and a niggling voice told her she should be finalizing an alternative plan.

Mitch was up at bat. It was the top of the eighth inning and, with a score of eight to three, the White Shirts were down by five runs. They already had two outs. Ebenezer Dahlmer, the only runner on the field, leaned into his knee at second base and yelled at Mitch to hit a homer. *It's up to me,* Mitch thought, flexing his shoulders and setting his bat.

On the pitcher's mound, Simon Carlson let fly with an inside curve that cut the corner of the plate and whirled right past Mitch's knees.

"Str-r-rike one!" Josiah piped.

Simon smacked his gum and grinned. For a little guy, he sure could throw a baseball. He rared back and hurled the ball, which headed directly for the center of the strike zone. Mitch swung hard and missed.

"Str-r-rike two!"

Mitch winced, circled the bat high over his head to take the tension out of his shoulders, and got ready for Simon's next pitch.

Mitch watched it spin into an arc. Although it looked like it was going to be high, Mitch didn't trust it. It was now or never. He swung the bat and caught the ball off center.

Jethro Smith nearly knocked Mitch over, getting into position to catch the pop-up foul. Mitch backed way out of the batter's box and held his breath. Jethro sat in a tight squat right on top of the croaker sack, his glove over his mouth and his eyes squinting into the bright sky. The white leather sphere kept climbing. *Damn!* Mitch thought. If only he'd straightened it out . . . if only Jethro didn't catch it . . .

When the ball started its descent it looked like it was aiming straight for Jethro's glove. Mitch closed his eyes and let the bat slide down his hand.

The ball hit with a loud thump. Enthusiastic cheers erupted, and Josiah hollered at Mitch to get back up to the plate. Mitch opened his eyes to see the ball rolling around Josiah's feet and Jethro scrambling to pick it up. How Jethro had ever missed catching it Mitch couldn't figure, but someone would tell him all about it after the game. For the moment he had one more chance to get a hit, and he was bound and determined that was exactly what he was going to do.

Kate's heart went out to Mitch as she watched him step back up to the plate. If the White Shirts wanted to win, they'd better start doing some catching up soon. And it was up to Mitch to get them going again.

She could see the tendons standing out on his neck and the deep lines crinkling around his eyes as he watched Simon Carlson wind up. There wasn't so much as a whisper among the crowd; just the sound of a lone mockingbird chirping away in a nearby tree. Even the wind hushed in deference to the moment.

The ball left Simon's hand with a *whoosh*. It moved so fast, Kate's gaze couldn't keep up. A loud crack rent the stillness, hurling the ball up, maybe eight or nine feet in the air, just high enough to prevent one of the infielders from catching it. At the speed and direction it was going, they probably couldn't have managed anyway, Kate thought. It flew toward right field, well over James Larue's head, and onward.

Kate jumped to her feet and cheered. Out of the corner of her eye she saw Eb hit the croaker sack at home base while Mitch rounded second. The ball hit the ground and rolled. Both Larue and Mort Moffet, who played first base for the Blue Shirts, chased after it. They ran into each other, jumped apart, and tumbled to the ground in a melange of flailing legs and arms. Before they could right themselves and get the ball, Mitch crossed the plate. The crowd went wild.

The two scores provided the momentum the White Shirts needed to catch up. Skip, who was next at bat, got a good, solid base hit, then Kelton Ziegler whacked the ball to left field for a double. Hardy's fly, which Obediah Stringfellow dropped, brought Skip and Kelton home and upped the score to seven for the White Shirts.

"We're only one behind!" Hardy called to Doc, who was up to bat. "Wallop me a good one!"

Though Doc put more strength behind his swings than Kate realized he possessed, he struck out. The White Shirts collected their gloves and took their places on the field.

"If we can just hold them," Julia said, "maybe we can score another couple of runs next inning and beat them."

"I wouldn't count on it," Kate said, watching a slow but true pitch leave Max's hand. Mort Moffet, who almost always struck out, hit it hard enough to get on first base.

Max shook his head and rubbed his right elbow. James Larue picked up the bat.

"Easy out," Julia commented.

Kate hoped so. But again, Max threw the ball too

slow, and Larue made a base hit. Max rubbed his elbow again.

Julia groaned. "We have to do something. Max's elbow is bothering him. Someone needs to switch places with him."

"Can anyone else on the team pitch?"

Julia shook her head. "Not nearly as well as Max usually does. Look!" She pointed. "They've called time out."

Mitch, Skip, and Doc converged on Max. When they split up Skip was left standing on the pitcher's mound and Max headed for Skip's position at short-stop.

"Oh, no," Julia moaned. "Skip can't pitch!"

Skip threw four consecutive balls to Simon Carlson, which loaded the bases. Mitch took over at the mound, and Jethro Smith stepped up to bat.

"We're in deep trouble," Julia lamented. "Jethro always gets a hit."

Jethro smacked the first pitch out of Mitch's hand and made it all the way to third base before Eb recovered the ball from center field and hurled it to Skip.

While Julia was moaning and groaning, Obediah sauntered into the batter's box. "Y'all might as well call it quits," he hollered, spitting out a stream of tobacco juice and backhanding his mouth. "Ya ain't got nobody can pitch worth a Gol-dern. Why, the mayor can pitch better'n any o' you guys."

For a split second Kate frowned in confusion. And then she knew that Obediah Stringfellow was among the men who'd egged her house. How else would he know how well she could pitch? She looked at him closely, watched him turn red in the face and heard him sputter something about how he'd *bet* she could pitch better. She jumped to her feet, intending to tell Mitch to arrest him, when she realized she had no proof and Stringfellow would deny having any part in the caper.

Mitch called time out again and motioned for the entire team to join him on the mound. They huddled up, and though she couldn't hear much beyond a general buzz, someone screamed out, "No way!"

It appeared they were taking a vote on something, and then Mitch was coming toward her—along with Doc and Max and Skip. Whatever could they want? Maybe they were going to ask her if she wanted them to take Stringfellow into custody.

They walked right up to her, so close she could count the beads of sweat dripping into their eyes.

"Stringfellow's right," Mitch said. "You can pitch better than any of us. Will you do it?"

Chapter Eighteen

"Pardon?" Kate asked, moving her head from side to side in an effort to clear it. She couldn't possibly have heard him correctly.

"We want you to pitch," Skip said. "Mitch says you're good, and we believe him."

"I don't know . . ." Kate hedged, looking down at her white handkerchief-linen dress and thinking she'd probably make a complete fool of herself out there on the mound. Besides—

"What if I can't hit the ball? And I don't know if I can use a glove, either."

"We'll back you up," Doc said.

"And you don't have to worry about batting," Max put in. "I can do that when it's time. I just can't seem to pitch anymore. My elbow is killing me."

"You have to try, Kate," Julia implored. "Please say you'll try."

Kate tried another tack. "I don't know how I can manage in all these skirts."

"Your dress is the right color," Doc quipped.

"All you have to do," Mitch said, his dark brown eyes warm and pleading, "is stand on the mound and throw the ball to the catcher. We'll do the rest."

"Let's play ball!" Josiah hollered from his umpire's spot behind the plate.

Kate took a deep breath and called herself nine kinds of idiot. "All right," she said at last. "I'll try. But don't expect much."

As though she were one of them, the men slapped her on the back, leaving dirty handprints all over the white linen. Mitch took her hand in his, laid the ball in her palm, and folded her fingers around it. He held her hand just a mite longer than was proper, but no one besides Kate seemed to notice. She dared to raise her gaze to his and read both encouragement and regret in his dark brown eyes. And then he winked at her and the regret disappeared. Suddenly he was a kid all over again, and she was the tomboy who had played ball with all the neighborhood boys in Topeka.

"You can do it," he whispered. "Just pretend you're throwing eggs."

Kate nodded, her throat too full for speech.

Max handed her his glove and then moved to the bench. Kate walked up to the mound amid much hooting and caterwauling. She slid her left hand into the damp leather glove and spit on the ball. People howled at that, but Kate hardly heard them. Her mind was on the ball, on her aim, on throwing a perfect strike over home plate, a strike Stringfellow couldn't hit.

She twirled the ball in her hand until the grip felt right, reached back over her shoulder, twisting her body to the right and raising her left knee almost as high as her waist. Then, in one smooth, fluid motion, her arm came around, her foot came down, and the ball sailed from her hand.

Mitch was so preoccupied with watching her movements, he didn't see the ball leave her hand. But he heard it hit Skip's mitt. *Whap!*

Skip fell backwards while Stringfellow blinked stupidly and looked first at Kate and then at Skip, and then back at Kate. "Well," Stringfellow said, working a wad of tobacco into the side of his jaw, "throw the ball, missy. I'm ready."

"She did throw it, you dimwit," Josiah said. "Strike one!"

Stringfellow shook his head and looked back at Skip, who rose on his toes and tossed the ball back to Kate. She missed catching it, removed the glove, and laid it on the ground when she picked up the ball.

The next two pitches came as fast, as smooth, and as accurate as the first one. Stringfellow never moved his bat. "You're out!" Josiah proclaimed, grinning and pointing toward the Blue Shirts' bench.

Kate, who seemed to have no trouble catching the ball bare-handed, struck out the next two batters almost as easily as she had Stringfellow. Mitch watched his team members crowd around Kate, most of them taking their turns at pumping her hand just like she was a man. He grunted and jogged from first base to the bench without so much as glancing her way again.

Where in the Sam Hill had she learned to pitch like that? he mentally grumbled. It wasn't natural for a woman to throw a ball overhand, much less do it so well. And catch bare-handed, too. He was almost sorry he'd suggested they let her pitch.

Even though Kate wasn't batting, several of the team members insisted she sit in the middle of the bench. Mitch, she noted, sat on one end and stared moodily into space. The men didn't give her time to question his strange attitude.

"We might just win this game, Miz McBride," Hardy said, his face beaming.

"Thanks to you," John Carey said. "I was the one

screaming 'no' out there in the huddle, but I was wrong. Where did you learn to pitch like that?"

"Back home in Topeka," she said. "Baseball was our favorite game. We didn't use gloves. I'm not even sure they were making them then." She rubbed her right shoulder, which was beginning to ache. "That was a long time ago."

"Aw, Miz McBride," Hardy said, "you aren't *that* old."

A loud crack resounded from home plate and they looked up to see Tully Patterson running for first. He made it—barely.

"My turn," John said, grinning. He got a base hit as well, and Max got up to bat.

"We've got 'em rattled," Skip said on a snicker. "If we can score five more runs, we can beat 'em, now that you're pitching for us."

"What's he doing batting?" Mort hollered from first base.

"It's my turn," Max hollered back.

"No, it ain't," Mort insisted. "It's Miz McBride's. She took your place. Remember?"

"She can't run in those petticoats," Doc said. "Let Max bat."

Mort called time out and gathered his team into a huddle. Nine heads bobbed, and then they broke up. Mort walked toward home plate. "He ain't gonna bat. If he does, then we win by default."

"There's no such rule," Skip said. "Besides, Max is on this team, too, and he played last inning. He gets to take his turn."

"All right," Mort said. "Max can bat. But the lady bats after him. You can appoint someone to run for her, but she has to bat."

"Now wait just a goldern minute! I'm the umpire," Josiah put in. In unison, the White Shirts turned optimistic looks his way. "And I say that sounds fair enough. Batter up!"

Max caught a piece of the ball a couple of times, but he ended up striking out. He shuffled back to the bench rubbing his elbow. "I'm sorry, guys," he said. "My right arm just doesn't want to work right today. But I can run for you, Miz McBride."

Kate nodded and moved slowly to the plate. She hadn't held a bat in so long, she couldn't figure out how to put her hands on it. Max showed her, and the Blue Shirts made no attempt to stifle their raucous laughter.

She didn't know when she'd felt quite so out of place. She squinted at the bright sunlight and called back the image of a ten-year-old girl wearing a baggy shirt tucked into Tommy Jaspar's outgrown trousers and a worn-out derby that belonged to her father and was so big she had to fold the brim up and pin it over her ears to hold it on. She called back the tension she'd felt standing at the plate, holding a bat over her shoulder and listening for the rush of wind the ball created as it came toward her. She called back the exhilaration of swinging the bat with all her tiny might, hearing the wood crack against the ball and feeling the bat's vibrations in her hand. And she called back the elation that came from whacking the ball so far out of the diamond she could make it all around the bases and still have time to stand and watch the outfield players scrambling for it.

The second she filled her heart with the recollections, Simon pitched the ball. Kate wasn't ready.

"Strike one!" Josiah bellowed.

The Blue Shirts in the field snickered and Jethro, the catcher, taunted her. "Easy out! Easy out!"

"Come on, Mayor," Max said from behind her, "swing at it!"

Kate nodded and braced herself. Simon released the ball. She watched it closely this time, swiped the bat at it, and missed.

"You're swinging too late," Max coached. "And keep the bat level. Here it comes."

That time, Kate hit the ball. She knew she did by the way the bat shivered and shook and transferred its vibrations to her arms and chest. But she couldn't see where it went. Max was running to first base, and the White Shirts on the bench were whooping and hollering. The crowd was cheering, and the Blue Shirts were all turned with their backs to her and shading their eyes with their hands, looking, she supposed, for the ball.

Where had it gone? So far out they couldn't find it?

From behind her, Jethro muttered, "You crazy idiots." Before she could question him, he knocked her to the dirt and tromped on her leg getting past her. From the ground she watched him pounce on the ball, which was lodged in the short grass no more than six feet in front of home plate. Laughter racked her frame so hard she had trouble sitting up.

She watched Tully hesitate on third base, run toward home, then turn around and run back. John stayed firm on second, and Max made it to first without any difficulty at all.

"Here, ma'am, let me help you up."

Kate looked up at the voice and into Eb's smiling face. She took his hand and he pulled her to her feet.

"You done fine," he said. "We've got 'em now."

Amid a chorus of cheers, she dusted herself off and returned to the bench. She looked straight at Mitch on her way past him, but he kept his eyes on the field and his mouth shut. What in heaven's name was wrong with him? she wondered. It had been his idea to ask her to pitch, and now all he wanted to do was pout. His odd behavior didn't make any sense.

"What happened?" she asked Skip the instant she sat down.

"You hit the ball, Miz McBride. You hit it hard."

"But you hit it almost straight down," Hardy added. "If you would've straightened it out, that would've been a homer for sure."

Eb got a base hit, which brought Tully home, and then Mitch hit the ball right into Mort's glove. Kate's heart sank. If they got another out before they got three more runs, the game would be over. There was no sense in the Blue Shirts batting again if they were ahead.

Skip got up to bat and Kate crossed her fingers in her lap. "Come on, Skip," she called. "Get us another run!"

He bunted.

Kate's words caught in her throat and she coughed, trying to clear them out. Her eyes stung and her chest burned, but through the haze of pain she saw Simon and Jethro both going after the ball, which had landed almost dead center between the mound and home plate and was rolling backwards. By the time Simon backed off and Jethro picked it up, John was sliding into home, and Skip was safe on first. Her swiftly released breath joined a chorus of similar sighs from up and down the bench.

Two, she thought, tightening her wrapped fingers. *We just need two more.*

Kelton popped three consecutive fouls, then got a base hit.

One. Just one more and we're tied.

Hardy picked up the bat and shuffled his big feet over to the box. He was so nervous, the bat trembled in his hands.

Poor Hardy! The pressure has to be killing him.

Kate held her breath. Simon threw an outside curve that missed the plate. Hardy stood his ground and Josiah called, "Ball one!"

Simon threw another ball, and then another. Kate breathed easier. One more and Hardy would walk.

But the next one wasn't a ball. It was, without a doubt, a strike—and Hardy didn't even swing. Simon threw another strike, and still Hardy didn't move. The count was full, and Hardy's knees were knocking together. The White Shirts were shouting encouragement and the Blue Shirts were jeering and the crowd was going wild.

"Come on, Hardy," Kate whispered, her own knees wobbling under her petticoats. "You can do it. I know you can."

Simon leaned way back and let the ball fly. Kate watched it glide through the air, smooth and swift and sure. Her chest tightened up and her stomach tied itself in knots and her fingers gripped each other so securely she wondered if she'd ever get them loose.

And then the ball curved inward. Before Hardy could move out of the way, it hit him in the ribs. He crumpled forward, and Doc dashed to the plate. Silence fell over the crowd as Doc mashed and Hardy yelped. Then Hardy unfolded to his full, gangly height and Josiah hollered, "Take your base."

That tied them up. Even if Doc got out, they were tied. And that would put the pressure on Kate to pitch a no-hitter inning. But Doc got on base, then Tully hit a home run, and the White Shirts were suddenly five runs ahead. John got a double and it was back to Max, whose right elbow was still giving him fits. He struck out, but it didn't matter. They were ahead. Way ahead.

"Go out there and do it again," Skip said, patting

Kate's shoulder. She stared at Mitch, hoping for a show of support, but he refused to look at her.

"Three up and three down!" Max hollered from the bench.

Now that most of the pressure was off, Kate relaxed. Too much. The first two batters got solid hits, but quick fielding kept them from advancing more than one base each. Then Mort got up to bat and pinned her with a look that said, "You can't strike me out any more than you can run this town."

She threw three straight strikes and Mort drifted back to the bench. As Julia had said earlier, James Larue was an easy out. That made two. One more, and the game would be over.

Kate spit on the ball and rolled it in her hands while Simon crouched low in the batter's box. The sun bore down on her back and sweat trickled off her brow and into her eyes. Resisting an urge to use her hem, she swiped at her forehead with the back of her hand and tried to blink out the salty drops of perspiration. She rolled her right shoulder back in an attempt to relieve the ache that had set in and didn't seem to want to go away.

The first ball she threw for Simon sailed wild to the left. The second hit the ground two feet in front of the plate. The third slid straight past his waistline and into Skip's glove.

"Strike one!" Josiah called.

The sound of those two words surged through her like a bolt of lightning, reviving, regenerating, electrifying, catching her spirit afire. She hurled two more neat strikes and found herself hurled skyward atop the uplifted hands of Eb and Skip and Hardy. The other six White Shirts joined the wave, and the crowd rushed onto the field.

But amid all the shouting and laughing and merrymaking, Kate's heart yearned to hear one voice, to see one smile, to catch the gleam of approval from one pair of eyes. Her gaze sought out Mitch Dawson, who jogged along with the team but was the only one whose eyes were not turned her way.

You're a damn fool idiot! Mitch silently berated himself as he jogged off the field with the team. *Why did you have to go and tell them she could pitch?*

Even as he thought it, Mitch knew he was being unfair. They had won, and winning was everything, he supposed. But to have a woman pull them out? If that didn't cap the climax, nothing did.

If it had been another woman, maybe he wouldn't feel so angry. But it was Kate, dammit! He wanted her to be soft and feminine—ladylike. He'd almost convinced himself she could be, and then, wham! She proved him wrong. Just like that. She proved once again that she belonged to the third variety. She could wear all the petticoats and carry all the scented handkerchiefs she wanted to, but those things didn't make her a lady. She could return his lust with more passion than propriety allowed and melt him with a smile, but she was too outspoken, too tough, and too smart to be a lady.

Well, what did you expect, Dawson? his conscience goaded him. *Did you honestly think she'd go out there and make a fool of herself in front of all these people? Did you for one minute think she wouldn't give it her best? How would you be feeling right now if she'd proved you a liar?*

"Aw, to hell with it!" Mitch mumbled.

"What's that?" Doc asked.

"Nothing!"

"Don't take that last bat so hard, Mitch," Doc said.

"That homer you hit was great. We all have our bad moments."

"Don't we, though?" Mitch heard the cynicism in his voice and made no effort to erase it.

If Doc heard it, he ignored it. "You coming over to our house for the celebration?"

"Naw, but thanks anyway. I've been away from the office too long as it is."

"If you change your mind . . ." Doc's voice trailed off as he moved among the crowd, shaking hands and inviting folks to the party.

Mitch watched him for a moment. Then he finally allowed his gaze to wander upwards to where Hardy's big hands held Kate aloft. She bounced along with the team, smiling and waving at people and acting just like the Queen of Sheba.

And then she turned her face to him, and in her eyes he saw more misery and sadness and bewilderment than he'd thought a body could hold.

He cut out of the crowd and ran lickety-split back to the hitching post, where Satan—and sanity—awaited.

Kate knew she should be feeling wildly exhilarated. After all, she was largely responsible for the win. And yet she felt as though she'd lost something terribly precious.

The feeling stayed with her throughout Doc and Sally's party. She smiled on cue, shook what seemed like hundreds of hands, and suffered through thousands of pats on the back—many on her sore shoulder—but all the while she ached deep inside.

Mitch's odd behavior was the cause of this tearing, gnawing sensation, she told herself. She wished he was at the party, and then again, she was glad he wasn't. She had to talk to him, but she didn't want to. It was her heart that was tearing in two. In time, broken hearts mend. Hers would, too.

She told herself these things over and over, but she didn't truly believe them.

The throb in Kate's right arm and shoulder, combined with the ache in her heart, masked the primary source of her pain for a long time. She was standing at the refreshment table, holding a nearly full cup of punch and talking to Liza and Stella, when the pain sharpened, intensified, and plunged like a knife into her abdomen. Suddenly she felt as though she had stepped out of her skin and was watching herself double over, watching the crystal punch cup tip and the red liquid spill down the front of her skirt, watching herself collapse onto Sally's polished oak floor.

Mitch stood in the center of the wide front hall, a vantage point that allowed him to survey both the dining room on his left and the parlor on his right while enjoying the hint of a breeze coming through the open door at his back. The sun might be down, but its relentless heat lingered. Damn, it was hot!

His wandering gaze sought a crown of strawberry-blond hair atop a tall, willowy frame among the sea of bodies. If Kate was there, she was hidden deep within the crowd.

She had to be here somewhere, he reasoned. Without her on the pitcher's mound that afternoon there would have been no reason to celebrate. Surely she was here, basking in her glory.

And it was a glory she well deserved, Mitch reluctantly admitted.

God, he'd missed her! His need for her burned bright and sharp, demanding his attention. He'd spent the three hours since the game walking aimlessly about town, grappling with his own image of what Kate should be. He wasn't yet willing to let go of that image, but he was ready to renew his efforts at developing a serious relationship with her. And, perhaps, in time, she would come to see things his way. His only worry was that she wouldn't take him back, that his realization of his burning need for her had come too late.

. . .

He strolled into the dining room. Suddenly a flurry of excitement erupted in front of the refreshment table. At first Mitch paid no mind, but when a female voice hollered for Doc his curiosity demanded closer scrutiny. Keeping a close watch out for Kate, he shouldered his way into the tightly packed throng and reached the table seconds before Doc, who'd come in from the kitchen.

Although he suddenly couldn't recall their names, he recognized the two councilwomen on the floor. One was on her knees, flapping a fan over the face of a prone woman, while the other held the woman's head in her lap. Women often fainted in such extreme heat.

He shrugged and turned away, and the gleam of reddish-blond hair flashed across the edge of his vision. His heart caught in his throat and a sense of dread dropped into the pit of his stomach. He whirled back around, pushing himself in front of a woman he didn't know and bending down for a closer look.

She'd just fainted. That was all. It was hot, and she'd exerted herself in the heat that afternoon; now she'd fainted. Doc was waving smelling salts under her nose. In a minute she'd come around.

Kate moaned and pushed feebly at the vial Doc held.

"She's gonna be okay," one of the women said—the one holding Kate's head.

"No, she isn't," Doc said. "She's bleeding."

"That's just punch," the woman with the fan said.

"I know blood when I see it!" Doc snapped. He looked up at Mitch. "Help me get her to a bed." Louder, he said, "You folks clear out of the way. We have to move her."

Mitch swallowed and fought back the sting of tears. Blood. That was Kate's blood all over her pale pink skirt. Oh, God! What happened to her?

Doc squatted at Kate's feet, waiting for Mitch to take her shoulders. Instead, Mitch pushed his arms under her ribs and hips. He staggered as he straightened up, then righted himself and followed Doc. Why was she so heavy? She'd been a featherweight when he'd carried her to the bedroom.

"Dead weight," Doc explained, as though he could read Mitch's thoughts. "I'll be happy to help."

Mitch shook his head. Doc led the way to his clinic at the back of the house and motioned for Mitch to lay Kate on the examining table. Sally came in right behind them.

"Oh, my stars!" she said, her mouth gaping and her eyes wide as she stared at the red stain that was quickly spreading over the pink silk.

Doc looked at Mitch, and a hint of consternation washed across his eyes and then disappeared. "Why don't you go on back out there and tell everyone she's going to be just fine."

That explanation might be good enough for the folks of Paradise, but it wasn't for Mitch. He set his jaw and dug in his heels. "Not until you tell me what's wrong with her."

"I've got work to do here, Mitch. She's hemorrhaging, and I'm not sure why."

"Then I'm not leaving until you do know why."

Mitch could sense the hesitation behind Doc's beetled brow. At least that was what he thought it was—until Doc shocked him to his toes.

"What's going on between you and Kate?"

"I—I don't know what you mean," Mitch hedged.

"I think you do. I think Kate is miscarrying. She sure didn't put a baby in her womb all by herself."

"Miscarrying?" Mitch asked, dumbfounded. "How can she be miscarrying when she's—" He caught himself, but obviously not in time.

"Barren?" Doc finished for him. "How did you know that?"

"Wilbur, come here!" Sally called. "You can discuss this with Mitch later. Kate needs you now."

"Go on," Doc said, shooing Mitch away with his hand. "Get out of here. But don't leave this house."

Satan, as strong as he was, couldn't have dragged Mitch away.

Kate rubbed her stomach, trying to make the pain go away. It didn't. Thinking a different position might help, she turned over on her side and pulled her knees into chest, then adjusted the cover, which, she realized, didn't smell right. It didn't smell bad; it just didn't smell like hers.

Awake now, she opened her eyes and focused on the shadowy shapes around her. She didn't know where she was, but it wasn't home. She closed her eyes again and tried to remember what had happened to her earlier. She'd gone home after the ball game, changed her clothes, and then gone to Doc and Sally's house for a party. There was a crowd of people; almost everyone in town was there, it seemed, except Mitch—and, of course, the Blue Shirts.

She recalled talking to Stella and Liza. They were

standing near the punch bowl and she'd just filled her cup . . .

And then . . . and then . . .

And then she'd dreamed. She remembered dreaming. Drifting and dreaming that Mitch had come, that he'd picked her up and carried her away. The memory caught in her stomach and wouldn't let go. She moaned from the pain and rolled over again.

"What's wrong, Kate?" a voice whispered from the darkness.

"Who—" Even talking hurt.

A match sizzled and flamed, and a lamp came to life. "It's me. Sally. Shall I wake Doc?"

Sally smoothed her palm over Kate's forehead, pushing her hair out of her eyes and telling her in that one gesture that the pain had been real. Very real.

"No. I must have hit my head. I can't remember."

"Your head's fine." Sally's voice came low, soothing to the ear, and her hand continued to move on Kate's brow.

"What happened?"

"You fainted."

Kate was convinced that fainting was only part of what had happened to her. An insignificant part.

"Why does my stomach hurt?"

"Just rest, Kate," Sally whispered. "We'll talk tomorrow."

"I don't want to rest," Kate insisted, but even as she said the words her voice trailed off and her eyelids drifted shut. "I want to know what happened to me," she mumbled. "Please . . . tell me . . . what happened. . . ."

"I want to know what happened to her, Doc. Everything."

Mitch rested his elbows on his thighs and propped his head on his slightly open fists. Doc wiggled in his chair, crossed one leg over the other at the knee, and gazed off into the shadows of his office.

"All these years," Doc began, "Kate thought she couldn't have children." He snorted in what Mitch quickly realized was self-derision. "Who am I trying to kid? *I* thought she couldn't have children. I told her that over and over. Apparently I was wrong. She was—most definitely—pregnant."

Mitch swallowed hard. "Was?"

Doc nodded. "She lost the baby."

"Will she be able—" Mitch couldn't finish the question.

"To have other children? I think so. Who am I to know? I was wrong before." Doc Myers stood up, walked to a cabinet, and removed a bottle of whiskey and two glasses.

Mitch stared. "Where did you get that?"

Doc laid a finger on his lips. "Sh-h-h," he cautioned. "I keep it for medicinal purposes only. I *am* a doctor," he added, as though that should be ample reason. He poured out two neat drinks and handed one to Mitch. "What I want to know is, are you the father?"

"I think so," Mitch said, frowning. Who was *he* trying to kid? He knew better than to think anyone else could be. "Yes," he said with more conviction, and then, "Yes!"

God! He was going to be a father. *Was.* Not anymore. A mere few hours ago he'd been well on his way to fatherhood. Kate—dear, wonderful, stubborn Kate—was going to have his child. And then, suddenly, before he'd ever had a chance to settle himself into this new role, it had been snatched away from him, leaving him feeling curiously empty.

"Were you planning to make it legitimate?"

It was Mitch's turn to wiggle uncomfortably. He downed the entire contents of the glass and shivered. "I would have," he said, "had I known."

Doc's eyebrows shot up. "Kate didn't tell you?"

"No, and I'd appreciate it if you wouldn't tell anyone else. The public knowledge can't do her any good."

Doc considered the contents of his glass for a minute. "I won't," he said finally, "but I think everyone already knows. You forget that most of the population of Paradise was here."

"So?"

"So, she was bleeding. She doubled over, fainted, and bled. Don't you think people will know?"

Chapter Nineteen

Everyone did know.

Paradise fairly buzzed with gossip concerning Kate's collapse at the Myers's party. Most folks agreed she must have lost a baby. And if that was true, they wanted to know who the father might be. Speculation flew among the scandalmongers on both counts, but especially on the latter.

Mitch heard the talk everywhere he went. At last he understood what Kate had meant by political suicide. Some of the voters were already distributing a petition for her recall, and Adelaide demanded that he arrest Kate on grounds of moral turpitude, which she called "perpitude." He ignored Adelaide and prayed the petition died from lack of signatures. Mitch still thought Kate had no business being mayor, but he didn't want to see her shamed with a recall vote.

If anyone suspected him as the father, they were careful to excise that information from the rumors they passed in his presence. For Kate's sake as well as his own, he wished they'd all find something else to talk about.

When Wednesday, which was the Fourth, rolled around, they did.

* * *

Independence Day festivities ranked high among the three major annual events in Madison County—Christmas and Election Day being the other two—and, as such, always drew a large crowd. Folks from all around started gathering early at the baseball field on the outskirts of town, and by the time Mitch arrived around nine a wide assortment of buggies, wagons, carts, and saddle horses littered the periphery of the field.

Mitch marveled at the Blue Shirts' preparations. They'd roped off the field, and in its center stood a temporary platform for the speakers. Red, white, and blue bunting decorated the platform. A variety of booths occupied two sides of the square while makeshift tables lined the other two sides. On the south side they'd dug huge barbecue pits, while on the north they'd set up a fireworks display. He wasn't sure what he'd expected, but it hadn't been such an orderly arrangement.

Womenfolk busied themselves covering the tables with red-checkered cloths and unpacking pickles, vegetables, breads, cakes, and pies from large willow baskets, while the menfolk hefted hunks of freshly butchered beef down to the pits. Many a gray-haired woman hastily created displays of jams and jellies, fresh fruits and vegetables, and handcrafted items in the booths, while many a gray-haired man carried firewood and footstools down to the pits. Children played chase, and young couples casually strolled among their elders, holding hands and gazing at each other all moony-eyed.

Watching the young couples reminded him of Kate and made him wish he could enjoy the festivities in her company. Although he discussed her progress with

Doc every day, he hadn't seen her since Sunday night.
Doc said they were taking her home at the end of the
week, when she would be well enough to fend for
herself. Although Mitch desperately wanted to see her
and talk to her, he decided he could wait until then—
would have to wait until then. There were too many
ears at Doc's house. Besides, Sally hovered over Kate
like a mother hen and refused to let male visitors into
the sickroom.

Mitch helped unload wagons, then moved down to
the pits to help tend the fires and turn the spits. After
a while he noticed that several of the men, especially
those who aligned themselves with Mort Moffet and
Obediah Stringfellow, kept disappearing for short
stretches. With each successive trip their eyes grew
glassier, their tongues looser, and their gaits less
steady.

The only reason he could imagine such behavior
was liquor. The only way he figured to find out for sure
was to follow one of them. Jethro Smith, the next one
to saunter off, became his target, but the only place
Jethro went was to the bushes to relieve himself.

Well, if that don't beat all, Mitch thought, wondering how long it would take the partakers to catch on
if he waited and followed another one. He figured he
might as well do some mixing and mingling, and
maybe he'd just stumble upon the source.

He wandered past the heavily laden tables, stopping
to sample a dill pickle and then a molasses spice
cookie. The tastes didn't sit too well on his palate, but
he hardly noticed as he strolled by the booths, stopping to speak to the ladies and complimenting them on
their handiwork.

Convinced he'd managed to lose himself in the
crowd, Mitch slipped between two booths and mean-
dered among the nest of wagons. Sure enough, he

spied two heavily muscled men on the far side, standing guard at a buckboard loaded with kegs and wooden boxes.

The two men looked familiar, but Mitch couldn't place them. However, he was fairly certain they weren't from Paradise. He weaved his way among the wagons and approached them from behind. Before they realized he was there, he'd dropped his left arm over the side of the wagon, popped the lid on one of the crates, and flipped a spigot on a keg.

"Hey! What d'ya think you're doing?" the taller of the two barked. A long, ugly scar blazed its way from the tip of his left eyebrow to the corner of his mouth, and his pale blue eyes glared at Mitch's badge.

"I'm gonna have to confiscate this liquor," Mitch said.

The two men hopped off the back of the buckboard and started toward him. "Why?" the other one said. His nose lay almost flat against his face and his eyes were nothing more than tiny black beads set deep in their sockets.

They were two of the meanest-looking ruffians Mitch had ever laid eyes on.

" 'Cause it's illegal. Ain't you two ever heard of Prohibition?"

They took another step toward him. "Yeah," Blaze scoffed. "We heard. But we don't pay that law no mind."

"We do here in Paradise."

They shrugged almost in unison as they continued to advance. Mitch almost wanted to laugh at them, and probably would have if they hadn't had such large, bulging muscles. His right hand wiggled, itching to snatch his six-shooter from his hip, but he resisted. "I'd rather just take this liquor peacefully," he warned.

"You're not gonna take this liquor anywhere, mister," Flatnose sneered.

They were so close, he could smell their stench, a combination of unwashed bodies and sour breath. *Might as well start with the big one,* Mitch thought. With the swiftness of an adder he snatched one of the bottles from the buckboard and brought it down on Blaze's head, shattering the heavy brown glass and slinging apple jack everywhere. Momentarily stunned, Blaze staggered backward.

Before Flatnose could react Mitch caught him on the jaw with a solid right hook. Like a jack-in-the-box, his head snapped back and then forward again, vibrating on its stem. Flatnose shook his head, which made his beady eyes wiggle. Mitch swallowed his laughter again, pulled another bottle out of the wagon, and splattered it on Flatnose's crown.

Out of the corner of his eye, Mitch saw Blaze grasp the edge of a wagon rail and pull himself upright. Mitch dropped the broken bottle neck and punched Blaze in the stomach. The big man didn't flinch. Mitch punched him again, then quickly backed away.

Flatnose hurled himself at Mitch, who kicked out with his right leg and caught the beady-eyed man square in the groin with the brass tip of his boot. Flatnose grabbed his genitals and hollered.

Mitch moved again, trying to put some distance between himself and the wagon, but other wagons and buggies were parked so close, he couldn't go far. Blaze came after him. Mitch hooked his arms over the bed of a farm wagon, heaved himself up, and kicked forward with both feet. The right one landed solidly on Blaze's stomach, but the left skittered off the man's ribs and threw Mitch off balance.

Before he could regain his stability Blaze came after him with a vengeance, fists flying and nails gouging.

The man dug one hand into Mitch's hair and pulled up hard, then walloped his chin with a powerful uppercut that sent Mitch's top teeth driving into his tongue. He gagged on the blood that filled his mouth.

Mitch could see Flatnose coming around, and he knew with the certainty that had kept him alive all these years that he'd better snap to himself.

Kate sat up in bed and smoothed the lightweight cover across her lap. "I wish you'd let me get up," she said as Sally carefully set a breakfast tray over her legs. "I feel fine, and I'd much rather eat at a table."

"I know, dear," Sally said sympathetically, "but I have to follow Wilbur's orders, and he says complete bed rest for two more days." She plopped down on an overstuffed slipper chair, propped her feet up on the edge of the mattress, and crossed her ankles. "Whew! I'm exhausted, and I still have to clean up the kitchen before I go to the barbecue."

"I'm sorry."

Sally's head snapped up. "For what?"

"For being so much trouble."

"You? Trouble? Why, Kate, I've hardly known you were here."

Kate nibbled on a cracker and stirred her soup. "But I have been an imposition."

Sally lifted a shoulder. "Oh, it's this heat sapping my energy, not you. Not even those three boys of mine are to blame." A broad smile wreathed her plump cheeks. "You see, I'm going to have another baby, and . . ."

She clamped her lips together and turned her gaze toward the window.

Kate took a sip of water—and then a deep breath. "It's all right." Sally looked back at her in disbelief.

"Really it is. I'm finally ready to talk about the baby I lost."

"You don't have to."

"I know. But I want to. I *need* to," Kate amended. "That is, if you have some time."

Sally worried her lower lip with her teeth, but Kate got the distinct impression she was trying not to smile.

"Do I have time? Let's see. You'll make me miss out on those delightful kitchen chores and then hours of soaking up all that heat." She laughed and tossed a hand at the light streaming through the window. "Can you make it last all afternoon?"

Kate loved to listen to the trill of Sally's laughter, so light and gay even when she didn't fell well, but she worried her own lip for a minute. "I—well, I don't know quite where to start."

"Why don't we not talk about the baby right now," Sally suggested. "Why don't we talk about Mitch Dawson instead."

Kate's brow stretched. "You know?"

"I had a pretty good idea."

Kate twisted a fold of the cover between her thumb and forefinger and waited for Sally's lecture. When it didn't come she said, "Aren't you going to tell me what a fool I've been?"

"What? For falling in love? I'm thrilled."

"No, for getting myself in this situation."

Sally leaned forward and took Kate's closer hand in hers. "We all know you thought you were incapable of bearing children."

"But now I'm an adulteress."

"You are not!" Sally squeezed Kate's hand. "Oh, maybe you are in some folks' eyes, but not in mine."

"There are those who will sit in judgment," Kate insisted. "They'll say I'm not morally fit to be mayor of this town."

"Yes," Sally agreed, "there are plenty of those self-righteous busybodies out there talking right now, I'm sure. Ignore them, Kate. Concentrate on getting well—and on mending whatever went wrong between you and Mitch. That is, if you truly love him."

"I do! But how did you know we aren't getting along?"

Sally smiled. "If you were, he would have known about the baby. He would never have asked you to pitch in that dratted game Sunday. And you'd probably already be married to him."

Kate's eyes misted and she fought back the sudden rush of tears. "I don't know if I can mend this particular tear, Sally."

"Remember how I fixed Mort Moffet?"

Kate frowned. "What does that have to do with this?"

"Maybe nothing. Then again, I may be able to help you with this. If you still want to talk about it."

Nodding slowly, Kate began with the day she had walked in to her office and seen Mitch for the first time.

Mitch gathered the blood and spittle in his mouth and launched it straight at Blaze's pale eyes. It landed right on target.

"Yeow!" Blaze howled, stepping back and swiping the red-streaked saliva from his eyes. Mitch took immediate advantage of the man's preoccupation and opted for the one choice he felt he had left open to him: He pulled his gun.

The second the hammer clicked, both Blaze and Flatnose threw up their hands in defeat.

"Look, mister," Blaze said, "we didn't come looking for no trouble here. We was asked to come over and peddle our wares, but if we're not welcome, we'll just take our stock on back home."

"Where, exactly, is home?" Mitch asked, his voice menacing. And if that didn't do it, he thought, the leveled barrel and cocked hammer ought to.

"Uh, Bagdad," Flatnose gulped.

"And if I let you take your stock, do you swear you'll never bring it or any other such stock back to Paradise? Regardless of who invites you to do so?"

"Oh, yes, sir," Blaze said. "We'll go and we won't come back. We swear."

Mitch waved the six-shooter at Flatnose. "Me, too," the smaller man added hastily.

Although he'd made his decision, Mitch pretended to consider the situation for a moment. Without taking his thumb off the hammer he said, "All right. I'm going to let you two go. But if you ever show up here again, I *will* confiscate the booze. And you two *will* go to jail."

The two bolted for the buckboard and scrambled aboard. Blaze took the reins and released the brake, then sat gaping at the lake of horse-drawn vehicles surrounding him.

"How are we supposed to get out of here?" he asked.

Mitch sized up the situation. "I guess you're going to have to get down and clear a path. Under my watchful eye, of course."

Flatnose glared at Mitch, started to say something, then shrugged and climbed off the buckboard. It took some doing, but they got the wagon out.

"Where're they going?" a male voice slurred.

Mitch turned to see Obediah Stringfellow standing behind him. "Back to Bagdad, I suppose."

Stringfellow narrowed his eyes and pinned Mitch with a feral glare. "And you sent them."

"I'm enforcing the law," Mitch said, holstering his pistol and starting to walk away. "That's my job."

Stringfellow clamped a hand on Mitch's shoulder and spun him around. "Not for long, it ain't."

Mitch scowled at Stringfellow's raised fist until the ex-marshal released his fingers and his right hand hung limply at his side. "What's that supposed to mean?"

"It means"—Stringfellow adjusted his chaw, turned his head, and punctuated his threat with a stream of tobacco juice that barely missed Mitch's boot—"that your days are numbered. Yours and Miss Priss Mayor's." And then, without further explanation, he turned and walked away.

Mitch stood staring after him for a long time. So far, Stringfellow had represented nothing more than a burr in Mitch's boot, but he wondered now if all that wasn't about to change. It wasn't just the threat. It was the sense that Stringfellow was not in this alone.

At one o'clock, the Paradise Brass Band assembled on the platform and played a rousing march. People moved in closer, and Mort Moffet mounted the platform. "Well, folks," he said, "I never thought I'd be up here again this year, welcoming you to the annual Fourth of July barbecue. But it seems your esteemed mayor has fallen into a spot of trouble"—he cleared his throat—"pardon me, illness."

The bastard, Mitch thought, anger deafening him to the remainder of Mort's speech. Mort stepped down and Thomas McWilliams, a fifty-year-old farmer and Civil War veteran, stepped up and delivered a long, impassioned speech on patriotism that Mitch didn't listen to. His mind was on Kate, who was certain to hear all about Mort's intentional slip of the tongue. If she had only been well enough to attend, Mort would never have had the opportunity to slander her.

Suddenly Mitch didn't think he could wait until Saturday to see Kate. Maybe he didn't have to wait. If Doc and Sally were at the celebration, then Kate was alone. He was searching the crowd for the two familiar faces when all hell broke loose.

Sally bit her lower lip. "You do have a problem, don't you? I agree with you, Kate—in part. If you sacrifice your values, you'll never be happy."

"And the part you disagree with?" Kate asked, holding her breath.

"That you can't ask Mitch to sacrifice his. I don't think Mitch's attitude is tied to values. Something tells me it's tied to experience. And if that's the case, a simple adjustment on his part will solve your problem."

"If the problem is his, what can I do?"

"Not much, I'm afraid. This is something he's going to have to work out for himself. Be patient. It's really far more complex than I'm making it sound, but there is hope, Kate. I know there is."

"And what if he decides to leave? His three-month probation is up at the end of the week."

Sally smiled. "Trust me. Mitch Dawson isn't going anywhere—unless you send him away."

Mitch forgot about going anywhere.

One minute Thomas stood rigidly before the restless crowd, talking about Bull Run and Gettysburg and Appomattox, and the next minute rockets whizzed through the air, arced high, then dived into the bunting that draped the platform. The fabric burst into flame.

Naturally, chaos ensued. The band members bumped into each other in their haste to get off the burning platform. Women fainted, children screamed, and people ran around without really going anywhere. In the surge, some people were knocked to the ground and trampled on. Mitch darted around, helping people up and begging for order. No one paid him any mind.

The platform collapsed and sparks flew everywhere, burning holes in clothing and tablecloths and breeding further panic. Occasionally, one of the sparks started a little fire in the grass, but the constant tramp of feet extinguished these flames before they could spread.

And amid it all rockets shot into the air high over-head and burst into colorful blossoms that rained more sparks onto the swarming crowd.

Fireworks didn't ignite themselves.

Though it was slow going, Mitch wormed his way through the melee until he cleared the booths that blocked his view of the spot where the fireworks had been set up. To his utter amazement, rockets continued to fire without assistance from anyone.

No one was there. No one.

He stood on one side of the display and watched a long, slow fuse burn its way down the line of rockets, which had been set into a cleared strip of ground. He whipped out his pocket knife and ran to the other end, where he cut the fuse just past its sparkling, hissing end. One last rocket discharged, but he had prevented at least a dozen more from going off.

Determined to prevent further catastrophe, Mitch snatched the unfired rockets out of the ground. A piece of paper came out with the last one. He dropped the rocket and unfolded the dirty scrap.

"See how easy it is to create bedlam?" he read. "If the lady mayor doesn't resign, more will follow."

He would have to warn Kate. For the first time since Sunday night, Mitch was glad she was staying with Doc and Sally. For the time being she was safe. And when she went home Saturday he was going with her. To stay.

"You are *not* staying with me!" she railed.

"Calm down, Kate," Mitch admonished in a voice he intended to be gentle but wasn't. "Can't you see your life is in danger?"

"No, I can't. I see a few men too cowardly to identify themselves who are perpetrating harmless pranks in an effort to scare me into resigning."

Or too smart to allow themselves to get caught, Mitch silently added.

She stomped around the parlor, turning her head to hurl her barbed comments but otherwise not looking at him at all. Mitch wanted to step in front of her and take her face in his hands and make her look at him, really look at him. Instead, he closed his eyes and lowered his voice.

"That fire wasn't harmless."

"No one was hurt," she countered.

"People *were* hurt. It's a wonder no one was seriously injured. You simply cannot stay here by yourself, Kate. It's too dangerous."

"Then I'll find another woman to move in with me."

"And you think that would make a difference? You'd just be putting someone else's life in danger."

Kate ignored him.

"Why are you being so stubborn about this?"

"I'm not resigning, Mitch. But if you move in here, the people in this town will recall me."

"We could be married," he offered. He meant it seriously, but it came out sounding quite casual.

Kate shot him a withering glare in response.

Mitch decided to try another tack. "Doc thinks it's a good idea."

Doc had said that, but in a different context than Mitch was deliberately leading Kate to believe. He cringed inwardly, detesting the implication, but he was at his wit's end. They'd been arguing about this off and on for almost an hour, and Mitch was making no headway at all. If this didn't work . . .

"Oh, so now we make Doc the culprit!"

Mitch bit back a retort, reminding himself that the best way to secure her cooperation was to maintain a composed front. "You're getting yourself into a dither over nothing."

"Nothing? You call this *nothing?*"

"I understand why you're upset, Kate—"

"You don't understand *anything.*" She whirled to face him, and he flinched at the green fire blazing from her eyes. "It's not your career that's on the line here. It's mine!"

"Oh, yeah?" he said, jumping to his feet and forgetting his resolve to stay calm. "Well, let me tell you something, Miss Know-It-All. *My* job is in jeopardy, too."

He hadn't meant to tell her that, but he was glad he had. He felt as though he had been relieved of a tremendous burden.

"That's not possible," she snapped. "I hired you, and I will be the one who fires you."

"Assuming you remain in office. In which case, neither of us has anything to worry about, do we?"

She blinked several times, and the fire seemed to die just a little bit. "I hadn't thought about it that way."

Her voice was much quieter, but it wasn't calm.

Rather, it carried the quality of fright, which threw Mitch. Was that why she blustered so? Because the prospect of losing the mayorship frightened her? She had a house and money in the bank. She didn't have to worry about where her next meal would come from.

Of course, there was another possibility . . .

"Don't tell me you're concerned about me." Mitch made no effort to soften the cynicism.

"And why wouldn't I be? I'm responsible for you."

Even through the heat of her anger, Kate discerned the slap to his pride. He was seething so, she could almost see steam belching out of his flaring nostrils. Jennie had warned her to press lightly so as not to bruise his ego. Kate took a deep breath and tried to soften the blow. "Forgive me. I didn't mean it quite that way."

"Then what did you mean, Kate?"

His voice was dangerously quiet. She shivered inwardly. "I didn't mean to hurt you."

"Let me tell you something," he said, coming toward her, his brow lowered and his lips curled into a snarl. "You are not now nor have you ever been responsible for me. I've been taking care of myself for thirty-four years, and I expect I can continue to do so without interference or assistance from a woman."

"I'm sure you can, Mitch," she whispered, wishing she could crawl under the settee. She'd been thrilled when Mitch had showed up at Doc's that morning and offered to take her home. All the way to Elm Street she had envisioned the two of them sitting down and having a long, productive conversation. But they'd barely cleared the door before Mitch had announced his plan to move in and take care of her. Since then the discourse had progressively degenerated, and now Kate wondered if it was possible to repair the damage they'd done.

"Look," she said, "I'm tired. We're both tired. And if we keep this up, we're both going to continue to say things that will hurt the other."

He gave her a long assessing stare, then said, "All right. But I'll be back. Before dark."

Chapter Twenty

In all the eight years Kate had lived in the house on Elm Street she'd never spent a single night anywhere else until the past week. As soon as Mitch left, she walked from room to room, her heart absorbing each color and texture and smell. She'd missed the house; she was glad to be home.

And yet the house didn't welcome her. Instead, it resounded with an emptiness that demanded to be filled, a silent void that begged for voices raised in laughter and song. It was much too large for one person, even too big for two. With every creak of a floorboard beneath her feet, every whisper of the light breeze brushing against the curtains as she opened window after window, Kate heard the plea.

Although Kate tried to ignore the appeal, tried to embrace the house and make it her home again, it balked. She had to set her mind to some task; anything to close out the voice. She'd promised Doc she would rest for another week, but surely a little light cleaning couldn't hurt, she reasoned. Besides, she was so tired of staying abed she couldn't stomach the thought of lying down again.

She collected rags and lemon oil and started dusting in the parlor, moving slowly and resting from time to

time so as not to overexert herself. When she finished
the parlor she transferred her supplies to the dining
room, and from there to her bedroom.

It was then that she thought of Hobo, perhaps because his favorite spot in the entire house was the foot
of her bed. How could she have forgotten him? she
lamented. While she had been gone, Doc had come by
daily to take care of the cat's food and water, but
Hobo had to miss her affection as much as she'd
missed his antics. And the cat was more than likely
furious at being forced to stay outside for a week.

She looked for the gray tabby in all his favorite
places: the front porch swing, the snapdragon bed, the
gazebo. He wasn't to be found, but then, he was adroit
at hiding, especially when his feelings were injured.
She put out a bowl of milk and called to him until she
was hoarse, then finally gave up and returned to her
dusting, all the while listening for his plaintive meows
at one door or the other.

Kate slept through most of the afternoon, then rose
refreshed and hungry. She scrounged around in the
pantry, which needed replenishment, and found a tin
of beef and a few small potatoes. She opened the beef
and gravy and heated it in a skillet, then diced and
panfried the potatoes.

Long shadows were spreading their gray tresses
across her back yard and a host of crickets were raising
their voices in a mighty chorus by the time her supper
was done. Hoping Hobo would come out of hiding
when he smelled the food, Kate filled a plate and took
it with her to the gazebo. The cat loved beef and gravy
almost as much as Kate did, but even the aroma of the
food didn't induce him to show his whiskered face.

Hobo had never acted so strangely. Reminding herself of the cat's extreme sensitivity, Kate wondered if,
perhaps, the tabby had given up on her ever return-

ing home and run off. The very prospect brought tears to her eyes and destroyed her appetite. She set her half-filled plate on the floor and leaned back on the chaise.

Immediately she sat straight up. Going maudlin over the cat was one thing; unleashing any more tears over Mitch was another, and if she stayed on the chaise, that was exactly what she was going to do.

She left the plate for Hobo and went back to the house, which had grown quite dark in her brief absence. Finding several of her lamps low on coal oil, she took one she had lit with her to the shed, where she kept her can of kerosene.

The shed door hinges creaked in protest. Kate was making a mental note to oil them when the light from her lamp caught a splotch of gray fur above a stack of crates in the rear.

"Hobo!" she cried, relief washing through her. "Come here, boy!"

A sudden, stiff breeze rushed through the open door and the hinges creaked again. But the creak was different this time. Not so much metal grinding against metal as a rope straining to retain its load.

The breeze ruffled Hobo's fur and he moved slightly to the right. "It's me, baby. I'm home," she said, her voice suddenly scratchy. The cat moved back to the left and then to the right again, and the hinges creaked, creaked, creaked with every movement.

Her hand shaking, Kate lifted the lamp higher.

She didn't know she had let go of the lamp. She didn't hear it shatter or see the flames leap from the puddle of oil at her feet. She didn't hear herself scream.

* * *

Mitch heard her scream from two blocks away.

His stride immediately stretched into a fast run and his breath came so shallow that within seconds his lungs were burning and his throat felt parched, but he didn't slow his pace.

Her scream reverberated so, Mitch couldn't tell exactly which part of the yard it was coming from, but the moment he rounded the corner of her house and hit the drive he saw the bright orange flames—and Kate standing in front of them. She just stood there, her body frozen, screaming into the burning shed.

His heart skittered to a halt, then restarted. He pushed himself toward her, his lungs burning, his legs aching, his boots feeling like leaden weights hanging on his feet. His mind grasped hold of one conscious thought and refused to allow another entrance: He had to get her out.

As though he was moving in slow motion, he reached her at last, grabbing her arms and snatching her away from the shed, away from the destructive, deadly flames. He threw her to the ground and rolled with her in the grass until they lay a safe distance from the flames. Even then she didn't stop screaming.

Not convinced that Kate had escaped unscathed, he sat up and used both his hands and his eyes to check for burning patches of clothing. When he didn't find any he laid her head in his lap and gently slapped her cheeks, talking to her in what he hoped was a soothing voice.

Gradually her screams turned into whimpers, and then she came alive, fighting and clawing and screeching like a cornered she-cat.

Fending off her blows as best he could, Mitch turned her around, sat her up, and shook her. "Kate!" he called. "Stop it, now!"

Behind her, the shed roof fell in, its impact propelling small pieces of burning wood upward and outward. Luckily, the wind was erratic and the shed was relatively isolated, but if they didn't put the fire out soon, it would very likely spread to the house by way of either the grass or flying debris.

"Kate!" he implored. "It's me—Mitch. I'm here to help you."

All the fight went out of her then, and she slumped against his chest.

"Good girl," he said, rubbing her back and smoothing her hair against her head until her trembles subsided. He stood up, pulling Kate with him, his gaze searching her face in the flickering light. Her eyes were wide, frightened circles, the pupils tiny dots, the green irises flat and dull. Her silent mouth hung open as though frozen in midscream. "Can you help me?"

Her mouth moved, but no sound came out.

"Where are your buckets?" he asked.

"Shed."

He shook his head. "What about a spade or shovel?" Those were in the shed, too, if he remembered correctly.

When Kate didn't answer Mitch took her hand and pulled her to the house and into the kitchen. Although he'd watched her prepare meal after meal, his mind went blank. He couldn't remember where she stored anything.

"Show me where you keep your pots."

As though in a daze, she walked to a cupboard and opened a door. Mitch grabbed two large cast-iron pots with bails and silently cursed their weight. He'd never be able to put out the fire with them, but maybe he could keep it from spreading too far.

"Stay here," he told her. Though she didn't respond, she made no attempt to follow him.

Back and forth Mitch went, from the pump to the

fire. He quickly gave up on putting out the flames and began drenching the surrounding ground instead, watching all the while for small fires started by drifting embers and dousing these before they grew. He worked until his arm and leg muscles were reduced to quivering strands and his shoulders ached so abominably he had to quit.

He filled the pots one more time, then left them by the pump and sat down on the wide back steps. While he was hauling water, the shed walls had collapsed. With nothing left to fuel the flames and the wind fairly calm, Mitch felt relatively confident that the fire was at last contained, but he wasn't about to walk away as long as a single ember burned.

The back door creaked open and he turned his head to see Kate standing behind the screen door. No light burned from within and very little burned from without, leaving her in deep shadow. He wished he could see her eyes, and shuddered to think they might still be dull and flat and empty.

Empty. If eyes were truly the mirrors of the soul, then her soul had been empty. For the first time since he had arrived, Mitch realized that Kate would never have lost control over a fire in her shed. He'd witnessed her staunch control too many times over far more serious matters. Something else had happened, something that had wrenched so forcefully at her soul, it had taken her wits away for a time.

She pushed open the screen and stepped down. Mitch reached up, and she took his hand. Her palm felt cold and clammy, and little tremors snaked their way from her hand into his. He clutched her hand tighter and pulled their joined hands onto his thigh as she sat down beside him. Though the combination of the summer night and the fire created a stifling wave of heat, she shivered. Mitch exchanged his hands so he could lay an arm across her shoulders and pull her closer to his side.

They sat in silence, watching the dying flames. After a while Kate sighed loudly, and when she spoke her voice came out harsh and unsteady.

"I dropped the lamp."

There was more to this than mere clumsiness, but Mitch didn't want to press. "It's all right," he said. "The fire's almost out now."

She shook her head fiercely, and her throat made a gurgling sound.

"They killed Hobo."

Those three simple words answered every question he had mentally posed and left him feeling vastly inadequate to the situation. "I'm sorry," was all he could manage.

"Me, too," she said, burying her head in his shoulder.

He tried to imagine how she must have felt, going into the shed for something, finding her cat dead, dropping the lamp, and not being able to move. He knew how devastated he would be if it had been Little Booger.

How had they killed Hobo? he wondered. There seemed to be no doubt in her mind that the cat had suffered from malicious intent, but again, he chose not to force her to talk.

"I'm staying," he said.

This time she didn't argue.

The next morning Kate awoke with a muddled head and a bad taste in her mouth. She blinked at the shaft of light streaming through a window and guessed from its slant that it was well past nine. A glance at the clock on the table by her bed proved her right, while the jar of sleeping powder and the empty water glass supplied the reason for her physical complaints.

Slowly she sat up in bed, propping her back on two pillows and willing her throbbing head to clear.

What day was it? she wondered, closing her eyes and rubbing her temples. Saturday. No, Sunday. The first time she'd awakened in her own bed in a week.

In a rush of pain, memories of the previous evening flooded in. Hobo hanging by the neck, his stiff gray body swinging back and forth in the wind. The shed burning out of control. Mitch . . .

Mitch! Where was he?

He'd said he was staying, but she couldn't recall anything past taking the sleeping draught, which had been at his insistence. The unruffled cover on the other side of the bed proved he hadn't slept there.

Kate slid her legs from under the sheet and stood up. She plucked her robe off the footboard, slipped her arms inside, and walked down the hall to the guest bedroom, where she stood in the doorway and smiled at his attempt to make the bed. It was neat enough, she supposed, but lacked the tautness and attention to detail most women employed.

In the kitchen she found a pot of coffee and a note: *7:30. Thought I should let you sleep. Will be back soon. Mitch.*

Stale coffee, she supposed, was better than no coffee at all. She poured herself a cup and took it to the dining room, where it was much cooler than the kitchen. No sooner had she sat down than the back door rattled on its hinges. Her entire body tensed, and she sloshed coffee all over the tabletop.

"Good morning," Mitch chirped, strolling into the dining room and looking inordinately pleased with himself.

Kate's breath left her in a rush, making her head

spin again. She laid an open palm on her throat and said, "Thank goodness it's you."

"Sorry I frightened you," he said, but he didn't look sorry. Kate watched him closely as he sopped up the spilled coffee with a tea towel he brought from the kitchen. No, he didn't look sorry at all, not with those twinkling eyes and smiling lips. Her heart fluttered against the wall of her chest and she found herself smiling back.

"Where did you go?" she asked.

"To take care of one of our biggest problems."

Her eyebrows shot up and she winced from the pain, then consciously lowered them in tiny increments. "Which one?"

"Obediah Stringfellow. I bought him a ticket to Denver. He leaves on this afternoon's stage."

Despite her aching head, Kate smiled. "How did you manage that?"

"I told him in no uncertain terms that he was no longer welcome around here and that I didn't ever want to see his plug-ugly face in Paradise again." He went back to the kitchen and started pumping water into the kettle. "I'll make us some fresh coffee," he called over his shoulder.

Kate followed him. "Does that mean you're staying?"

"If you'll have me."

She sat down. *Oh, God! I'm not ready for this.*

He set the kettle on the stove, replenished the wood in the firebox, and checked the reservoir before joining her at the table. "Will you have me?"

Though he wiggled his eyebrows and grinned, his dark brown eyes bore a degree of apprehension as he watched for her reaction.

Certain he could see her wavering thoughts, Kate

dropped her gaze to her cup. "As marshal, yes, I want you."

She heard his sharp intake of breath and braced herself for his next question.

"And otherwise?"

No matter how much she resisted it, this answer required eye contact. Slowly she raised her chin to his expectant gaze. She watched his Adam's apple bob and knew he was as nervous about this conversation as she.

"I'm not sure yet," she said, swallowing hard herself.

He stood abruptly, collected the coffeepot, and rinsed it at the sink.

"I ground enough coffee this morning for a second pot," he said, dumping coffee into the basket and reassembling the pot. He was treading water and they both knew it.

When he turned to her and opened his arms Kate rose unsteadily and moved into his embrace. Whether she liked it or not, he drew her like a magnet. She leaned into his hard chest, slipped her arms around his waist, and let his warmth wash through her.

"I love you, Kate," he whispered in her ear. "I never thought I'd say that to a woman, but it's true. I love you."

Kate wanted to believe him. With all her heart, she wanted to believe he offered her his love unconditionally, and though she had to know, she wasn't quite ready to let go of the heady feeling his declaration produced. She hugged him tighter even as she held back the tears of joy her eyes wanted to shed.

His hands slipped over her back, his palms rubbing, massaging, promising a lifetime of physical pleasure if she'd only accept it. Oh, how his caress tempted her to toss out everything she represented and become the proper lady he wanted her to be.

They both jumped when the kettle whistled.

For a moment they stood apart, Kate's hands on his ribs, Mitch's on her shoulders, their gazes locked. But the shrill, insistent whistle demanded attention. Mitch moved to the stove, Kate to the table.

He poured the water, then sat across from her and reached across the narrow table to lay an open palm on her cheek. "Do you want to talk about it?"

"Have you changed your mind about anything?" she asked.

Mitch hesitated, then pulled his hand back. "No."

Kate took a deep, fortifying breath. "Neither have I."

He stood up, shoved his hands into his back pockets, and started pacing. "Why, Kate?"

She heard the tears in his voice and was surprised at how calm she felt inside. "Because I am who I am. I can't put on personality like a dress, Mitch. I can't wash away my identity like so much dirt. I can't empty my soul so you can fill it up with traits and beliefs you want me to have. I tried that once, and I failed miserably. You have to accept me for who I am, not for what you want me to be."

"I can't do that."

"Then we have nothing further to discuss."

Oh, God! That sounded so final! She considered amending her statement, then quickly discarded the notion. No matter how much she wanted Mitch Dawson in her life, she couldn't allow herself to fall right back into the same trap with which Arnold had snared her.

"What if your adversaries collect the required number of signatures on the recall petition?"

She hated to squelch the sudden hope in his voice,

but she had no choice. "There will be a special election and I'll run again. But I won't magically change into another person when I'm no longer mayor, Mitch, any more than you were a different person while you were working for Western Union."

"What about children? Don't you want children?"

The reminder of her recent miscarriage burned a hole in her chest. "Yes," she whispered. "I want children."

"But not enough to resign."

She flinched at the bitterness in his voice. "That's not what this discussion is about, Mitch, and you know it. You're skirting the issues."

Breathlessly, she waited for Mitch to say something, hoping he'd understand, hoping he'd capitulate. Instead, he offered a brief nod, turned, and walked out the door. The screen banged against the frame twice before settling down.

Pain, sharp and acute, knifed through her chest, ripping her heart in two.

Around midafternoon, the doorbell awakened Kate from a nap. *Mitch!* she thought, her spirits soaring. She scurried out of bed, not bothering to put on her shoes as she hastened to let him in. To her complete surprise, Adelaide stood where Mitch should have been. While Kate blinked away her disappointment, Adelaide pushed past her and stomped into the parlor.

What kind of bee has she got in her bonnet? Kate wondered as she followed her mother-in-law.

Never one for exchanging pleasantries, Adelaide plopped herself down on the fragile love seat and jumped right into the purpose of her visit.

"What do you mean getting yourself with child?" she demanded.

Hot tears stung Kate's eyes and a huge lump threatened to choke her. The loss of her baby, now coupled with losing Mitch, was still too fresh, too raw to discuss with this unfeeling woman.

Adelaide poured more salt into the wound. "All those years when Arnold so desperately wanted a child and you didn't give him one. Then, poof! He's not even cold in his grave, and you go gallivanting in bed with another man and prove what I've always known about you, Kate Gillis: You're nothing but a slut. To think my son saved you from a life of poverty, then left you comfortably wealthy, and you repay him with such lewd behavior. Don't you ever call yourself a McBride again."

Blood rushed to Kate's head and she turned her own indignation on Adelaide. "How dare you—you, you . . . pompous ass!"

There. She'd said it. And felt better for having said it. The words dried her tears and melted the lump and filled Kate with a wonderful sense of power. She heard Adelaide gasp, but she plunged ahead, not caring what the woman thought of her anymore. She moved toward the love seat, shaking an impolite finger at her mother-in-law.

"Get this straight, Adelaide. Your son saved me from nothing. Had it not been for him, I would have finished my degree. And had it been up to him, Arnold would have left me with nothing more than the mortgage on this house. *I* was the one who raked and scraped and did without so we could put some money by. *I* was the one who insisted Arnold take out that life insurance policy. If I am—what did you call it?— 'comfortably wealthy,' it's because I planned it that way."

Adelaide's black eyes blinked several times and her lower lip quivered. When she spoke her voice was considerably lower, yet tinged with accusation. "You make it sound as though you planned his death."

Kate flung her right arm out and pointed to the door. "Get out of my house, Adelaide."

The woman regained her volume. "Your house? This house belonged to my son—"

"And now it belongs to me. Your son is dead, which means we have no further relationship." Kate marched into the hall and held the door open until Adelaide huffed out, then she stood on the front porch and watched until the McBrides' buggy disappeared from sight.

She knew she should be ashamed of herself, but a part of her felt cleansed and whole again.

A little over two weeks later a short man with a handlebar mustache walked up to Mitch in the café, clapped him on the shoulder, and put a forefinger on his badge.

"Quite a step up for a cowboy. When did you become marshal of this town?"

"The name's Dawson," Mitch answered, trying to remember where he'd seen the man before. "And you are—"

"Jenson. Melvin Jenson. I thought we'd met before."

Of course! The owner of the Red Dog Saloon in Bagdad. What was he doing in Paradise? Mitch smelled a rat.

"Perhaps we have," Mitch answered evasively. "Can I help you with anything?"

"No, thanks," Jenson said, twirling the end of his mustache. "Just transacting a little business over here."

Yeah, illegal business, Mitch thought, recalling Flatnose and Blaze from the Fourth of July. They'd said they were from Bagdad, and he remembered thinking he'd seen them before. Mitch would bet they were two of Jenson's men who'd been in the Red Dog when he was there. He'd have to keep a closer watch on Mort and Ned and some other Paradise businessmen he didn't trust. But he couldn't let Jenson get away without letting the saloon owner know that he knew who he was and what he suspected Jenson's business in Paradise entailed.

"You know we enforce Prohibition here," Mitch said.

"So I've heard," Jenson said, his chin bobbing. "So I've heard."

As the summer progressed, Kate saw less and less of Mitch. His concern for her safety seemed to have left town along with Stringfellow. The absence of further threats lulled Kate into complacency on that matter as well.

She missed Mitch; missed his tenderness, missed their long conversations, missed all the little things they had shared so briefly and yet so completely. She understood why he avoided her, for she avoided him, too. Being in the same place together hurt; being in the same place *alone* together spelled nothing short of risking severely damaged emotions. Frequently, Kate questioned her tenacious hold on the preservation of her identity, but each time she talked herself into maintaining that hold.

She missed Hobo; missed his warm weight on her feet at night, missed his meowing and his antics. She considered acquiring another cat, but there would never be another Hobo, just as there would never be another Mitch.

She missed the child she had lost, and she missed the children she knew now she could physically bear but might never have for want of a father.

She hid all her regrets, all her sorrows, all her grief behind a mountain of work. She prepared impassioned speeches extolling equal rights for women, which she delivered to the Paradise Woman Suffrage Association. She authored article after article for various state and national women's movement newsletters. She answered the many letters she received, spent hours on end in discussion with the townsfolk, and breathed easier when the recall petition failed.

She traveled to Topeka and lobbied for a property act that would give married women control over their own earnings. There, she saw Jennie Clark again, but the two were so busy they never found time for the kind of long, sisterly chats they had enjoyed while Jennie was in Paradise.

She took whatever sustenance she could squeeze out of every municipal improvement, every forward step in the suffrage movement, every positive newspaper report, and she told herself that in the great scheme of things, this was enough. Deep down, she knew she lied, but she hid from that truth as effectively as she hid from the sadness.

Thus she survived the long hot days of summer.

Somehow, Mitch survived those days as well. He cursed the blazing sun while he blessed the work that kept him out in it. And there was plenty of both.

With Stringfellow gone, things settled down somewhat, but almost every day found him acting as peacemaker in one situation or another. He watched out for Jenson, but he didn't see him again, nor could he catch Mort or Ned peddling liquor, although he had a gut feeling both of them were. When he wasn't involved in his official duties he joined the current street crew.

Not only had Mitch never been involved in the process of paving streets, he'd never even seen it done before. The streets of Dry Creek, like most western towns, were in no better shape than those in Paradise.

Once the shallow, V-shaped rain gutters had been dug on each side of the streets, the gas lines laid, and the ditches lined with bricks, the preparation for paving began. Marty Pence, now wearing trousers legally, supervised the construction. Though well deserved, the respect she garnered from the townsmen amazed Mitch.

Marty purchased a box grader with town funds. A team of horses dragged the box grader along the streets, forming a crown in the middle to allow for proper drainage. When a two- or three-block segment was crowned men moved in with additional teams of well-watered horses, which they walked back and forth, back and forth over the segment to compact the soil.

"It's the urine more than the walking that does the trick," Marty explained to Mitch, who wondered how much of the smelly stuff the soil actually absorbed in the shimmering heat. But Marty seemed to know what she was talking about, so he didn't argue with her.

Crushed rock, which the townsmen hauled by the wagonload from a quarry near Bagdad, was used as paving material. The men put down the crushed rock, graded it out, and again, walked teams of horses back and forth over it until the stone was sufficiently compacted.

All in all, it was a simple enough process, but one that could only be accomplished efficiently by a huge work force of both men and beasts. In the beginning the men grumbled about being forced to take time out from their own work in order to fulfill the four days' street service the town ordinance required, but once the first segment was finished and they saw the actual fruits of their labor they stopped grumbling and started working with pride. Indeed, many gave additional days to speed up the work.

As was to be expected, there were a few who blithely ignored their obligations. Mort Moffet was one, and most of the rest were his pals. Since the ordinance gave them until the end of the year to serve their four days, neither Mitch nor Marty could do anything about it.

"I hope it's snowing or sleeting or raining buckets while they're working," Marty said. "That would serve them right!"

Though Mitch agreed, the performance of street service for this particular group of men was the least of his concerns.

Though he'd always been a loner, he'd never felt so alone. He couldn't avoid seeing Kate on occasion, and each time he felt as though someone were driving a blade into his chest. He thought he'd eventually get used to it, but he didn't. He wanted Kate more than ever, but under his conditions, not hers. She taunted him by doubling her efforts with the women's movement, proving to him that she was, indeed, another Jennie Clark, a woman of the third variety, a lima bean he couldn't change into an English pea no matter how much he wanted to.

As summer droned to an end, he grew increasingly restless, yet he exerted no effort toward making a change. Instead he devised all sorts of excuses: the heat; the street work; Little Booger's new kittens, born in early September.

Then, almost a month later, an opportunity for new employment fell right into his hands. Had it been an offer from one of the employers whose advertisements he'd answered, Mitch probably would have sent a polite no-thank-you.

But it wasn't. It was an offer to resume his duties as marshal of Dry Creek.

Chapter Twenty-one

That night a cold wind blew across the prairie, chilling Kate to the bone as she hurried the horses home from the monthly suffragists' meeting. No sooner had she put the team away and started a fire in the stove than her doorbell rang. Kate's heart did a flip. No one except Mitch ever came to see her after dark, nor had he come since the night she found Hobo hanging in the shed. And Mitch never used the bellpull.

It was, therefore, with a degree of trepidation that Kate opened the door. But her fear fled at the sight of Mitch standing on her porch, a large basket overflowing with kittens in his arms. He held the brass knob of the bellpull in one hand, while he used the other to scoot a frisky ball of gray fur back into the safety of the basket.

"They're only about a month old," he said, letting go of the knob, "and not ready to wean."

Kate nodded as though she understood everything—when, in reality, she understood nothing—and held the door open for him to enter.

"Put them in the kitchen," she said. "It's warmer in there." She followed him to the back of the house and watched him set down the basket in the corner closest to the stove. "Would you like some coffee? I was about to make some."

"Yes, thank you," he said, far too formally.

What was Mitch doing here? she wondered, thrilled and yet saddened at the same time. She couldn't believe he would have exposed the kittens to the stiff, cold wind without good reason. Perhaps he'd changed his mind about their relationship. Perhaps, finally, he'd decided he could accept her for what she was.

"How have you been?" they asked at the same time. Neither answered, and they both fell into an uncomfortable silence while Kate filled the kettle, ground the coffee beans, and prepared the pot.

"So, Little Booger had kittens," Kate said when she'd finished.

"Yes."

She knelt in front of the basket and counted, forgetting her nervousness as she observed the playful litter. "Gosh! Seven of them. Aren't they cute? This one looks like Hobo."

"And well he should," Mitch said. "I'm sure Hobo was his sire."

"Can I have him?"

"You can have them all."

His answer stunned and confused her. "All? I don't want them all. And you just said they weren't ready to wean."

"I know. I'm leaving Little Booger with you, too."

This was not good news. She still didn't have a clue as to what he was doing, but the fact that he was giving up Little Booger didn't bode well.

"What do you mean?" she asked, steeling herself for his reply.

"Come sit down," he said.

The kettle whistled, and she poured hot water into the pot, then pulled out one of the Windsor chairs. Her pulse raced and a chunk of cold dread settled in her stomach.

"I'm leaving Paradise," he said without looking at her. Instead, he stared off into nothingness, and his speech rang of rehearsal. "I got a letter today from Earl Woody. He was my deputy in Dry Creek and took my place as marshal. He said he fell and broke his hip and can't get around anymore, and the town council has decided they'll hire me back."

She supposed she'd known something like this was coming, but that didn't make it any easier to take. "So you're going? Just like that?"

"Just like that. I hate to leave you in the lurch this way, but I've already spoken to Skip, and he says he'll fill in until you can hire someone else."

Kate didn't want to see him go. God, how it hurt to even think he was leaving. So long as he stayed, there was hope for a reconciliation. Once he was back home in Dry Creek he'd never return to Paradise. Kate knew he wouldn't. But she wasn't going to beg him to stay.

"I'll never make it back to Dry Creek with Little Booger's litter. Will you keep them for me? See that they all get good homes later?"

Her mouth had gone so dry she couldn't speak. She gathered moisture and swallowed, then wet her lips. "Yes," she managed. "I'll take good care of them."

"Thanks," he said, pushing his chair back and rising.

"You aren't going yet. You haven't had your coffee."

For the first time since he'd walked in with the kittens he looked into her eyes. She saw sadness in the dark brown depths; sadness and regret. This was hurting him as much as it hurt her.

"It won't work, Kate. You and I both know it. There's no sense in prolonging our agony."

"I love you, Mitch," she said.

"I know."

"I never told you before. I couldn't let you leave without my telling you."

A flare of hope lit his eyes. "Is there something else you want to tell me?"

For a moment her heart battled with her soul, but in the end, she said, "No."

He turned away, adjusting his hat, his shoulders sagging. She wanted to get up and run to him, throw her arms around his neck and beg him not to go. But if her declaration of love couldn't hold him, neither would her embrace. He was right. There was no sense in prolonging their agony.

She listened to the front door close behind him and knew she would never see Mitch Dawson again.

Four days later Mitch flipped Satan's reins over the hitching post in front of the Dry Creek marshal's office and stood still for a minute, soaking in the peeling yellow paint, the smell of boiling coffee, and the sound of Earl Woody's bellowing voice.

What was Woody doing at work? Mitch wondered. He took the boardwalk in two long strides and pushed open the door.

Woody sat with his feet propped up on the desk. The second he saw Mitch he dropped his feet to the floor and rushed forward, extending a meaty hand in a warm welcome.

"Damn, it's good to see you!" Woody hollered, pulling Mitch against him in a bear hug. "What are you doing back here? I heard things were going great for you in Paradise."

"I got your letter," Mitch said.

Woody pulled away and frowned. "What letter? You know I cain't write much past my own name."

"Yeah," Mitch said quietly, frowning now himself. "But if you didn't write to me, who did?"

"Hell if I know, but what difference does it make? You're here." Woody's frown dissolved into a wide grin; he slapped Mitch on the back and left his hand on Mitch's shoulder. "Come on, let's go get a beer. Shorty will hoot when he sees you, and we've got a lot of catching up to do."

"Somebody's got a lot of explaining to do," Mitch said, scratching his head.

A few minutes later Mitch, Woody, and Shorty sat slurping dark, foaming beer in the Webfoot Saloon, and Mitch felt like he was home—almost. But something wasn't right.

Absently, Mitch answered their questions while his mind whirled with possibilities, none of which made any sense to him at all. Finally he told them to just hold their horses for a minute until he got back. He collected Woody's letter from his saddlebag, but when he showed it to Woody the marshal took to scratching his own head.

"I done told you, Mitch. I didn't write no letter." His gaze skimmed over the contents. "This here says I broke my hip. Now why would someone want to go and tell a barefaced like like that?"

"That's exactly what I want to know," Mitch said.

"Let me see that," Shorty said. He read the letter to himself, then looked at the envelope. "This ain't even postmarked Dry Creek. This here says Bag-some-thing, Kansas. I can't make it all out."

"Oh, my God!" Mitch said, gasping. He snatched the letter out of Shorty's hands and drained the rest of his beer in one long swallow. "I've gotta go."

"But you just got here!" Earl Woody objected.

Mitch settled his hat on his head. "I'll write you a long letter and explain it to you later. But if I don't get back there now, something bad's gonna happen to Kate. If it hasn't already."

"Kate? Who's Kate?" Shorty asked, his eyes twinkling.

"What are you babbling about, Mitch?" Woody asked.

"Don't you see?" Mitch said. "Whoever wrote that letter wanted me out of Paradise."

"Cain't you just send a wire?" Woody asked.

"That's what I should have done in the first place. If I'd wired you, I wouldn't be here. Hell, if I'd looked at that postmark, I wouldn't be here. I'll send a telegraph to Skip, warn him on my way out of town."

"You coming back?" Woody called.

Mitch waved from the door. "I'll write to you. That's all I can promise."

Mitch had been gone almost a week. To Kate it felt like a year.

Funny, she thought, how just knowing he was there if she needed him made all the difference. She'd gone days on end without laying eyes on him, often from one council meeting to the next unless she'd happened to pass him on the street or see him at the Madison House. As long as he was in Paradise, she carried hope in her heart. But the moment he left something in her went with him, and she didn't know if she'd ever get it back.

At first the idea that she was now on her own terrified her. She'd leaned on Mitch mentally, counted on his standing behind her and protecting her regardless of their conflicting viewpoints. Oh, she had Skip, but it wasn't the same thing. The badge had little do with it. Skip wasn't going to keep the close watch on her Mitch had. Skip wouldn't have been there to pull her out of the burning shed.

She took her fears to the gazebo, her place for solitude. There, she began to realize that she'd gained something with Mitch's departure. With him gone, she had no choice but to rely on her own wits, her own inner strength.

Stringfellow might be gone, but she didn't dare let down her guard. Mort Moffet and his friends had never stopped grumbling, and now that Mitch was out of the picture she fully expected them to start harassing her again.

As time went by, she tried to convince herself, she'd get over Mitch Dawson. It wasn't the first time she'd had to pick up the pieces and go on. It was just the hardest.

The third day on the trail back to Paradise, Mitch spied a lone gray wolf on a rise that was still way off in front of him. Oblivious to his approach, the wolf danced and frolicked in the dying sun, as graceful and beautiful an animal as Mitch had ever seen.

In the course of his life he'd spent too much time on the trail to fear a single wolf, and he harbored very little fear—though a great deal of respect—for an entire pack. As a general rule, wolves, as Mitch well knew, killed only what they could eat; but let them get hungry, truly hungry, and they'd go on a killing spree the moment food was available. This happened most often in the early spring, especially if the winter had been long and hard and food scarce.

As he watched the wolf, Mitch found himself comparing wolves to people. Mort Moffet and his gang were like a pack of wolves, presenting no cause for

alarm until they'd been practically starved for lack of
fair game. Then, when the game ran out—and it had,
thanks to him—like cunning trappers, they'd set a
snare. And he'd walked right into it. With him out of
the way, there was no telling what they'd do—to Kate,
the five councilwomen, and the segment of the Paradise population who supported them. Kate was like
the lone wolf playing on the rise, blissfully unaware
that potential danger lurked so close, for were Mitch
like most men, he'd take his rifle and shoot the wolf
out of pure-dee ignorance.

Mitch pushed Satan harder. As horse and rider
started up the rise, the black snorted and balked, while
the wolf turned lonely, frightened yellow eyes to Mitch
before bounding off down the other side and across
the prairie.

"Easy, boy," Mitch soothed, slowing Satan to a trot
and patting him on the neck. "He's scareder of us than
we are of him."

To himself, he added as though sending the thought
to Kate, *Run. Run like the lone wolf for whatever shelter
you can find. And wait for me there. I'm on my way.*

The first Monday in October marked six days since
Mitch had left town and six months since Kate and her
petticoat government had first taken office.

That afternoon, as Kate spent a leisurely hour in the
tub, she practiced her midyear report, which she expected to deliver to a record crowd. To her amazement, folks had never stopped coming to town council
meetings. She didn't think they came out of either
curiosity or a lack of confidence. Not anymore. Now
they came simply because they were interested. If the
petticoat government hadn't accomplished anything

else, at least they'd gotten people off their mental duffs and involved in municipal government.

But they had accomplished other things; lots of other things. In a mere six months the town's operating fund balance had grown from thirty-six cents to almost fifty dollars, with no outstanding bills over thirty days old. Fully operational now, the gas plant served both businesses and residences all over town. Almost half the corners boasted street lamps, and before the year was out every corner within the town's corporate limits would have one. The rain gutters were 90 percent complete, and crushed stone paved far more than half the streets.

Townsfolk could traverse the boardwalks without fear of falling through; trees, shrubs, and grass had been planted on the courthouse square; a majority of the commercial buildings bore fresh paint on their walls. A new sign greeted strangers coming into Paradise, while happy faces and friendly townsfolk made them feel welcome. Though the town might not ever completely live up to its name, it was a darn sight closer to paradise than it ever had been before.

As Kate saw it, Mitch's resignation was the only blight on the petticoat record. Despite the article Herman Stockley had carried in Saturday's *Chronicle,* which included a statement from Mitch about hating to leave Paradise but wanting to return home, folks were certain to pose questions at the council meeting. Some were bound to accuse her of running Mitch off, while others would express concern over the town's ability to find and hire another marshal with Mitch Dawson's efficiency and experience.

These things she considered while she dressed for the meeting. People had learned to expect honest, straightforward, nonpolitical answers from her, and she wasn't about to disappoint them. Yet she knew she must choose her words carefully so as not to unduly arouse discontent.

"I have the utmost confidence in Skip Hudson," she said to her reflection as she ran an oversized hat pin through the bun she'd fashioned on the top of her head and then back through the low crown of her hat. "And rest assured that I and your council are actively seeking a well-qualified man to—"

The words hung in her throat and Kate frowned into the mirror. To do what? she questioned. To fill Mitch Dawson's shoes? No one could do that. Not for her. And probably not for Paradise. Nevertheless, she already had three applicants for the job, and one looked very promising.

She lifted the watch pinned on her bodice and checked the time. Six-fifteen; time to go. Suddenly panic snatched at her insides, and she didn't know why. The meeting didn't start for forty-five minutes; she'd hitched up the horses before she took a bath, and all she had to do was collect her reticule and the leather case in which she carried her paperwork, then lock the doors and be on her way. In ten minutes she'd be there. She had a good report to make, and she'd banished the butterflies from her stomach ages ago. So why the sudden anxiety?

It didn't make sense, yet she couldn't deny the tightness in her chest or the knots in her stomach or the flush in her cheeks. She wet a cloth and held its damp coolness over her face for a minute while she told herself to calm down. Neither measure helped.

As though from afar, she heard a voice tell her to run. Run and hide. And wait for Mitch.

This is madness, she thought, turning out the lamp. She headed for the back door, picking up her purse and portfolio from the dining room table, and telling herself to stop thinking such foolish thoughts. Mitch was gone. He wasn't coming back. Stringfellow was gone and he wasn't coming back, either. She had nothing to worry about. Nothing at all.

These things she mentally repeated on her way to the carriage house. By the time she got there she'd almost talked herself back into her usual state of well-being. She picked up the wedge she used to hold the door back, grasped the handle with her free hand, and pulled.

Then something struck her on the back of her head and the world went black.

The night was black. Ominously black. Mitch turned his face to the sky and watched gray clouds scud across a crescent moon, obscuring whatever little light it and the stars might have shed. Thunder boomed almost directly overhead and a bolt of lightning stretched its long, jagged brilliance from the sky to an elm tree nearby. A loud crack rent the air, and the treetop burst into flames.

Satan reared and whinnied, and Mitch could feel the gelding's flanks quivering against his legs.

He needed to find shelter fast.

The light from the burning elm illuminated his immediate surroundings. All Mitch could see was grassy prairie. Then another slash of lightning ripped the black night asunder, revealing a rocky outcropping off to the right. Mitch turned Satan's head toward the rocks and urged the horse onward.

From way off in the distance came the lonely cry of a solitary wolf, and Mitch wondered if it was the same one he'd seen earlier. Once he'd likened Kate to the wolf, he couldn't shake the comparison.

Like the wolf, Kate was sleek and beautiful, comfortable with herself, confident in her ability, canny and wise and strong. Yet alone on her own rise, she was far more vulnerable than she'd ever imagined.

He drew Satan to a halt before the rocks, jumped down, and led his faithful steed under the narrow overhang. Quickly, he tethered the horse, then scouted for firewood before the rain started. The night wasn't so cold that it demanded a fire, but he sure did want a cup of hot coffee to wash down his jerky.

When he had the fire going and water from his canteen heating in the small pot he'd taken from his saddlebag Mitch sat down, leaned his back against a boulder, and stretched out his legs.

He didn't know why he was so worried about Kate. He'd telegraphed a warning to Skip and he'd be back in Paradise by noon the next day. Of course, he reminded himself, he'd been gone for six days. Anything could have happened to her well before he'd arrived in Dry Creek on Saturday, but somehow he didn't believe that. For one thing, he hadn't had a really bad feeling until just a few hours ago. For another, if something had happened earlier, he felt sure Skip would have wired him a message in Dry Creek, but none had awaited him. And Joe McIntosh, who'd taken his place at the Western Union office, had assured him nothing was wrong with the telegraph lines.

Then why did he feel so uneasy? Especially about the telegraph?

He poured the hot water over the ground coffee he'd bought in Dry Creek and listened to it drip, drip into the bottom of the pot, but all the while his mind was on telegrams.

"Son of a bitch!" he hollered into the night, throwing his torso forward and slapping his thighs hard.

How could he have forgotten about Simon Carlson? The man could lose his job over failure to deliver a telegram, but Simon could always say part of the

transmission had been distorted or swear up and down
that he'd recorded the message exactly the way it had
come in, even if he'd intentionally written it wrong.
Mitch hadn't hung around long enough to witness the
dispatch. It would be Joe's word against Simon's, and
in the end no one at Western Union would give a
tinker's damn.

He'd be willing to wager Satan that Skip received a
falsified version of his original message and had absolutely no idea that Kate's life might very well be in
danger.

The rain came then, in unremitting, slanting, slash-
ing sheets that doused his fire and splattered against
his poncho. He folded his legs beneath him, pulled his
hat down over his forehead, and filled his tin cup with
coffee from the hissing, steaming pot.

Out on the prairie the elm tree crumpled to the
ground amid a few recalcitrant sparks, which the
blackness and the rain quickly swallowed up.

A loud crash lifted Kate from a deep sleep into
semi-awareness. She was conscious enough to feel the
intensely throbbing pain in the back of her head, just
above the nape of her neck, but too groggy to question
why it was there. She groaned, let her head flop forward, and returned to the comfort of oblivion.

Mitch cursed the storm, not so much because it kept
him awake as because it prevented his getting back on
Satan and riding on to Paradise. Even if he could
convince the beast to move in such weather, the complete obliteration of the sky thwarted his sense of direction. He'd wind up hopelessly lost and perhaps far-

ther away from his destination than he was now. He had no choice but to stay put until dawn.

The high, narrow overhang provided little shelter from the rain's fierce attack. Mitch huddled beneath his poncho and worked at piecing together the puzzle. The more he could figure out now, the better his chances of dealing with the situation tomorrow.

Mitch harbored no doubt that something grave had befallen Kate. He knew it in his heart and felt it in his bones.

He went back to the letter. Someone wanted him out of Paradise; someone who knew about Earl Woody. He couldn't remember talking about Woody to anyone except Kate and Skip, and neither of them would have sent the letter. But anyone, he realized, could have learned that Woody was the marshal of Dry Creek, Nebraska, and that he'd been Mitch's deputy. And virtually everyone knew that Mitch had come to Paradise from Dry Creek.

The letter had been mailed from Bagdad, which didn't mean squat. Hell, it was only an hour's ride away. Anyone could have ridden over there and posted the letter.

He wondered if Melvin Jenson could have anything to do with this. He'd seen the little man in Paradise back a couple of months ago, and Jenson had said he had business there. Mitch racked his brain, trying to recall their conversation. He'd said something to Jenson about enforcing Prohibition. What if Jenson wanted to build a saloon in Paradise? Mitch didn't believe Skip could be bought, but he wasn't the least bit sure Skip possessed the guts to put a stop to such an operation. Faced with such a situation, Skip would more than likely turn in his badge and tell Kate to hire someone else.

That idea presented a whole new realm of possibilities. Although the bid to recall Kate had withered on the vine, Mort had said he planned to regain his post as mayor next year. All this time, Mort could have been looking for a man to slip right into the marshal's position when Mitch resigned. Completely unaware of Mort's manipulations, Kate would hire him, possibly already had. If he was Mort's man, he'd take the bribes and follow Mort's orders.

But Kate was smart. She'd catch on. And then she'd fire the new marshal just like she'd fired Stringfellow. No, there had to be something more. Something sinister, or else he wouldn't feel this tremendous urgency, this awful sense of impending doom.

All right, he thought, *so Mort's behind the letter.* Mort wanted him out of Paradise because he presented a constant deterrent to Mort's plans. But the former mayor had to know that Kate wouldn't let him get away with anything for very long, which meant he had to get rid of her.

Mitch shuddered at the thought.

But Mort was smart, too. He'd know Mitch would find out that Woody hadn't broken his hip the minute he got to Dry Creek. Maybe Mort had counted on Mitch hanging around for a few days. Maybe he'd hoped Mitch would stay in Dry Creek once he got there, or even go somewhere else.

Regardless, Mort knew now that Mitch was on his way back to Paradise. And he had a pretty good idea when he'd arrive because Mitch had told him. The instant he sent the telegram, he showed Mort his hand.

God! He was walking right into another trap! But at least this time he could see it coming, could plan for it.

Maybe Mort hadn't planned to do anything to Kate at all. Maybe this whole thing was a setup to get Mitch. Folks in Paradise thought he was in Dry Creek, and folks in Dry Creek thought he was in Paradise. If he wasn't careful, he might spend eternity buried somewhere on the prairie between the two towns, and nobody except the men who put him there would ever be the wiser.

Mitch checked his rifle and his six-shooter to make sure they were both fully loaded, then slipped the saddlebags that held his ammunition over his thighs.

It was going to be a long night, but Mitch didn't dare allow himself to fall asleep.

Chapter Twenty-two

"Hey, missy, wake up!"

The voice sounded like it was coming through water. She felt a current tugging her along and heard the cascading thunder of water falling. Was she in a river? She couldn't be underwater; she couldn't swim.

Kate gulped for air, but she couldn't breathe. Her lungs were like hot lead weights in her chest—burning, heavy, uncooperative. Glittering stars danced on the red screen of her eyelids and pain knifed through the back of her neck when she turned her head, trying to find the surface, trying to find air. In her mind she became a fish—a golden sun perch, struggling to make her gills work, struggling to flip her tail and move her fins, struggling to pull life-giving oxygen into her lungs. Struggling to survive.

Water splashed across her face and she gasped, sucking water into her nostrils and her dry mouth. The water burned a trail up her nose and down her throat. She was drowning, but she wasn't giving up yet. Not without a fight.

She lashed out with her hands and feet, kicking, punching, flailing her limbs, trying to hold her head above water, trying to breathe.

The lead weights transferred themselves from her

chest to her elbows, pinning them to the ground. But at least she could breathe. She stopped struggling and inhaled deeply, relishing the scorching air that filled her burning lungs. Slowly she let it out, terrified she wouldn't be able to take another breath. Time after time she sucked in air, slowly exhaled, then filled her aching lungs again, until at long last the burning sensation subsided.

Gradually the glittering lights dimmed, and she opened her eyes enough to see the golden glow of a lantern hanging over her head and a familiar face hovering so close to hers, she could smell the man's rancid breath.

Obediah Stringfellow!

The air left her lungs in a *whoosh* and she struggled to breathe again.

"It's just me, missy," he cackled. "Ain't no reason to be afraid of old Obediah, so long as you do what you're told."

He pulled her up against a rough-hewn post, splinters piercing her bodice and shoving themselves into her skin. Kate gasped in agony even as her mind labored to assimilate the circumstances into which she'd fallen.

She wasn't in a river; she was in a barn. Or maybe a stable. She was sitting in smelly straw that prickled her legs below her skirt and petticoats, which were twisted around her knees. The walls of the decrepit building rattled under the assault of a storm, and the waterfall she'd heard was rain pouring off the leaky roof. Fortunately, where she sat was fairly dry.

"Here now," he said, shoving a piece of paper onto her lap and a pen into her right hand. His long, dirty fingernail tapped the sheet. "Just write a little letter for me and I'll let you go back to sleep."

She moistened her lips and swallowed. "What do I write?"

"What's on this here paper," Stringfellow said, handing her another sheet. "Just copy it and sign it. It's got to be in your handwriting."

Writing filled the paper he handed her, but she couldn't read it. She tried to focus her eyes, but the words wavered and swam together. "What does it say?"

"Don't pretend with me, missy. I know you can read." A pistol hammer clicked next to her ear. "Now write it."

She had no doubt Stringfellow would gladly pull the trigger, given half a reason. Kate squinched up her eyes and gasped when she realized the message said she'd run off to Dry Creek after Mitch and was resigning as mayor. With sudden clarity she knew Mort Moffet had dreamed up this whole scheme. There might be some way to foil it, but only if she lived. She scrawled a similar note, signed her name across the bottom of the page, and Stringfellow snatched it out of her hand.

"That's a good girl," he sneered. "Now you can go back to sleep."

She watched the lantern swing at his side as he walked away, and then the darkness swallowed her up again.

Mitch fought the darkness that threatened to swallow him up. He told himself he couldn't afford to doze off, even for a few minutes, but his eyelids seemed bent on falling shut and his mind on skimming through images of Kate in peril: Stringfellow pulling his gun on Kate; the message tied to the rock—*Quit or die;* Kate on the floor in front of the punch table, her life's blood staining pale pink linen; Kate screaming and standing frozen amid leaping flames.

Twice he'd saved her life. Once she'd almost lost it because of him. He had to get back to her. He had to touch her and hold her and know she was alive. If he had to spend the rest of his days protecting her from danger, he would. It didn't matter; nothing mattered so long as he was there for her. He couldn't stand the thought of something happening to Kate because he hadn't been there to do his job.

The moment daylight broke, Mitch hit the trail. The storm showed no signs of abating, and after a while he wasn't the least bit certain he was headed in the right direction anymore. He watched the sky for a break in the gray clouds and wished he carried a compass. Nonetheless he pressed on, praying he wasn't veering too far off track.

He'd been traveling about an hour when a gray wolf darted out in front of Satan. Miraculously, the horse never seemed to notice. The wolf dropped back so that it was running parallel to the horse. It turned its golden, almost mesmerizing eyes to Mitch, who would have sworn the wolf was trying to tell him something. Then the animal plunged ahead, keeping its parallel course but pacing itself so that it ran just a few feet ahead of Satan's nose.

The rain was so heavy, Mitch couldn't see farther than eight or ten yards in any direction. For all he knew, an entire pack surrounded him. Or, perhaps the wolf was mad, though it didn't snarl or otherwise act rabid. In fact, it seemed almost tame. Regardless, Mitch didn't trust the wolf. He tugged the reins and headed Satan in a slightly different direction.

Within minutes the wolf was back at his side, gazing up at him again with a pleading look in his yellow eyes.

Again Mitch changed direction; again the wolf came back.

What the hell, Mitch thought. *I don't know where I'm going anyway.*

For the remainder of the morning and into the afternoon he followed the wolf. Was this the same wolf he'd watched the evening before? he wondered. The one that had frolicked on the rise? The one he'd likened to Kate?

He watched the rain pound the wolf's back, watched the animal stretch its legs in smooth, long leaps, and thought again about how graceful and strong the wolf was, how at peace with himself and his environment. But if he captured the wolf and penned it up, he would become feral. He would do anything he had to do to release himself, to regain his freedom. Mitch knew it would. He'd seen the evidence in too many steel traps that held nothing more than chewed-off feet.

Was that what he'd tried to do to Kate? Pen her up and turn her into something she wasn't, something she never could be? Did she, like the wolf, prefer to live her life minus a foot if that was her only route to freedom?

God, yes! That was exactly what he'd tried to do! The acknowledgment brought tears to his eyes. The tears trickled down his cheeks and mixed with the rain. He'd accused Kate of having a penchant for controlling people without seeing the same trait in himself. And now, due to his blindness and stupidity, her life might well hang in the balance. He had to get to Paradise, had to find Kate and tell her he loved her unconditionally, tell her she could run for governor—hell, president—if she wanted to. But he had to get there first.

The rain turned the prairie into a lake and slowed his pace, but when Mitch didn't reach Paradise or any other town by midafternoon he started worrying that perhaps the wolf was leading him on a merry chase to nowhere. And then Mitch realized he was on a coach road, trudging between parallel ruts that were overflowing with water.

Damn! He wished he could see! How long had he been on the road, and where was it leading him? he wondered. Sometime soon, he'd have to stop, have to feed and rest Satan before the tired horse gave out completely, have to fill his own empty stomach and rest his own body before he collapsed in the saddle. Somewhere along the road there ought to be a house or a barn or a shed, or even a lean-to. Something, anything that would provide a roof, a modicum of shelter from the pouring rain, though he didn't know how he'd ever see it through the deluge.

Satan's legs sank up to his forelocks in water, and Mitch's poncho had long since failed to hold back the rain. Water ran in a long rivulet down his spine. Mitch shivered with cold and a prevailing sense of uneasiness.

Someone yanked her head up by her hair, and Kate screamed in protest. Immediately the back of a hand crashed into her cheek, the knuckles colliding with her jawbone and sending shards of pain rushing to her ear.

"Shut up!" a male voice hissed. "What do you want to do? Wake the dead?"

She stifled a whimper and peered through the dimness, her eyes searching for a face to go with the unfamiliar voice. A match scraped across the sole of a boot and hissed to life, revealing a man with a wicked white scar that ran from the corner of one eye almost into the corner of his mouth.

The man touched the match to the wick of a lantern,

then put the still glowing match in his mouth to put it out. .

Kate shivered. "Who are you?"

"What difference does it make?" the man snarled. "I brought you some food."

He shoved a tin plate of beans into her stomach. Before she could grasp the plate he let go of it, and most of the beans slipped into her lap. The man with the scar laughed at that, much louder, Kate thought, than she'd screamed. He moved away, though not far, and hung the lantern on a nail sticking out of a post. He pulled a cigar out of his pocket, lit it with the fire from the lantern, then sat down and leaned his back against the post.

Kate eyed him with distaste, then plucked the greasy beans off her dirty skirt and dropped them back onto the plate. She eyed the now gritty beans with distaste as well, but she was hungry enough to eat the tin plate. "May I have something to eat with? A spoon or fork?"

"There ain't nothin'.."

"Then how am I supposed to eat?"

"With your fingers, I reckon."

"But they're dirty," she argued.

"So's your face, lady. You're a sight." He laughed at that. She wondered if he only laughed at things that caused someone else misery. But a few minutes later, as he watched her lick the bean juice off her fingers, she saw the savage gleam in his eyes and wondered if perhaps she shouldn't be concerned about something more than what he chose to laugh at.

"Here's something to sop up the juice with," he said, digging a crust of bread out of his pocket and tossing it at her. It landed on the filthy straw next to her hat.

Her stomach rumbled, and she eyed the crust with both hunger and disdain. In the end she decided she had enough dirt in her mouth and left the crust in the straw.

He shrugged. "Suit yourself."

The nauseating smoke from his cigar curled around her head, but her instinct told her not to show any weakness to this man. She swallowed hard, forcing down the bile.

He made no move to collect her plate, no move to leave. Kate suspected that someone had guarded her since the moment she had opened the carriage house door. She wondered how long ago that had been. From the emptiness of her stomach and the lessening of pain in her head she figured at least a day, maybe more. She wished someone would tell her something. Perhaps this strange man would. It wouldn't hurt to try.

"Where am I?" she asked.

He snorted. "In a barn."

Kate bit back a retort and tried again. "Who brought me here?"

"Some men who don't like you very much. And if you don't shut your trap, I ain't gonna like you much, neither." His gaze flittered over her, taking in her bare ankles and calves, a long tear she'd just noticed in her bodice, and her disheveled hair spilling onto her dirty face, and he whistled low and long. "On second thought, maybe I am gonna like you."

He crushed the end of his cigar against his boot heel and crawled toward her. The light from the lantern shone on his back, casting his face in deep shadows, but Kate didn't need to see his face to recognize the danger she was in. She braced her back against the rough post and drew around herself an invisible armor of wit and inner strength. Poor weapons, she supposed, to take into battle. But they were all she had.

*   *   *

As the dying sun took with it the little light it had managed to shed, the rain yielded to a steady, foggy drizzle. Way off in the distance Mitch could discern first one light and then another through the dark mist, a sure indication that a town lay ahead. He turned his head to thank the wolf, but the animal had disappeared.

Satan plodded along, raising his head occasionally to snort, whether in pleasure or pain Mitch didn't know. He knew that he ached all over. His head throbbed and his eyes burned. He was in no condition to help Kate, but he dared not move on if this town wasn't Paradise.

The closer he came to the lights, the more certain he was that the wolf had led him astray. Nothing looked familiar . . . and yet it did, somehow. Apprehension crawled down his spine again, and he was thankful the darkness, combined with his drab poncho and Satan's black coat, masked his entrance into the town. Even the mud cooperated, absorbing the normal clip-clop of iron horseshoes.

Mud. No lamps to light the streets. The tinkle of a piano and the clamor of raucous laughter. Definitely not Paradise.

Mitch leaned low over the gelding's neck and whispered in his ear. "Sh-h-h, boy. Don't make a sound."

From what he could tell in the dark, he was on a street of businesses mixed with houses. The stores were all dark, but the tinkling piano was closer than before. He turned Satan down an alley and slipped silently to the ground. Hugging a building with his back, Mitch sidled his way over to the next street.

And there, on the opposite side in the middle of the block, stood the Red Dog Saloon.

Bagdad! Shit! What am I doing here?

Well, they certainly weren't expecting him in Bagdad, but that didn't mean he could just walk right into the Red Dog and order himself a beer. Melvin Jenson was sure to recognize him, and if the saloon owner was involved in the plot to get Mitch out of Paradise, then he might as well be walking into a nest of rattlesnakes. Probably Flatnose and Blaze were in there, and they'd recognize him, too. It might have worked if none of the three had ever shown up in Paradise, especially since he'd maintained anonymity the one time he'd been to the Red Dog. But his chances of getting out of there alive now were nil.

So, what was he gonna do? Get back on poor old Satan and try to find Paradise? At least he was only an hour away, but that was in the daylight, when he could see where he was going. Try to find the wolf and ask him to lead him to Paradise? He laughed at that, silently and without humor.

Well, he wasn't going to stand here in the drizzle all night and watch the Red Dog. Maybe he could find the livery stable and bed down there with Satan, then skedaddle before the sun came up, and Jenson would never know he'd been in town. He'd like nothing better than a bath and a hot supper, but his needs could wait. Satan's couldn't.

He was fixing to turn away when a man came out of the Red Dog and struck a match against the door facing. Something about the man rang a familiar bell, and when he put the match to the cigarette stuck between his lips Mitch knew why. Stringfellow. What was he doing in Bagdad when he was supposed to be in Denver?

Suddenly Mitch felt like he'd swallowed an andiron.

* * *

With a knee on either side of her legs and his palms on the ground, the man with the scar inched closer. Kate could smell his rancid armpits and his fetid breath, and she fought back the revulsion rising in her throat and sapping her strength.

"You shore are a purty thing," the man said, "even with all that dirt on your face. 'Course, I've always had a soft spot for redheads."

It took every ounce of willpower to keep her gaze locked with his, but Kate knew better than to shift her eyes even for a second. Slowly, hoping her movements didn't attract his attention, she eased her arms out from her sides before he could trap them with his own. She wasn't sure what she was going to do, but she wanted everything possible at her disposal, and that included the use of her hands and arms.

When her right hand grazed her hat a tiny spring of hope welled in her breast. She heard Billy Fink tell Mitch that he was arresting her for wearing a device capable of lacerating the flesh. Thank goodness she'd used her largest, most deadly pin to hold her hat in place on Monday night.

Her heart lurched when his gaze dropped and she stilled her hand, but he merely licked his lips and leered at her partially exposed bosom. "I'm gonna have myself a good ole time," he said, sitting back on her thighs and grasping the torn cloth in his hands. He pulled at the fabric, and it ripped from shoulder to waistline. Kate felt her cheeks bloom hot with anger and embarrassment. "Yes, ma'am. This shore is gonna be fun."

She repressed a shudder of loathing and moved her fingertips along the narrow brim of the hat and up to the crown. The end of the pin pricked the pad of her finger, and she winced before she considered the reaction. But the man with the scar never seemed to notice.

He buried his face in her bosom, slobbering all over her chemise as he took the thin cotton in his teeth and tore it open.

Kate slipped her fingers over the cool shaft of the pin until she touched the ornament on its head. This she grasped tightly between her thumb and forefinger. She pulled, and the pin squeaked through the straw.

Scarface flinched and raised his head. Kate's heart pounded out of control in her chest and her blood ran cold. If he saw the hat pin in her hand, she'd never get out of this unscathed.

Where was Stringfellow going? Mitch wondered, keeping to the shadows as he dogged the former marshal's trail, hoping that Stringfellow wasn't leading him on a merry chase to nowhere. But that's what he'd thought the wolf was doing, and look where he was now. He didn't know why Kate would be in Bagdad, but he figured Stringfellow was somehow tied to the letter that had gotten him out of Paradise in the first place. He wasn't about to lose the rascal.

Stringfellow disappeared inside a livery stable and came back out a few minutes later leading a saddled horse. Mitch silently cursed his luck. By the time he doubled back to the alley and collected Satan, Stringfellow would have disappeared and he'd never find him again in the dark. He supposed the best he could do was note the general direction the man took and hope Stringfellow wasn't in a hurry to get wherever it was he was going.

To cover her attack, Kate managed a weak smile, moved her free hand to one of his buttocks, and gently squeezed. Intentionally caressing him made her sick to her stomach, but it was the only way she reckoned her plan would work. She refused to consider failure.

Scarface grinned. "I knew you was gonna like it," he said, smirking at her and then burying his face in her bosom again.

Kate fought back the sudden stiffening of her limbs, whipped the pin around, and drove it into his other buttock. The man howled and bit her breast, which only served to fuel Kate's ire. She pulled it out and speared him again.

"What the hell!" he bellowed, sitting up and raising his hand to strike her. But Kate was quicker. She slashed the palm of his hand wide open; then she went for his unscarred cheek with the lethal hat pin.

He went for his gun.

Stringfellow headed out of town, toward Paradise. Mitch dashed back to the alley where Satan, as faithful as ever, awaited him. In a flash he was in the saddle and heading the black after Stringfellow. He rode for a couple of miles and was about to give up on ever finding the scoundrel when a thin shaft of light appeared and then disappeared not far off the road. From the best Mitch could tell, the light came from a barn.

He eased the gelding toward the spot where he'd seen the light. It was probably only a farmer, he reasoned, checking on his livestock, but he had to make sure. He slipped off Satan's back, sank in muck up to his ankles, and crept toward the building, where he leaned into a rough board and listened. A low keening eddied against his ear while male laughter reverberated through the walls.

His six-shooter in his hand, Mitch stole his way through the mire to the door, but someone had dropped the bar on the inside and it only creaked in protest when he tried to open it. He considered kicking it in; it was certainly rotten enough to give way with ease, but he didn't want to announce his entrance if he didn't have to. After all, he couldn't be positive it was Stringfellow he'd seen slip inside, although he knew in his gut that it was.

But God! Don't let that wailing woman be Kate!

Perhaps there was another entrance . . .

His heart hammering with fear for the woman and his head throbbing with anger, Mitch moved as quickly as he could through the oozing sludge. He stopped from time to time to peer through a crack in the old, warped planks, but none was wide enough to allow him to see inside.

As he neared the back side of the barn, the voices grew more distinct.

"Shut her up!" a familiar male voice barked. He'd been right; it was Stringfellow.

The woman screeched, and a man bellowed in pain.

"She done stabbed me again!" Another male voice. A vaguely familiar male voice, but Mitch couldn't place it.

"Well, take that goldern hat pin away from her."

A vision of Kate sitting in Billy Fink's cart and wearing the biggest damn hat pin Mitch had ever seen flashed before his eyes. Billy had arrested her for wearing it and Kate had thought to use it as—what had Billy said?—"a device for lacerating the flesh."

If he hadn't been so worried about her, he might have laughed out loud at the very notion of a woman holding off two men with nothing more than a simple hat pin. But the thought of what they might be doing to her now clamped his jaw so tight it hurt his eyes and propelled him forward.

By the time he turned the corner of the barn he was

madder than a peeled rattlesnake and terrified that something would happen to Kate before he got a chance to tell her he understood. He wished he could call out to her, let her know he was there. If she could just hold them off for a moment longer . . .

A lopsided rectangle spilled pale yellow light from the back wall onto the wet ground. He sidled up to the window and chanced a peek.

His gaze first lit on Stringfellow, who stood barely within the circle of lantern light and appeared relatively harmless at the moment. The scar-faced man he'd fought at the Fourth of July barbecue, the one he'd dubbed Blaze, stood over Kate, his feet planted on either side of her hips. Blood dripped from a fresh cut on his cheek and off the hand that held a peacemaker against Kate's temple. His other hand, which was raised above his shoulder, held her hat pin. She sat perfectly still, her face ashen and her eyes open but glazed.

"I'm gonna get you now, bitch!" he said, lowering the hand that held the pin.

Mitch's heart leapt into his throat and his grip tightened on the gun. Without thinking about what he was doing, he shoved his pistol into the window opening, aimed the barrel at Blaze's chest, and pulled the trigger.

He'd killed other men in his day. In his profession, he'd been offered no choice from time to time. He'd learned over the years that it never got any easier. Never before had he enjoyed watching a man die. Until now.

Like a poppy opening to the sun, blood bloomed bright red on Blaze's chest. The man's eyes flew open and his jaw dropped. He released the hat pin, which fell harmlessly onto Kate's bosom, but he held on to the gun.

For a split second Mitch's heart stopped beating as he watched Blaze's finger tighten on the trigger. But then the man's lank body twisted in the air, and he fell onto the straw, right on top of Kate's hat. He kicked once and then was still.

Mitch tore his gaze away from Kate and searched the circle of light for Stringfellow. The man had disappeared. If Stringfellow had slipped out the door on the opposite side, he could even now be sneaking up behind him. But if Stringfellow waited in the shadowy interior of the barn, he could mow Mitch down the second he opened the door on the other side of the window. Mitch was damned either way he went.

He chose to move.

In the space of a heartbeat Mitch kicked open the door and dove to the left, away from the light. And away from Kate. He rolled over, hauled himself onto his knees, and trained his pistol on the dark expanse between him and the front of the barn.

A horse neighed, the barn shuddered, and then the muck quickly absorbed the pounding of departing hoofbeats. Mitch held his breath and listened, but the only sounds he heard were the wailing wind bashing against the rickety barn and Kate's soft whimper.

Although he was convinced Stringfellow had fled, Mitch crawled cautiously toward Kate. The chance that still another scoundrel lurked within the shadows was too great to risk getting shot before he could get her out of there.

Finally he reached her. Her glassy green eyes stared at him, and for a moment he thought that, perhaps, he'd been too late after all. Tenderly, he smoothed a palm over her clammy forehead, brushing the hair off her face and tracing her brow with the pad of his thumb.

His heart caught in his throat when a solitary tear

rolled out of one eye and her lips moved in a silent plea.

"I'm here, darling. I'm here to take you home," he whispered. "I'm here to take us both home."

Epilogue

November 12, 1912

"And he threw you over his shoulder like a sack of potatoes and you lived happily every after."

Sixteen-year-old Maggie tossed her younger brother a withering glare. "You make it sound so commonplace, Everett," she accused, "when it's the most romantic tale I've ever heard."

"Love!" the twelve-year-old spit back. "Since you sprouted bosoms last year that's all you think about."

Kate grinned despite herself, then shooed her youngest child off. "Go see what's taking your daddy so long. I'm eager to leave."

Everett nodded—almost sullenly, Kate noted with surprise. He was her most obedient child and the spitting image of his father. If he continued to grow at the rate he was going, he'd be equally as tall by the time he reached his majority. He rose from his chair and left the kitchen.

"Everett always ruins your story," Maggie complained, pouting. "Tell me how it really ended."

Kate smiled indulgently and leaned back in her chair. "It didn't end, dear. That was like the first day of the rest of my life, the beginning of everything that truly holds meaning for me." She sighed wistfully and closed her eyes for a moment, calling back the memories.

"Then tell me the beginning," Maggie insisted, "as much of it as you can, anyway, before Everett comes back and spoils it again."

Kate looked at her daughter and smiled. Maggie had heard this story before, all of it, so many times Kate couldn't count them. Yet she never seemed to grow tired of hearing it. And, Kate realized, she'd never grown tired of the telling.

"You should have seen the look on Mort Moffet's face when your daddy and I walked into his office the next day." Kate's smile blossomed into a hearty chuckle. "His eyes bulged and his throat worked like he was trying to swallow a bullfrog. Mitch figured Obediah Stringfellow would come straight here, to Mort, and he did. The rapscallion was sitting right there, wiggling and squirming like a three-year-old at a brush-arbor meeting. Of course, the second he saw us he jumped up and made a dash for the door, but your daddy just casually reached out and snagged him by the sleeve and hurled him back into his chair."

Kate refilled her cup with coffee and stirred in some cream. " 'You ain't going nowhere 'cept to jail,' Mitch said. That was the first time I'd heard your daddy use poor grammar in months, and I realized that the lapses always occurred when he was really angry or frustrated—or when he just wanted to needle me." She sipped her coffee. "I had just begun to realize how much I didn't know about Mitch, but I was learning. Once he finally started talking and I started listening, anyway. I think he must have talked nonstop from the time he found me until we got back to Paradise."

Maggie raised her eyebrows at that. "Nonstop, Mother? Really?"

"Well, almost. Anyway," she hurried on in an attempt to cover her sudden embarrassment, "Mitch got the truth out of Mort and Stringfellow. They'd hatched this plan to convince the town that I'd run off after Mitch."

"And that's why they made you write the letter."

Kate nodded. "I'm sure they planned to kill me eventually. We never did understand why they let me live as long as they did. Maybe they just didn't have a taste for killing."

"Did they go to jail?"

"Oh, yes. And it's a good thing they did. I think if the jury had acquitted Stringfellow again your daddy would have killed him. And Mort, too."

"When did Daddy tell you about Jennie Clark?"

"That night."

"Weren't you jealous?"

Kate stared into her coffee cup. "To be honest? Yes. At least at first. And then I was mad at Jennie for causing him so much pain."

Maggie shook her head. "I don't understand how you could work with her after that."

Kate gazed at her daughter for a minute before replying. Maggie never minded saying exactly what she thought, which was one reason the two got along so well. "It wasn't as though your daddy had come to my arms from hers. A number of years had passed, and I couldn't help wondering if, perhaps, Mitch hadn't blown their relationship out of proportion. But I did almost drop out of the movement."

"You never told me that before."

Kate shrugged. "That night in the barn, when I thought I wouldn't live to see another day, I realized that nothing meant quite as much to me as your daddy. Later, when he told me about Jennie and I understood why he was so dead set against marrying a woman with a cause, I told him I was planning to retire from both politics and the suffrage movement. But he wouldn't hear of it. He kept saying it would be like penning up a wolf. Of course, once you kids started coming along, I did retire." At her daughter's twisted grin, Kate added, "Well, sort of."

"I'm proud of your accomplishments, Mother. There aren't many girls who can say their mother served two terms as mayor and then was largely responsible for Kansas giving women the right to vote in the presidential election. But I'd be just as happy to be your daughter if you were a regular mom." Maggie's eyes sparkled with mischief. "I'm just glad you and Daddy finally came to your senses."

Kate laughed. "Otherwise you wouldn't be here. You know, I used to dream of having a little girl with hair just the color of yours and eyes the color of robins' eggs."

"Sorry, Mom. Mine are hazel."

"I know. And they're beautiful eyes."

"But at least I got your hair. Except I wish I didn't have these twin cowlicks at my temples like you do."

They both laughed at that.

"Thanks for not giving up," Maggie said.

"I almost did after Wilbur was born. My fourth boy—and a breach at that. Dr. Myers saved my life."

"Which is why you named Wilbur after him. He hates that name, you know."

They were silent for a minute, but it was a comfortable silence. Kate loved all six of her children, but she and Maggie shared a special closeness she'd never had with the boys.

Maggie broke the silence. "Who are you going to vote for?"

"Who would you vote for, if you were old enough?" Kate asked.

Maggie didn't hesitate. "Roosevelt. He was a good president, he's a strong man, and I like his ideas."

"So do I."

Cold wind invaded the warm kitchen. Kate looked up to see Everett closing the door. "Daddy's got the team hitched up," he announced, then gave Kate a mulish glare. "Do I have to go?"

His objection astonished Kate. Everett was a quiet, happy child who seldom questioned his parents' judgment or decree, yet she'd always sensed that a fire smoldered somewhere deep inside him. She hoped it did. A little rebellion once in a while was good for the soul.

If Kate was merely astonished, Maggie was truly horrified. "Why, Everett! This is the most important day in Mother's life! Of course you have to go."

Everett ignored his sister and directed his argument to Kate. "But I can't even go in there with you. We got a day off from school and I didn't even get to sleep late. Gosh, Mom! It's not even six o'clock and I've been up for hours."

"I know, son," Kate said, her voice soothing yet firm, "but I want to be there when the polls open. One day you'll thank me for insisting you witness this momentous occasion."

The back door opened again and Kate watched Mitch stomp his feet on the top step before scurrying inside. Kate never grew tired of feasting her eyes on his rugged face. Except for a few wrinkles around his eyes and a modicum of gray lightening his dark blond hair, he looked much the same as he had the day he'd arrived in Paradise.

"Br-r-r. It's cold out there," he said, rubbing his hands together and reaching for the coffeepot. "I can't remember it ever snowing this early before." Mitch winked at Kate, and her stomach quivered. "I suppose that was the momentous occasion you were talking about."

"You know better, Daddy," Maggie teased.

Mitch grinned and ruffled Everett's hair. "When you're old enough to vote, son, you'll understand. It's not every day that a person is allowed to vote for the President of the United States for the first time. Your mother's been waiting fifty-two years."

"But this is not the most important day in my life, Maggie," Kate corrected her daughter, "although it is up there with the day I met your daddy, and our wedding day, and the days you all were born. . . ."

"And one day," Mitch added, "this country will grant women in every state the right to full suffrage. Who knows? The population of the entire country may get as smart as the people in Paradise and elect a woman for president."

Kate felt herself glow.

"Yeah," Maggie said, puffing out her chest, "and maybe it will be me."

Without hesitation, Mitch smiled at Maggie, his brown eyes gleaming with pride.

"Maybe it will, sweetheart," he said. "Maybe it will."

Author's Note

Most of the authors I know have at least one story simmering on the back burner, waiting for some cataclysmic event to occur or something to click that will demand it be removed, examined, and possibly—perhaps finally—committed to paper.

I dreamed up the premise for this story years ago, decided it was illogical and unbelievable, and relegated it to a back burner. And then one day last fall a fellow writer brought me a rather tall stack of old historical magazines she'd rescued from her mother's trash pile. The one on top contained an article that provided the historical background I needed for this story but had never actively searched out. I squealed. I screamed. I hugged her neck. And she, I'm sure, thought I had, finally, lost it.

But, oh, what I had gained! I knew that Victoria Woodhull was our first female presidential candidate (1872). I knew a bit about the suffrage movement and some of the strides those brave, far-seeing women accomplished a century or more ago. But I didn't know that much of what I'd dreamed up about a group of women taking over a western town and cleaning it up had actually happened in a small town in Kansas in 1888.

Scarcely a year before, following several years of pressure from the Equal Suffrage Association, the Kansas state legislature granted women the right to vote and run for office in municipal elections. Shortly thereafter, Argonia, Kansas, elected Susanna Salter the first female mayor in the United States, and the following year, Oskaloosa elected an all-female ticket, the first "petticoat" government.

Although the Paradise in this book is intended as a fictional town (there is a small community named Paradise in Kansas), and the characters are certainly fictional, many of the accomplishments of Mayor McBride and her council and the problems they faced are founded in history—not only that of Oskaloosa, but of other frontier towns, as well.

I hope you enjoy reading *Prairie Paradise,* and that you will write to me, in care of Zebra Books, 850 Third Avenue, New York, NY 10022.

> Elizabeth Leigh
> Alexandria, Louisiana

Taylor—made Romance From Zebra Books

WHISPERED KISSES (3830, $4.99/5.99)
Beautiful Texas heiress Laura Leigh Webster never imagined that her biggest worry on her African safari would be the handsome Jace Elliot, her tour guide. Laura's guardian, Lord Chadwick Hamilton, warns her of Jace's dangerous past; she simply cannot resist the lure of his strong arms and the passion of his *Whispered Kisses*.

KISS OF THE NIGHT WIND (3831, $4.99/$5.99)
Carrie Sue Strover thought she was leaving trouble behind her when she deserted her brother's outlaw gang to live her life as schoolmarm Carolyn Starns. On her journey, her stagecoach was attacked and she was rescued by handsome T.J. Rogue. T.J. plots to have Carrie lead him to her brother's cohorts who murdered his family. T.J., however, soon succumbs to the beautiful runaway's charms and loving caresses.

FORTUNE'S FLAMES (3825, $4.99/$5.99)
Impatient to begin her journey back home to New Orleans, beautiful Maren James was furious when Captain Hawk delayed the voyage by searching for stowaways. Impatience gave way to uncontrollable desire once the handsome captain searched *her* cabin. He was looking for illegal passengers; what he found was wild passion with a woman he knew was unlike all those he had known before!

PASSIONS WILD AND FREE (3828, $4.99/$5.99)
After seeing her family and home destroyed by the cruel and hateful Epson gang, Randee Hollis swore revenge. She knew she found the perfect man to help her—gunslinger Marsh Logan. Not only strong and brave, Marsh had the ebony hair and light blue eyes to make Randee forget her hate and seek the love and passion that only he could give her.